THE
BELOVED DEAD

THE
𝕭ELOVED 𝕯EAD

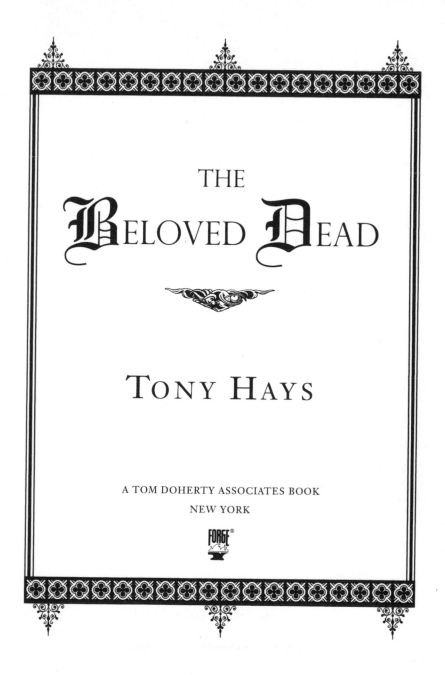

TONY HAYS

A TOM DOHERTY ASSOCIATES BOOK

NEW YORK

FORGE®

This is a work of fiction. All of the characters, organizations, and events portrayed in this novel are either products of the author's imagination or are used fictitiously.

THE BELOVED DEAD

A Forge Book
Published by Tom Doherty Associates, LLC
175 Fifth Avenue
New York, NY 10010

www.tor-forge.com

Forge® is a registered trademark of Tom Doherty Associates, LLC.

Library of Congress Cataloging-in-Publication Data

Hays, Tony.
    The beloved dead / Tony Hays.—1st hardcover ed.
       p. cm.
    "A Tom Doherty Associates book"—T.p. verso.
    ISBN 978-0-7653-2628-7 (alk. paper)
    1. Arthur, King—Fiction. 2. Britons—Fiction. 3. Murder—Investigation—Fiction. I. Title.
    PS3558.A877B45   2010
    813'.54—dc22

                                       2010036259

First Edition: April 2011

Printed in the United States of America

0 9 8 7 6 5 4 3 2 1

For Red and Carrie Nell Shelby,
good and true friends

$\mathcal{A}$CKNOWLEDGMENTS

Any novel that reaches publication owes a debt to many people. A novel is, to a certain extent, a giant collaborative enterprise, at least in terms of getting it through the necessary steps so it can be published. I will be forever grateful to my agent, Frank Weimann, and the folks at Literary Group International and to my editor, Claire Eddy, and her assistant, Kristin Sevick. Writers, by and large, have been labeled a jealous breed. But I am happy to say that the advice, encouragement, and friendship of fellow writers C. W. Gortner, Brendan DuBois, Rebecca Cantrell, Michelle Moran, Karen Essex, and all the great members of the Historical Novel Society have done much to see me through the challenges that come with writing historical fiction. Arthurian scholar and author Geoffrey Ashe has never failed to keep me pointed in the right direction. To everyone else who has played a role in getting these novels in print, a tremendous "thank you"!

TONY HAYS
Savannah, Tennessee

CASTELLUM ARTURIUS

1. the unfinished church
2. Arthur's Well
3. barracks
4. Kay's house
5. metal-working site
6. Accolon's house
7. Cuneglas's house
8. main gate
9. Malgwyn's house
10. Arthur's feasting hall
11. Arthur's kitchen
12. Merlin's house
13. watchtower

Via Caedas

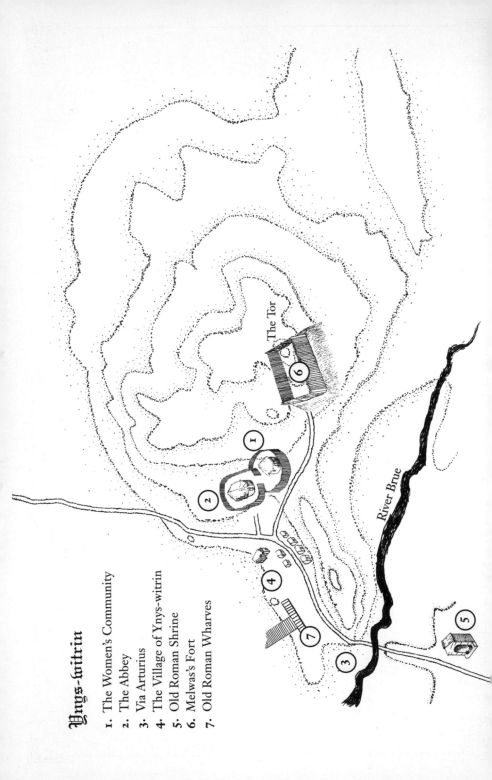

Ynys-witrin

1. The Women's Community
2. The Abbey
3. Via Arturius
4. The Village of Ynys-witrin
5. Old Roman Shrine
6. Melwas's Fort
7. Old Roman Wharves

The Tor

River Brue

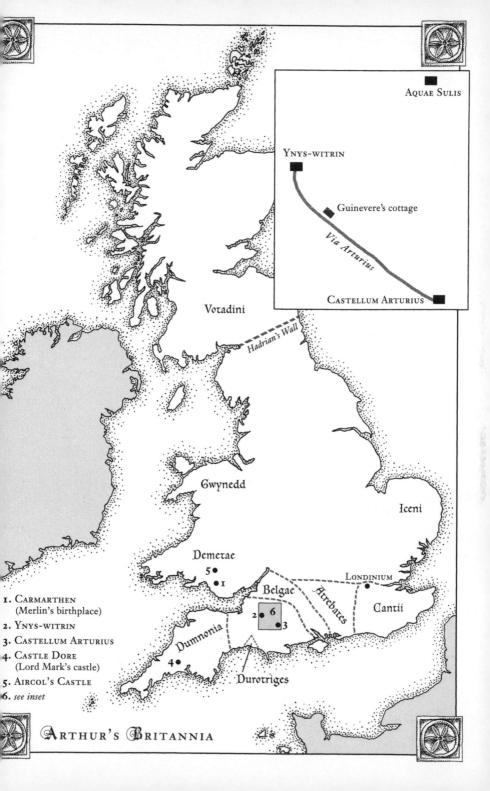

AQUAE SULIS

YNYS-WITRIN

Guinevere's cottage

Via Arturius

CASTELLUM ARTURIUS

Votadini

Hadrian's Wall

Gwynedd

Iceni

Demetae

5

1

Belgae

LONDINIUM

2   6

Atrebates

3

Cantii

Dumnonia

4

Durotriges

1. CARMARTHEN
   (Merlin's birthplace)
2. YNYS-WITRIN
3. CASTELLUM ARTURIUS
4. CASTLE DORE
   (Lord Mark's castle)
5. AIRCOL'S CASTLE
6. *see inset*

ARTHUR'S BRITANNIA

THE
Beloved Dead

GLASTONBURY

uperstition is a powerful thing. I have fallen victim to it myself on more than one occasion in my ninety winters of life. But with age has come skepticism, about almost everything. In truth, I have seen many things in my life that I could not explain, things not even Merlin could explain, and he was the wisest man I have ever known.

Omens are plentiful in our lands and legends. Our people, in the dim past, looked to the stars for guidance. The Romans, it is said, studied the entrails of dead animals, though truly, I never understood what the white, pink, and purple bits could tell anybody about what was to come. I prefer that empty feeling in the bottom of my stomach when I know that something bad is going to happen. That is an omen I can trust, for it has proven its worth many times.

But I have learned too that to ignore superstitions widely held by the people is to risk calling down some unseen power upon you. I do not believe in the shades of the dead, nor do I believe that the cry of a screech owl on a full moon is a harbinger of some disaster. But once, near the River Dubglas, I was directed away from a road and down a seldom-used lane by a strange old man with tufts of white hair *poking from his ears. It turned out later that a Saxon party had lain in ambush down my intended path. When I tried to locate the old man and thank him for saving me from certain death, I could not find him, but was told that a man similar to that description had lived in the wood many years before. But he had been dead for ten winters or more. A shade of the dead? All I know is that I am still breathing because of that warning.*

A fortnight ago, I climbed atop a horse belonging to the abbey and rode to the chapel just beyond the bridge over the River Brue. It is grown over now, disused and derelict. The abbot had told me that he planned to have it demolished. He is a good man, if a young one. But then, at my age, nearly everyone seems young. He lets me live in a house owned by the Church, near unto the abbey. Occasionally he counsels with me when negotiating with the Saxons; I have dealt with them so often over the years that I can tell what they are thinking from the look on their faces. Some days, when the weather is not too damp, I go to the scriptorium and copy a manuscript or two.

I have traveled far, from farmer to warrior to councilor to a king, and now I am just an old, one-armed man who has traveled many roads. I wanted to see the chapel before it breathed its last. I thought it an ill omen to destroy a place of worship, but then, my old friend Kay had destroyed a Roman shrine to build this chapel. I remember another place from those days, of worship, of sacrifice, buried deep in the woods of our land. I wondered what remained of that place. That had been a season of ill omens, among the worst of my long life.

To this day, I believe that all the death and horror that accompanied Arthur's marriage during his second year as Rigotamos could be traced to our journey to Londinium in the late summer. It was at the least an unwise quest from the first step and at the most a tempting of the gods, and each of us knew it. Yet we followed our high king, our Rigotamos, Arthur ap Uther, despite those misgivings, because above all else we loved him.

PART ONE

THE

White Mount

C<small>HAPTER</small> O<small>NE</small>

T his is not wise, Rigotamos," I cautioned. "Not wise at all."
I pulled my fur cloak closer about my neck, my fingers
brushing the crossbow fibula that Arthur had given me years
before. A mist hung over the countryside, as thick as any I had
ever seen. Early morning at Londinium was often like this,
not that I had traveled much in these parts. The Saxons had
encroached on our lands to the south, east, and north. Londinium was like a finger of high ground amidst the waters of
the Saxon flood.

The White Mount, where we now stood, was on the eastern edge of the Londinium of Rome, above the flowing waters
of the River Tamesis. Most of the wondrous buildings had
fallen into disrepair. As we rode in from Castellum Arturius
far to the west, our mood had been dampened by the decay of
a once beautiful city, replete with baths, temples, a governor's
mansion, shrines to the entire pantheon of Roman gods. The
great circus in the northwest now held pigs owned by a local
farmer. Not far to the east of us lay a large temple, but our scouts
said that the buildings had tumbled down and the altar destroyed, probably by a Saxon raiding party. But now yellowed

grass grew out from the broken stones, and reeds smelling of snakes and mud crowded what had been a clean riverbank, and purple thistles grew where Roman soldiers had walked. And among those abandoned buildings, where once colorful mosaics and bracing baths held sway, were the wattle-and-daub huts of our people, of Britons.

❖

I was not the first to caution him. All of his councilors had told him this. Aye, when word of his intentions had reached the other lords of the *consilium*, four of them sped riders to urge him against it. But he was much out of sorts with me (and I with him) and persisted in his belief that this was a good thing. So, on this late summer morning, with three troop of horse in formation around the base of the White Mount, Arthur ap Uther brushed our arguments aside, dismounted, and approached the stone that marked the burial place of Bran's head.

Bran was a remarkable man, or god; no one was quite sure which. I had heard many stories about him as I grew up, spun by the old folk around the fire, late at night. The ancient tales had it that Bran was a king of all Britannia in the long distant past, long before Arthur or Ambrosius or Vortigern. He had gotten in some family dispute with a Hibernian king over the betrothal of his sister, Branwen. I could not keep all the details straight—he had a brother of unsound mind involved as well— but I knew that it prompted a war between Hibernia and Britannia, and that only Bran and six others were left of the Britons. They became known as the Seven, but curiously, only Bran's head had survived. Even my old dad looked askance when told of how Bran's head continued to live even after it had been parted from his neck, often regaling his companions with stories and jokes. But, in time, the head, like the rest of Bran, died and was buried here at the White Mount, facing Gaul to protect Britannia from foreign invaders.

And so Arthur had determined to recover Bran's head from the mount in order to show the people that they should depend upon the Christ and the consilium to guard Britannia's shores, not old skulls.

The Rigotamos was nearly alone in believing that this venture was wise. We had all tried to tell him, his foes, his friends, but especially those who cared little for Arthur or any noble but cared deeply for a people bruised and battered by decades of battle and death.

I remembered the recent visit of Coroticus, abbot at Ynyswitrin, to Castellum Arturius. While I had my own differences with Coroticus, on this issue I agreed with him. "You do not stab a dying brother in the throat to hasten his death," Coroticus had told the Rigotamos, referring to the chaos that still marred our lands, brought about by the Roman departure. We struggled yet with the incursions of Picts and the Scotti, and the more immediate threat of the Saxons. Our lords, at least most of them, were bound in a consilium, headed by a Rigotamos, or high king. First, we had had Vortigern, who betrayed the people and brought the hated Saxons to our shore. Then came Ambrosius Aurelianus, a tall, sturdy leader who cared for the people and carried himself with *Romanitas*, and, with the help of his *Dux Bellorum*, Arthur ap Uther, checked the Saxon advance across our lands. Now, after Ambrosius's rather eventful retirement, we had Arthur, a man who deeply believed in the Christ and cared even more deeply for the people.

"My 'brother' is not dying, abbot," he had answered. "And you, of all men, should not encourage the people to look to an ancient talisman to protect them from harm. Rather they should put their faith in the Christ and the consilium to keep them safe." And that had been his argument against all opposition. Bran's head represented dependence on the old ways. The Church and the consilium (though it was not of one mind on the Church) represented a new path. Hence our quest to Londinium, where Arthur intended to dig up Bran's head and move it to a more suitable burial place.

For my part, I saw no harm in leaving the head where it lay. In truth, it was nothing more than a symbol, just as the Brutus Stone and the Diana Stone were symbols. That the people put faith in its protection was no different than having a favorite tunic or dagger. I knew of men who would not go into battle without their favorite brooch firmly affixed to their cloak. It hurt nothing and calmed their fears.

But, despite all of this opposition and argument, Arthur was still the Rigotamos and we were still bound to follow his orders. So now we had arrived at the White Mount.

Arrayed beside me were Kay, Bedevere, Merlin, and Gawain. "Rigotamos," Merlin began, "it is late in the day. We have almost lost our light. Perhaps it would be better if we camped and you completed your task on the morrow."

Merlin spoke the truth. The afternoon sun was fading in the western sky, and we had not had time to prepare torches. Word of our mission had filtered through as well and a group of the local folk had gathered, their faces grim and foreboding.

Arthur's face was set in hard lines. The muscles at his jaws

THE BELOVED DEAD / 25

pushed at his skin, burnished a deep brown by long days in the sun in recent months. The tension among our entire company was as thick as the mist which oft coated our mornings. After the abortive rebellion by Lauhiir, Teilo, and Dochu (and Lord David, if the truth be known) more than a year before, Arthur no longer indulged his desire to avoid the trappings of rank and to travel, at least outside Castellum Arturius, with only the most modest of escorts. We had three troop of horse, enough to deal with any bands of *latrunculi* or marauding Saxon parties, but not so many as to worry the Saxon leaders that an invasion of their Canti lands was imminent. Vortigern had granted those lands to the Saxons for their help with the Picts and Scotti.

Finally, his eyes softened a bit and he nodded to Bedevere, who commanded our horse. Barking orders right and left, our soldiers dismounted and began establishing a camp on the summit of the mount. Merlin and I climbed down from our horses as well and stretched our legs. Although Arthur loved his Romanisms, like vigiles and posca (that horrible vinegar and water concoction that soldiers drank), he bowed to reality and to the limits to which he could push his men when it came to making camp.

As a lad, my father once took me to a field near our farm. There you could still easily see the double ditches, grown over and filling up with dirt and debris, that surrounded an ancient Roman marching camp. He walked me around the field and showed where the gates had been and how the defensive ditches had worked. I often wondered how he knew so much, as he had been but a babe when the legions left. He was long dead, though, and I tried not to ponder things that had no answer.

As the men busied themselves with putting up tents and preparing campfires, Arthur motioned to me to join him. With a sigh, I answered his call. I knew what he wanted, and I had no interest in discussing it further.

We walked out from the bustle of the growing camp to a point where we could look over the river. In the distance I could see the twinkling of lamps at a handful of farmsteads. The summer's heat was oppressive, and my face and body were covered with dirt and sweat from our journey. The dampness in the air soaked through to my stump of an arm, causing it to ache and tingle.

"Malgwyn, you know I have no other choice," Arthur began.

"My lord, I know that you are the Rigotamos, the highest chieftain in our lands. You have all the choices. No man has more."

Now it was Arthur's turn to sigh. "You are smarter than that, Malgwyn. Do not pretend to be unlearned and ignorant. The consilium will not stay together without compromise, and compromise requires sacrifices of us all."

Sacrifices. I rubbed the remnant of my right arm, remembering that sacrifice. A long time before, I was a farmer. But then the war against the Saxons stole my young wife from me and made me a soldier in the command of Arthur ap Uther, now the Rigotamos, the High King of all Britannia; he was but the Dux Bellorum then, the leader of battles, for the consilium of lords that held our fragmented island together. My knack for reading battlefields and my zeal for killing Saxons raised me in Arthur's esteem, and I quickly became one of his lesser lieutenants. But a Saxon sword cleaved my arm along the River Tribuit and took my bloodlust away.

Arthur stanched the flow of my life's blood and saved me,

when I wanted nothing more than to die. He took me to Ynys-witrin, and the *monachi* bound my wounds, healed me, and taught me to write with my left hand, gave me something of a trade since farming and warring were lost to me. Death still seemed my only haven, and I bore Arthur a grudge for my salvation, a grudge that blighted my days and sent my nights reeling into a waterfall of drink.

It was only on the eve of Arthur's election as Rigotamos, in the wake of the deaths of Eleonore, my wife's sister, and Cuneglas, my younger brother, that we were reconciled. But with that reconciliation came another with my young daughter, Mariam, whom I had abandoned, and that was worth all that had gone before.

The current rift between me and Arthur had nothing to do with all of that, but it did concern family. While nobility had avoided my branch, another, distant line of the family was indeed noble. In that brood was a female cousin, a pretty young thing, but headstrong and temperamental. Her father had arranged a marriage with a brother of Lord Mark at Castle Marcus. But she rebelled at such a match and ran away to the women's community at Ynys-witrin, pledging her life to the Christ.

And true to her nature, that lasted nearly as long as it took for her to settle in to her new duties. She found the rules of the community stifling, aye found them threatening to choke the very life from her. The community was one that vowed poverty and chastity. Poverty was not a problem for my cousin; even the most noble of families in those days often had little. Chastity, as her young body matured into a woman's, became a major concern, one that the sisters could not ignore.

Of course, male visitors to the community were few, but

among those was a young tax collector for Ambrosius Aurelianus, a handsome young officer. And he noticed my cousin as she toiled in the garden. Suddenly, he found more and more reasons to visit the sisters. Inevitably, the two entered into an affair, and just as inevitably, they were discovered. My cousin, Guinevere, was cast out of the community in disgrace. The young tax collector, Arthur, suffered little; his sin was but one of lust. Hers was the greater. It was not an uncommon story, but this one was different.

You see, Arthur truly loved Guinevere, and she loved him.

Determined to care for Guinevere, Arthur provided a good cottage along the road from Cadwy's Castle (which Arthur soon inherited) to Ynys-witrin. The cottage was nestled off the lane far enough to be invisible to travelers. Merlin, even then protecting his young friend, put word about that it was inhabited by a sorceress, an evil woman with the ability to turn a man to stone simply by looking at him.

But that had been years before and few now credited Merlin's stories. Arthur's subsequent promotion to *Dux Bellorum* allowed him the luxury of being seen in public with Guinevere. He could never consider marrying her, though, he believed. She was a disgraced sister of the community, and the people would not accept her as his wife. A Rigotamos must be seen as nearly perfect, Arthur thought. And consorting with a fallen sister also damaged the image of piety that he hoped to project. Never mind that many of our people did not yet embrace the Christ and, indeed, still clung to the old ways, the old gods.

Our present discussion was caused by an envoy from Lord Mark at Castle Marcus who had arrived some weeks before. The young envoy had carried a parchment that only Arthur,

Merlin, Kay, and I had been privy to, and its contents had been closely guarded ever since. Even Bedevere had not been acquainted with its message, though that was bound to happen as soon as our task at the White Mount was completed.

The message was simple. Mark, David, Gawain, and a number of other lords believed it was time for Arthur to take a bride. To that end, they proposed an arranged marriage between Arthur and the young daughter of a northern lord, Aircol, who paid no obeisance to the consilium. The group of lords believed that an alliance with Aircol would not only strengthen the consilium through numbers, but would help protect the north. The girl was but fourteen, less than half of Arthur's age. Still, she was of an age to marry.

Their argument was well spoken and logical, too logical. Such marriages were not uncommon among the nobles, allying families and property. Aircol's lands were well placed to help defend against Saxon encroachment, and should the Saxons invade our lands, his men could flank them or even come into the Saxon lands to their rear, wreaking havoc and disrupting any invasion.

So Arthur had acceded, and I had erupted.

"But you love Guinevere!" I had shouted.

"Yes. But there is nothing I can do, Malgwyn, and you know that!" came his reply.

"Explain that to my cousin, whose pleasures you have certainly enjoyed for many seasons!"

He turned from me then, unwilling to discuss the matter further, unwilling, I guessed, to risk a complete break.

And so it had remained between us, few words passing and then but grunts and shrugs. Seeing Guinevere, so happy with Arthur, stabbed at my heart, but this was not my message to deliver. If her heart were to be broken, then Arthur would have to do it. I would have no part of it.

Now he wished to discuss it once more. We found a fallen log and both sat, not looking at each other, looking instead to the lands to the south, Saxon lands.

"Malgwyn," he began finally. "You know that I do love Guinevere, but you know too that the decisions of a Rigotamos are not always his own."

I chuckled. "Is that so, my lord? Strange that Vortigern never worried about such things. He threw away his woman in favor of a Saxon bride, and no one urged him to do it. Aye, everyone was aghast! But he cared not!"

"True. And he was betrayed! And no one stood with him! Malgwyn, no matter how much I love Guinevere, no matter how much you love her as your cousin, she is still a woman cast out of the Christ's community. A Rigotamos cannot marry such as her. A Rigotamos must be perfect. And marriages are about strengthening one's position. Guinevere knows this. And though she be of noble birth, Cadwy is long dead, his property split among his sons. I must make the marriage most advantageous to our people!"

Lord Cadwy had been Guinevere's guardian after the death of her father. Castellum Arturius had once belonged to Cadwy, but the old man had given it to Arthur. The rest of his lands had gone to his sons, a wastrel lot who never amounted to much.

"My lord, I will concede that a marriage to Guinevere brings no advantage to our strength or our defense. Only a fool would argue that. But I reject your argument that you cannot marry her, that she is unacceptable. You well know that she is favored by the people. They truly love her, and I see no reason why they would object to your marriage."

Arthur nodded. "That is true. Guinevere is well thought of by the people. But being a beloved woman is just not the same as being a queen. The people would expect more of her, more of me in my choice."

I was arguing with an oak tree. In truth, he had already decided and no matter how much I challenged him, he would not be swayed. "Tell me what it is you wish of me, Rigotamos, in this matter."

He sighed and looked off at the twilight, back toward the heart of our lands. "I need you to go with Bedevere and Merlin to escort Aircol and his daughter back to Castellum Arturius for the wedding."

I started to protest, but his wool-wrapped hand had already raised to stop me. "Malgwyn, I need to show my resolve in this matter, and pay proper respect to Aircol. To do that, I need my most trusted advisors to provide the escort."

"What of Kay?"

"As Seneschal, he has many duties to perform in preparation for the wedding." He stopped and smiled. "Already he is finding it a daunting task."

I could not help but laugh. The Seneschal served as keeper of the Rigotamos's household. Kay, tall and slender as a willow, was one of my favorites, but he had an infamous temper and had been much out of sorts lately, dealing with the chore of handling Arthur's servants. He was always more a soldier than an administrator. But after a moment the laugh caught in my throat, and I turned away from Arthur.

"What else troubles you, Malgwyn?"

Off in the distance, to the southwest, I saw a single lamp lit at a farmstead, bursting into life. "I thought you were going to ask me to explain this thing to Guinevere."

He studied his wrapped hand, the one missing his middle finger, taken at the joint by a well-aimed Saxon spear. "No, that is a job I cannot delegate to another. Do not think that I find any pleasure in this, Malgwyn. I have loved Guinevere for more than ten winters. But marriages for kings are affairs of state, not affairs of the heart. You have no idea how I wish it could be otherwise."

"You are wrong, Arthur," I said, taking a liberty I would never dream of taking among others. "Kings are men with the power to do what they please. But you have never understood that."

"Remember your friend Patrick?" The good Patrick, *episcopus* to the Scotti across the sea, had died some months before in a sordid affair at Ynys-witrin. I had not known him long, but I came to consider him a good and true man, and that can be said of so few in the world.

"How could I not?"

"You are asking me to be the sort of *tyrannus* that he denounced."

"I am asking you to be the kind of king that our land is filled with."

With that, I felt his hand on my shoulder, wrenching me around to face him. We were close enough that I could smell the mint leaves he had chewed to freshen his breath.

"I am not like them, Malgwyn. I do not want to be like them." No anger sparked his eyes; no blood marked his cheeks. He said it earnestly and with an intensity that marked a young man, not a war-hardened chieftain.

"I will go for you, just as I came here for you. I know that you mean well, my lord." My next question was a difficult one. "How will you tell Guinevere of your decision?"

A sad and dark look clouded his face. "Gently, not easily. Part of me wishes to maintain our relationship, but I would not dishonor her nor my marriage to Gwyneira by suggesting it."

"She would not agree to that at any rate."

Arthur chuckled. "I know. She already senses that this is coming. She is your cousin, after all, Malgwyn. I cannot think of a good way to tell her this, so I will just tell her and pray that she does not have a dagger near at hand. But know this and know it well, Malgwyn, no dagger she could wield against me would strike any deeper or any truer than the one that this matter has already struck me with."

"Tell me, Arthur. When you first determined that you wanted to be the Rigotamos, did you think that it would come without costs?"

The corners of his mouth turned up in a half smile. "Trying to do right for the people has forever been weighted down with costs. But I will admit that the vision of sunny days shone more brightly than that of the rainy ones."

A good answer. An honest one. "I know that you are trying to do the right thing, and that counts for much in this world."

He rose then, his hand lingering on my shoulder. "Aye, old friend, I do mean well. I fought across this land to bring it peace. But even in peace, there are often wounded and dead left on the battlefield."

CHAPTER TWO

We returned to the others then, our new camp a bustle of activity. Kay was supervising construction and Bedevere was busy setting guards. Merlin was overseeing the cook. The ground was littered with bricks and stone, remnants of Roman buildings. A broad expanse of the old wall surrounding Londinium still stood, below the mount. It once ran across its summit, but, since it had fallen into disrepair, people had taken the bricks to use in their own modest huts. You could always tell a Roman wall; it was principally built from regular stone, but every so often a course of red stone was laid.

A new face was among us, though—Morgan ap Tud, Arthur's new physician. With his vast store of knowledge on herbs and healing, Merlin had generally taken care of most of those duties. But with Arthur's election as Rigotamos, the old man had been called on for other chores. Lord David argued that Arthur needed a trained physician; I suspected that David needed a spy in our midst.

But Morgan, a short, slender fellow with a closely trimmed beard, seemed a good man. I say "seemed" as I did not know him well enough to truly judge him. He had trained in the north with a renowned physician named Melus. And he bore himself well. But time would answer my questions about him and this was his first journey with us. At that moment, I noticed him scurrying about the campfire in some sort of frenzy.

As I approached the fire, I saw old Cerdic getting our meal ready, dodging Morgan, who seemed to be everywhere at once. Poor Morgan! He had not been among us long enough to make many friends, and since he was often without duties to perform, he spent his time trying to be helpful, and further aggravating a forever annoyed Cerdic.

The old *servus* had been with Arthur longer than anyone, I think. Merlin once told me that Cerdic had been a gift from one of Arthur's kin many years before. He was a stout man with a barrel chest and a thin fringe of white hair encircling his bald head. He had few of his teeth left and those seemed to just barely cling to his gums. Though not a short man, he was not as tall as I, and he always wore a deep blue tunic. I suspected that it had some significance, but I knew not what it might be.

Arthur had brought Cerdic along to make our meals. Now the Rigotamos's head steward, he had cooked for our campfire during the war. The cooking was not difficult; it was finding something to cook that often made it a trial. And Cerdic was a master at scavenging. This night he had concocted a stew of deer meat with leeks, with some loaves of bread he had stashed on our wagon.

I stole up behind him and whispered, "I trust not a cook who does not eat his own food."

He chuckled, and without turning answered, "If you had gnashers like mine, you would steer clear of tough meat and hard bread."

"If I had gnashers like yours, I would crawl in the grave and pull the dirt in on top of me."

"I thought you had already done that, but 'twas wineskins that you pulled over the top of you."

'Twas only two years before when that had been true. I had already become accustomed to such jests, and Cerdic and I traded them now in the manner of old friends. "Where is Talorc?"

Talorc was a Pictish slave of Arthur's, a stubborn and bitter youth whom I had first encountered in the events surrounding the conspiracy against Ambrosius Aurelianus and Arthur. He knew not his place. Kay had begged Arthur to sell him, but the Rigotamos was not much of one for buying and selling slaves. Cerdic had brought him on this journey to try to teach him humility. Or to take the chance to drown him in the river. I was not sure which.

"I sent him out to find some pig and cabbage for tomorrow. We are staying longer than I expected, and I did not bring enough provisions."

"May I help, Cerdic?" an incredibly solicitous Morgan offered.

The old servus rolled his eyes. "If you could go and find Talorc and see what is keeping him, Master Morgan, that would be help aplenty."

And the little fellow bounced off, glad to have a task set for him.

"Sold what you had to the locals, I expect," I said once Morgan was out of earshot. We all suspected that Cerdic stole from Arthur's table to add to his own coin hoard.

He just grunted and moved on about his chores.

"What did you tell Arthur?" The voice at my shoulder was as familiar as my own—Merlin.

Turning, I took him by the shoulder and drew him away from the others. "What you wanted me to tell him. What else could I say? I serve Arthur."

His wrinkled visage smiled at me. "I knew that, but Arthur worried." The old man paused, the corners of his mouth drawing down. "You should know, Malgwyn, that I counseled Arthur against this match. I advised him to marry Guinevere."

At that, I took a step backward and cocked my head at him. "In truth?"

He nodded, his wispy white hair rustling in the breeze. "No one loves Guinevere more than I. She is as my daughter, and I do not believe that this arrangement will bring Arthur the benefits he seeks. Once," and his eyes grew watery and dim, "I loved one as he loves Guinevere. And I did not act until it was too late. This is why I have urged him to make Guinevere his queen."

"Then why has he agreed to the match?"

"Mark and David threatened to withdraw from the consilium if he refused."

I felt the blood rising in my face; a tingle ran across my skin. "He said nothing of this to me!"

Merlin's fragile hand touched my tunic. "Lower your voice! He would call for my head if he knew I had told you this. Arthur knows too well how you feel about David."

"I spoke the truth at Ynys-witrin!"

The hand grasped my shoulder. "I do not doubt you, and you raised doubts in Arthur's mind. But there was no certain proof that David lied about his involvement in Lauhiir's treachery. And you have never been an ally of David's. Then, there's the other."

He did not need to say more. Merlin was no believer in the Christ, and he thought Arthur's devotion was not wise. Aye, he thought it decidedly unwise. Though he had his differences with Druids, he was more aligned with them than the Church. In truth, Merlin was a child of the forest and field, who believed that they provided all a man needed for survival. I could not and did not argue with him. Arthur loved Merlin as a father and chose to ignore his religious beliefs.

But "the other" that Merlin referred to was Aircol's devotion to the Christ and his support of the Church. It was nearly as famous throughout our lands as Arthur's. In truth, some said that he had given far more to the support of the Church than the Rigotamos. But Arthur's problems with the Church stemmed more from the corruption within than a lack of faith. It would please him to strengthen his ties with another soldier of the Christ, especially since so many of the other lords in the consilium did not share his beliefs.

As I sorted these things in my head, we retreated behind one of the two wagons we had brought along to bear our supplies. Servants and slaves listen too closely to things we say. More than once, when we warred against the Saxons, slaves had sold crucial information to our enemies. We had discovered their treachery before much damage had been done, and Arthur had taken their heads, but it was wise not to create the opportunity for such betrayal.

"And what of the contract? What has Arthur promised?"

"Nothing as yet. One of our tasks will be to negotiate that. Aye, that is the main reason he wishes you to go."

Again, the blood flushed my face. "He said nothing of this!"

"Of course not, Malgwyn!" Merlin chided me in his teacher's voice. "That would not have been wise. To convince you to support his decision was quite enough of a chore for him to perform. My task was to conscript you as a negotiator."

"Some wine, my lords?" Talorc had appeared at my elbow, a wineskin in hand. Merlin gave him a withering look and the boy melted away, back toward the fire.

"That child is a menace!" Merlin snorted.

"I see Kay has been abusing your ear." Kay had never much liked the boy, but since taking over Arthur's household, the dislike had grown to intense hatred. Still, the Rigotamos refused to let him be sold. "So, what will be our instructions? How much of Arthur's lands will we have to give away?"

"Whatever it takes to assure that Aircol joins the consilium. That is the only reason Arthur has agreed to this match."

I frowned. "That could mean giving up a great deal."

"That is why you are coming, to make certain that I don't give away all of Britannia," he said with a wink. Merlin paused then and brushed a strand of white hair from his face. "You think Arthur weak."

"No, I think Arthur underestimates his strength among the people. I think Arthur worries too much about placating the other lords. Answer me this, Merlin. In all of your years have you ever seen the people take to a lord as they have Arthur? Have you ever seen them surge to touch his tunic as he passes?"

It was true. Arthur was an uncommon man, and the common people adored him.

Old Merlin shook his head. "No, Malgwyn, but it has not been that many moons past that four lords of the consilium conspired to overthrow him! And by the strength of those who support Arthur and an abundance of good fortune, they were defeated."

"But Guinevere does not deserve this, not when we all know that Arthur adores her."

Merlin nodded slowly. "Were Arthur you, he could marry whomever he likes; some might grumble, but that would be all. Arthur, though, is not you. He is the Rigotamos, the head of a council of other lords who snipe and bait and attack each other, all maneuvering for some advantage, some secret channel through which they can ascend to become Rigotamos. And beyond that, he is a believer in the Christ, and one who believes in Him more strongly than others do." He paused. "Do you know what a king is, Malgwyn?" Merlin asked after a moment. "He is someone whom people admire and trust enough to place their security and that of their families in. Arthur earned people's admiration as the *Dux Bellorum*, our leader of battles. But it was his fervent belief in the Christ and those messages He champions that brought him the people's trust. Should he marry a woman who had been cast from a believer's community, they would begin to question if their trust was well and truly placed. A simple pebble thrown in a quiet pool causes ripples that eventually spread across the water, perhaps even sending water over or through a levee."

"Vortigern believed in the Christ! And he went his own way."

"People are mistaken about the causes of Vortigern's downfall," Merlin spoke even more quietly than usual. "People think his gravest error was bringing in the Saxons to fight the Picts and Scotti. And that was indeed an error. But what brought Vortigern low was when he abandoned his wife for the Saxon woman. They viewed that as a betrayal. And when he most needed their support, the people turned from him."

"Will not Arthur's betrayal of Guinevere cause the people to question their judgment?"

Merlin shook his head. "He is not married to Guinevere. And if he were to marry her, David, Mordred, Melwas, Mark and the others would latch onto that and turn it against him. In normal times, there would be no questions, but these are not normal times, Malgwyn. And what would not be an issue elsewhere, his enemies will make an issue. They will sow seeds of doubt. So, tell me this, my dear, dear friend. Is Britannia better with Arthur at the helm or with some other?"

I dropped my head at that. The old scoundrel knew all too well what my answer would be. "But what of equality and justice, of doing what is right, not necessarily what is the most expedient?"

"Why," Merlin laughed, "he has you for that!"

"Malgwyn!" Bedevere's voice broke across the camp. He saw us and tramped over. He was dressed only in his simple warrior's tunic and iron-studded belt, his hands wrapped in scraps of wool.

Twisting around, I heard a sudden gabble of voices in the distance. Merlin had stolen my attention and my ears as well, it seemed.

As Bedevere approached, I took stock of him. Shorter and stouter than Kay, he was not a man to whom words came easy at any time, but he was just the sort to whom men turned in times of danger. We had warred over much of Britannia together, and he had blocked more than one battle axe aimed for my neck. And I for him as well. He was known too for his honesty and honoring his word, something that often annoyed me when I was seeking the truth of an affair. If he promised not to reveal a confidence, no number of Saxon warriors could pry it from him.

I would never be as at ease with him as I would with Kay, whose bursts of temper and irritability were matched only by his kind heart, but, in his own way, Bedevere was just as dear to me. He had been with Arthur since near childhood, and no man loved the Rigotamos more.

At his back were a half dozen soldiers, arrayed in their gray tunics and red cloaks, spears in hand.

"What is wrong now, Bedevere?"

He pulled up short, planted the tip of his sword in the ground and leaned on it. I saw the beginnings of a grin flirting beneath his beard and mustache. But I was in no mood for levity.

"A group of the local people are seeking an audience with the Rigotamos. Arthur wishes you to counsel him as he treats with them."

My shoulders dropped then, and I surrendered to my duties.

<hr/>

The people gathered had committed a grave error from the outset of their mission. Leading them was a Druid, though bard or mere acolyte I could not tell. He was one of those men who could be young or old. His hair was white, to match his robe, but his face was mostly unlined. The robe was wrapped at the waist with a cloth belt; in his hand he carried an elaborately carved walking stick. The others were a mixed lot, in their faded and worn tunics, some barefoot, some wearing tattered sandals.

During the Roman days, I knew, the Druids had almost

been eliminated. I had heard some of the brothers at Ynys-witrin say that Julius Caesar, first of the many Caesars to come, had learned to hate the Druids in Gaul. I never understood it. The Romans had been pagan, idol worshippers for long years before they adopted Arthur's faith. You could still see hundreds of abandoned shrines around the countryside dedicated to the many Roman gods. Many, but not all, had been converted to worship of the Christ. The Romans, my father had told me, did not like to waste things.

Arthur joined me, and I saw him frown at the sight of the Druid. He saw Druidism as a blasphemy and sin, a false religion that sought human sacrifice to appease its gods. With a determined sigh, he crossed his arms and turned his head at the approach of the Druid.

That was my signal to step forward and begin. "How are you called?" I ventured.

He bowed his head, his long, freshly brushed hair nearly touching the ground. "I am called Wynn." His voice was gentle, befitting a man of peace.

"I am Malgwyn, councilor to the Rigotamos, Arthur ap Uther. You wish to treat with him?"

"Aye. The people of the villages hereabouts have asked me to bring their petition to the Rigotamos."

The Druid Wynn was not making it easy to reject his entreaties. He was acting very properly, very diplomatically, exhibiting no arrogance. "And what would their petition be?"

He looked about, almost nervously, and then turned back to me with a grimace. "Is it permitted that we all sit? I injured my back some time ago and standing for long periods pains me."

"Perhaps I should look at it," interrupted Morgan ap Tud,

appearing suddenly at the Druid's side. Arthur silenced him with a pointed look and the little physician slipped away.

I turned to Arthur. "My lord?"

Already the muscles in his jaws were twitching beneath the skin. This was not a good sign. He only did that when frustrated or angry.

Finally, Arthur nodded his assent and we moved to a pair of oak logs placed opposite each other at the campfire. The local folk ranged behind the Druid as I took up my place next to the Rigotamos.

"Now, good Wynn, what petition do your people have for Lord Arthur?"

The Druid priest smiled. "They protest the removal of Bran the Blessed's head from this his grave. To do so will only bring disaster to our lands."

I knew that no amount of pleading would change Arthur's mind. But their entreaty could not be simply rejected out of hand. Arthur would not speak; he would leave this to me. It was my job—and sometimes Merlin's—to communicate for him. This allowed us to explore alternatives without Arthur having to take a public stand. "And what sort of disaster do you foresee?"

The Druid shrugged. "I do not pretend to see the future, Master Malgwyn. But I, like these good people, see only madness in tempting the fates."

I sensed rather than saw Arthur stiffen. This Druid, for all his smiles and obeisance, had just taken his life into his hands. To accuse a noble, let alone the Rigotamos, of insanity was more than a dangerous course; it was akin to placing a sharp, naked blade against your own throat. But I also saw the shrewdness of his action. Arthur knew that he truly courted disaster by killing this emissary before the people, no matter how low the esteem in which he held Druids.

Despite his many disagreements with the Church, Arthur was a true believer in the Christ. Of that no one doubted. A simple glance at the crosses on the shields of his men told that story well. He believed too in ruling with a fair hand, a just hand. Yet, while he thought these things signs of strength, his rivals and critics saw them as weaknesses.

With all of that said, what Wynn had done was force Arthur to deal with him directly and not through me. And deal he did.

"Madness, is it madness to deal with reality and not superstition? Is it madness to look to the Christ for protection, not some rotten skull?" Arthur exclaimed. His blood was up, and I could see that the Druid's head was still in danger.

But the fool simply sat there and smiled, even as the people at his back grumbled warningly at Arthur. One thing I had learned over the years, you did not mock Arthur ap Uther. I rose quickly, to forestall the coming explosion.

"Wynn, your quest is not one that will be successful." Better, I thought, to bring this to a conclusion quickly than risk a number of summary executions. Besides, Arthur's beliefs were widely known and these people had affronted him by presenting a Druid as their representative. "On the morn the Rigotamos will unearth the skull of Bran and proclaim the entirety of Britannia under the protection of the consilium and the Christ."

The gathered throng sucked in air noisily, and even Arthur stirred nervously beside me. This was going further than he had planned, much further.

One man stepped forward, his garments carrying the mark

of some little wealth. Beneath his gray-and-black unruly hair, his eyes showed both fear and a quick mind. "My lord, I beg you not to do this. The Saxons will hear of it and will retaliate, and we are much closer to them than you. We will feel the bite of their battle axes." He was well spoken for a common farmer.

Arthur rose then and threw a quick smile my way. He saw immediately what I was about. The Druid was forgotten now. "How are you called?" he asked this new man.

"Fercos, my lord."

"Come, let us talk," and Arthur draped his arm around the surprised farmer's shoulder and led him away from the campfire into the decaying light.

The remainder milled around aimlessly for a moment, until I spied Cerdic. "Cerdic! Some bread and cheese for our friends. And some skins of good wine!"

He shouted for Talorc and the two of them fussed over the gathering, distributing, I noticed, Arthur's best cheeses and wine.

"You overstepped, Malgwyn," Merlin said softly, appearing at my one elbow.

I grimaced. "I feared that Arthur might do something rash. The Druid owes me his life."

"Aye, and so do the others. But," he grudgingly admitted, "by threatening something that Arthur had no intention of doing, you have successfully used the Saxons to our advantage."

"Come, Merlin, you know that in a negotiation you always ask for more than you want."

But the old man just shook his head in amusement at me. "One day, Malgwyn, you may go too far."

I saw that the Druid, Wynn, was still seated on his log, looking for all the world like a satisfied man. He saw me appraising him and smiled. I took up a wineskin and cup and joined him.

He waved off my offer of wine and considered me, still with that smile on his face. "You think you have accomplished something here."

I could not help but smile in return. "I did what it is my task to do."

"Your task is to create problems where none, in fact, exist and to ignore those problems that do lie on the table?"

My stomach grumbled and I filled the cup for myself. "I serve the Rigotamos. My tasks are many." I did not like his question.

Wynn smiled yet again. "Tomorrow, just as you begin to dig, they will remember what brought them here. And by the time that you are striking your camp, the people will realize that they were tricked. Fortunately for your Rigotamos, the deed will have been done. But it will leave the taste of soured wine in their mouths, and they will not forget it. And that does not count the other."

My face showed my complete confusion. "What 'other'?"

"Why, tempting the fates by removing Bran the Blessed's head. I doubt not that your Arthur will bring the wrath of the gods down about his head and on his people."

I did not like this Wynn. His Latin was good as was his grasp of our language, but I heard a Gallic accent in his words. A Druid from Gaul in our lands? 'Twas not impossible, but it made me ponder his history.

He carried a walking stick or some such thing with three faces carved into it, symbolic, I supposed, of his religion. Of true Druids, I knew little. Of false ones, I knew my fair share. I knew too that Mordred, David, and others of the consilium were sympathetic to the recent reemergence of the Druids.

The return of the Druids had not surprised me. Aye, it would have surprised me had they not spread across our lands. When the Romans had withdrawn our legions, ages before my birth, they left behind a confused and fragmented collection of tribes. The Dumnonii, the Durotrigii, the Canti, the Belgae, the Demetae, the Votadini, the Atrebati, the Dobunni and all the rest. And within each of those were clans. Some, like the Dumnonii, the Durotrigii and the Dobunni, had banded together in the consilium. But the Canti had succumbed to the Saxon invaders. The Atrebati walked a shaky plank, bordering as they did the Saxon lands. The Votadini were too far north to have truly felt the bite of the Saxon axe as yet, though they had their own difficulties with the Picts.

Merlin once told me that the Druids had maintained a great school on an island in the north, but that the Romans had destroyed it. The Saxons, themselves pagan, welcomed the Druids and that, plus the feeling among the people that abandoning the old gods had caused our current miseries, made our island fertile ground for Druids.

All of these things ran through my mind as I sat across from the Druid Wynn, still smiling. Many of us, Arthur, Bedevere, and myself, believed that a bloc of the Druids worked as spies for the Saxons. Few questioned them in their travels; fewer still wanted to challenge their right to travel. I suspected that Wynn was among these. He seemed too happy at the possibility of trouble for Arthur.

"If you question the manner of Arthur's rule, perhaps you should visit his seat on the River Cam."

The smile became broader. "I care too much for my head to make such a journey. The word of how you deal with Druids has spread far and wide."

"You mean the word of how we deal with false Druids, for that is what they were. Arthur is no friend of the Druids, that is true, but he has not and will not ban them from his territories. Dictating what gods a man should worship is a path to trouble."

"Truly? Your Arthur believes this."

Not exactly, I said to myself, but I would not let Wynn know that. "Truly."

"Then perhaps I will visit you." He stood and looked about at Cerdic and Talorc still feting our visitors with wine and cheese and bread. "It seems that my friends' complaint has been successfully shunted to the side." He squinted at me with curiosity. "You are skilled with words. I wonder if you have other abilities? I will take my leave now."

And with that, he turned and made his way out of our camp, Morgan ap Tud chasing after him, to offer him help with his injured back, I supposed. The Druid worried me, and I knew that I would see him again soon.

❖

We shuffled the local folk off after Arthur had treated with Fercos, and they seemed happy now that the Rigotamos had given his assurances that we did not intend to spark a war with the Saxons on this journey. But I feared that Wynn had not been wrong in his judgment. Their old fears would return on the morrow.

Cerdic and Talorc prepared a mighty meal. Someone had caught a great salmon and found some oysters to go with our deer stew. The salmon had been cooked up with some leeks and herbs. What had seemed a simple meal was turning into a feast. We ate silently at Arthur's campfire, though the noises from the soldiers' fires filled the night sky. Not even the screech owls could be heard above their din as they played at dice and drank *cervesas*. The breeze from the river was fresh and clean, though, and for an expedition near unto the edge of Saxon lands, we were relaxed.

I spread out my cloak on the ground. We all slept that way. Arthur had been told once that Caesar slept on the earth with just his cloak for comfort. That had been enough to convince him that he should do the same. But, in truth, Arthur was never one to put his own comfort over his men's. "War," he once told me, "is not supposed to be pleasant."

The others had gone to prepare their own beds. Though the meal had been good and the atmosphere much less tense than before, no one seemed inclined to talk. Bedevere had gone off to see that the guards were posted for the eve. The night air had put a chill in Merlin's bones. Arthur, somber and grimacing, kept his own counsel. Poor Morgan ap Tud cast about for someone, anyone, who welcomed his presence. I was melancholy at best, sad at being away from my daughter, Mariam, sad at being far from Ygerne, not yet my wife but the holder of my love.

Our path had been stony. She had been my brother's wife for many years, but he had been killed more than a year before, during the events surrounding Arthur's election as Rigotamos. Our attraction had been swift and intense, but that she had been my brother's woman was as a mountain for me. And it took me many moons to climb it.

It did not help that our journey was not of my choosing. And I did not like the way that I had treated with the people. It was not honest. I found myself serving not the truth or my *patria* but Arthur instead. This was not what I had bargained for, what I had told myself when I accepted Arthur's commission as his scribe and councilor. I had hoped for some honor, but I was finding none. The task that Arthur had set for me when this journey was ended added to my melancholy as well.

A rock beneath my cloak poked at my back. It did not hurt, but brought me wide awake. The soldiers' fires were dying and the sounds of a marching camp fading. I rose and went to the edge of the mount, looking down at the River Tamesis below.

Beneath the moonlight, it glowed and sparkled in yellow and white as it continued to the sea. A few farmsteads in the distance still had candles burning. Somewhere a dog barked.

And then, close by, a woman screamed.

CHAPTER THREE

The cry had come from the west, near the settlement on the riverbanks. Something in the mournful bleating alarmed me, touched some part of me. I dashed back to my cloak and snatched up my dagger. Without even thinking, I ran down a path and out of our camp. Behind me, I heard shouts and the sound of leather slapping against packed earth.

One, two, and then three dots of light appeared below me as I burst through some brush and into the collection of houses, our peculiar kind of round-shaped huts so at odds with the angular buildings of the Romans.

A half dozen or so people stood in their doorways, their shadows dancing in the flickering torchlight. Between two of the houses I saw the yellow globe of three or four torches illuminating a large group of people.

As I drew closer, I recognized Fercos and one or two others from the afternoon. They were gathered around a lump on the ground, a lump covered by a gray cloak.

From beneath the cloak, a dark blob shone under the torchlight. I knew it all too well. Blood.

Pushing my way through, I could see by the ankles and

feet poking beyond the cloak that they were those of a young woman or boy. I glanced around quickly and saw that Fercos was crying.

Two men fronted me, blocking my path. "You are not welcome here! This is our affair!"

"I mean no harm. I wish only to help." The tightened muscles in their faces told me that the arrogance of a king's councilor would win no battles here.

One, an honest-faced man with the sadness of the ages written on his countenance, said softly, "How can you help? The maiden is dead by another's hand, and one of your fellows probably did it. We know all too well how soldiers take what they want."

I cursed Mordred under my breath. His tenure in this region the previous year had turned many people against us. He wielded little control over his men, and they pillaged the land freely. Kay had most recently been in command here, but he had had too little time to set aright the relationship between our soldiers and the people.

"He is skilled at such things," a voice behind me said. Deep and gravelly, it yet conveyed a tenderness. I knew it well—Arthur.

The group spread out then, surprised by the Rigotamos's appearance. He had thrown one of his older tunics on, rushing, it seemed, as I had, to find the source of the scream. Behind him I saw Bedevere and another soldier, alarm written on their faces, but Arthur raised a hand to stop them in their advance.

The man made to protest, but thought better of it. Arthur brushed past me and laid a hand on his shoulder. He turned to one of our soldiers. "Go fetch Morgan ap Tud." To the poor villager, he said, "First, tell me what has happened here."

Another man, one who seemed more composed than the others, stepped forward. "Fercos's wife had gone to throw some water out behind their hut when she found her daughter, Hafren, lying dead here."

"From what cause?" I asked.

Fercos, tears still streaming from his eyes, saw us now, in truth for the first time. "No one can help her. Go and leave us. We must prepare her for burial."

"Do you not care who did this?"

"And how would you discover that?" Fercos fairly spat at me. "Just leave us be."

Bedevere slid in between Arthur and me. "My lord, I am not certain we wish to involve ourselves in this matter. We have nothing to gain and much to lose," he whispered.

That decided it for me. I was tired of doing things because of what advantage they could or could not bring us. I did not even wait for Arthur's reply. I stepped up to Fercos and laid my one hand on his shoulder. "I would do this because I too once lost a loved one to murder, and because I have some experience with searching out the doers of these deeds. Would you have this happen to another man's daughter?"

"He has handled these sorts of affairs before," Arthur said. "I would consider it a favor to me if you would allow him to help you."

The Rigotamos was one of the most perceptive people I had ever known. He saw in a blink of an eye that this was important to me, and though he could have stopped me in a second, he allowed me to pursue it. I was appreciative.

Fercos met my eyes with a look as intense as any I had known, searching for truth, honesty, something. Whatever he sought, he must have found, for his expression relaxed and he stepped away.

"Has aught been touched?" I could not remain silent; my mind was already trying to grasp the situation.

"Just a cloak thrown across to cover her," someone answered.

I knelt and tried to block out the noises of the gathered crowd: whispers, low exclamations, and grumbled curses. Pivoting on my heel, I searched out Bedevere and with my eyes and a shake of my head silently asked him to disperse the people. He looked to Arthur, who nodded his assent.

Turning back then, I surveyed the area without touching anything. She lay partially on her back and partially on her side; I could tell that from how the cloak was pushed out by her knees. Apart from the puddle of dark blood leaking from beneath the cloak, I could see the scuffs of sandaled feet and drag marks in the mud.

I stripped away the cloak and stumbled back. A dirty strip of cloth had been tied about her head and across her mouth to keep her from crying out. Beneath her pale, pointed chin gaped what seemed another mouth, but I knew it was not that. Her throat had been cut and I needed no closer look to see that it was deep. Aye, any deeper and the blade would have severed her head.

It was only then, when I had seen that horrible wound, that I looked at the rest of her. She was a pretty girl, long brown hair plaited into two strands and large eyes. I caught myself thinking how her pale tone suited her, but then I realized that 'twas the blood drained from her that made her appear as a piece of Roman marble.

Her hands had been tied behind her back with the same sort of cloth, as had her ankles. Quickly, I took a knee and felt her head with my one hand. It took but a second before I pulled my hand away, bloody. Her attacker had struck her from behind, not fatally, but fiercely enough to render her senseless. She had been dragged, alive, to this refuge.

Her dress, of a fair brown cloth, was torn and bloody. On each upper arm was a shale armlet, black and shiny. They were old and held the marks of many winters. Still, I thought it said much of Fercos's prosperity that his daughter would have two such baubles.

Too many people were yet about. I looked to Bedevere. "Have some torches brought and," I added in a lower voice, "move these people away. I must needs examine her."

His eyebrows rose a bit, but he nodded and went about his task. He understood what I needed to do and why I needed privacy.

Some minutes passed as the torches were gathered. I spent the time studying the earth around the body. Again, I noted the sandal prints, the two drag marks where someone had moved the maiden's body to this place. I saw that the copse from which the marks led was near unto the houses, barely enough room for two men to stand arm in arm. Ultimately, I would have to search in the wood, but for now I restricted my investigations to the poor maiden's body. For the first time in his short tenure with us, I wanted Morgan with me. I had learned much from the monachi at Ynys-witrin about our bodies, but Morgan had spent a lifetime learning.

"Where is the medicus, Morgan ap Tud?"

"He has been sent for," Bedevere reminded me.

Finally, all the people had been cleared and the torches put in place. Arthur had sent for a dozen men from our camp. He had not spoken to me since I had brashly thrust myself into this affair, but I knew he would not remain silent forever.

As I approached the unpleasant task of inspecting the maiden's body, I heard the raspy, abrupt sound of a throat being cleared.

"Malgwyn, Bedevere is right," Arthur began. "This is not wise. You did well in putting down this protest and eliminating the Druid as a factor, but I cannot spare you to sort out this crime, even if you can. And that is much to risk your purse on."

I turned to face him. "Yes, my lord, I understand the problems. And I do not pretend to believe I can find the killer of this girl before we leave tomorrow. But I should be able to learn much and leave that with these good people so that they can continue the search. It costs you nothing. And it may do you some good, or your reputation. In these lands, the people live with a fear brought by the Saxons. That you are seen to be sensitive to their problems may bring their tribe closer to the consilium. It will cost me a sleepless night, but at least it will be one spent in a good cause."

"Malgwyn." Bedevere joined us. "The father himself may have done this thing."

"No. I saw his eyes. They held true pain, Bedevere, not the evil of a man who would kill his own child."

The Rigotamos and Bedevere exchanged fleeting looks. "You make a strong argument, Malgwyn. And, as you say, it will be your night's sleep disturbed. But be ready on the morrow." Arthur turned to his Master of Horse. "Stay and provide whatever assistance he requires." His orders given, he spun on his *caligae* and headed back up the path.

"You can be an aggravating man, Malgwyn," Bedevere

grumbled. "The time is not long past when you cared for nothing but from whence your next drink and your next woman would come. Now, you care about so much more."

"Would you have the drunk back?" I asked, kneeling down beside the maiden's corpse.

"Ask me tomorrow," my old warrior friend replied.

With that, I turned my attention back to the poor girl. Pulling the dress away, I saw what I feared. She had been foully abused. But it was more than that. Great bruises marked the inside of her thighs, and that most private place was ripped and torn in a manner I had never seen before.

"Bring a torch closer," I ordered. Bedevere brought it himself and knelt next to me.

"In the Christ's name, Malgwyn!" he exclaimed. "What has been done to her?"

I did not answer, but swallowed my disgust and looked closer. The flesh was torn and bloody. I gestured for the torch to draw closer yet. This was beyond belief! Splinters of wood and bits of bark were imbedded in those shocking wounds. That someone could do this to such a young girl was simply beyond my ken. What purpose could it serve?

Then I realized that my backside had become damp. I had fallen backward onto my rump in my surprise and hadn't even noticed it.

"Bedevere, a hand please." I felt very old then and willingly took his wool-wrapped hand in mine and struggled to my feet, letting the cloak fall back over the child's mangled body.

"Post a man here with instructions to allow no one near. I will not have anyone, including her parents, see the truth of this."

"But they will need to prepare her body for burial," Bedevere argued, and rightly so.

"Then bring me some water and cloth," I paused, "and some ochre, chalk, and such as well."

The stocky warrior looked at me as if I were insane. "Malgwyn, where shall I find such as that? I keep it not in my bag."

"Please, Bedevere, just find some and bring it to me."

The water appeared in just a few moments. I had spent the time plucking the splinters and bark from her flesh. One splinter seemed odd, with a shiny, smooth surface to it, as if worked. The edge on one end was frayed; the other end was pointed as a normal splinter. I kept it.

While I washed the dirt and grit from her, Bedevere appeared with the items I had requested. I wanted to ask him where, indeed, he had gotten them, but the grimace on his face stayed my question.

Another few minutes and I had done all that I dared toward covering up her shame. She had not been dead long, nay her body yet held some warmth, and so I arranged it more pleasingly, removed the gag and smoothed the terror from her face and washed the blood from the ragged cut at her throat. The rest I left for her family. I wished only to hide the nature of her abuse; that was something even one so cynical as I found shocking.

I took the chance to think about what had passed in the maiden's last moments. This thing had not happened here. She had been bound and abused elsewhere, then, gagged, dragged back here and her throat slit nearly on her father's doorstep. That left an odd question floating before me: Who was being punished (if anyone)—the girl or her father?

After tucking the gag and two of the larger splinters into my pouch for later study, I walked slowly along the edge of the wood. That no one heard anything was not a surprise. The ground was carpeted in cedar needles, the residue of more years than I cared to count. My own footfalls were virtually silent.

Finally I found what I sought—a broken branch, low-hanging and freshly-snapped—the point where the murderer slipped back into the wood. It was located on the side nearest our camp, but that meant nothing by itself. Or, I realized, it might mean everything.

Bedevere reappeared with two soldiers and I directed them to remain on guard, keeping the folk away from the corpse for a bit longer. "Come, Bedevere. Let us see what we can find."

Each of us carried a torch, and we plunged into the darkness of the wood. Even in the torchlight it was too dark to see much by way of footprints and the ground was too hard to show much, much harder than the earth behind the huts. So, we looked for other signs, broken twigs, perhaps a bit of cloth torn from a tunic. Anything. Nothing. Beyond that one broken twig, nothing else hinted at his path of retreat.

Would that the spot where he committed this foul deed be as easy to find, I thought.

And it was.

We came upon the clearing almost by accident. It was marked by a large boulder in the center, and it took but a few seconds to find the blood smeared on its surface.

As I walked around the large stone, I could see how the affair had played out. He had either arranged to meet her here or had come upon her by surprise, but either way, he approached from behind. With Bedevere's help, I found what I sought—a rock, flat on one side and curved on the other, and bloody on the flat side. He had slammed the rock against her head, knocking her senseless.

Before she could recover, he had bound and gagged her. We found where he had lain her on the ground, and though I had not thought we would find it, discovered the branch with which he had abused her.

One end was marked by jagged edges and giant, bloody splinters. I shivered. I could not imagine the pain and horror that the young girl had felt. What must she have thought? The evil of it struck at my heart.

He must have knelt over her, staring into her face as he thrust it again and again into her. She had wanted to scream, but the blasted gag had dammed up her cries for help. Finally, she had lost consciousness; she must have. The blow to the head. The binding of her hands and legs. The gag. The pain. To have remained conscious throughout all of that was the act of no god I could ever worship.

Why? Rape. I understood rape, if not the impulse then the act. I could never do it. It was about power, anger, but not pleasure, not in any honest way. I learned that long ago, at the first Saxon village we raided.

⁂

We had been told that two of the Saxon lords were meeting there to marshal their forces for a strike deep into the heart of our lands. Mordred and I were detailed to take a small detachment to attack them. Our orders were to lie in wait in a wood just outside the village, to strike them at dark when they would be tired after a day's riding.

It soon became obvious that only half a dozen Saxon soldiers were there. Mordred's men and mine were tired as well, tired from hiding all day, hungry. I do not know who started it, but just at nightfall some of our men began the attack without orders. They dispatched the Saxons quickly, but then started in on the people.

I found two of Mordred's and one of my men having at a pretty young Saxon maid. It had nothing to do with sex. It was as if I could see the anger flash from their ears as they attacked her with a ferocity I did not believe possible. The looks on their faces were ones of unhappiness, not pleasure. The Saxons were not there for them to punish so they would punish the maiden.

I still had both arms then, and I waded into their midst as a hot dagger into butter. One I backhanded against a hut. The second, one of Mordred's, scampered backward, falling and blubbering for mercy. I kicked him beneath his chin with all the force in my leg. The last was my own man. He fell to his knees and bowed his head. He offered no apology.

Without a pause, I grabbed him by his hair and dragged him to where the girl lay whimpering against one of their odd, sunken huts. Though I knew it would frighten her, I held his face just inches from her own. I leaned over and whispered in his ear, "What if that were your own daughter?" And then I kicked him so hard I felt a rib break under my foot.

No, those men were angry, but they weren't to be denied their pleasure, either. This killer cared only about pain and torture and fear. He did not even try to take any pleasure from the flesh, at least not in the way we had always judged such things. This was another creature altogether.

Taking advantage of her state, he dragged her back to the

place behind the huts, snatched her hair from behind and slit her throat. All that too had a purpose, though I could not reckon what it might be.

"Malgwyn?"

It was Bedevere.

"Aye."

"Fercos's woman wishes to prepare the girl for burial."

I nodded. Daybreak was but an hour away now. I could tell them much about how their daughter had died, perhaps a bit about the kind of man who had done the killing, but nothing about who he was. The odds that I would have been able to were not good from the beginning, but I had needed to try. I felt no sense of failure for myself, but a sadness for Fercos and his woman. In my heart, there had been no hope for success. Death was too much a part of our world and I needed to do something clean and pure. But the strangeness of this death made that sadness so much greater. I truly wanted to bring this killer to justice, but I knew that was not going to happen. It could have been one of our men, though I could not think of one capable of this brutality. It could have been a stranger passing by. Finding this beast was not going to happen. Though it gave me no comfort, I knew that, and I knew I would not be able to dismiss this affair from my mind.

"Let them. While they are about their burying, Arthur can remove Bran's skull. We should be finished by the time they are finished. Someone should gain something from this."

Bedevere slipped into the darkness.

After a moment's pause, I turned to go, holding the torch in my one hand, when it happened; someone rushed me from the darkness, knocking the torch to the ground and shoving me into the underbrush.

I scrambled in the loose leaves and vines, falling back twice before making it back to my feet.

"Bedevere!" But he had already gone back to the village, and it took me only a second to realize that I was alone too.

Whoever my assailant had been, and I could not help but believe it was the killer, he had been waiting in the forest. But why? And why had he not killed me?

My torch was out and the forest blocked any moonlight. I knew then how a blind man felt. "Bedevere!"

And almost as I spoke, I could hear his welcome voice calling in return.

But a hand touched me from the blackness, and I grabbed for my dagger.

"Malgwyn, it is me, Morgan!"

Ah, so the little medicus had finally arrived. Then I spotted the growing point of light from Bedevere's torch and heard the low-hanging limbs tear at his cloak.

As Morgan helped steady myself, I shook his hand off.

"Next time . . . make yourself known, or you'll find a dagger . . . between your ribs," I snapped as sharply as my breath would allow, and immediately felt bad. "I'm sorry, Morgan. I have . . . just been attacked, and you startled me."

"Malgwyn!" Bedevere was still searching.

"Here!"

He grew close enough then for me to make out his square figure. As he and Morgan looked me over quickly, his torch warmed us all.

"What happened?"

"Someone . . . was . . . hiding here, in this copse." My breathing grew less ragged, more even; I could still feel my heart pumping in my chest. "He rushed me and knocked me to the ground."

"The man who killed the girl?"

"Who else would fear discovery and hide here?"

"But why not kill you, too? The advantage was his."

"I know," I said, my head shaking almost against my will. "But that is not the most troubling thing."

Even in the torchlight I could see the contours of Bedevere's face take on a puzzled look. "How so?"

"The killer fled toward our camp."

"Then we must follow!" he sputtered, making to leave.

"No, in the night we would not find his trail. And, if in our camp, by now he has had time to cover his crime. For all we know, he changed direction as soon as he toppled me."

The lines at Bedevere's mouth told me he was not satisfied with my answer. In truth, neither was I; too much time had passed now and answers would come slowly if at all. That was of little comfort to me and would be of even less to the people of the village.

And then I went to Fercos and his wife and told them what they needed to know of Hafren's death.

✤

A few hours later, we watched as two of Arthur's men dug at the stone marking Bran's skull. A dozen or so local people stood nearby, uneasy and restless, but Arthur's assurances of the day before and the burial of Fercos's daughter had deplenished their numbers and stolen their fear, of Bran's revenge at any rate. The Druid was nowhere to be seen.

After a few minutes, one of the soldiers stopped digging

and motioned for Bedevere. He trotted over, peered closely into the hole, and nodded at Arthur. The Rigotamos waved for Merlin and me, and we joined him.

They had discovered what appeared to be a square wooden box. There was only one thing it could be, and from the holes rotted at its joints, it was old enough. We all held our breaths as Merlin waved his arms about, mumbling what must have been some incantation. I laughed under my breath. Though Arthur did not believe in such things, he was obviously taking few chances.

Finally, my old friend struggled to his knees and recovered the dark box, handling it gingerly. He set it to the side and opened it. We all drew closer.

Indeed, there was a skull there, resting on what had once been a velvet lining. I tried to remember what I had heard about Bran's skull, anything that would aid in identifying it. But it was not really necessary. After all, what other skull would be buried in a box on the White Mount?

Arthur moved to take it from its box and hold it high for all to see. Merlin stopped his arm in mid-motion. "Do not act as a champion. Simply remove it with humility. To do otherwise could be seen as belittling their beliefs."

"You sound as if you would rather I not do this."

Sometimes Arthur amazed me.

"I would rather you put that back in the ground and cover it up," Merlin snapped, but softly. "I have told you, Bedevere has told you, even Malgwyn has told you that this is not wise. You should not challenge forces that you cannot see."

"He's right, Rigotamos," I proffered.

"Why, Malgwyn, I thought you were a man of logic and

reason? Surely you do not believe in such as the protection of Bran's skull?"

"As a general thing, my lord, no. But there is no reason to do this, either. If you must, do not bash these people over the head with it. Honor their beliefs, even in dismantling them."

"He's right, Arthur," Bedevere joined in.

Something in Arthur's eyes grabbed at mine, a twinkle that I could not define. But he thrust Bran's skull into the air anyway as all those watching, including some of our own soldiers, gasped, and the grumbles grew louder.

Until Arthur spoke. "We now place Bran the Blessed's skull under our protection, so that it may never be taken by our enemies, so that it may forever be honored and respected."

And the grumbles changed to murmurs of agreement, then of approval, but approval tinged with reservations.

"Worry not about Bran. He shall be revered."

Without waiting for any of the ceremonies that we had planned, Arthur placed the skull back in its decaying box, handed it to Bedevere and remounted his horse.

He trotted over to where I stood. "This is better, faster. Let's ride."

We were off, our soldiers scurrying for their mounts. Cerdic and Talorc had already prepared the wagons for the journey back.

As we crossed the River Tamesis, a figure appeared on the far side, standing atop a bank above the road. As we drew closer and I could better see who it was, I cocked my head in surprise.

Wynn, the Druid.

He still wore his white robe, belted at the waist, and held his oddly carved staff. No smile graced his face as he clambered down onto the lane and stood in our path.

Arthur raised a wool-wrapped hand and halted our party. "What do you want with us, Druid?" No softness in his voice now. Wynn stood alone.

"You may have charmed the people with your words, Arthur, but you have disturbed the spirit of Bran and, in time, he will pay you for your sacrilege."

The Rigotamos laughed grimly. "Bran the Blessed is long dead. The people will realize that only the consilium and the Christ protect their freedom. Now step out of our path before I take home your skull as well."

"A curse is upon you, Lord Arthur, and the fools who allowed you to do this thing. They are as guilty as you, and you will soon feel its bite as well," he answered, but he also moved to the side, out of our path. He was not stupid.

On down the road, but not far, I turned back in my saddle and saw his figure, still standing by the side of the road. I wondered about Fercos's daughter, and the Druid, and his cryptic warning that his curse would wound Arthur "as well."

PART TWO

THE
LAND OF THE
DEMETAE

CHAPTER FOUR

ather!"

My daughter, Mariam, her golden hair flowing behind her, ran across the market square and leapt into my arm. She wrapped her arms about my neck and kissed my cheek, giggling as my beard tickled her.

"And have you behaved?"

"Of course, Father. You have gained weight! Mother will be pleased."

Events in the last year had taken their toll on me physically, and I was just now beginning to regain my health. Ygerne had insisted that I eat at least one meal a day at her home. I was living in a modest wattle-and-daub hut, across the lane and down the slope a bit from Arthur's hall, with Merlin, whose mind sometimes wandered and who oft needed a helping hand. After my brother's death, Arthur had proclaimed Ygerne and her family as part of his household and hence they were eligible to draw from his kitchen stores. As his councilor, I too could eat from his table, but, in truth, Ygerne cooked better than Cerdic.

While Ygerne and I shared a bed now, we had yet to be married, more a formality than a necessity in those days. But she had been mother to my daughter since nearly Mariam's birth. Gwenyth, my dear wife, had been killed by the Saxons when Mariam was but a year old. Obsessed by revenge, I had left Mariam with Ygerne and Cuneglas, my brother, and went off to join Arthur's war. The loss of my arm and, I believed, my honor and dignity at the River Tribuit sent me spiraling into drink and self-pity, and I was ashamed to reclaim my daughter. It was not until years later that I came to my senses. By that time, Ygerne had become the only mother she had ever really known.

But holding her now, seeing those bright eyes, it was as if my Gwenyth were alive still. I swung her down and took her hand in mine. One of the young boys who lazed about Arthur's stables or the barracks when not getting into other mischief took my horse's reins from me, and Mariam and I started across the dirt-packed square toward the back lane where Ygerne's house lay.

"A council will be held after the feast, Malgwyn," the Rigotamos reminded me, joining us from within the stables. "We have much to discuss."

I tightened without realizing it. Aye, and there was much that I did not relish discussing. "Yes, my lord."

"You are not happy with Lord Arthur, Father?" Mariam missed nothing. Her tiny fingers gripped my hand a little harder.

"The Rigotamos and I often disagree about things, Mariam. It is of no consequence."

"Then why are you grinding your teeth?"

I squeezed her hand gently. "Little girls who ask too many questions are given to the Druids for sacrifices."

"Father! You're not going to give me to the Druids." Her voice was confident.

"Oh, but I am. Ask Master Merlin. It was his idea."

"Father! Master Merlin would give you to the Druids before he would me. Master Merlin loves me."

My teeth were not grinding then. I was laughing. She knew us all so well. Just a few minutes in her presence and I was as relaxed as after a good night's rest.

But as we turned from the market square and down into the by-lanes of town, an image of that poor child, so vilely abused, hardened my face yet again. I glanced down, but Mariam was not looking and I was glad.

The feast was a disaster. Cerdic had not had time to prepare the food as he liked, and Arthur's face was strained, the muscles at his jaws working vigorously, a sign that something had gone amiss. Guinevere, wearing her favorite green gown, was with him, and she seemed disturbed, yet not distraught. They had fought, but not over the marriage. Something else had brought them to angry words.

As I chewed my roasted pork, I wondered at this. Like any pairing, they had their troubles. But for the most part, they were well matched and had few difficulties. Nimue, a young Gallic slave, smiled at me as she filled my beaker with wine. She was growing into a lovely lass and, Arthur willing, would one day be a good wife for some young man.

Our journey, some two weeks in length, had tired me, and I hoped that this feasting would end in a reasonable time. Though I loved Ygerne, I longed only for my own bed this eve.

Merlin would have to put up with my snoring yet another night. But after listening to the squeaky refrains of the lyre player, singing some ancient song of heroes near the hearth, he would welcome it.

I chuckled in a grim sort of way. Here I denounced Arthur for not taking Guinevere to wife and for taking this child of the Demetae for only political reasons, and yet I took my pleasure in Ygerne but seemed unable to move into her house and enter into a marriage myself, something I knew she would favor.

Instead, I avoided the topic, sidestepped the issue. In truth, I had no acceptable reason for doing this thing. I loved her. Of that I had no doubt. But to marry her meant to move into her house, my brother Cuneglas's house. And that was more than I would do. Perhaps once I had constructed a house of equal or greater size, I could. But Arthur's business kept me so busy I had little time for such an undertaking.

And, still, there was Arthur's offer to make me a lord of the consilium by granting me the lands of Dochu and Teilo, who had rebelled against Arthur with Lauhiir some moons before. I had not answered him as yet. To accept the title meant moving to their lands and establishing my own dominion, which also meant moving Ygerne, Mariam, and the other children there as well. I was not prepared to do that. Castellum Arturius provided a safety that a new fortress, long days away to the north, could not.

So I had avoided answering Arthur's offer, and I think that he was glad of it. We had grown closer over the past year, nearly as close as we had been before I fell at Tribuit, and in some ways closer. But late at night, as I lay on my furs, and the stump of my arm ached in the damp air, I thought of the men I had left on that green hillock, their blood mixing almost festively against the new grass. I had not served them well.

I kept to myself this night. Normally, my charge was to observe the proceedings, watch any visitors, try to read the purpose in their eyes. But we were treating with no other lords. Indeed, the only "visitor" was Tristan, young son of Lord Mark at Castle Marcus, and he was not with us by choice.

Tall, handsome Tristan was a "guest," or more appropriately hostage for his father's good conduct. More than a year before, Mark had tried to force the consilium to treat with the Saxons, to give them free passage across our lands for trade. But then Tristan had involved himself in the death of my wife's sister, Eleonore, a death which led to the discovery of a conspiracy against Ambrosius Aurelianus, then the Rigotamos.

Because of Tristan's father's mischief, Arthur had used Tristan's part in Eleonore's death to hold him as surety of his father's good behavior. That made Tristan a very unhappy man, and it did my heart good to see him in such a state.

Once we had been punished by a bard's song—some ancient refrain of a king who had gone mad—Kay, as was his duty as Seneschal, slammed his cup against the table, calling all to attention.

Arthur stood and held his hands out for silence. He was an imposing figure, cloaked in his crimson tunic and flowing robe, his hands wrapped in wool with those stubby fingers poking forth.

"I am not one for speeches, so I shall not bore you with one now. Nimue! Come here, girl!"

The serving maiden nearly dropped her pitcher of wine. Fear flowed from her every pore; her eyes turning from those of a girl content with her lot to those of a cornered cat, seeking escape. She stepped back.

But Arthur smiled at her. "Come, girl. You shall not be sorry."

Nimue approached Arthur with head bowed.

"Kay has come to me on your behalf several times in recent months. My councilor Malgwyn has spoken well of you. Merlin, too, has oft mentioned you. The sum total of their advice has been this: you were wrongfully enslaved and you should be freed. All gathered here know that I will not buy and sell slaves. But I will free them when it is deserved. And this I do now for you. Your life is your own. Do well with it."

As Arthur signaled for Nimue to rise, I saw the truth then. Guinevere and Arthur had argued about his decision to give Nimue her freedom. As I have mentioned, Nimue was quickly becoming a pretty young woman, and Guinevere did not like that Arthur showed her any favor at all, just as she had felt about Eleonore, my Gwenyth's sister. Sadly, Guinevere was really more beautiful than Nimue or even Eleonore had been, but she would not, could not, recognize that. I dreaded the day that she found out about Arthur's impending marriage.

I turned my attention back to Nimue then, and Arthur was advising her. "You may stay here or go as you please. Perhaps you would wish to return to Braga, in Gaul. I am told that you have family there. I can arrange safe passage and an escort."

Nimue was still stunned by her emancipation, but she answered him quickly. "If it pleases you, Rigotamos, I would like to stay here and continue serving in your kitchen. What family I may have in Gaul are all but certainly dead. Here, I have friends, more, it seems, than I knew." She kept her head bowed, but I saw a smile beginning. I was happy for her.

"If you are sure that is what you wish?"

She nodded.

"Then we have the added problem of a suitable guardian."

I had not thought of this. An unmarried maid needed a guardian, someone legally responsible for her, not that laws held much sway in our lands in those days, but like many things, the appearance of structure and law was about all we could muster then, and as Arthur's Romanisms comforted him, this illusion comforted us all. The obvious answer was that Arthur should serve, since she would be working in his kitchens, but he seemed a bit flustered, his cheeks reddening. And then I caught the look in Guinevere's eye, a look as sharp as a Saxon axe.

Arthur was no fool. He had not navigated the politics of the consilium and the treachery of his fellows without being crafty. "As this is a special occasion," he began in a rumbling voice, "I shall grant you a special favor. You may choose your own guardian."

The scene before me was, simply, laughable. Guinevere did not know whether to be pleased or not. Kay preened, assuming, I suspected, that he would be her choice (and then her husband in a year or so, unless I missed the mark). The others at the feast, Bedevere and our friend Illtud, who had come down from Ynys-witrin, looked amused. Merlin was poking at something in his bowl of mashed pork, flicking some offending bit away. A dog had wandered into the hall and was nudging my leg for some food, completely unaware of the drama then unfolding.

I watched Nimue closely; I was curious whom she would choose. She raised her head then, adjusted her rose-colored servant's gown, a peplos-cut like Guinevere's but of less finely woven cloth, and faced Arthur.

"With your permission, my lord, I would ask that Master Merlin be named my guardian. He is already as a father to me."

I could not help but smile. Kay's face drooped. Bedevere and Illtud hid their own smirks behind woolen-wrapped hands. Guinevere cocked her head to the side and nodded approvingly, appraising Nimue, for perhaps the first time, as something other than a potential rival.

"What say you, Merlin? Merlin?"

My old friend looked up from his bowl and nodded as if irritated. "Of course, of course. It is my honor."

And with that, the feast ended, all except for our council after.

⁂

As the now free Nimue and the others began to clean away the night's meal, Bedevere, Merlin, Kay, and I moved to Arthur's private chambers, separated from his great hall by a thin wooden wall. He planned a more substantial construction, but his time as Rigotamos had left him little freedom for such things. Aye, his beloved cruciform church was still little more than muddy foundation trenches, although that was more the fault of Coroticus, the abbot at Ynys-witrin.

So Arthur had sent Guinevere to her home on the Via Arturius, the road between Castellum Arturius and Ynys-witrin, with Illtud as her escort.

Arthur's quarters were not fancy. Aye, other than one weaving, there was little in the way of decoration but his shield, bearing the chi rho symbol of his faith, mounted on the wall. We sat about a wooden table, our faces grim. I am not sure that any of us relished our task.

"Bedevere, you, Malgwyn and Merlin will depart tomorrow. Take two troop of horse. That should be enough to discourage any *latrunculi* bent on mischief or a Saxon raiding party. On your way north, stop at Ynys-witrin and add Coroticus, the abbot, to your party."

I started to protest, but Arthur held his hand up, his irritation showing through. "Enough, Malgwyn. I know that you do not like him, but I am beginning to wonder if there is anyone you like. You hate Coroticus. You hate David. You hate Aircol's daughter."

With that, I rose sharply. "You forgot yourself, my lord. I have hated you for longer than all the rest!"

And we stayed like that for a long moment, our jaws both grinding, staring at each other with narrowed eyes.

"Stop it! The both of you!" Merlin admonished us, like the teacher he so often seemed to be. "Arthur, you brought Malgwyn to your service because you respected his abilities to reason through matters, his wisdom. And he has proven that it was a wise choice. Malgwyn, you came to Arthur's service because you realized that at this time in our world, he is the best suited to lead us. You know that as well as you know how to breathe."

It was hard to argue with the thin, wrinkled little man. I did not feel calm, but I felt foolish at my anger. And I felt foolish standing like a peeved little boy. I sat.

"I want to impress upon Aircol," Arthur continued in an apologetic tone, "the strength of my devotion to the Christ. Bedevere, take Cerdic with you to prepare the meals. And take double the meat, butter, milk, and leeks, and mushrooms, all the foods. Allow Cerdic to distribute the extra to the people on your return trip as he sees fit. Oh, and take Morgan ap Tud. I would have him with you if someone falls sick. Besides, I have little for him to do here."

I could not remain quiet. "Rigotamos, I understand your desire to impress Aircol, but these actions seem but empty gestures, false even."

Though I expected to be chastised again, help came from an unexpected quarter—Bedevere.

"Rigotamos, Malgwyn is right. If you wish to grant food to the poor, that is noble. But do it because they are in need, not because you wish to make Aircol happy. I thought better of you. He is a noble, yes, but he is not Rigotamos, and he should wish to impress you. Do not lower yourself like this."

For the first time in a long time, I realized that Arthur was still young in a sense. We were about the same years, but where I was born a poor farmer, he was born a noble. And he wanted so much to succeed. I had simply wanted to survive. Until Tribuit.

But in other ways, Arthur was wise beyond his years. As a youth, I had been told, Merlin was his teacher. Little was really clear about Arthur's early years. I knew that his father was a noble named Uther, a friend of Ambrosius and Lord Cadwy and that Uther died fairly young. Beyond that, I knew nothing, and to ask was something not done. Merlin, too, was quiet about those days. His willingness to impress Aircol stood in marked contrast to his attitude toward the Saxons. And, for that much, I was thankful.

He considered Bedevere's words. "Agreed." Stroking his mustache, Arthur turned then to me. "Be prepared to grant Aircol command of any northern army gathered to repel another Saxon invasion, but do not agree to it unless you must. Allow him to speak for the consilium with the other northern tribes, but do not agree to let him treat alone with the Saxons under any circumstance."

"What of additional lands?"

Arthur smiled beneath his beard. "'Tis time for you to decide, Malgwyn. Will you accept Teilo and Dochu's lands and become a lord of the consilium? Or will you remain my scribe and councilor? If you refuse the title, you may grant Aircol those lands."

Bedevere and Merlin looked at me intently. Arthur still smiled. He already knew my answer, knew it by my hesitancy in answering until now.

"I will stay here, Rigotamos. Though I know that I am not as obedient as I should be, I am fit more to be your scribe than a lord," I reminded him, lifting my half arm.

"You are fit to be what you wish to be, but I will not argue with you. I know we have our differences, Malgwyn, but I welcome your presence in my councils. Give Aircol the lands."

Bedevere cleared his throat, his woolen hand fingering the brooch at his shoulder. "That will give him a very large power base in the northwest, Arthur. Is it wise?"

Arthur's thick eyebrows rose and fell and he shrugged. "What is wise in these days? You know as well as I that we have few allies in the north. While I do not hate David as Malgwyn does, I do trust Malgwyn's instincts and judgment. David is not to be depended upon. Allying ourselves to Aircol puts a friend at David's back gate. And a little whisper in the wind tells me that Aircol and David are rivals.

"After all," he continued, "we will have Aircol's daughter in our midst. I would not choose to think of her as a hostage against his good behavior—as Tristan is for Mark's—but her presence serves a similar purpose."

"You assume that Aircol will feel a need to protect his daughter," Merlin countered. "Daughters are for marriages and alliances."

"He is a father, too," I said, coming to Arthur's defense in this matter, oddly enough. "It might not be enough to guarantee his goodwill, but it will give him pause."

Arthur nodded. "So it is decided. Bedevere, you will command the party for the journey. Kay will remain here and see to the preparations."

"And you, my lord?" Kay asked, innocently.

The Rigotamos rose, pulling his tunic down and cinching his iron-studded belt tighter. "I will go to Guinevere's cottage and do what must be done."

※

"She will need you, Malgwyn," Merlin told me later that night as we settled into our beds.

"Who?" My mind was still wrapped around the poor, ravaged body of Hafren back at the base of the White Mount.

"Guinevere. This will be a savage blow to her. You are the only family she has left."

"Yes," I agreed. "And Arthur has conveniently arranged for me to be absent when Guinevere needs me most."

Old Merlin cocked his head to the side. "I did not think of that. Arthur did not, either. But it would not matter. He has his mission to complete as we have ours."

He stopped and looked across the room at me. "Have no fear, Malgwyn. She will need you just as much when we return."

But I did worry, because I knew Guinevere better than Merlin. She had abandoned her vow of celibacy for her love of Arthur, though she had been but a child when she undertook it. She had borne her disgrace with nobility. And I did not believe that she would give up the role of consort easily or well. In truth, I did not know what she would do. And that made me fear for her. For Merlin's point was double-edged: Just as I was all the family that Guinevere had, she was all the blood kin left for me, save Mariam.

❧

"Why must you leave now?" Ygerne was much out of sorts with me. I had just cinched a leather pouch on my saddle and was preparing to mount my horse. We were standing in the flat below Arthur's hall, just inside the main gate. Nearby, Cerdic and Talorc were guiding a cart pulled by oxen, loaded to bursting with our food and supplies. Merlin was leading his horse through the gate to meet Bedevere, who was waiting in the levels below the castle with our troops. "You just returned from the White Mount."

"And now I must leave for the Demetae."

She eyed me closely, that red hair shining in the summer sun. "Guinevere did not stay at Arthur's hall last night. Does that have something to do with your journey north?"

Ygerne was clever, accomplished at putting facts and events together, drawing some meaning from them. Arthur would allow the word of his impending marriage to be spread later on that day, but until then, we were sworn to secrecy. She knew from the lines in my face that my mission was important, and she knew too that I was not pleased by it. Most important, she knew that I would not tell her without Arthur's permission. I think that frustrated her the most.

Her red hair swirling about her in the constant wind, she took my face in her hands and kissed me. "Take care. I would have you come back to me, and Mariam worries so when you leave. She fears that you will not return and often cries in her bed at night."

I pulled her hands away with my one. "There will be fewer trips after this, I hope. I have told Arthur that I will not accept the forfeited lands and become a lord of the consilium. He has agreed that I may stay here in his service."

The smile that brightened her face was more than I could have desired. "Then you deserve a better kiss, for I have hoped you would do just that." And she gave me one.

Moments later, Merlin and I were atop our horses, leading them through the massive double gates and winding down to the levels below. The wind had shifted, and I caught a whiff of the woad-making, such a horrid smell. In my heart I prayed that it was not an ill omen.

CHAPTER FIVE

W e have not met Arthur. What think you of that?" Bedevere asked as we passed the narrow lane that led to
Guinevere's cottage.

Indeed, we had not seen Arthur on the road, nor did we
have time to stop to see Guinevere. Our journey on this day
was much longer than our trek to the White Mount and would
take more than a week to complete. Stopping to retrieve
Coroticus would make the journey that much longer.

I shrugged, tucking the reins under my half arm as I wiped
the streaming rainwater from my face with my one hand.
"Perhaps she took the news better than we thought," I answered,
knowing that the likelihood of that was slim at best.

The rains had held off for some time, but in recent days
they had returned, soaking the ground like some great sea
sponge, the likes of which I had once seen far to the west,
where the great seas touched our lands. Part of our path took
us along ancient wooden track ways, paths that kept us from
the sodden mess of the bogs where our horses' hooves would
sink beyond recovery in the foul, ill-smelling muck. Some
people in another time had created wooden causeways to help

them. Their waterlogged boards, dark against the bogs, were marked here and there by blazes of white and yellow wood, freshly cut to repair damaged planks.

We had passed our outpost near the hills between Castellum Arturius and Ynys-witrin and were descending along the track toward the old Roman bridge before beginning the ascent into the village. A wisp of grayish-white smoke arose on our left from a small community of women dedicated to the Christ's mother, Mary. They had a timber chapel and a small group of huts. These women were not of the same beliefs as those in the larger community above the abbey, and they kept to themselves, not mixing with either the brothers or their fellow women.

That thorn tree from Joseph of Arimathea rose starkly against the skyline on our right as we made our way along the lane. The last time I had passed this way, we had been greeted by a steady stream of merchants and pilgrims, all coming to Ynys-witrin to see the famous Patrick, episcopus of the Scotti. And some had seen him. Others had attended his burial in the simple graveyard beside the *vetustam ecclesia* in the abbey.

As we neared the abbey precinct, marked by its vallum, I noted a gathering of soldiers wearing red and gray tunics, the uniform of Lord Melwas, commander at the great tor. He was poised to take over from Illtud, who had consolidated our holdings in the wake of the recent revolt, but whose talents were many, and he was now needed for other tasks.

In the distance, atop the mist-shrouded tor, I could dimly see the small wooden chapel and huts recently built by Arnulph and Ogmar, Patrick's companions. They had been granted permission to establish a small hermitage on the summit in honor of the old episcopus.

Much to my surprise, as we started up the slope to the entrance of the abbey, I saw that the bank and ditch had been
strengthened and the old timber rampart replaced with a new,
thicker, taller one. I saw too that Melwas's men stood watch,
something the abbot had not welcomed or permitted when
Liguessac, or Lauhiir as we called him, had commanded the
tor. But Lauhiir was trapped inside the abbey after claiming
sanctuary. His men had killed three of Arthur's soldiers. It was
also believed that he had killed the old monachus Elafius for
interfering with his plans to rebel against Arthur. But that ac-
cusation had been convenient, not truth. So, now he sat within
the vallum, unable to leave for fear of his immediate arrest and
execution.

A figure stepped out into the lane before us. At first I did
not recognize him, dressed as he was in a plain brown tunic
and a hooded cloak. Coroticus, the abbot. Behind him, I saw a
smallish figure, hustling clumsily in pursuit.

"No robes and trinkets, my lord?" I asked, swinging down
from my horse and splashing into the mud. My tone carried a
hint of insolence. I was no friend of the abbot's nor he of mine,
though it had not always been that way. But time and events can
sever even the most intimate of relationships, so what chance
does mere friendship stand in a turbulent era?

"I thought it better to travel incognito."

I nodded. Arthur enjoyed traveling that way, though circumstances rarely allowed it. That Coroticus would choose to
go about dressed plainly was a bit surprising; he so loved his
abbot's gold chain and cross and his fur-lined robes.

Coroticus must have seen the confusion on my face or sensed
the hesitancy in my manner. "Scotti raiders are reported along
our path. The deaths of Teilo and Dochu have left their lands

fragmented and unguarded. My capture would not be a good thing."

No, I said to myself. For Coroticus that would not be a good turn of events. But, instead of commiserating with him, I simply said, "And whose fault would that be?"

His well-fed cheeks glowed red, and he turned to berating young Ider, who, it appeared, had been chosen to accompany the abbot.

"Bedevere!" I called to my friend, who was even then arranging to incorporate the abbot's horses and wagon into our own. He turned from his task and trudged through the mud to my side. "I need a favor."

"Anything, Malgwyn."

"Send three men under a flag of truce to my bandit friend Gareth," and I gave him the location. "Have them bring him to us along the way."

That square face, lined from the demands of a life at arms, wrinkled up into a frown. "For what purpose?"

When I told him, he smiled and nodded his assent. "That is wise. I would never have thought of that, Malgwyn."

"It is risky for Gareth and his band."

"Then why will he agree?"

I grinned. "Because he will see it as great fun, a chance to tweak the Scotti's nose."

With a laugh, Bedevere sent a patrol off to fetch Gareth while we waited the brief time it took for Coroticus and Ider to join us. As we continued on through the village, headed northeast, I noticed a gaggle of soldiers crossing the lane and headed toward the Roman wharves to the southwest. At its center was the unmistakable form of Melwas, a little lord who was as broad as he was tall. Part of Lord Vortimer's faction who opposed Arthur's election as Rigotamos, Melwas had wisely kept his distance from his comrades. After Lauhiir's ill-fated rebellion, Arthur had no reason to deny him the command at Ynys-witrin.

I knew little of his history. His family originally came from the lands of Iceni, now overrun by the Saxons. But he had lived among the Durotriges for many years now, and Melwas was popular among the people in the way that only truly ugly men can be popular. His brown hair was perpetually greasy, and his attempts at growing a beard were laughable. His plump, reddened cheeks bore witness to the wineskins he had drained, and he was given to boring guests at his feasts with his recitations of imaginary women conquered. Some considered him a buffoon, but there was a sparkle to those eyes, set deep above those fat cheeks, that made me wonder.

He stopped, holding his hand out to halt his followers, and turned as we passed. With a slight bow, he nodded to me and I to him. Until, that is, I saw his group more clearly. Until I saw the thin man in the white robe, a rope tied about his waist, turn and look toward us.

Wynn.

The Druid from the White Mount.

With great strength, I forced myself to make no sign of recognition, but the red in my cheeks must have told the entire story, for Wynn smiled at me.

Blast him! And blast all Druids! How could they feel smug when they had to rely on the likes of Melwas and Mordred for noble support? 'Twas a question without answer.

But my horse, with the rhythmic rise and fall of his hooves, carried me past. I did not like that Wynn had appeared in our country, nor did I like that we were leaving for the Demetae with him yet in our midst. And I could not forget the curse he laid on Arthur.

Looking around, I saw a soldier I knew, one who had fought with us in the wars and had been at the White Mount. With a jerk of my head, I called him forward from the ranks. "Take a message to the Rigotamos. Tell him this, 'Druid. White Mount. Ynys-witrin.' Do you understand?"

He was a likely enough man, with good, strong features and a seasoned eye. The nod came swiftly and a quick glance around made it firmer still as he saw and recognized Wynn. "As you command, master," and he was off without bothering to seek Bedevere's approval.

"What is that man's name?" I asked Bedevere as he rode up next to me.

"Aidan. Where have you sent him?"

I jerked my head back and to the left. Bedevere's raised eyebrows told me all.

"To Arthur?"

"It may be a small thing, but he should know. We have had our troubles with Druids in the past, and this one cursed him."

"Agreed."

We continued along in silence for a bit, following the road as it turned and headed toward Aquae Sulis, the only sounds those of the leather and chains of our saddles and the wagon.

"You are no friend of the Druids," Bedevere began, "and no friend of the Christ. In what do you believe, Malgwyn?"

I was silent for a moment. It was a question that had troubled me greatly of late. In truth, I was not certain. I knew only that I had a great yearning for something to believe in. The Druids were wise men, and there was much to be said for their philosophy. But I could conceive of no god or gods that would demand human sacrifice for their pleasure. Yet the Christ was something as elusive as the morning mist that was here and there and everywhere, but slipped through your grasp like river eels. And though I was not a well-educated man, I knew that the Christ represented God's gift to man and that He had been sacrificed, but had arisen. This troubled me too.

"Malgwyn?"

"It is not an easy question, Bedevere. Nor one that I am yet prepared to answer. I respect the Christ and those beliefs, for if believing in the Christ makes men like you and Arthur and Kay, then it is truly good. But, as the Druids do, I believe that there is something godly in the fields and forests and wind and rain and sun. Yet I tell you frankly that their practice of sacrificing humans, of the Wicker Man, chills my blood. I have seen too much killing on the battlefield to appreciate gods who demand it to stay in their good graces."

"The Christ is about faith, Malgwyn. And faith is something that you can neither see nor hear nor feel. It is in your heart."

As time had passed, I had grown much closer to Bedevere. Kay had always been my favorite, but his temper and his youth would forever separate us. He was a pleasant companion, but Bedevere was not just a friend, but a seasoned partner, one whose eye caught things that I had not seen and whose mind grasped connections that eluded other men.

As we rode along, I saw that Morgan ap Tud was riding apart from the rest. I still felt bad for being so sharp with him at the White Mount, so I nudged my horse up to join him.

"Arthur is not letting you stay in one place long," I offered.

Morgan turned to see me. "Malgwyn! It appears neither of us gets to stay in one place."

"I would ask you how you are settling in, but you've hardly had a chance."

He nodded. "It is difficult. I spent many years studying with my teacher, Melus. I knew everyone within a day's ride, intimately. And now . . ."

"Fear not, Morgan. Once the issue of Arthur's marriage is settled, you will have time to make friends among us."

"When Lord David recommended me to the post, I was so honored that I'm afraid I did not consider everything."

"You are close to Lord David?" I tried to pose the question as innocently as possible.

Morgan beamed. "Yes, our families have been friends for years. My father was one of David's lieutenants in his younger days."

"Yet you have become a medicus."

The little physician dropped his head. "I was never very good with the tools of war, but I have always been bright and curious. 'Twas Lord David himself who suggested the healing arts. He always said that there were many ways to serve."

"Indeed."

I rode on a few minutes later. With such close connections to David, Morgan would bear watching.

❖

We had been some three hours on the road, if it could be called that. This was no Roman road, built to last a thousand years, layered for strength and evenness. This was more a wide path, uneven, muddy, and rough on our wagons, which bounced and rumbled along. Cerdic's wagon had already become mired twice, requiring our soldiers to dismount and lift it onto drier ground.

I thought that is what had happened again, as I heard cries

behind us and the creaking and rattling of our column as it stopped. Turning in my saddle, I saw a sight that made me laugh out loud.

Approaching us were the three soldiers Bedevere had sent in search of my friend Gareth, the thief. But they had been disarmed, their arms and hands bound, and their mounts taken. Herding them along from behind was Gareth, atop the best of the horses, with a dozen of his men as escort.

"Malgwyn, I am insulted!"

The entire column was laughing now at the soldiers' predicament, even Bedevere, who did not often laugh.

"And why is that, Master Gareth?"

"You sent only three men to capture me? Surely you knew that my head has a much higher value and only three men were doomed to fail. Besides, all you had to do was ask."

"Well, Gareth, they were sent to invite you, not arrest you."

The little bandit cocked his head to the side and placed his hand on his dirty red tunic. "Oh! They should have made that clear. Really, Lord Bedevere, you must teach your men more manners. They were very impolite."

Bedevere was laughing out loud now. He and I knew things about Gareth's service to Arthur that others did not. And Gareth was allowed much liberty. Ider was confused, but Coroticus was not. He knew something of Gareth's worth. Indeed, Gareth yet stood accused of a murder that he did not commit, accused by the abbot.

With much shouting and many jests from their comrades, the three soldiers were released. We all dismounted, and Bedevere and I met with Gareth away from the others. I no longer trusted Coroticus in many things, and the safety of our party was one.

We squatted in a clearing just off the road, the three of us—Bedevere, me, and Gareth.

"How are you, Malgwyn? Much time has passed since we last met."

"I am sorry for Lynnfann, Gareth. He was a true friend and served me well."

A dark cloud covered Gareth's face. "One day, I would have you tell me of his end."

"I will. He died with honor, though his killing was not honorable." During the hours leading up to the rebellion, I had conscripted Lynnfann to do some spying for me. He was accomplished in slipping in and out of places unseen. But he had been captured by the rebels, as was I, and it was only his quick thinking that spared my neck. Later, during our imprisonment, he had met his end under torture, loyal to me to the last.

Gareth nodded. "What need have you of me? I have purses to lift this day." Ever the bandit.

"We need some of your men to cover our flanks."

"You have three troop. Send one to each flank and keep one in your escort."

"We do not want them seen," Bedevere explained. "We need to know if anyone follows or approaches, but it is best that such a man not know that he has been spotted."

"You want spies."

"Call them what you will. Our need is still the same."

Gareth's manner was worrying. I knew that he would mourn the death of Lynnfann, and I hoped that it would not damage our friendship, but I seemed to have been wrong.

"It will cost you. I am not a wealthy man who gives favors for free."

Bedevere and I exchanged looks. How foolish we had been! "How much?"

"Lynnfann had a wife and child. The Rigotamos must pledge to ensure their feeding and upkeep. From what I know of his last days, he was of some service to Arthur. Let his family be cared for."

A wife and child? I had never known. But I was not empowered to grant such a favor. Only Arthur himself could do so.

"It is done." Bedevere surprised me with the speed and firmness of his answer. "And if Arthur objects, then I will make them part of my household. I know enough of Lynnfann's sacrifice to honor him thus." He offered his hand to Gareth who took it in his own, more delicate, fingers.

"I have heard it said that the great Bedevere has no heart but much honor. I am glad to see that such was only half right. I would have granted the favor for Malgwyn's sake alone, but Lynnfann's family deserves better than I can give them. And, perhaps, his son will not have to steal to scrape out a living."

"Then you may rest easy."

I reached across and tousled Gareth's hair, at which his somber face finally broke into a major grin. "Will that suit you, you thief?"

"Quite well. 'Tis good to see you again, Malgwyn. You've stayed away too long."

"Arthur keeps me busy. And I have little time for outlaws like you."

Gareth stood and motioned for one of his men. "My lord," he addressed Bedevere, "tell this one where and how you wish my lads to be used."

With that Bedevere took Gareth's man aside, as Gareth

and I eased to the edge of the clearing. "Tell me of Lynnfann's death."

So I told him the whole tale, a story that I have told elsewhere and will not repeat here. Suffice it to say that much of Arthur's success in defeating the rebellion raised by Teilo, Dochu, and Lauhiir could be credited to Lynnfann's deeds. I left nothing out and Gareth listened with great interest.

"I never told you this, but Lynnfann was my brother's son. My brother is long dead, and I had taken the task of raising him. It was a sad day when I learned he had been killed."

My face blazed red in shame. I had never known that, and because of my own situation with Mariam and my dead brother Cuneglas, I would have flown like the wind to tell Gareth immediately of the boy's death.

He must have read my thoughts, for he grasped my shoulder. "I do not blame you for his death. I am certain you did all you could. But let us swear together that, one day, we will truly avenge his killing."

"On that, you have *my* word, Master Gareth."

We rejoined the rest and all remounted our horses. Gareth reined his mount, jumping and neighing, to our side. "Now, you unseemly lot, keep Aircol's daughter safe on your return."

Our mouths agape, we watched the little bandit ride off, singing some old song. "How does he know about Aircol?" Bedevere asked, more amazed than I had ever seen him.

I shrugged. "I am sure I do not want to know how."

Our flanks now protected by Gareth's men, we proceeded on our journey. The roads and the weather, and any trouble we might encounter, could easily stretch our one week journey into two. The cloudy, dark day matched my mood, and I considered it an ill omen, not the way you want to start an important task.

❖

At dusk, as we made our camp, properly this time with the soldiers preparing a hastily dug ditch and bank, I wondered at their stamina. They were not Roman soldiers, of whom I had heard so much during my life. Roman soldiers, my old father had said, could march all morning, battle all the afternoon, and build a proper fort by sunset. I thought he stretched the truth a bit, but I had seen the ruins of Roman forts. They covered our landscape, it seemed, almost as pestilentially as their villas. And I knew that, in the north, some were sturdy and strong enough to be used yet by chieftains there, nobles of those tribes.

All of us had at least a little Roman in our blood, an officer here, a common soldier there. They had been among us too long not to have left their mark. We, here, in the far western lands, were less tainted by their blood, but Arthur, Ambrosius Aurelianus, Guinevere all had Romans in their ancestry. My father said that even we were descended from a Roman soldier named Pantera, long, long ago.

But, much to Arthur's chagrin, our soldiers did not have the discipline that legend assigned to the men of Julius Caesar. He tried, and to an extent, he succeeded. And that was why we had been successful against the Saxons. But with the Saxon armies at bay for the moment, our men were beginning to resent the discipline on which Arthur relied.

Bedevere, Merlin, and I shared a campfire near the center of our enclosure. Coroticus and Ider had their own, served by a pair of slaves from Melwas, I presumed, as I did not recognize them from my days at the abbey. Cerdic and Talorc kept trudging back and forth between the wagon and the fire, grumbling about this thing or that which they had forgotten to pack. The soldiers, now preparing their own fires, were grumbling, too. Only one troop was fresh. The other two had made the journey to the White Mount with us. They were Arthur's sharpest troops and he had wanted to make the best impression on Aircol, so no rest for them.

A screech owl cried in alarm off in the forest. Many considered it an ill omen, but I liked it. After all, there was much in the world to be alarmed about, but the cry of the owl meant I was home and so I found comfort in it. On this night, though, it reminded me of another owl, crying into the darkness as I lay on the hard ground. But it had not been an owl, rather the piteous cry of a mother, wailing over the body of her dead daughter. It was a memory I would have eagerly wished on another.

Our supper was boiled beef, leeks, and cabbage, not a pretty meal, but filling. Talorc had just taken our platters away when one of the soldiers posted on guard appeared at our fire with a prisoner in tow.

"Who is this that you have dragged into our midst?" Merlin was grumpy, aggravated that his bed must wait.

"I am sorry, my lord. But he insisted that he see Master Malgwyn," the guard apologized.

The prisoner wore a faded, ragged tunic and seemed drunk, but I had spent too many years in that state not to recognize an act when I saw one. "Go back to your post. We will deal with this one."

As soon as the soldier was out of hearing, I turned to the

drunk. "You are one of Gareth's men, but I do not remember your name."

"No need," he said, straightening himself. "I bring you word."

"Already. 'Tis only been a few hours."

He shrugged. "We were told to be on the lookout for any strange ones following you or coming near to your party."

"Aye," Bedevere agreed. "You were."

The thief pointed to the west. "Not a ten-minute walk over that way is a single traveler. He seems to pace himself with your party, and as soon as you stopped for the night, so did he."

"A single man?" Why would a single man follow us? "Do you know him? What lord does he serve?"

Gareth's man grinned. "He serves no lord, Master. He is a Druid priest. I have seen him about Ynys-witrin of late, supping with Melwas and his men."

CHAPTER SIX

W ynn! Would that Druid never go away? I was beginning to wish that Arthur had run him through on the
road near Londinium. It seemed that that would have solved
a great many problems. First, he tries to foment discontent
among the people at Londinium. Then, he curses Arthur. Later,
he appears at the side of a lord suspected of no good. Now, he
was found following our party at a distance!

"Shall I kill him?" Gareth's man said it simply and plainly.
Bedevere and I exchanged looks. No matter how tempted we
were, this was not something either of us was prepared to order.
Bedevere believed in the Christ and had no love for Druids, but
I did not think he would countenance killing this one. In truth,
other than the insult to Arthur, we had no reason. Besides, alive
he might be a source of information. Dead, he would be no
good at all.

"No. Leave him be," Bedevere ordered. "But watch him
closely, and if he seems about to do some harm to us, dispatch
him. Otherwise, just keep us informed on what he does and
who, if anyone, he meets or talks to." He looked then to me
and Merlin for confirmation. We each nodded.

"Go then. Be vigilant."

And, much like my old friend Lynnfann, he disappeared as though he had never been there.

"What do you make of this?" I asked Merlin, who knew far more about the ways of Druids than I.

"This does not smell of Druid practice to me. Something else is at work here," he judged. "The Druids of my acquaintance have been, generally, honorable men, not conspirators and plotters."

"How so?"

Merlin leaned back on his cloak, propping his old skinny body up on an elbow. "Druids do not like this new religion. It denies the very basis of their beliefs, and it replaces them as the men of the most importance in society. I have heard it told that Julius Caesar feared the Druids because of the sway they held over the people, as religious leaders and as the holders of ancient laws and rituals.

"But in reality, it has not been the Christ who has challenged the Druids for power, but, like Caesar did, the lords. Belief in the Christ has been one of the ways they have stolen from the Druids. Lords are generally about power, wealth, and territory. As this religion gains converts it will gain lands and power. The lords who at least appear to support it will gain as well. What Wynn may be doing is attempting to make converts among the lords, whose military power would make his order's standing stronger."

Something was missing in his recitation. "I do not disagree with you, Merlin. But what of their beliefs, their faith? What of the Christ? Of the divine sacrifice? What of the Druid's beliefs, their gods and rituals and festivals?"

Merlin smiled an old man's smile of jagged teeth. "Except

for such as Arthur and Ambrosius and our friend here, Bedevere, the truth of religion is unimportant to lords, only how
they can use it to consolidate their positions, to increase the
heft of their purse.

"The Druids I have known relished their position, their
role in society. They held themselves above petty matters.
This Druid does not." Merlin paused. "And I tell you, Malgwyn, if the Druids have turned themselves to conspiracy and
power, we are in for more of a challenge than the Saxons ever
posed."

And I had thought that I was a cynical, embittered man.
Merlin had obviously given these things great and serious consideration, and the answers he derived were dark and grim. "You
do not believe in the Christ, Merlin, yet you follow Arthur.
Why?"

He shrugged. "I was entrusted with his instruction when
he was but a boy. He grew to be a clever, honest man, a man of
great gifts and a sense of humanity. Others have seen it in
him. Look at that old fool Sidonius, in Gaul. Arthur's reputation for justice and fairness in dealing with people is as wide-
spread as the wind can carry it. I take pleasure in having had
a hand in building those beliefs. I love him as I would a son.
It is as simple as that."

"But you claim to love Guinevere like a daughter, and yet
you support Arthur's decision to cast her aside like old bread."
I still felt the sting of Arthur's actions. Though I knew that his
heart was yet with my cousin, the fact that he would forsake
her for politics still left me soured and I could not escape the
feeling.

"I have explained that, Malgwyn. Yes, I support his decision, but only after trying with all my might to change his

mind." The edge to Merlin's voice told of his irritation, but something in it told me that it was not intended for me. "Arthur is like my own child." He paused for a second, chewing his lower lip so intensely that I feared he would harm himself. "Children always disappoint their parents, at some point, on some issue."

I took no comfort from his words, as I knew Guinevere would not, could not, be consoled. I feared for her, for when she learned of Gwyneira. She was a passionate woman, and such women often acted rashly.

Little could be said after that, so we ended our day with more questions than answers and a long road ahead of us, with Arthur's bride at the end.

❖

I knew as soon as I saw her that she was trouble. Not in the same sense that Arthur's slave Talorc was trouble, but a looming problem nonetheless. Gwyneira, daughter of Aircol Lawhir, king of Dyfed and of the Demetae, was beautiful. A petite young girl of fourteen years, her golden hair shone brightly in the sun as she stood proudly next to her father when we rode into his city.

Aircol's lair, perched like Arthur's atop a windswept hill, was slightly northeast of Merlin's birthplace at Carmarthen. An odd place, in the autumn and winter I was told that the hill took on a reddish hue from the ever-present bracken. And, unlike Arthur's fort, Aircol's was really two forts, an upper and a lower.

The settlement in the lower town was of wattle-and-daub houses, some sturdy enough for two stories, and a number of old roundhouses scattered about the town. Roman ways had not taken hold in Dyfed as they had in our region, and the Demetae still built the old round-style homes. In the upper enclosure, near to Aircol's timber-built hall was a pleasant, wooden chapel, very plain, but standing as a monument to his devotion to the Christ.

We rode in file through the gates and along the main lane, leading up to the hall where Aircol and his daughter stood to greet us. Unlike Arthur's hall, no market square lay before it, just a large open area. Some of Aircol's servi had led our supply wagons away from the procession so that only Coroticus, Bedevere, Merlin, and I, with our three troop of horse, approached our host.

"We cannot argue that Aircol has disrespected us in any way," Merlin murmured, nodded his head in approval at the warmth of our reception.

Aircol, tall with fair hair, strode forward with arms spread and palms turned up in welcome and supplication. "Welcome, to our home," he said in a very, very deep voice, so deep that it seemed to echo off the walls of the buildings.

Bedevere glanced at me with a widening of the eyes. Even the old, stone-faced soldier was impressed.

We dismounted and, allowing Coroticus to take the lead, approached our host as the crowd cheered. I was a little puzzled. Aircol was approaching this as an arrangement already agreed, and yet we had not even begun negotiations. I did not know whether to welcome this or fear it.

I will not bore you with details of the feast. Suffice it to say that it was designed to show two things: the bounty of Aircol's lands and his generosity with his guests. Oysters, salmon, lamb, and pork, fresh-baked bread. It was a pleasure of a meal, properly prepared and properly served. As visiting cleric, Coroticus was asked to bless the food, a task he did with great aplomb and dignity, and much to the approval of Aircol. Two *sacerdotes*, of Aircol's chapel I presumed, seemed impressed with Coroticus.

Our roles had not been discussed with the king as yet, so other than a few looks of sympathy and a few more of fear, I was left alone, honored for my status as a councilor to Arthur, but the object of puzzlement because of my missing arm. In those days, aye even in these, a missing limb was viewed as a sign from God that I had sinned in some way, or that I was cursed. I did not mind. Once I had agreed with those who felt that way, but now I understood that it meant only that I had not been agile enough when the Saxon swung his sword at me.

One thing that I did notice among the guests at the feasting was a general feeling of happiness. Oh, a few of Aircol's young nobles seemed to mope about, unhappy I am sure that they were not chosen to marry young Gwyneira. But they were in the minority. Dyfed and the Demetae seemed happy with this new turn of events.

As the feasting ended, I stood and glanced about for Merlin and Bedevere. We would be joining Aircol to begin our negotiations.

"Excuse me, master?"

I looked down to find a little boy standing next to me, the finery of his tunic and breeches marking him as some kin of Aircol's. He had narrow eyes and something of a hawk's face. "May I help you, young sir?"

"Yes," he said in a particularly grown-up voice. "Why is a man such as you arrayed in a noble's clothing and joining us at a feast?"

Rarely have I taken an instant disliking to someone. I think perhaps Gildas, the young monk at Ynys-witrin and even yet a splinter in my aged hand, was the only other person. "And, my young lord, might I have your name. 'Tis not often that I am confronted by such a brave man."

His narrow eyes narrowed even more. "Why am I brave?" A little uncertainty began to raise its ugly head.

I leaned down close to his ear. "Because I am a warrior, who has killed more Saxons than you have years with one arm and two. And unless you make yourself scarce, I will add you to the list."

His eyes grew large, and he turned and ran straight into Aircol, who was then approaching. From the way the little one wrapped his arms about Aircol's legs for protection, his identity became apparent.

"I see you have met my son, Vortipor. You are Malgwyn, Arthur's scribe and councillor. Welcome to my hall." He extended his hand with a smile and I took it the same. "My pardon for my son's youthful arrogance. He has not yet learned humility or good manners."

That this child, Vortipor, was Aircol's son seemed out of sorts, for the father was a good man. One look told that tale. I wished that I could say the same for the son.

He took me by my half arm then and led me away from Vortipor and the rest. "You will be negotiating for Arthur?"

I nodded.

Aircol glanced about and lowered his voice. "I am eager for this match to be made. You will find me very agreeable."

Immediately, a tingle set upon me. For one about to enter into negotiations to make such a statement was more than strange. "My lord, I appreciate your candor but does telling me this gain you some advantage that I do not see?"

He laughed deeply, throwing his head back and letting his long, straight white hair hang down his back, over the bearskin he used for a cloak. "You are just as I have been told, a straightforward, honest man. I will tell you. Of all the lords of the consilium, Arthur is known as the most devout and steadfast believer in the Christ. Until his election, I feared that Vortimer or another who favored the Druids or the pagan gods would succeed Ambrosius as Rigotamos. Call it irresponsible, but I could never ally myself to a lord who did not share my beliefs.

"I know you fought with Arthur against the Saxons, and I know that together you thrust them back into the land of the Canti and along the eastern coast, earning our people a breathing spell. But they will return, Malgwyn. You know this. I know this. Arthur knows this. We must be ready, and for Arthur's forces to succeed, he needs an army capable of defending the north. I have a strong force, but more importantly I have connections with the northern tribes that can bring them to our banner. They know me and trust me."

The more he talked, the more I liked this man. He had a strong face, wrinkled though it was, and his blue eyes were bright, almost mischievous.

"This is all politics and warfare, my lord," I said finally. "I am a father as well. I know that arranged marriages are a part of our world, but do you not worry about sending your daughter many miles away to marry a man you don't truly know?"

His smile was a good one too. "Arthur's reputation for fairness and equity have spread far and wide. I cannot help but believe that he will treat my daughter well." Aircol's hand moved up to my shoulder. "I know of his relationship with your cousin. May I speak frankly?"

Another twinge of warning touched my spine. I nodded.

"I think Arthur was wrong in not marrying her. She was but a child when she committed to the sisters, far too young to make such promises. But he has made his decision and I am glad for the opportunity it presents to join our two houses." He paused, stroking his mustache with a finger. "I understand that you are no friend of Lord David's."

The smile touched my face before I realized it. "We have different views of some things, and I know that he champions the match between your daughter and Arthur."

"You will be glad to know, then, that I am no particular friend of David's, either. I find him a duplicitous snake. I fear that his role in arranging this match is simply to sow dissent among Arthur's men. That it also strengthens Arthur is of little matter to him. I have heard that you believe him part of the late rebellion against the Rigotamos. My own agents tell me that this is so. You will quickly discover that I am your friend and ally. Together, we may help to hold off the hounds baying for Arthur's blood."

This Aircol made it difficult to dislike him, even if I were so inclined. With yet another smile, he ushered me to his private quarters where Bedevere, Merlin, and Coroticus waited.

❖

The negotiations took little time. We were almost required to force Aircol to take Teilo's and Dochu's forfeited lands. But he gave such a substantial dowry, including a share of his gold mines in the north of his lands and a sizable donation to the abbey at Ynys-witrin, that we felt it only fair to grant him the lands. It was most puzzling.

Aircol agreed to command the northern armies but to take

his lead from Arthur and the consilium when negotiating with the northern tribes. It was as much or more than we could have wished for.

We were done within two hours.

❖

"Malgwyn," Aircol said, throwing his arm over my shoulder. "You seem less like a victorious negotiator and more like a defeated enemy! Rejoice! Arthur's position in the consilium is secure. All of our lands are safer still."

"I am happy, my lord," I answered, despite the gloom I felt down to my very bones. "I am happy for all of us, but it is in my nature to worry."

"Then change your nature, my new friend," he advised with a smile.

"My lord," Bedevere interjected. "We should leave for Castellum Arturius at your earliest convenience. I know that we just arrived, but I doubt that anyone guessed that we would have reached an agreement so swiftly. A quick departure could confuse our enemies and put us a step ahead."

Aircol's blue eyes grew a question. "Lord Bedevere, our enemies are few and far away. I have had no serious challenges to my authority in years. Arthur's victory against Lauhiir's rebellion is too fresh in people's minds to allow another so quickly."

That is when I saw it. All great men have flaws. After all, they are men. Aircol was naïve. Hard to believe that a man who had risen to lead a great people could be naïve, but perhaps he grew that way over time, through complacence. I liked him, so I turned and faced him. "My lord, when you think yourself without enemies, they have already won."

We left it at that for two more days of feasting and hunting.

�֍

The night before we departed for Arthur's castle, Aircol held a great feast, one that Arthur had never matched. Though Arthur had good quantities of imported wines and goods, Aircol seemed determined to best him and every lord. I, for one, was not complaining. As the servants hurried about Aircol's hall, I dug into the assembled dishes with a relish—salmon baked in salt dough, whole trout, pork ribs, chicken wings soaked in a garum-like sauce, suckling pigs roasted on great iron spits. The air was filled with those smells, some sweet, some bitter. The scent of leeks and fresh-baked bread was all around.

We had lent Cerdic and Talorc to Aircol's chief steward, and they had joined the legion of servants. I saw Cerdic now testing one of the suckling pigs. He caught my glance and winked. The red in his cheeks said that he had been testing the wine as well. And there was plenty of wine, from Aircol's lands, from Gaul, even from Judea. Ever the accommodating host, Aircol had provided a goodly selection of cervesas and mead as well.

And I was well on my way to a truly delightful evening when I felt a tug at my sleeve.

"Malgwyn?"

It was Bedevere.

"Come outside."

We left the feasting and stepped out of a side door into a narrow lane beside the hall. One of our soldiers was waiting there with our friend the spy. "What have you for us?" Then was not the time for pleasantries.

"The Druid came into the city this eve. I lost him in the lanes."

"Where has he been the last few days?"

"Meeting with three other Druids near the coast. They came by boat, from the north."

"Were you able to get close enough to hear them?"

Our little thief shook his head. "No. They were wary and posted lookouts."

"And he comes here on this night?" I did not see a purpose behind the Druid's actions. He follows us here to Aircol's seat and meets with other Druids. Then he enters the town on the last night of our visit.

"Let us advise Aircol. He is no friend of the Druids. He will order a search and we can apprehend this man," Bedevere said.

"No," Merlin intervened. "He has done nothing so far. Aircol is well pleased, and we will return to Arthur with not only a new bride but a strong alliance with a powerful lord. Disrupting this may be just what the Druid hopes to do."

I was not certain that arresting the Druid would cause problems with Aircol, who had no more love for the Druids than Arthur, but Merlin was right that we needed no further distractions. These were not our lands. We were yet strangers.

"See if you can find him—"

"Dylan, Master Malgwyn," he said with a rotten-toothed smile. He was a different sort from my dead friend Lynnfann, more serious, older, but he carried himself well. Many of Gareth's men came from good families, but fortune had thrown stones in their paths and caused them to take a different trail.

I nodded in return. "See if you can find him and keep a close eye on him. Use your fellows. On our way back we can detail two small squads to watch our flanks and Aircol will be bringing a troop of his own horse with him. 'Tis more important that we know what this Druid is about. Watch and note what he does and who he speaks to."

He nodded and slipped away into the darkness.

We turned to go back to the feast, and then something happened that I did not expect at all.

A woman screamed.

CHAPTER SEVEN

At first I took it to be part of the merriment from the feast, but as I glanced at Bedevere and Merlin and saw alarm in their eyes, I knew it was not. I started toward the sound, but Bedevere put out a hand to stop me.

"This is not Arthur's fortress, Malgwyn. Aircol's men will see to it. Probably just some soldier dipping too deep into the mead."

But something in the scream reminded me of another, a scream of a pain that ran deeper than injury, a pain borne of mortal grief. 'Twas a scream just like that which I had heard on the White Mount. I shook off Bedevere's hand and headed at a trot toward the sound. From the scratching of metal on metal and creaking of leather, I knew that Bedevere and Merlin were following.

Others were running too, toward a large roundhouse along one of the lanes. I saw two soldiers wearing Aircol's tunics warding off onlookers from a huddle of people at the rear of the house.

The soldiers straightened a bit as we approached, but relaxed when they saw our tunics. "My lords, there has been a killing, nothing to concern yourselves with."

"They are welcome here," spoke a voice from behind us. Aircol. I brushed past the soldiers to a narrow area behind the house and between it and a storage shed, next to a pen where the pigs were kept. Stuffed into the confined space was a young girl, obviously lifeless from the paleness of her skin, with an older woman crouched over her.

"Bring torches and keep the others away."

Aircol came up beside me. "It is the daughter of one of the local decurions. He was with us at the feasting."

I nodded and knelt beside the girl's body. I really did not have to look. Lifting her limp head, I found the same horrid wound that Fercos's daughter had carried, right across her throat, to the very bone. With a heavy sigh, I pulled away her simple dress and saw that which I had hoped not to see, that most private of places ravaged and bloody, great splinters protruding from the now dead flesh.

The metallic smell of blood and death made me dizzy, and I fell onto my backside. Two young girls, hundreds of miles apart, killed in a most savage manner. The method the same. The reason unfathomable. Killing was common across the land. I had seen much death, both rational and irrational. Life was cheap. We had all said it, and it was true. I had seen women of low repute killed by men. I had seen wives killed by husbands with vicious tempers. They were punished by what courts we had, by whatever noble ruled the land, or else they bribed their way free.

But this was different. Two young girls. One the daughter of a leader of a small village. The other the daughter of a decurion. Neither quite yet old enough for marriage. Neither of a kind to solicit this sort of death. Yet both in the wake of our travels. And . . . I pushed myself to my feet quickly as I realized that the killings held one other thing in common—Wynn, the Druid.

"My lord," I said to Aircol. "A Druid was seen entering your town earlier today. I have good reason to believe that he may have a hand in this."

Aircol cocked his head to one side in confusion. "How could you know that?"

"Trust me in this matter, my lord."

He turned and looked to Bedevere who nodded.

"Very well, Malgwyn." He turned to several soldiers who had gathered. "Find this Druid and bring him to my hall."

"I apologize, my lord, for disturbing the feast."

The old lord shook his shaggy head. "You disturbed nothing. Whoever did this deed is the guilty one. Tell me of this Druid."

"I know but this, my lord. Some weeks ago, Arthur led an expedition to the White Mount at old Londinium. While we were there, a young girl was killed in the same manner as your decurion's child. She was the daughter of a local leader as well, who had brought a delegation, including the Druid, to treat with Arthur. The Druid followed us here to your seat and now this has happened. I cannot help but think that there is some connection."

"Lord Aircol," Bedevere intervened, "Malgwyn has a talent at discerning the truth in these matters. He is often appointed as a kind of investigator . . . an *iudex pedaneous* . . . by Arthur." My warrior friend had not the love of Latin titles that Arthur did, and it took him a moment to find the right one.

"Ambrosius has told me of this. Very well." He turned to

the gathered soldiers and townsfolk. "Malgwyn has my ear in this matter. Render unto him all the cooperation that he needs." With that Aircol returned to his hall.

"Malgwyn, you know that Druids only kill in ritual," Merlin said after Aircol had departed, chiding me.

"Who knows what this Druid is about, Merlin? Can you argue that he was nearby when the girl was murdered at the White Mount? Or that Dylan saw him entering this town?

"No. I cannot," he conceded, pulling at his beard. "But that still does not make him guilty of these crimes."

"We can worry about that when we have bound him to a stake and set the dogs on him."

"These attacks have touched you closely, haven't they?" Merlin knew me so well. When you share a house with someone, you come to know them, whether you want to or not.

"I cannot discern a reason for them, Merlin," I said after a moment. "They are so brutal, so savagely brutal, and committed on girls so young as to be almost helpless."

"Do not forget," Merlin warned, "that they could simply be separate killings that, no matter how horrible, are not necessarily linked to some broader conspiracy."

I turned back to the poor girl then, shutting out all the noise. Kneeling, I motioned two of the torch-bearing soldiers closer.

Her face was frozen in a grimace of pain, her eyes rolled up as if willing herself somewhere else. Bruises above her slashed throat made me believe that he had held her throat to silence her while he did his savage business. That was different than Fercos's daughter. She had already been dead when this madman raped her, if it was the same man, and I could not help but think it so.

"We found this lying against the side of the house," Bede-vere said behind me, passing a rough cut branch. "Malgwyn, this is just like the killing at the White Mount. Could the Druid have done this?"

"I confess, Bedevere, I do not understand this at all." And I did not. "While Merlin could be correct, that the two killings are not connected, I find that difficult to swallow. But killing for greed, to gain power, in battle, even by accident, I can fathom. But this is not about any of those things. This seems an act done by an angry man. But how could a man be this an-gry at these girls? Perhaps he knew Fercos's daughter well, but if it was the same man, and I cannot believe it to be otherwise, he could hardly have known this girl so well. The anger then must be directed against someone else." I was thinking now as I talked. "Who else could that be but Arthur? If the Druid did these things, he has done them to somehow damage Arthur."

"Or," Merlin interrupted, "this could be vengeance for the removal of Bran's head."

My face burned red and I thrust the piece of wood at Mer-lin. "You think Bran's spirit slit this girl's throat and raped her with a stick of firewood?"

"I think someone might wish others to think that, that someone wishes others would think that Arthur is no longer favored by his god or any gods."

I calmed. Merlin was right. And I was right. This could all be an elaborate scheme to turn the people against Arthur. Every lord of the consilium knew of his plan to remove Bran's head. Any of them, David, Mark, Melwas would have been bright enough to think of it. It seemed, somehow, too subtle for Mor-dred, who was even then languishing on our western shores, supposedly putting down pirates and incursions by the Scotti.

Perhaps I was thinking in too narrow a vein. But, even at that, it was an odd thing. Only someone truly depraved would inflict such pain on innocent girls for political reasons. The one thing that I knew for certain was that I would beg no mercy for the culprit when he was found, nor would I show him any mercy should I find myself alone with him.

"We will find the Druid, Malgwyn," Bedevere assured me.

"And I shall go and repair any damage this might have done to our plans with Aircol," Merlin said, patting me on the back with a frail hand.

"Has there been trouble?" Morgan's voice broke from the darkness. Our little medicus emerged into the torchlight. "May I help?"

His voice was so solicitous; his face reeked of concern. Bedevere looked at me. Merlin looked at me.

"No, Morgan, I am sorry, but this poor child is beyond your skills."

"What happened to her?"

Morgan was fully in the torchlight now, and I ventured an answer to his query. "Her throat was slit and she was raped with some object. Come, look for yourself."

I watched closely as his eyes widened in amazement.

"Oh, my dear!" For a moment, I thought he might faint. "Excuse me, please." And he jogged back into the blackness.

Merlin and Bedevere looked to me.

"Either he did not do this, or he is a skilled liar," I said finally.

"He is a creature of David's," Bedevere reminded us. "And he was at the White Mount."

I nodded. "We need to know more. Let us keep someone near him so we know what he's about."

"I'll see to it," Bedevere answered.

They left me alone then, and I studied the stick of wood in the flickering torchlight. Like the limb I had found at the White Mount, this one held bloodstains and bits and pieces of flesh. I tossed it away in disgust and irritation with myself, but a whiff of something odd flitted past my nose as the piece of wood thudded against the house before falling in the mud. "Fetch that again!" I shouted at one of the soldiers standing nearby.

With a quizzical look, he did so and I held the unbloodied end up to my nose. How very strange. The wood smelled of onions!

The feasting abruptly ended in the wake of the girl's death. Funny, I do not know her name. I never knew her name. But her wounds would haunt my dreams for years. They did not find the Druid. Whatever his business, whether the murder of the girl or something else, he had slipped into town and out as if a spirit. Which made me wonder about Merlin's question. Did Arthur, by removing Bran's head, awaken some spirit? Did he bring some curse on himself? The gods knew that I had warned him. Merlin and Bedevere warned him. I had seen him and Gawain nearly come to blows. But in that bullheaded fashion of his, Arthur had disregarded all of us. And only the gods knew what evil he had brought down on us.

We rode out the next morning, headed east. In better days we might have gone south to the great channel and crossed it in boats, arrayed for a king such as Aircol. But Scotti and Saxon pirates ranged freely in the waters. Mordred's charge had been to establish a fleet of boats to patrol, but his dispatches claimed difficulty in finding men to build the necessary vessels, a lie as he was probably being paid a tribute by the pirates.

Despite the dark mood the girl's killing had laid upon me, I was pleased that it was a bright morning and portended well for the journey. My eyes had grown puffy, and I knew if I looked into a still pool of water, I would see dark half moons beneath each. I had been up all night, questioning the girl's mother and father, trying to trace her movements so that I could find a clear path, but no one had really seen anything. She had been present at the feasting—her parents had last seen her there. But at some point she had simply disappeared. No one could remember quite when they last glimpsed her. One man, barely able to speak for the quantities of mead he had drunk, believed he saw her leave with a man, but his account was so garbled and confused that it was useless. She was at the feast, and then she was dead. The chances that the killer was of Aircol's lands were almost none; almost.

Careful, subtle questioning had found that Morgan had been at the feast, but then left before the killing. Without asking him directly, and thus warning him, I had no way to discover where he went. I understood the situation well enough to know that I would cause only trouble for myself if I accused one of David's men of these horrible deeds without proof. I sent one of our men in search of Gareth, to thank him for his help and to release his men.

I feared not for our safety on the return. Aircol brought three of his troops of horse as his escort. Together we had six. In those days each troop held thirty mounted men. So, on that day, we had 180 or more in our escort, a formidable force. Saxon or Scotti raiding parties rarely exceeded twenty or thirty souls.

The lord of the Demetae brought a sizable entourage with

him—slaves, a number of his lesser lords, the child Vortipor and, of course, Gwyneira. The two young ones rode in a large, creaky wagon, covered by well-scraped hides emblazoned with Aircol's symbol, and pulled by strong oxen. Aircol himself rode a handsome horse and spent much of his time riding next to Merlin, to whom he had taken an obvious liking.

Odd, that. For Merlin was certainly not a believer in the Christ, though he did not mock the new faith as did some. But the old man had a charm all his own, and he was born of Carmarthen, so the two had many friends in common. Now that we shared a house, he spoke often of his childhood in the forests of his birthplace. His mother had died young, and Merlin had been raised by a wild man of the forest named Lailoken. Not much of a life for a boy, but Lailoken had taught Merlin much about medicinal herbs and cures. In many ways it was not very different from the education he might have had living with the brothers at an abbey or monastery or from a *rhetor*, in private classes.

"What has you so deep in thought?" I jerked at the surprising voice on my left. 'Twas Bedevere.

I shrugged. "Merlin. Aircol. The dead girl. I have no lack of things to think about."

"You mean the two dead girls," Bedevere pointed out.

"Aye. Toss in Bran's head to fill the bag up." I paused as a farmer drove some cows across the lane before us. "Merlin believes it may be a plot by David and some of the other lords to discredit Arthur, make it look as if these killings following in our wake are a scourge laid on by the gods for Arthur's desecration of Bran's grave.

"But if that is so, Bedevere, why choose young girls and why abuse them so horribly?"

"The more devastating the deed, the more innocent the victim, the more displeasure the gods are showing Arthur?" Bedevere, like me, was unsure as well.

"Perhaps. Or perhaps it is the Druid, exacting his own revenge against Arthur, or putting teeth to his curse? Arthur's hatred of the pagan religions is well known. Any power accorded them is power taken from Arthur."

Bedevere laughed, unusual for him, and it was a bitter, cynical sort of laugh. "Trying to do what's right, what you believe in, can certainly give a man many enemies."

"That is a lesson I have learned from bitter experience. But what is left to us? To do evil is, simply, to be evil. To do nothing only allows evil to work its way among us. Better, I think, for a man to do what he can and accept that he will be condemned by some for doing it."

"You are beginning to sound much like Arthur, Malgwyn," Bedevere chided.

"Perhaps Arthur is starting to sound like me." I could not allow the jibe to go unanswered. I was still troubled over Arthur's decisions in this matter—digging up Bran's head and acceding to the demands of the other lords to marry Gwyneira.

I lowered my voice. "We must keep an eye on Morgan. I want to like him, but he is of David's tribe."

"Just as we must watch for the Druid," he answered. "It seems we spend most of our time, Malgwyn, watching other people." Bedevere laughed again, and it was good to hear it. I sensed that somewhere in his past he had suffered some great tragedy, but he talked so little at all and even less about himself that I knew I would never learn those secrets that had made him so taciturn.

We rode in silence for a bit, the only sounds those of creaking leather and jingling chains, and the slurping sounds of wagon wheels rolling through mud and oxen hooves sinking up to their shanks as they struggled along the road. On our left, off a distance in a field and shrouded in low-lying mist, a fire burned brightly in the remains of a Roman villa, its once plastered walls now looking as diseased as a plague victim. The villa had been a fine one in its day, with a central range and two wings framing a large courtyard.

The family, dressed in poorly woven clothes and rough-cut animal hide cloaks, stood in the shadows and watched our procession pass. I caught a hint of roasting venison in the wind. Someone had gotten lucky on the hunt and snared something bigger than a rabbit. A child, though girl or boy I could not tell from that distance, lifted a hand in a tentative wave, but oddly her mother, I assumed, slapped the hand down and hustled them all back into the safety of their once splendid home.

Their fear and plight humbled me. We spent our time struggling to bring order to chaos, to strengthen Arthur's hold on his title and lands, and they struggled to survive. Arthur wanted a better life for our patria, but that had taken second place in our efforts. There had been corruption and injustice under the Romans, but there had been education, structure, a sense of justice, even if illusory.

For a reason I cannot describe, I turned my horse and trotted across the field to the old villa. Behind me, I heard the sounds of Bedevere's horse sloughing through the mud as he followed.

Off to our left were the remains of the bathhouse. I dismounted and walked over, sidestepping piles of sheep dung, and peered inside. This must have been a wealthy man's villa. The colored tesserae, now faded from weathering, formed a picture of the Greek chi rho, a symbol of Christianity. Odd, I thought idly, to put a symbol of your religion on your bathhouse floor.

A man came out then, fearfully at first, and then his expression changed quickly, his shoulders slumping as if relieved. "Master Malgwyn!" he shouted, throwing up a hand in greeting.

I have met many people in my life, but I did not know this man. Of that much I was certain. But he strode forward with a smile on his face, forcing me, without my even realizing it, to dismount and meet him on equal terms. I took his hand in my one and studied his face, but beneath the beard, sprinkled with white, it was nothing more than a landscape of poverty and toil, and an unfamiliar one at that.

He realized then that I was trying to place him and his smile grew wider. "You do not know me, master. We have never met."

"Then how do you know me?"

And the smile grew wider yet. "The whole land knows of Arthur's one-armed warrior and scribe. You are famed for your wisdom and courage. You are most welcome in our home."

"But your woman stopped your girl from waving to us. I thought you hostile."

Discomfort grew on his face and he looked down. "At first, master, we did not know it was you. She was just being cautious and . . ."

"And what—"

"Rhodri, master."

"And what, Rhodri? There is something else?"

Rhodri had the look of a good man, one who cared for his wife and children. I looked at his hands and saw they were callused and rough, the hands of a man for whom toil was a daily experience. With his mouth set in a stern expression, he finally raised his eyes to meet mine. "My daughter is a strange child, master. I do not know how or why, but she sees things that others do not." The words came out slowly, haltingly.

"What did she see, Rhodri?"

Before he could answer, the little girl, so little and pale, the redness of her hair making her paleness even more so, stepped from behind a tumbling villa wall. "I saw a dark cloud above your big wagon." Her voice was soft, almost a whisper.

I knelt before her and searched her face but saw no mischief there, simply sadness. "A dark cloud? Does that mean something?"

Rhodri cleared his throat and looked away.

"What?" Bedevere asked.

"It means someone is going to die," came that same little soft voice.

"And how do you know this?"

She shrugged. "It always does."

Rhodri's wife hurried forward and clasped the girl against her gown. "There have been . . . other occasions when she has seen the clouds and someone has died. I cannot explain it, master, only affirm that it is true."

"Who? When?"

"A year ago, a sacerdote was passing through and took a meal with us. He was on his way to the abbey at Ynys-witrin. As we ate, Vala, my daughter, suddenly became rigid, her eyes fixed and strange. I thought her ill, but she pointed at the sacerdote and said, 'The cloud will soon claim him.' I punished her for being rude to a holy man, but the next morning, the sacerdote was dead. He had passed sometime in the night. I do not know the cause, but he had not appeared of a healthy pallor.

"Then, a fortnight later, a friend from a neighboring village came by to visit. Vala saw the cloud surround his head as well. Within three days he had choked to death on a bit of food."

I shook my head. Omens and superstitions! Our lands were full of them, yet no one could really claim to understand them. Everyone knew something, some omen, but it was rare to find an instance where the omen and bad happenings could be seen together. But why should I be surprised that the girl had seen her cloud over our procession? We had tempted the fates horribly of late and some retribution was bound to befall us.

"You have been helpful, Rhodri. Should you ever need my assistance, send for me at Castellum Arturius and I will give you what aid I can. We are sorry to have disturbed you and your family."

Remounting my horse, I saw Bedevere begin to speak and shook my head sharply. In a moment, when we were out of their hearing, he asked his question. "What do you intend to do with this?"

"Nothing. A little girl saw something. Little girls see many things."

The expression on Bedevere's face said everything. He was aghast that I would withhold this information. "But . . ."

"But nothing, Bedevere. The men are already grumbling about curses and bad omens. Giving them yet another to add to their collection only stokes the fire."

"They deserve to know, Malgwyn. Aircol deserves to know."

"Aircol believes in the Christ, and so do you, I thought. He will place no credence in pagan superstition."

"Perhaps not, but you are playing with hot coals, Malgwyn;

however, I will hold my tongue for now." He stopped and looked toward the sky. "We should make camp. The sun wanes and it has been a difficult night and day for us all."

With that, we turned our mounts and trotted across the field back to the lane. Merlin and Aircol met us at the edge of the road.

"This seems a likely place to make camp," Bedevere announced.

"There is yet an hour of light left," Merlin protested, but by then Bedevere and I had already dismounted and so had most of our men. The pleasures of abandoning the saddle were too great for them to argue. My own fatigue made an early end to the day seem desirable. Aircol did not mind. And that was that.

Within two hours the camp was established, with the difference that this time there were three enclaves instead of the two on our journey to Aircol's lair—Bedevere, Merlin, and me at one, Coroticus and Ider at another, and Aircol and his children at a third. Yet all were encompassed by a hastily prepared defense ring.

Cerdic and Aircol's cooks prepared a wonderful meal, which our boy Talorc grudgingly served. Poor Talorc! Kay's badgering had made a bitter nature all that much more bitter.

We feasted on deer that night. Our newfound friend, Rhodri, had graciously shared of his venison, but I could not help but notice that once he had delivered the meat, he hurried back to his home.

Even his daughter's vision was not enough to dispel our good mood. Two beakers of mead into the night, I stopped worrying about omens and murdered girls and enjoyed a soft evening with my friends as the fire crackled before us. Even my displeasure with Arthur faded with each beaker. And I fell asleep upon my fur cloak, my belly full of mead and venison, almost content. My sleep was peaceful and deep.

Until they fell upon us two hours past the midnight.

CHAPTER EIGHT

At first I thought I was reliving the screams of the mothers of those young girls murdered by this madman. But as my eyes flashed open, I barely had time to snatch my dagger and thrust it into an attacker's stomach before his entered mine.

I struggled from beneath his body and clambered to my feet. In the black of night, I could see little but dark forms clashing and hear naught but metal rending flesh.

A body came hurtling from the dark and I dodged the gleam of a spear point. My dagger found purchase in another stomach and the warmth of his blood coated my hand.

"Malgwyn," came a hiss from the dark. Bedevere.

"Here!"

"Scotti raiders. They must have silenced our guards."

My night vision was growing sharper, and I could discern bodies scattered around our fire, some Scotti, some ours. Shouts and curses filled the air.

And then another Scotti burst into view. Before I could confront him, his face curled into a howl as a blade appeared from nowhere and blood sprayed from his chest.

I turned in surprise to see young Talorc brandishing a

sword quite effectively. 'Twas his blade that saved me. I nodded quickly and returned to the battle.

The Scotti attacked on three sides, but primarily from the west, leaving only the road and the ruined villa where Rhodri lived free. In the dark I could not accurately judge their numbers, but it was a large raiding party, and bold.

Bedevere was rallying a troop to support Aircol's men who were valiantly encircling his wagon. The king himself was nowhere to be seen, nor Merlin, but I knew my old friend well enough to know that he was giving a good account of himself. The little girl, Vala's, vision instantly sprang to mind, and I snatched my own sword from the ground, rushing to aid our defenders.

"Whence came they?" I asked Bedevere as I crossed swords with a young Scotti raider.

"They must have landed in the great channel and worked their way east."

A Scotti burst out of the darkness. I sidestepped his spear as Bedevere bent over and caught him in the abdomen, then flipped him onto his back. I dispatched him with a single blow across his throat.

"Look!"

I turned toward where Bedevere pointed to see a Scotti climbing aboard the wagon. In the confusion, he had slipped inside our lines unnoticed.

But before either I or Bedevere could move to stop him, a figure sped past us, almost as a blur. We watched in stunned silence as the figure ripped the Scotti from the wagon, threw him to the ground and rammed his blade into his enemy's chest. He was not skilled, but he was effective.

It was Talorc, the servi boy.

In battle, the most unlikely man can become a hero. I smiled at him even as I realized that the sounds of clashing swords were abating.

Others of our men staggered and limped back into camp. Bedevere sent a troop to pursue the Scotti, but they were reduced in number and fleeing as silently as they came.

Aircol and an exhausted Merlin came in. I had forgotten about Merlin in the confusion. But it looked as if the old man had acquitted himself well, and at some cost to his person. His right arm held a nasty gash, but with luck he would only bear another honorable scar. Aircol looked none the worse, and a smile broke across his face as Gwyneira and Vortipor poked their heads out from within the wagon.

"My lord, it seems that we have given you more excitement than you desired," I stuttered, still out of breath from my labors.

He stretched his back and rolled his shoulders forward. "I am growing old for this kind of fight. But I am grateful for all of you. You saved my children."

"Talorc saved your children, my lord. He came from nowhere and fought boldly." I decided it was time that the servi boy drew praise rather than criticism. Kay would be outraged that Talorc had proved him wrong.

Aircol brushed his long hair from his face and stepped in front of Talorc. He placed a fatherly hand on the boy and smiled. "I do not own you, but I will plead with Arthur for your freedom. You have done me a great favor and I will not forget it."

Cerdic and Morgan emerged from the surrounding forest then, a look of confusion on their faces.

"What is wrong, Cerdic?" Merlin asked with a grin. "Did you lose some leeks in the trees?"

The cook's pudgy face turned so bright a red that we could see it even in the flickering campfire. He carried a club in one hand and scowled at us. "I was chasing the Scotti!"

"As was I!" Morgan echoed.

We all laughed at their discomfiture, but it was a laugh tinged with the knowledge and relief that we were still alive. Two soldiers appeared, looking winded and weary though the battle had been brief. They drew Bedevere aside and spoke to him for a few moments.

"How many?" I asked.

"Six," he said, hanging his head, "and as many wounded. Too many to bring back with us. Let us bury the dead here. The wounded still able to sit a saddle can return with our party. We will leave the worst here with Rhodri and give him supplies to keep them and his family fed until we can send a wagon to fetch them."

I nodded my agreement. Aircol gave me a curious look as Bedevere went to see to the wounded.

"A question, my lord?"

"You are unusual, Malgwyn. Bedevere is Arthur's Master of Horse and yet he seems to seek your approval."

I stopped and thought about what he said. "My lord, Bedevere and I warred together for many years. We fought side by side against the Saxons. In that time, we came to know each other only as brother warriors can. I would not have called us friends until recently, but we have always understood each other. For us, it is not about who is the superior."

"That speaks well. For a man with but one arm, you command the respect of others. Many among us believe that your loss of that arm is God's punishment for your sins."

"My lord," I said with a smile, "if God wished to punish me for my sins, I would have neither arms nor legs."

Aircol shook his head in amazement. "Have you that many sins? You are indeed an uncommon man to have sinned so much but maintained the respect of your fellows."

I merely smiled and grunted. Even a few moments of battle could be exhausting, and I suddenly felt the effort deep in my bones. Aircol took my grunt with good humor and patted me on the back.

With guards posted and patrols set, we returned to our sleep as best we could. I found no rest as my mind reeled from the cascade of events that had befallen us. And so I sat, with my sword across my lap, waiting for the false dawn.

Even as I tried to pass the night, the memories of those poor ravaged girls refused to leave my mind. Were it rape, I could understand though not condone it. Such impulses were a part of every man's being. Most could control it. Some could not. Man needed that sort of release, needed it so much that he would even take it when not offered. But this was not about that. It could not be. This was about something else altogether. Whoever did these things was making a point. I knew that when I discovered the doer of these deeds I would understand the why of it. When? I laughed to myself. If? That was the more proper question.

I spent the few hours till dawn contemplating the why of it, and wondering if I would ever find the answers I sought.

The morning light brought a clearer view of the night's carnage. We had dispatched some ten or fifteen of the Scotti. I noted a handful of blood trails that indicated that our attackers had dragged another half-dozen or so away with them. Bedevere and Aircol clashed on the question of the disposal of the Scotti. Bedevere wanted them left to rot. Aircol believed they deserved proper burial.

I sided with Bedevere but kept my own counsel. Coroticus sided with Aircol, and Bedevere eventually relented. In all truth, he did not press his argument very hard and there were no ill feelings over it. There would be more important arguments later, I feared.

"What think you, Malgwyn?" Bedevere asked as work parties were organized.

"I think the Scotti were fortunate. We are not but a few hours' ride from the coast. They were probably intent on raiding some of the inland villages and stumbled across us."

While the men, both ours and Aircol's, dug the graves, I took the chance to ride a scout farther on down the road. To my surprise Ider volunteered to go with me. We had had little time to talk on this journey. He had been of great assistance to me in the events surrounding the rebellion at Ynys-witrin, and I prized his friendship. He was young and eager, but a bright lad nonetheless.

"Malgwyn, I saw you ride out to the family across the road from our camp yesterday," Ider began. "Did you learn aught from them?"

I shook my head. "Not really." I had decided to share the little girl's vision with no one else. "They are but simple folk."

He nodded and smiled, but it was a sad sort of smile, and he chewed on his upper lip.

"Does something trouble you, Ider?"

"You have always treated me well, Malgwyn."

"You are a good man. I have never had reason to treat you otherwise."

Again, Ider chewed his lip, and he rubbed a hand across his tonsure, that shaved spot that ran from ear to ear across the top of his head, marking his membership in the brotherhood.

"What is it, Ider?"

He frowned then and dropped his head. "I am young, Malgwyn, and I know there is much that I do not understand."

I turned my head then, looking at him truly for the first time since he had joined me. "What troubles you?"

"You are known to be an honest man, and a strong one. You follow the Rigotamos, yet you do not embrace his faith."

"I can have faith in a man without believing in the same things that he does."

"But Coroticus says that anyone who does not believe in the Christ is a sinner."

I was touched. Ider was concerned about my fate in the next life. "Coroticus says many things, Ider. Some are more true than others."

It took only a glance to see that my answer did little to assuage his fears. "It is not easy to change a lifetime of beliefs, Ider, and it should be given all the time for thought and reflection that it requires."

That seemed to placate him, though it shouldn't have. I really had said nothing. After a few more minutes, when it seemed there was no danger lying immediately ahead, we turned and began the short ride back to our camp.

While dismounting, Ider turned to me again and said something odd. "Malgwyn, where did Cerdic and Morgan go last night?"

"What do you mean?"

"I was awakened by a noise about the supply wagon, probably some one hour before the Scotti raided. I looked and saw Cerdic slip into the forest and then Morgan after him."

Cerdic and Morgan left the camp and then a short time later the Scotti raided. After the Scotti fled, they both reappeared. Might mean nothing. But at the same time, it might mean everything. Perhaps the Scotti knew who they were attacking.

I smiled at Ider. "Probably needed to relieve himself."

"But he did not return until after the Scotti attacked us."

"You didn't return to your sleep?"

Ider shook his head. "I tried but could not find rest again. Then the Scotti came."

"I'll ask him, Ider, but I doubt it was anything noteworthy."

"But Malgwyn, so many ill omens cannot be wrong! The Rigotamos removed Bran's head and almost immediately bad things began to happen—the Druid cursed Arthur, the young girl was murdered at the White Mount, another girl murdered at Aircol's fort, the Scotti attacked us! Surely Arthur has called demons down among us by his actions!"

"Ider! Take hold of yourself! Do you truly believe that a Druid has the power to curse us? If so, then you deny the basis of your own faith. Do you not believe that God and his son, the Christ, control all things in the world?"

The young man looked up at me, frustration etched on his face. "I do believe that. I have given my life to His service."

"Then why these doubts?"

"Many people believe in curses and omens, Malgwyn. You know that. Can they all be wrong? How do you account for all these horrible events?"

I was not sure how to answer him, but I had to find a way.

If someone as dedicated to the Church as Ider could be swayed, then we were entering into a dangerous realm. "Coincidence. People are killed every day in our land, Ider, young girls among them. The Scotti raid often. This time, we just happened to be in their path. And lucky too, had we not been there, they might have massacred poor Rhodri and his family."

Ider's face smoothed then, relaxed, and I felt bad. He was relieved because I had lied to him. The murder of the two girls was certainly not coincidence. The attack by the Scotti might be, but I would not wager my next meal on it, especially now that I knew that members of our party had acted strangely just before the assault. And though we had failed to find the Druid, Wynn, that did not mean that he was not somewhere close by.

I told myself to remember to find Gareth's men to see what they knew of this. We had released them for the return journey, out of fear that Aircol would not understand why we used thieves to guard our flanks. And with the addition of Aircol's men, it would have taken a very large force indeed to overwhelm us. The Scotti party was a good size, but the men were pirates, not trained soldiers. They had fought bravely, but not that well.

Sighing, I watched as Ider reported to Coroticus, who glanced in my direction and nodded, a thin smile on his face. Men with long histories together often share many secrets. Such was my relationship with the abbot. It had been into his care that Arthur delivered me after that horrible day at Tribuit. And it had been Coroticus who had first recognized my curious skill at sorting out these affairs.

In those days as in these, the position of abbot was as much political as religious. The Romans made it so when they adopted the faith. One thing that I had learned from my long-dead father and Coroticus, whenever the Romans were involved in anything it became political. In the past, I had praised Coroticus's grounding in the real world. But I had also learned recently that he could be as much a zealot as the most passionate of believers.

Some said that politics was what had doomed the empire to failure; the politics, and unbridled ambition. Roman emperors spent most of their time seizing power and then fighting off pretenders to their throne. They argued so much that Alaric and his barbarians bashed down the door to Rome, causing the Romans to withdraw their troops and their protection of Britannia. We were left with a mess. My old dad had been a boy, but he had remembered well the chaos that resulted. Perhaps, with Arthur at the helm, the last of those days was behind us.

I handed my reins to one of the soldiers and searched through the throng for Bedevere.

"You are Master Malgwyn," a soft voice said to me. I turned and it was Gwyneira. She was tall for her age and blossoming into a beautiful woman, with an already fine figure and the deepest blue eyes I had ever seen. For traveling, she wore a heavier tunic, dyed blue with woad, and belted at the waist. Her cloak, a deer fur with a rounded cut was pinned with a beautiful silvered brooch marked with her name. She smiled pleasantly, and it was the kind of smile that immediately endears one to its bearer.

"Yes, my lady."

"My brother was rude to you the other night. I apologize for him. My father has told me your story. You are a man of much experience."

"I am a man, Lady Gwyneira. And not a particularly

accomplished one at that, unless you count the amphorae of wine and mead and cervesas that I have drunk."

She laughed then, a little girl's laugh, which made her all the more endearing. "Tell me of Arthur. If I am to marry him, I would like to know more."

I needed no looking glass to know that my face had turned a deep red.

"Please," Gwyneira said, touching me lightly on the sleeve of my tunic. "I know that his consort, Guinevere, is your cousin, and I know that you have fought against this match. That is why I ask you these questions."

"My lady?"

"You will tell me the truth." She had a habit of pursing her lips in such a way that the expression seemed a symbol of an earnest nature.

"I could ask Merlin or Bedevere, but they will couch their answers so as not to cause offense. You will tell me straightaway what I wish to know, without embroidering Arthur's virtues."

Despite her youth, she had an uncanny talent for assessing those around her and tailoring her questions to achieve the best possible result. I suspected that was the result of her father's teachings. You did not rise to be the ruler of the kingdom of Dyfed without being adept at diplomacy.

I looked about and saw a fallen tree, old and devoid of branches. With a wave of my one hand, I directed her toward it. "What do you wish to know?" I asked as we sat.

"Arthur is renowned for three things—his devotion to the Christ, his prowess in battle, and the sense of fairness by which he reigns. But those are the things spread by his friends. You know the man. Who is he?"

Her question was earnest and I could not lie to her. "He is

all those things. He is also stubborn and certain that he is right even when he is wrong."

"Is he often wrong?"

"He is often quick to make decisions when he should take more time for consideration." My half-arm twinged, as it often did in the dampness of early morning, and I stopped long enough to massage it.

"You received your wound in his service?"

"Aye. On the River Tribuit."

"Is Arthur a good man, as good as my father tells me? Or is he just an ordinary man that fate has raised high?"

In some ways, she reminded me of my Mariam. Her questions were blunt and asked as if she expected a lie in response, skeptical always.

"He meets the challenges facing him in more than an ordinary way, and he looks beyond the obvious when seeking answers. Arthur has good and loyal men serving him, and they give him good counsel as well. Most important, he is not afraid to listen to his men. That, in this age, is exceptional in a king."

"And how do you serve him?"

"I have served him in and out of battle, as the need arises. I have charge of preparing his documents, and I give him counsel when asked."

She cocked her head to one side as if displeased at my answer. "My father tells me that you are a man who serves a higher purpose, even if that purpose runs counter to your lord's desires, yet you do not believe in the Christ."

"I thought we were discussing Arthur?"

Gwyneira stood, facing away from me for a long moment. Finally, just as I was about to speak, she turned. "Soon after our wedding, my father will return to his home. I will be alone in a strange place, no real friends. I will need someone that I can seek counsel from, a kind of guardian. Of all the men in Arthur's service, you are seen as the most independent, the one most willing to speak frankly, without fear of reprisal."

"Lady Gwyneira, I am humbled by your request. Have you discussed this with your father? What if Arthur objects? As your husband, he will be your guardian."

"You misunderstand me, Malgwyn. I am speaking of an informal arrangement, an understanding between you and me. But to answer your question, yes, I have spoken to my father. It was he who suggested you."

And probably Ambrosius who had suggested it to him.

I frowned. Not over displeasure at her request, but that I immediately favored it. Becoming this child's guardian, in public or private, was like thrusting a dagger into Guinevere.

I did not answer immediately, trying to sort out the conflicting emotions at battle within me. Though my heart was pained and my stomach knotted over Arthur's treatment of Guinevere, this girl was not to blame. It was difficult not to be taken with her. She wore her beauty as she would an old, common tunic, comfortably and with grace. I suppose I fell a little bit in love with her at that moment. She would need a friend, of that I had no doubt.

"If you desire it and your father has no objections, then I pledge to do what I can for you within my abilities."

Gwyneira smiled then. "I can go to Arthur now, confident that I have a friend. I know what I have asked is not easy for you personally—"

I raised my hand to silence her. "You are not at fault, my lady. You are a good person, and that is enough for me."

Standing, I moved next to her and she wrapped her hand about my arm. We walked together back to the camp as Merlin and Coroticus cast quizzical looks at us and Aircol simply smiled.

With the dead buried and appropriate prayers given for their souls, we resumed our journey for home. I, for one, would be glad to put the land of the Demetae behind us, in favor of the relative safety of Castellum Arturius.

PART THREE

CASTELLUM ARTURIUS

CHAPTER NINE

"Are you ready for this?" Bedevere asked as we crossed the River Cam and Castellum Arturius came into view.

"I do not know," I admitted. My stomach was wrapped into a knot. Behind those rock and timber walls were Guinevere, Ygerne, and Arthur. And I did not want to face any of them.

We headed straight for the main gate in the southwest. A messenger had been sent ahead the night before to herald our arrival, so the road to the gate was crowded with people. And I forced a smile as I looked up at the top rampart, the one holding the parapet for the guards, and saw little Mariam perched on a soldier's shoulders yelling and waving at me.

The rest of our journey had passed uneventfully but for the general hazards of traveling, the roads in this part of Britannia being more treacherous than in others. Bedevere, reluctantly, sent to Melwas at Ynys-witrin for another troop of horse.

We all knew Melwas, at least to some extent, but we were not certain of his loyalties. He had come of age only in the last years of Arthur's push against the Saxons, and his prowess in battle had gone nearly unmeasured. I remembered him as a bold soldier, one who did not shrink from battle. Kay had once termed him reckless, but Arthur thought him just young and burdened by a young man's enthusiasm for war.

Command of the great Tor at Ynys-witrin gave him great influence in the heart of Arthur's lands, called by some the "summer" country. That he was ambitious was assumed. The only real question was how far he was willing to go to realize those ambitions. Consorting with Druids, as we had seen him do, gave a hint to his intentions, but only a hint. There had been no sign of the Druid Wynn. Perhaps I had misjudged him. Perhaps not. I could not shake the thought that he had committed those horrendous murders at the White Mount and in Aircol's city, but without a witness or other evidence, I could prove nothing against him.

At any rate, Melwas's troop of horse finally arrived when we were but a day's ride from Ynys-witrin. That we had sent for them several days before did not bode well for Melwas, but after the Scotti raid I welcomed any and all help as we brought Arthur his bride.

We arrived at Castellum Arturius about ten days after the Scotti had attacked us. Our procession was a slow moving one, burdened as we were with three ox-drawn wagons and a larger than normal escort. In some villages our journey took on the trappings of a triumphant procession as word had leaked out about our purpose. Folk would gather by the road and shout well wishes as little girls threw flowers. It was strange to me, but I suppose that times had been so bad for our people that they would grasp any opportunity to celebrate.

With great ceremony, Coroticus and Ider had split off from our group at Ynys-witrin; they would rejoin us in time

for the wedding in two days. We had stopped soon after crossing the River Cam to arrange our order of entry. Aircol and
Gwyneira were placed in the vanguard of our column as befit-
ted their rank. I, Bedevere, and Merlin rode behind with the
great wagon containing young Vortipor following. The child
had demanded to be allowed to ride with us, but his father
denied him. The boy sulked inside the wagon, and I, for one,
did not miss him. How Aircol could produce offspring as different as Gwyneira and Vortipor was something I would never
be able to fathom. But then I did not understand how Mariam
could be my child; she was so much more than I.

❖

As we approached the gate, I saw that Arthur had had great
banners posted on the ramparts, bearing a red cross against a
white background. Obviously, he wanted no mistake about his
devotion to the Church, at least not in the face of Aircol's
strong reputation as a believer in the Christ. Arthur's faith
was strong, of that there was no question, but I suspected the
banners were more for Aircol's sake.

Because of the narrowness of the approach, Aircol and
Gwyneira dismounted and walked the last leg of the journey,
up the lane and through the massive double gates. Bedevere,
Merlin, and I followed suit. I saw with approval that Arthur's
workmen had prepared and then covered over one of our best
defensive measures.

Rock cutters were kept busy, busting rocks into smaller
ones with sharp, pointed edges. These were then embedded in
the ground with their sharpest edge pointed up. Arthur had
thin blankets of sod cut and laid over the points, hiding them
from view. When horses were ridden, the sod quickly gave

way, effectively hobbling the horses and often tumbling the riders to the ground. Only the lane was kept clear, greatly reducing the numbers an enemy could bring to bear on a single point.

I did not know where Arthur would choose to meet us. Protocol dictated that Arthur be positioned in front of his timbered hall. But he was so obviously anxious to please Aircol that his enthusiasm might bring him to the very gate.

And I was right.

Arthur stood in the middle of the lane, framed by the open gates. He wore his best tunic and cloak. As was his wont, he had abandoned his helmet and his chestnut hair flapped in the ever-present breeze. To a new acquaintance, he looked strong, confident, and handsome. But I could see lines in his face and dark circles beneath his eyes that had not been there before. Whatever had gone on in our absence had worn on him. Of that much I was certain.

Kay and Illtud stood behind, flanking him on the left and right. Their faces looked less worn than Arthur's, and contrary to his example they wore their helmets of bone and leather.

"Lord Aircol, Lady Gwyneira! Welcome to our home!" Arthur proclaimed in his deep voice.

Aircol stepped forward and grasped Arthur's forearm as Arthur grasped his. Smiles broke over both of their faces, and Gwyneira turned her head slightly and smiled at me. The message was clear; she was pleased. Now extricated from greeting Aircol, Arthur offered Gwyneira his arm, which she took, and the three of them walked along the main road, the Via Caedes, as it wound below the summit where Arthur's hall stood.

For some reason I resented the festival atmosphere, although I had no right to. My mind was still focused on those two poor dead girls that I had left along the road. There would be no more festivals for them, no husbands and no children. Some madman had ripped those possibilities from them as quickly and as cleanly as a well-forged sword could cleave a man's head from his shoulders. And I had no more answers now than I did when I stood over their broken and abused bodies. At that moment, all the self-hatred and darkness and helplessness that had marked me as Mad Malgwyn came rushing back.

The procession fell apart just inside the gates. The people who had climbed the ramparts for a better view now descended. Bedevere and Merlin followed Arthur and his guests up the lane and around the curve to the market square. I was left standing in the middle of the lane, just inside the walls, and I could not think of where to go next. Only the bobbing blond head of my daughter, Mariam, returned my sanity.

"Father!" she screamed, running toward me. I scooped her up in my one arm as she wrapped her arms about my neck.

"Have you been a good girl?" I asked, brushing her ear with my lips.

"Of course I have, Father." She leaned forward then, her lips planting a kiss on my cheek. "But Mother worries that you have not been a good boy."

"Well, let's see. I did not drink. I lied only a few times and then for good reason. I only killed a couple of Scotti raiders. And I made a new friend, two really."

"Who?"

I carried her up the lane behind the great parade that now filled it. "Lord Aircol and his daughter, Gwyneira."

She pursed her lips. "We do not like them."

"And why is that?"

"They have made Aunt Guinevere very sad. She has left us and gone to live elsewhere."

Obviously, I needed to talk to Ygerne and then Arthur soon. "Where did she go?"

"To Ynys-witrin, Mother says."

So Guinevere had returned to the women's community. It must have seemed the only course left to her. She could have remained in her cottage, along the road to the abbey, remained as Arthur's mistress. It was not uncommon. But I knew my cousin well enough to know that her pride would not allow her to settle for that. Noble blood still ran through her veins, and the pride to go with it as well.

"You must go and fetch her back. I miss her." Mariam, like her own mother, the mother she had never really known, had the habit of deciding things for me.

"We will see." I put her down then and took her hand as we reached the market square before Arthur's hall. A great crowd was still gathered, angling for a good look at Arthur's new queen. The next few days, until the wedding, would be one great celebration. Were Arthur less respected, I doubt that many would care. But the people liked him, liked that he administered justice with an even hand, liked that he taxed the Church more than he did them.

"Where is Ygerne?" I asked, searching the crowd for her welcome face.

"She is at home. Mother said she would not celebrate a sin." Dear, dear Mariam. She knew neither guile nor subtlety, and I hoped, forlornly I knew, that she would stay that way.

"I would not say that where Lord Arthur can hear you, child. It would not be a good thing."

"Oh, but I already have, and so has Mother."

I winced. It sounded as if my troubles had only just begun. "Run along home, Mariam. I must go to my house and then to Arthur's hall. Tell your mother that I will be there soon."

She squeezed my hand hard. "Promise?"

"I promise. If you behave yourself, I will take you to meet Lord Aircol and his daughter."

Mariam puffed her lower lip out in a pout.

"They are good people, Mariam. Guinevere's pain is not their fault."

"All right. But do not be long."

So, with my marching orders in hand, I parted her company and crossed the hard-packed earth of the market square, elbowing my way through the crowd.

"Malgwyn!"

The cry came from a gaggle of nobles near the front entrance of Arthur's timber hall. I craned my neck, trying to see who called my name. A smile broke across my face as I saw the source. Kay.

"How are you, old friend?" I asked, looking up into his face, looming far above. He was the tallest man I had ever known, a full head taller than I.

Kay locked me in a tight embrace. "I have missed you, Malgwyn. You are spending too much time with Merlin and Bedevere. They love the traveling life too much."

"Believe me, Kay, I have dreamt of quiet nights here at home. Too much excitement is not good for my old body."

"Bedevere told me of the Scotti raid. Think you that there is more to it than a chance encounter?"

I shrugged. "I do not think so, but I cannot say for certain. If it was but chance, then they were very unlucky."

"So I have heard," Kay said with a bitter smile.

"And did you hear about the part your friend, young Talorc, played?"

I would have given one hundred Roman coins for the look on Kay's face. He was disgusted.

"Yes, Bedevere and Merlin just told me."

"Be at ease, Kay. With any luck, Aircol will convince Arthur to give Talorc his freedom and you'll be rid of him forever."

"If Arthur had sold him a year ago, we would not be worrying with him now." He stopped. "Tell me of Aircol and his daughter. Are they worth all of this trouble?"

"Aircol is a good man, much like Arthur in his way, true to the Christ and worthy to be trusted." I paused and considered my answer. "No. He appears worthy to be trusted. There has been no chance to test that judgment."

"And the girl?"

"She is a daughter of nobles and her actions show it. In truth, she seems to hold a wisdom beyond her years and has an accurate understanding of her position. She knows of Guinevere and feels bad for her."

"We all feel bad for Guinevere, Malgwyn," Kay said with a touch of sadness in his voice. "But that will not change the situation. Nor will it make this child any more welcome by many of our people. I told Arthur at the beginning that he underestimated the people's love for Guinevere."

And he had. We all had. But the rebellion of the previous year was still too fresh, and Arthur had seen a way to consolidate his position as Rigotamos as well as bring a new ally into the consilium. In practical terms, Arthur had been right. Most marriages among the nobility were matters of arrangement, negotiated to strengthen one lord or another's position or wealth. But the one thing that set Arthur apart from all the others was the one thing that he could not afford right now—a heart. His heart told him he loved Guinevere at the same time that his head said he must marry another. I did not envy Arthur. Still, I suspected that Arthur would easily come to love Gwyneira.

But none of that rescued me from the oath that bound me to Gwyneira. "Give her a chance, Kay. She has just arrived."

Kay cocked his head to one side. "I did not expect to find you defending her."

"She is just a young girl, being forced into a marriage to satisfy her father. She holds no blame in this."

"Still, life here will not be easy for her at first. After that, it will be totally up to her as to how she is treated."

"Not totally," I murmured, but Aircol and Gwyneira had turned to face the people milling about the market square, stealing both my and Kay's attention.

I elbowed my way through, moving to a position behind and to the side of our visitors. Arthur's soldiers cleared most of the area of the market square as Arthur, Aircol, and Gwyneira pivoted and faced the gathered crowd. After a long second, as the crowd cheered, Arthur stepped forward.

"In two days, I will be married to Gwyneira, daughter of Lord Aircol of the Demetae. In honor of my wedding, I declare a general amnesty of all prisoners and two days and nights of celebration!" And that brought the crowd to its feet.

Men and women alike shouted and chanted Arthur's name. The whirling blues, reds, greens, and blacks of their tattered clothes nearly made me dizzy.

Holding up his hands for silence, Arthur turned a smile on Aircol and his daughter. "Our guests have endured a long journey to be with us. We should give them rest before tonight's feasting."

As the crowd continued to cheer, Arthur led them into his hall. I felt a hand on my shoulder and turned to see Kay at my side. "Arthur wants to meet with us at my house. He'll be staying with me until the wedding, giving Aircol and his children the hall."

"Who will keep them safe?"

"Bedevere is charged with security."

Kay was somber, more so than I had seen him for many months. He seemed to have aged years in the fortnight we had been gone. But I held my tongue.

We made our way through the now dispersing crowd as merchants hawked their goods to people who could not afford them, their cries rising above even the constant din of the metalworkers at their hearths at the far end of the lane.

Kay and I were silent for the first few minutes of our short walk, but something in his manner told me that he wanted to speak, so I started.

"What is wrong, Kay? You seem about to choke on something."

"You could always read me well, Malgwyn. I did not know how to tell you this, but Arthur has decided to release Tristan and return him to Lord Mark."

I shrugged. "That's probably wise. He has held him here for more than a year, and if he is to grant a general pardon to all prisoners, he can hardly continue holding Tristan."

The frown on Kay's face told me he did not like my answer. The tall warrior had been in love with Eleonore, whose death had marked Arthur's election as Rigotamos. And it was partially Tristan's participation in that horrid murder that allowed Arthur to use him as leverage to keep Mark and the other lords in line. "Look, old friend, while Tristan bears some responsibility for Eleonore's death, he is far from the most culpable. Others, still free, hold the most guilt. I am no more fond of him than you, but it is time to let him go. Besides, Bedevere tells me that Mark himself is about to remarry."

"I had not heard this. Who will he marry?"

"Some Scotti girl named Iseult. I do not like it; I think any link with those Scotti scum is unwise. But Arthur can hardly tell another lord whom he should or should not marry."

Kay chuckled, but grimly. "But, Malgwyn, that's exactly what Mark and David and the rest are doing to Arthur."

I felt my face flush. "Arthur is marrying Gwyneira for his people's sake. An alliance with Aircol brings us nothing but more security for our people."

Kay stopped in the middle of the lane.

"What?"

"Malgwyn, just a fortnight past you nearly came to blows with Arthur over this marriage! And rightly so! Bedevere and I agreed with you, but we had not your courage!"

"Or my stupidity," I mumbled. "My arguments made no difference. Arthur is an odd sort of man. He is so concerned about being a good man, a good lord to his people, that he gives no weight to his own wants and needs. He sees this marriage as essential to stabilizing his position and securing peace. That he loves Guinevere is, really, of little importance."

I stopped and looked up at Kay. "I cannot fault his intentions, Kay. I want to. I wanted so desperately to find fault, but I know that his love for Guinevere is real, and I know all too well that he sees his marriage to Gwyneira as necessary and unavoidable."

"And she? What does she see?"

I turned from him and continued walking. "How would I know? She probably sees only her duty to her father."

"You are a poor liar, Malgwyn."

"About some things," I agreed. "Kay, she seems a good person, without the airs of so many of her station. Her young brother, on the other hand, is the spawn of the devil."

By then we had reached Kay's two-story house along the lane that ran from Arthur's hall to the barracks. Kay's old servus, Cicero, met us at the door.

"The Rigotamos is awaiting you," he told us in his ancient, rasping voice. Kay had given him his freedom years before, but Cicero stubbornly refused it. "Where would I go?" he had asked Kay. And that had been that.

Kay dropped his head to enter the house. I had no need. Kay's quarters were not large, just three rooms on the ground level and one above. One corner of the hard-packed earthen floor was covered with a fur, over one of Kay's storage pits where he kept his cheese, bread, wine, any vegetables. A sturdy wooden table sat to one side. A whiff of wood smoke lay in the air. I knew that Cicero kept his cooking fire at the back of the house.

Arthur sat in a sturdy chair, hunched over the table. He rose at our entry and stepped quickly to us, laying his hand on my shoulder. "Malgwyn! It is good to have you back."

"It is good to be back, my lord." I took his measure in a single glance. Close to, like this, the dark circles beneath his eyes were all the more pronounced. Wrinkles had deepened in his cheeks and along his neck. Arthur had aged ten years in a fortnight.

He turned away from me quickly, feeling uncomfortable at the strength of my stare, I was sure.

"I know, I know," he said, waving a hand absently as he resumed his seat. "I look ill."

"You look as if you have had the plague and yet survive. Arthur, what has happened?"

Merlin emerged then from the back of the house with Bedevere on his heels. "Yes, Arthur, tell us."

"Guinevere has not taken the news of my marriage well," he said flatly.

"And you thought she would?" I could not help myself.

"I am not stupid, Malgwyn," he snapped at me. But then, before I could respond, his shoulders sagged. "Perhaps I was stupid." It pained me to see him so.

"Perhaps hopeful is a better word," I answered at long last. "But that is all past now. We must focus on what is, not what could have been."

Bedevere, Kay, and Merlin all nodded. "He is right, my lord," Bedevere agreed.

"Did you receive my message about the Druid Wynn?"

Arthur nodded. "I did. But he has not shown his face here."

"He wouldn't have. He followed us to Aircol's domain, where another girl was murdered exactly like the girl at the White Mount." I stopped, hanging my own head.

"And?" Arthur prodded.

"And, nothing. Once again there were no witnesses. The town was searched afterward, but the Druid could not be found."

"Are you certain it was Wynn? Druids have never seemed to me to be the sort that would assault a woman, at least not unless it were a ritual killing."

"I am certain of nothing in this. But I know that Wynn holds ill will toward you. And I know that he was in the vicinity of both killings. That alone makes him worthy of consideration."

Arthur nodded. "We must put this aside now and concentrate on other matters. Tristan will represent his father at the wedding and then I will allow him to leave. I think we have proven our point. Messengers arrived yesterday indicating that Lords David, Mordred, Gawain, and Gaheris will arrive by tomorrow."

"And Melwas?" Bedevere asked.

"Melwas is not invited, nor do I suppose he would attend if he were."

"And why is that?" I could not remain quiet. Melwas was always anxious to better his standing in the consilium and one such as he acting outside his normal character was more than worthy of note.

"Guinevere," Kay said with a frown.

"Guinevere? I understood that she has returned to the women's community at Ynys-witrin."

Arthur raised his head, his brown eyes marked by a question. "The women's community? She is not there. She has taken up with Melwas at the great tor."

Chapter Ten

I do not believe it! Guinevere would never allow a snake like Melwas to touch her!"

Normally, raising my voice to Arthur would infuriate him, but he scarcely acknowledged me. "She went to him two nights after you departed. Apparently Melwas had been trying to press his suit with her even before, but she had rejected him until I told her of the marriage to Aircol's daughter. Less than a day later, she had taken residence in Melwas's fortress."

And so the explanation for Arthur's melancholy became apparent. His woman, once rejected, had quickly found another benefactor. It was not an uncommon story. The Lady Nyfain, young Owain's mother, had suffered a similar fate. But I knew my cousin, and I was certain that there was more to the story. I could not imagine that she willingly sought solace in the arms of Melwas, whom I and most others considered little more than a toad. It would, though, explain his apparent reluctance to send aid when we were on the road. He probably weighed the risks of not responding and determined that making a complete break with Arthur was not in his best interest. Perhaps Melwas was smarter than I thought.

I pushed the knowledge from my mind. I could not address that problem yet; other things took precedence.

"Rigotamos, you should alert all patrols about this Druid. Regardless of whether he killed these girls, he means you nothing but harm. We used Master Gareth's men on our journey to Caer Goch, to watch our flanks and keep an eye on the Druid. With as many troops as we had on our return, I saw no need. But I would like to bring two or three here to, umm, watch over us." At this juncture, I saw no need to cast suspicion on Morgan.

"Or has Gareth bribed you to get his men here to pick the pockets of my guests?" Arthur was not serious, and it brought welcome laughter to the room. "Very well," he agreed. "Bedevere, see to it."

I breathed a sigh of relief. For the first time since this entire affair had begun, I heard that special confidence in Arthur's voice, that essential confidence that had first drawn me to his service.

"The visiting lords will be encamping between Castellum Arturius and the River Cam," Kay said into the pause. "We have laid in enough food to care for them for up to a week."

"The celebration will not last quite that long. Two days before the wedding and one day after. More than that would not be appropriate. Bedevere," Arthur said, turning. "Triple our patrols in the countryside, especially the roads to the east. This is the first major gathering of our lords since the consilium met more than a year ago. I do not want any surprises."

"I will see to it. What about vigile patrols within the town?"

Arthur's eyes narrowed as if pondering something unseen. "Double those as well. I would have our town peaceful."

"Will that be necessary with Malgwyn's spies about town?" Kay asked.

"I would rather have too many eyes," Arthur decided, "than too few."

"Has that been a problem of late?" Merlin asked. I barely heard the question, still stunned that Guinevere would ever seek refuge with Melwas.

"No more than usual," Kay answered. He turned back toward Arthur. "I will see to that also. Personal bodyguards for Aircol and his children?"

"He has his own, but assign Paderic to them as well."

Paderic was Arthur's cousin, a good man but one slow in mind. Given a specific task, he could be counted on to sacrifice his own life if needed to fulfill his duty. As a drinking companion, he had no equal. He was funny and full of life.

The next few minutes were spent outlining the activities. Kay, despite his volatile personality, had obviously worked everything out. Finally, we had no more business to discuss. I rose to leave, but Arthur's hand caught my one good arm. "I would speak with you alone, Malgwyn."

I just nodded. Bedevere, Kay, and Merlin left us alone, but not before Kay gave me a knowing look. When we were by ourselves, Arthur motioned to a chair and I took up my seat once more.

Though the sky was cloudy and the scent of rain rode on the breeze, Arthur's face and neck were slick and shiny from sweat. He was not looking forward to this conversation and nor was I.

"Malgwyn, I do not know what to do about Guinevere," he confessed, hanging his head so low that his chestnut locks brushed the tabletop.

I shrugged. "Why should you do anything?"

His head jerked up. "I cannot let her stay with Melwas!"

"You have no say in the matter, Rigotamos. You rejected her and she chose another." I was not predisposed to make anything easy for him. "You have known Guinevere long enough to understand that she controls her own actions."

"Do not pretend that I cared nothing for her, Malgwyn." His tone hardened, nearly as hard as the look on his face.

"And do not pretend that your decision to marry Gwyneira has no consequences."

"Will you go to her on my behalf?"

"No," I said flatly. I knew that he would ask such of me, though I wished with all my heart that he would not. I was one of the few people that Guinevere might actually listen to. "Arthur, I have followed you into battle and would gladly do so again. Though I disagreed with the decision you made, you had solid reasons behind you. I will not argue that point. Besides, the decision is done. The negotiations completed. You have done what you had to in order to strengthen both your position and the consilium. The Saxons do not want us acting as one. 'Twould be far easier to eliminate us tribe by tribe, lord by lord. I recognize that the decision you made was not easy. And I know that it is not unusual for a king to have mistresses. But I will not go to Guinevere and convince her to take the lesser role. She is my cousin and I love her. She would have made an excellent queen."

"You would have her in Melwas's arms?"

"No, but neither would I have her in yours, as your second choice."

"That is not fair, Malgwyn."

"What is fair, Rigotamos? Life is not fair. And affairs of

the heart even less so." I stopped. "I went to market one morning a husband and father, and returned to find my woman dead and my life destroyed. Is that fair? Arthur, I have sworn my allegiance to you, and that has been a good thing for me and, I hope, for you. But I must draw a line somewhere, and becoming involved in your relationship with my cousin is that place."

His shoulders grew rigid at the affront but then sank in acceptance, and he stood slowly. "You are right. I have handled this situation badly." He moved to a window and looked out on the lane through the cloudy swirls of Roman glass, salvaged I guessed, from an abandoned villa. "Give me an army and a battlefield and I can act with courage and cunning. I know how to deploy my soldiers, how to sense weakness in the enemy. But when it comes to dealing with women, I am an infant."

"All men are infants at that, Rigotamos. None more so than I." Arthur was indeed a man of action. His quiet confidence in the face of the enemy drew men to his banner like bees to honey. And he prosecuted those battles with a passion and an iron will unmatched by any general I had ever seen. As the Rigotamos, the overking of lands that stretched from our southern coast nearly as far as the great wall in the north, built by the Roman Hadrian an eon before, he was popular for his faith in the Christ and his evenhanded dispensation of justice.

"I will resolve this myself, Malgwyn, when more time is available. But should you chance to speak with her, let her know that she remains close to my heart."

In all the years that I knew Arthur, from battlefield to timbered hall, I will never forget his silhouette in that window nor the pain in his voice. That was the most vulnerable I had ever or would ever see him. "I will."

He straightened suddenly and turned. "Now, Malgwyn, we have much to do in preparation for this wedding. How do you find Aircol and his daughter?"

"They are good people. The girl is young and beautiful, but she carries herself as a much older woman. She understands the responsibilities incumbent upon one in her position. Aircol appears to love the Christ every bit as much as you, and it was apparent from the start that he desired this alliance as much as you."

Arthur nodded. "That is good. Now tell me of the negotiations and I will give you leave to return to Ygerne. She is eager to see you, I am certain."

And the memory of her face beckoned me as well, so, without delay, I gave him the details.

✤

"You missed me," Ygerne said later, nuzzling under my good arm. Owain had taken the children to the market square where vendors had set up shop and the festival was already beginning, leaving Ygerne and me to reacquaint ourselves.

Despite my long journey, I had but to look at her once to feel that special warmth in my loins. Her red hair glowed in the flashing of the fire and the press of her full breasts against me threatened to ready me for action again.

"I am not ashamed to admit it."

"You could scarcely hide it," she teased.

We had long been drawn to each other, even before my brother Cuneglas died. And that fact I was ashamed to admit. He had been killed during the events surrounding Arthur's election as Rigotamos, but he was known throughout the town for being untrue to Ygerne. After the death of my Gwenyth and before Ygerne, I had found my pleasure where I could, usually among the serving girls. We were all lonely, I suppose, looking for what comfort we could find in this world. But those days were over. Ygerne and I had not yet married, nor did we yet live together. Though I had finally taken my brother's place in bed, I could not bring myself to move into his home.

When we were sated with each other, I told her of the strange murders I had encountered on my journeys. I found Ygerne to be an excellent ear, and I needed badly to talk about what I had seen.

"How strange! And there was no sign that they had been truly bedded?" she asked when I brought my story to a close.

"No. Nothing that I could mark down as evidence of that."

She propped her head up on her hand and narrowed her eyes. "No one saw anything? A stranger lurking about?"

Something in her voice said she had more to tell me but she wanted answers to her questions first. That was her manner.

"Nothing. But, in both situations it was dark and we were on unfamiliar ground. And," the words almost caught in my throat, "we were there on other business."

The flash in her eyes should have caught my tongue in mid-flight. Trouble was brewing.

"Then it was not about pleasure. The killer had some other reason for abusing them thus."

"I thought so too, but I cannot fathom what that could be."

"Perhaps if you had spent more time seeking this monster and less playing matchmaker, you would have." She could not hold back any longer.

I knew that the words then on their path from my mouth were destined for disaster, but I could not stop myself from speaking them. "Mariam tells me that you counseled Arthur against this marriage," I said after a few moments of silence. My nose twitched at the scent of wood smoke heavy in the air.

Ygerne moved away from me a bit. "He asked me what I thought. I told him. He did not like it."

"I do not suppose he would."

"Why?" She rolled completely away from me then and gave me a frown.

"He was already committed to this before he asked your thoughts. No man likes to be told that he is wrong about the path he is already on."

"No *man* likes to be told anything by a *woman*," she snapped.

"You are not being fair, Ygerne!"

"I am a woman, Malgwyn. And I know how much a woman's opinion counts in this world."

"Arthur has done this because he feels it is in our people's best interests."

"Then Arthur needs to spend more time among the people. What man wouldn't leap at the chance to bed a beautiful young girl? Arthur is no different than any other. And she is just a pampered child who knows nothing but a life of privilege." The bitterness of her tone surprised me. She spoke the words with the sharp tang of acid on her lips.

"Ygerne! Give the child a chance. You have not even met her. She has only just arrived."

And then Ygerne bolted to her feet, pulling a fur about her. "What? You too are abandoning Guinevere, your own kin, your own blood? Why do you defend this child? Did Arthur commission you to initiate the girl, teach her how to pleasure him?"

"Ygerne! That is not fair!"

"Go! And do not show your face in this house until . . ."

I bounded to my feet. "Until what?"

"Until I give you leave!" The fire in her eyes was matched only by that of her hair, and her breasts, bound now by the animal hide, shook with her anger.

"Ygerne!"

"Go!"

I pulled on my *braccae* and tunic and left, more puzzled by her anger than upset by it. Once outside the door, I looked hard at the planed boards. Were I to live past a hundred winters, I would never understand women.

❖

Merlin frowned at me as I entered our house. "I did not expect to see you for a fortnight." I had moved in with him after Arthur's election as Rigotamos and my commission as his scribe. Merlin could be forgetful, and he needed someone to watch over him. I needed to be needed.

"Nor did I expect to see you so soon." The irritation in my voice bothered even me. "Ygerne is out of sorts with me over this damnable marriage!" I tossed my pouch in a corner and slumped in a rickety chair. Against the far wall was a long table, covered in pots and vials filled with innumerable cures that Merlin provided for the sick. From the sharpness of the headache growing between my temples, I would be hunting his pot of willow bark extract soon.

"You expected her not to be opposed?" The question in Merlin's voice was a surprised one.

"Maybe. Perhaps. I do not know, Merlin! How could I have known?"

The old man shook his head in mock exasperation with

me. "Malgwyn, you are an intelligent man, but you know little about women."

"Then, teach me, master." The sarcasm lay heavy in my voice.

He crossed the room, limping a bit I noticed, and stood over me. "Now, Malgwyn. When has any man understood a woman? This is a gift that the three gods have not granted us."

"Nor Arthur's one god?"

He chuckled and nodded. "Nor the one, nor any. We are forever fated to be left in mystery about the inner workings of the female mind."

"So I am wasting my time in the trying?"

"There is only one thing you can do—remember those subjects that have infuriated her and never bring them up again."

It was my turn to chuckle. "Well, Master Merlin, since the topic at hand is Arthur's marriage and that will be the only subject under discussion for the next week at least, I am not sure that I can see a clear path to avoiding it."

"Nor do I, Malgwyn. It would seem that you, my friend, will be without the good Ygerne's pleasures until enough time has passed to calm these troubled waters."

"Your ability to prophesy is uncanny." I stood and walked to a corner of our wattle-and-daub house, tossed back an animal hide covering our storage hole. For a couple of minutes, I rummaged around for some cheese and bread, but found neither. "What am I to eat?" I grumbled.

"You will eat as I eat, from Arthur's larder. If you will recall, we have both been away for the last several weeks. Restocking our food stores will have to wait for a few days."

"I have eaten enough of Cerdic's food. I was hoping for something with more flavor than a piece of firewood."

And Merlin laughed loudly as he slapped my back.

We wandered up the lane to Arthur's kitchen, where Cerdic was berating Talorc for some horrible travesty he had apparently committed. Along one wall, I saw pots of milk, sour milk, and I knew that if I looked closer I would find wood sorrel mixed in, used to help the milk curdle for cheese making.

"Cerdic, be of good cheer! We are home at last," I encouraged him.

He grimaced and stepped back from Talorc. "You do not have to prepare three nights of feasting with a staff of worthless servants." Cerdic eyed us carefully, yet another frown growing on his face. "Why are you here?" He grunted and nodded as he looked us up and down. "Seeking scraps from Arthur's table, I suspect." Cerdic turned to the Pict. "Boy, go fetch them some bread and cheese, and some of that pig meat." Talorc scampered off.

"Why so unhappy, Cerdic?" I asked as Merlin and I settled into a pair of chairs. The old slave was often in an ill humor, but today he seemed especially so.

"Why? I have hundreds of people to feed and I am shorthanded."

"Aircol brought servants. I will speak to him about lending some of them to you," I said, glancing around at the bustling scene, servi carrying platters, amphorae. A familiar face was missing though.

"Cerdic?"

"What?"

"Where is Nimue, the slave girl that Arthur freed?"

Kay and Arthur entered then from another door, one facing Arthur's hall, across the lane.

Before Cerdic could answer, Arthur interrupted. "What? What are you asking about?"

"Nimue, the slave girl." Merlin and I spoke almost at the same time.

Kay and Arthur looked at us quizzically. "She is dead. No one has told you? Poor child. She scarce had time to enjoy her freedom. They found her, what, Kay," Arthur looked to his friend, "two days after they left?"

CHAPTER ELEVEN

y mind whirled and I nearly fell from my chair. Nimue
dead! "How?"

"It appeared that she drank too much, perhaps in celebration of her victory. Paderic found her in one of the old houses
in the village below." Arthur must have seen the fury on my
face. "Malgwyn, we all liked Nimue, but she was a simple serving girl. From all indications, she was drinking to celebrate her
freedom, drinking with the wrong companions, ones who cared
not for her safety."

My eyes shot to Kay. What he must have gone through!
Kay had loved Eleonore, the ill-fated sister of my own dead
wife, and she had been murdered. We had all watched with
pleasure as he quietly, indeed tenderly, paid court to young
Nimue. And now the deepened lines in his face and his brusque
manner had an explanation.

My judgment was true. Kay did not even look at Arthur or
agree with him.

"You should have sent for me!"

Arthur shook his shaggy head. "Your mission to Aircol was
more important. In truth, Malgwyn, I never gave a thought to

sending for you. People die. Some violently. Some not. I am sad to lose such a girl, but you were already nearly two days on the road before she was discovered, and it was not an unusual death."

"You mean it did not appear to be unusual, my lord."

He nodded absently. "We have more immediate problems, Malgwyn. I know that you liked the girl, and as I have said, I mourn her loss, but what is done is done. Focus on those still above ground."

The way he so easily dismissed the poor girl rubbed me as raw as a tanner worried a hide with his scraper. I detested too the way in which he disregarded poor Kay's feelings. But there was nothing I could do about it. Arthur was right, as he normally was, about that which was important and that which was not. I had other, more important things to worry about: the coming wedding and Ygerne's anger. Such was enough to occupy any man. Still, I would miss young Nimue; she was a pleasant sort, the kind to brighten a man's day with her smile. Though a slave, she had rarely bemoaned her condition, which made the granting of her freedom by Arthur all the more sweet. Bittersweet now, it appeared. And I mourned her death for my old friend Kay.

I sometimes wondered why God or the gods or fate spared my life and not those of folk more deserving—like Nimue. But in the end, that way led only to madness as there was no answer, at least not one that we were equipped to understand.

"Yes, Rigotamos, you are correct." I rose and headed for the door.

"Your food, Malgwyn?" Merlin called after me.

Stopping, I swiveled my head just a bit and answered without really looking at him. "Food holds no interest for me suddenly." That Arthur was right did nothing to lift the darkness then burdening me.

Despite the protests of Arthur and Kay, I left the kitchen and walked up the lane to the uppermost rampart, climbing then the parapet. Over the months of Arthur's tenure as Rigotamos, I had come to consider this my favorite place, that site where I could think without distraction. But as the wind whipped about me, it seemed a hateful place, and I felt as dark as I had in all those days when I would not let the sun brighten my day no matter how hard it tried.

With the growing gusts of wind, the clouds descended across the land, obscuring the signal fire on the great tor at Ynys-witrin. And with the clouds came pebbles of rain, forced into my hair and my beard until my head felt like a sodden mass. I thought of nothing, really, as I allowed the gods of nature to assault me. A weight pressed against my forehead, but it seemed from the inside out and my eyes lost focus of all around me.

I do not know how long I stood like that, leaning against the timbered walls, the world nothing but a jumble of greens and browns and grays. I had never told anyone, but I did not really like the wine and mead and cervesas of which I drank so much. But it made time pass more quickly and kept me focusing on my pleasure and not my sorrow.

Lately I had begun to think of those times with a wistfulness, a longing. No Arthurs. No Ygernes. No Druids. No complications. Just an occasional manuscript to copy, a skin of wine to drink, a string of forgettable women to bed. I did not fool myself. I was as forgettable for them as they were for me. We sought solace, a little tenderness, from each other. And, generally, the trade was a good one. But the tenderness lasted just a moment, a wink of an eye.

"Malgwyn?"

Startled, I turned and saw that young Owain had joined me. The orphan was growing into a tall, spindly lad. He was the son of Nyfain, a once noble lady whose first husband had died in battle. She then married Accolon, who in his youth had been one of Arthur's first followers. But he fell in love with Arthur's sister, Morganna, a woman whose fancies were as changing as the wind. Morganna left it to Arthur to turn Accolon away, and the warrior blamed Arthur for the whole mess. But, late in his life, he returned to Arthur's service. Indeed, Arthur's election as Rigotamos had rested on Accolon's shoulders. In his last hours, he served Arthur faithfully and well, giving his life in the end. Nyfain too died during that affair, leaving poor Owain, who had never really known his true father, an orphan.

I had become close to the boy and let him help me with my duties as a scribe. He lived now with Ygerne and her brood, and Merlin was seeing to his education.

"Yes, Owain. What is it?"

"Are you ill?"

I glanced down at him, his smooth child's face marked now with lines of worry.

"I suppose so, in a manner. Why?"

He screwed his face into a frown and leaned on the rampart next to me. "I am used to seeing you grumpy, unhappy, even angry, but I have not seen you look like this in many moons, not since before Mother and Father Accolon died."

"It is good of you to notice, boy. But I have no easy answers for you." There was much more I wanted to say to him, but I could not expect him to understand. What I would say was about sacrifice, pain, lives lost, and for what? No one had any more to eat than they did before. No one paid fewer taxes. The healers knew no more about curing illnesses. I found myself asking a question that I could not ask and maintain my sanity.

Had the land truly prospered under Arthur's reign?

The Saxons threatened us less, but in the lull Arthur's enemies within the consilium had simply seized the opportunity to work their mischief. The only one I could see who had honestly profited by Arthur's ascension was Ambrosius, now retired and living the truly good life.

But none of that was for Owain. His world consisted of Castellum Arturius, the boys and girls with whom he played, me, Ygerne, Merlin, the secret out-of-the-way places where he refought battles. Once, before we went to the White Mount, I found him behind one of the old buildings below the fort. He had prepared a credible model of the River Tribuit and, using bits of tesserae from a broken mosaic as soldiers, recreated our victory there, hollow for me though it had been.

Owain was stunned at being caught, but I had knelt with the shaken boy and showed him how to correct his troop placements. For an hour, I taught him the lessons that Tribuit had taught all of us; I even showed him where my arm had been taken and how it had occurred, things I had never before relived for anyone.

His grasp of things military had surprised me, and I had seen the budding general within him. But I worried for him.

Now I just smiled. "'Tis just a mood, Owain, and it will pass in time."

"Because of Nimue?"

"She is certainly a part of it. I just learned of her death. It is bound to make me melancholy."

He nodded in his little boy way. "I liked her. She was always kind to me. Malgwyn, she was very young. Why did she die?"

"I do not know, lad. Some people die young of too much drink. Sometimes something in their bodies goes awry. Sometimes there just is no explanation."

"Surely God knows."

We were on tortuous ground here. I had not embraced Arthur's faith, at least not in any meaningful way. Nor was I a believer in the old ways. Yet, I felt a great yearning, a desire for there to be more to this existence than random chance. "There is reason in all things, Owain, though we may not be able to understand it."

He nodded. Death was nothing new to him. It was an all too familiar visitor in those days. My father used to say that we had been cheated of our youth when the Romans left, that while affairs had not been perfect under their rule, there had certainly been less death and violence. The world into which Owain had been born was one where Death did not tiptoe through the lane, stealing into an occasional door and visiting its sorrow on those within. In this world, Death boldly marched from village to village, kicking in doors and terrorizing everyone.

"Why is Mother Ygerne upset with you?"

"I do not know for certain. She is upset that the Rigotamos is marrying Gwyneira. I know that much. But somehow I feel there is more than that. It bothers me, but I am not certain that I know how to mend the rift." I cuffed him on the ear. "Any suggestions?"

Owain leaned against the rampart and frowned, shaking his head. "Women are difficult to understand, aren't they?"

The severity of his look sent me into laughter, a good, belly-deep laugh. One sentence from young Owain and my ill mood fled like a falcon in flight. I tousled his hair with my one hand and then led us both down the ladder and off the parapet.

❖

I kept my distance from Ygerne throughout the rest of the day and evening. Mariam came to my house late in the afternoon and sat in my lap as Merlin amused her with stories of Gwynn ap Nudd, the faerie king who lived inside the great tor at Ynys-witrin. Long before the feasting, her yawns threatened to overtake her and she rode my shoulders back to Ygerne's house. I let her down and knelt beside her.

"Mariam, do you know why Mother Ygerne is upset with me?"

My daughter pursed her lips again and frowned at me. "Mother warned me that you would ask me questions. She said to tell you that you are a grown man and should understand women better."

Before I could answer, the door flew open and Ygerne appeared, snatching Mariam from my arm and slamming the door in my face. That she was upset about Guinevere I understood. But that had been Arthur's decision, not mine. Frustrated and worried, I trudged back up the lane toward home.

Because our return journey had taken so long and been so tiring, the feasting on the first night was fairly subdued. Despite Cerdic's blustering, he prepared a more than adequate table, simple foods to be sure like pig, chicken, leeks, potatoes, flat bread and mead spiced with apples and flecks of fennel.

The air held little of the festive atmosphere it should have, I noted as I walked through the lanes. The wedding of the Rigotamos should have heralded the greatest festival in recent memory. But that night was strangely calm, though the flickering of the torches made shadows seem to dance along the lanes. Granted, none of the other lords of the consilium would arrive until the next day, along with other guests: the bishop Dubricius, two of Vortimer's brothers—Faustus and Riocatus (both sacerdotes)—an envoy of Sidonius Apollinaris from Gaul, an envoy from Pope Leo in Rome, and one from the Roman emperor. I cannot now remember if it was Avitus or Majorian or Libius Severus. It was before Anthemius, I am almost certain. Emperors changed so often in those days that one needed a sharp mind to remember them all. Arthur, anxious to solidify his status as Rigotamos, had sent out fast riders as soon as the decision was made, before even our trip to the White Mount.

I heard that three horses and one rider had died in the race to reach Rome, but, as with so many rumors, there was no way to prove it true. That the dispatch rider had flown with the wind was obvious, but even extraordinary acts were often exaggerated. I never understood why.

The vendors with their wooden stalls had not yet filled the market square, near the still unfinished church. But the people from the outlying villages had just begun to arrive. Those who first gathered in their colorful patchwork clothes were more interested in the wine than in buying or trading for brooches or new tunics. Indeed, I saw more than one old and frayed toga among them. Good wool was not meant to be abandoned, even if its style was outdated.

"Malgwyn!"

A voice called to me from near the main gate. Craning my neck around, I saw a tall, slim man approaching. He wore the tunic and *camisia* of a noble and the belt at his waist was studded with iron. Tristan ap Cunomorous (or Mark as he preferred).

Though I had no interest in talking with him, courtesy dictated that I do so. "My lord."

He trotted up to me then, his Pictish hair flowing about his shoulders, a smile planted firmly on his face. "I have just heard that Arthur is releasing me to return home."

"Yes, it is only just," I muttered, with little sympathy in my voice. I took the chance to study him a bit, though, and I noticed that he had more lines in his face than I remembered. Perhaps his stay with us had matured him. "I hear that your father is marrying?"

"It is true. As with Arthur's match with Gwyneira, there is more than a little controversy about it."

"Aye?"

He leaned in closer. "She is Scotti, daughter of some tribal chief or other, named Iseult. I do not yet know the whole story of it, but she is either very beautiful or very rich."

I had to chuckle at that. Mark was known for two things: his appreciation of beautiful women and his devotion to treasure. "Well, I am sure it will be good for you to get back home to Castellum Dore."

My good wishes paid, I made to turn away, but Tristan's hand caught my shoulder.

"Malgwyn," he said with a stammer.

"What is it, my lord?" Something in his eyes held me to the spot: pain.

"I need you to know that I truly did not wish any harm to Eleonore. My passion drove my hands in ways that my brain could not control. But you must understand that her death was not my intention."

Despite the earnestness of his voice, I was not inclined to treat easily with him. In truth, he had not killed Eleonore, but I had let him believe that he had. He certainly contributed to it, but others bore more blame than he. "Yet, Tristan, she did die." I stopped. Tears streamed down his smooth cheeks. "Here, here! Steady yourself, Tristan. Her death is long past, and you have borne your punishment with grace. When you are my age, I expect to see you high in the consilium." My words held not the ring of truth, but so upset was the young lord that he did not hear the lie among them. Yet his grief was convincing and my hard old heart softened a bit.

"May I seek you out for counsel in the future, Malgwyn?"

"Of course, my friend."

With that, Tristan wiped his face with a wool-wrapped hand, straightened his stance, and left me with a nod. I watched him walk back through the main gate and sighed. Perhaps it was time to lay my anger over Eleonore aside.

The wind shifted out of the northeast, and the acidic stench of the tanner filled the lane. My nose crinkled at the sting, but at least it was not as bad as the smell of the woad-making. I headed toward the barracks at the far end of the town, next to the metalworkers' hearths. For once, the ringing of their hammers did not echo throughout town.

I saw a familiar shadow passing through the stout gate to the barracks. Illtud, another of Arthur's cousins but smarter than all the rest combined. And he looked much like Arthur, tall with a full head of chestnut hair. But where Arthur went bearded, Illtud did not. And where Arthur was a born general and hungry for position, Illtud was a skilled soldier with little in the way of common ambition. He had been a frequent visitor at

Ynys-witrin when I lived there, but he spent no time with the abbot. No, Illtud sought out the oldest and wisest brothers and conversed with them for hours. I never asked him what he found so interesting. He was a private man, and I respected that.

"What say you, Illtud?" I called after his shadow. He stopped and turned toward me.

"Malgwyn? What brings you to the barracks this late?"

"Idleness. I have nothing to which I can put my hand. My latest mission is finished and my charges guarded by Bedevere's sword."

"And your daughter?"

"Asleep by now, enchanted into a deep slumber by one of Merlin's stories."

"So you'll play at dice and drink yourself to sleep?"

I laughed. "Just visiting old friends, Illtud. And you? What brings you to the barracks at such an hour?"

He smiled then, a good smile. "I am confused, Malgwyn. I would have your counsel."

"Of course. We have warred together too often for me to deny you that."

Illtud looked away, nodded, and took my good arm in his hand, guiding me away from the barracks and toward the northeast gate. Now he had my attention. We exited the gate and descended the lane, but only to the second rampart, where he led me from the path and to the well there. Few came here at night; it was one of the only places in the town where you could be assured of privacy.

The soldier Illtud released my arm and walked over to the earthen bank, surmounted by its timber rampart, and dropped into a squat, resting his back on the bank. Neither the tanner's

stench nor the choking odor of fermenting woad or that of the fuller penetrated here, only fresh-cut timber and rich earth flavored the air.

"What is it, Illtud? Why have we come here?"

"The town is a very small place, Malgwyn. Everything we say, whether intended for one pair of ears or many, is heard by the many. What I wish to speak of is not something that I want to have as the subject of town gossip."

Now I was concerned. Perhaps Illtud had heard of some new plot against Arthur. "Tell me."

"I am thinking of leaving Arthur's service."

And then my mind did race! Illtud leaving Arthur's company might mean any number of things—an alliance with another lord, a sign of even further unrest among the soldiers. That Illtud, cousin of Arthur and one of his most loyal men, could abandon him was unthinkable!

"But, Illtud!"

He waved a hand at me wearily. "Be at ease, Malgwyn. I do not leave his service in dissatisfaction with Arthur, or to ally myself to any other lord, no earthly lord at least." It was as if he could read my mind.

"Then why?" If the reason was not among those, I could not see in which direction it lay.

At that question, Illtud covered his face with his wrapped hands and shook his head. He did not answer me for a long moment, and I gave him his time. Finally, those steady brown eyes reappeared. "I mean to enter the Christ's service."

"In truth?"

Illtud nodded. "I have tortured myself with this decision for many, many moons. But I am drawn to Him as a child to sweets." He bounced to his feet then and paced before me.

"We have warred throughout this land, Malgwyn, you and I. We have done everything we could to bring peace. But I see in the Church a way to do so much more, to educate our children, to teach them a better way to govern our lands."

"I cannot argue that education is one answer. What are the Druids but an order dedicated to knowledge? Knowledge is power. But, Illtud, the land must be secured first. Peace must be attained. And you are far too important to that quest."

He jerked to his feet in frustration. "If not now, Malgwyn, then when? By any reckoning, I have passed half my years in this life. When will the time arrive?"

"Do not tell Merlin how you count a man's years. He would disagree, violently." But such was too quick an answer for the serious question Illtud had posed. This evening had gone from an effort to fight boredom to one of surprises. First Tristan apologizes and now Illtud turns sacerdote. I should not have been surprised at all. He had long been turned different to the rest of us who followed Arthur's banner.

"Are you certain that this is the path you desire?"

"I know this and only this, Malgwyn. I am never happier than when in study and reflection and at prayer. No doubt clouds my mind; no hesitation enters my thoughts." For one of the few times in my life, I could detect no deception in another man's words, no hint of a falsehood. My soldier friend was sincere, and that counted for everything.

"Then you are a fortunate man, Illtud. We will miss you at the war councils, but you are right. Life is too short to ignore such a strong calling. Perhaps you can bring some decency to the clergy," I quipped.

But Illtud didn't smile. "With abbots like Coroticus," he said, "it needs decency."

"Promise me this. Wait until after Arthur is wed and all the other lords have returned home before making your intentions known. Right now is not a good time for yet more turmoil in our ranks."

He nodded. "Agreed. A few more days will not matter."

I clapped him on the back with my one hand and left him to the solitude as I returned to the road leading through the gates, a bemused smile on my bewhiskered face. If men as honest and decent as Illtud could find a home in the clergy, perhaps I should revise my attitude.

Straightening my shoulders and my tunic, I began the ascent through the final rampart, oddly at peace with myself.

Until a voice interrupted my journey. A most unwelcome voice.

Arthur's cousin, Mordred.

"Malgwyn!"

I thought for a moment of some reason to ignore him, but I could not find one. So I turned and nodded. "Lord Mordred. I see you have returned to the nest for Arthur's wedding." More pleasant than that I could not be.

"Rest easy, Malgwyn," Mordred assured me. While rumors had spread that Mordred had put on great weight while commanding our western defenses, he appeared to me to be the same man I had accused of murder and treason some two years before. Mordred, yet another cousin of Arthur's, was thin with an equally thin face and long nose. His eyes were set a bit too close together, and he looked as a hawk. What concerned me most, though, was his hair. It had always been straight and greasy, but now he wore a braided lock that fell from the center of his scalp and across one or the other of his eyes. At first I immediately took it for the sort of topknot that

Saxons wore—not that that would have surprised me—but on closer inspection I saw that I had been mistaken.

The last time I had seen Mordred had been in Arthur's hall, immediately after the attempt on Ambrosius Aurelianus's life, an attempt by the Saxons to derail Arthur's election as Rigotamos. He and I had clashed then, and Ambrosius had banished him to the far western coast. This was the first time he had returned to Castellum Arturius since.

"I do not think it would be wise for me to rest easy just now, Mordred. You always make things more interesting."

He laughed and wrapped his arm about my shoulders, sending a chill down my spine. "Malgwyn, Malgwyn! We are not enemies. Just adversaries." He had been at the mead; I could smell it on his breath.

"As you like, my lord. I was headed home, and you?"

"My lads and I thought we would see what drink and food might still be available at Arthur's hall."

I glanced behind us to see a pack of young nobles, most unfamiliar to me. They were the sort that, try as they might, could not hide their sneers. But one stood out from the rest, not a noble, a priest, a Druid priest, with a wide smile on his face.

Wynn!

CHAPTER TWELVE

I shrugged from beneath Mordred's arm and pulled him from the center of the lane to the edge. Behind me I heard a grumbling from his young toughs, but I ignored it.

"Mordred, are you crazy? Bringing a Druid to Arthur's hall! And this Druid?"

"You know him?" For the first time in my acquaintance with Mordred, he spoke with true and utter innocence.

One of the guards at the innermost gate rushed to my side. It was one of the men who had fought beside me in the late rebellion. "Captain?"

I pointed out the Druid. "Arrest him!"

Mordred grabbed my shoulder and twisted me around. "Malgwyn, you cannot! He has asked for and been granted my hospitality. By our laws he is sacrosanct!"

Regardless of law and custom, the soldier was ready to ignore Mordred and arrest Wynn at my command. I considered my options for the briefest of seconds. Once a man had been granted a lord's hospitality, he became as one of the lord's family, safe from but the most severe of crimes, such as murder. But I had no absolute evidence of Wynn's guilt in the deaths of the girls. Mordred was truly shocked and taken by surprise by my reaction. And Druids in general were held sacrosanct by many of our people. Treading carefully was called for here.

"Forgive me, my lord," I said after a moment. "I was not aware that he was here under your protection. But I would ask your leave to speak to this priest at some future time."

Mordred's narrow eyes narrowed even further. "If he has no objections, I see no reason why you shouldn't. We will go now to Arthur's hall and make our presence known. 'Tis good to see you again, Malgwyn." But his voice held a queer tone, a questioning tone, though it did not paint his words as false.

❖

I returned to the castle well where Illtud was still enjoying the solitude, relieved, I suspected, that he had finally told someone what he wished to do. "Come, Illtud! We have a problem."

Without a question or a word, he bounced to his feet and followed me back up the lane and into the town. As we wound between the houses toward Arthur's hall, we found Kay and Bedevere walking together. They stopped, surprised, I guessed, to see us.

"What, Malgwyn? You look as if you'd seen a spirit," Kay chided.

"The Druid Wynn, from the White Mount, is here in the castle."

Bedevere's eyes narrowed and his broad shoulders straightened beneath his tunic. "There is no need for concern, Malgwyn. I will deal with this. Where is he?"

I grabbed his shoulder. "You cannot, Bedevere. He is here under the protection of Mordred. I just saw them at the northeast gate."

He brushed my hand aside. "Then perhaps I should settle with that snake as well."

I dipped my head, embarrassed and ashamed of what I was about to say. "I do not think you should, Bedevere. I don't think Mordred has any idea who he has brought among us. And a blood feud between the two of you now would bring nothing but dishonor on Arthur and his guests."

"What of it? You saw those two girls, their honor torn to bits by a stick of wood! That Mordred would protect the doer of those deeds strips him of any rights his nobility gives him!"

I watched in amazement as Bedevere, the stolid, taciturn soldier, turned as red as the cross on his tunic. His chest puffed out and I thought for a fleeting moment that he intended to strike me. In reflex, I threw my arm up to ward off any blow.

But Kay, whose fits of anger were renowned, stepped between us. "Bedevere!" He glanced about and saw that the few people about the lanes had turned in our direction. "Let us discuss this somewhere more private."

Mine and Merlin's house was the closest, so we headed, almost at a trot, for it.

Once inside, I lit an old Roman lamp made from terra cotta and fired a grayish-white. Our hearth, in the middle of the room, still held the glowing embers of a fire. Merlin was not there, probably over at Arthur's hall, across the lane and up the slope.

Bedevere slumped then into a rickety old chair, fashioned from trimmed tree branches and lashed together tightly with leather. He leaned forward and put his face in his hands, much as Illtud had done. "I am sorry, Malgwyn. You are right."

"There is the other still, Bedevere." He knew that I meant

Morgan, who had been scarce since our return. "We cannot be certain that the Druid did these things."

Bedevere's long-vaunted stoicism hid a passionate man beneath it. I learned this many moons before, when Bedevere and I commanded troops of horse for Arthur. After a Saxon raid, we were searching a village for any survivors or lingering Saxons. They had been especially destructive, setting thatched roofs afire, the yellow and blue flames licking at the heavens. The wind carried the sickeningly sweet odor of burning human flesh. On the edge of the village, we had dismounted our troops and began a sweep. After about thirty minutes, I circled one of our ubiquitous roundhouses and found Bedevere, sitting on the ground, holding a child who had been butchered by the Saxons. The famous soldier with the iron heart was crying. He did not see me, and it was not the time to intrude. I slipped away.

Now I was seeing a glimpse of that Bedevere, the one who cared enough to cry for a child.

No one spoke for a long moment, until Bedevere raised his head and searched the dimly lit room. "I am sorry, Malgwyn. I cannot erase the image of those poor girls from my mind. Nor can I forget the curse that Druid laid on Arthur. He stands for all that I abhor in the world, in our world. Pagan beliefs that demand human sacrifice. And Mordred? We should have killed him when Ambrosius stepped down."

"You do not think that I agree with you? Of course I do," I told him. "I would have choked the life from him with my one hand! But I did not, and the time is now past for that. This time, I do not think he knew exactly who he was bringing among us."

"No. I did not."

Mordred.

In our confusion, we had not seen him enter. He crossed the room and took up another chair, pulling his sword from his belt as he sat. Illtud's hand shot to his own blade, but Mordred waved him off. "I am not here to fight. I am here to listen."

None of us knew exactly how to take this. Mordred seemed almost reasonable and none had seen this side of him before.

He pushed his braided lock from his face and smiled at me. "Malgwyn, you and I will never be friends. Indeed, I fear that before all is said and done I will have to kill you. But none of that is important now. I desire this match between Arthur and Aircol's daughter as much as anyone. We need strong, dependable northern allies, and Aircol is both strong and honorable. I would have married the girl myself to secure his entrance into the consilium, but only the hand of the Rigotamos would do.

"Merlin has told me something of what happened at the White Mount and in Aircol's city. And that Wynn shadowed you all along the way. I embrace our old ways, our old gods. But I would not have agreed to bring him here had I known what Merlin has related."

"How did that occur?" If Mordred was disposed to be agreeable in this affair, then I could do nothing less.

"I stopped at Ynys-witrin before coming on here. Melwas introduced him to me and asked if I would bring him in my party. I think Melwas knew that there was bad blood between Wynn and Arthur, but I do not think he knew all of it."

"If he knew there was bad blood, then why would he want to complicate matters here?" Illtud asked.

"Melwas is not disposed to be agreeable to Arthur right

now," Mordred answered with a chuckle, and we all exchanged knowing looks.

Guinevere.

"I do not deny that I want to be Rigotamos, but I am not, yet." Mordred added the last word with a certain emphasis. "But now is not the time for Arthur's authority to be usurped. Now is the time to consolidate and solidify our holdings. But once offered, I cannot withdraw my promise of hospitality, not without some evidence." He turned that thin, hawkish face toward me. "I take it you have no more evidence against Wynn than you had against me."

"Less, my lord. But there is always time."

Mordred chuckled. "I will offer this. He will continue with my party, but we will keep him under constant watch. I brought a troop of horse, and they will encamp outside the castle. I will stay with them for the most part. And I will personally see that he does nothing of the sort here. If you can prove his guilt in these other deaths, I will deliver him to you. Otherwise, he will simply be an annoyance; he will do nothing more."

"Not even make a little mischief at Arthur's expense?" Bedevere queried.

My enemy narrowed his eyes and smiled in that sly way of his. "A little mischief never hurt anyone."

He stood, replacing his sword in his belt. "Agreed?"

Kay, Bedevere, Illtud and I exchanged looks. We had little choice actually. "Agreed," I answered for us all.

"Then relax, my lords. We have a wedding to celebrate." With a smile and an almost imperceptible bow, he left.

"What now?" Illtud voiced what all of us were thinking.

"Now," I said, "we wait for my old friend, Gareth, to send help."

"The thief?"

"He'll lend us a few men again to keep our own eye on the Druid, Mordred, and Morgan."

"The medicus? Why he?"

Bedevere and I exchanged looks. Kay and Illtud should know. "Morgan was with us when both girls were killed. On at least one of those occasions, his whereabouts cannot be determined. And do not forget that Morgan is a creature of Lord David, newly thrust into our midst. I will not bore you with my own doubts about David, but . . ."

"You do not believe Mordred." Kay made it a statement, not a question.

"My heart tells me that he is not lying this time, but my head tells me that I should never trust Mordred."

We swore Kay and Illtud to secrecy about Morgan, but the more I considered him, the more he made a certain sense.

✦

We stayed up late, discussing our developing problems. Aircol, whose mind was already poisoned against Wynn by our suspicions, would not look with favor on the Druid's presence, and he would look with even less favor on the man who brought Wynn into our midst. And that, we agreed, was good.

Gareth's men arrived, using their varied skills to slip past our guards and through the gates. We set one to watch the Druid and the other to watch Morgan.

Before I took my rest, I walked the lanes to Ygerne's house. I wanted so badly to be with her; I wanted so badly to know what I had done to raise her ire. But the dark windows and stiff breeze sent me back to my own hut, a sad and dejected man.

The next morning brought a clear sky and a bright sun. A hint of chill flavored the air as Merlin and I prepared for the day, reminding my bones and joints that old age was not too far in my future. I had already been abed when Merlin came home the night before, and, as was our wont, we did not speak upon arising.

Pulling on my braccae, I fell backward onto my fur blankets, as Merlin snickered at my discomfiture. "I have not killed anyone yet today," I warned him.

A knock sounded at the door as I scrambled to my feet and wrapped my belt around my waist. "Enter!"

The door swung open to reveal Lord Aircol, dressed rather plainly, an odd, confused look on his face as he saw me tugging on my braccae and securing my belt awkwardly with my one hand.

"Malgwyn, pardon me!"

"No pardon necessary, my lord. How may I serve you?"

"I wondered if you might take your morning meal with Gwyneira and me? We have some things we wish to discuss with you."

Merlin gave me a jaundiced look. We had shared a house long enough to know almost immediately what the other was thinking. He smelled something unpleasant in this.

"Of course, my lord. But you could have sent one of the slave boys to fetch me. You surely didn't have to come yourself."

Aircol smiled grimly. "This is to be a confidential discussion. Join us in Arthur's private chamber if you will." Without further comment, he spun and started back up the rise to the hall.

"Walk carefully, Malgwyn. Aircol is not a happy man," Merlin cautioned.

I nodded, slid my dagger into my belt, and followed in Aircol's wake.

❈

Gwyneira looked more lovely than ever. She had taken a length of hair from the back of her head, braided it and then wrapped it around the top of her head like a crown. The rest she wore swept back behind her ears.

Arthur's chambers were modest, taking up the rear third of his timbered hall. He had recently enlarged his own space, walling off two extra rooms. The wall of each was covered with one of his banners, the red Cross on white linen. Each also held a simple bed and table with chairs, better constructed than those gracing mine and Merlin's home.

Blackberries had come into season, and I noted a bowl of them on the table in Aircol's chamber along with bread and cheese. Gwyneira sat in one of the chairs and Aircol pointed me to the other. Whatever the source of his displeasure, be it the Druid or some other irritant, this was not the happy, almost giddy lord I had met in the land of the Demetae.

For a long moment, Aircol held his tongue. Then he whipped around and threw a bit of parchment in my lap.

Scrawled across its smooth side in a crude hand were two words—*abeo meretrix*, the rough Latin word for a woman who sells her body. "Die whore."

"Gwyneira found that on the floor beside her bed this morning!"

I had no words; I just sat, dumb, looking at the hateful message. "My lord . . ."

"You must find out who has done this, Malgwyn. You gave my daughter your sacred promise to be her confidant, her protector."

I did not remember it exactly that way, but this was not the time to argue. My brow furrowed into a frown. The issue here was not the insult to Gwyneira and her father. No, the issue in this was that someone had gained access to her chamber at night, while she was there, right under the very noses of Bedevere's guards.

"My lord, that such a message would be left does not surprise me, not really. My cousin Guinevere is popular with the common folk, and I know that there are many who oppose this union. I feared that Gwyneira would be subjected to this sort of name calling, but I thought it would come out in public, embarrassing but hardly dangerous. This, however, is different. With your permission, I will tell Bedevere of this."

"Bedevere! I will see Arthur now! Or I swear that I will pack our wagons and return to Dyfed!"

I leapt to my feet. "Lord Aircol, we cannot allow our enemies to drive a sword between us! Forgive me, lord, but if you speak to Arthur in anger, you could irreparably damage this union, and it is one you both desire. Please remember why you came here. Give us a chance to take new measures. Give yourself a chance to calm. I take full blame for this. Let me tell Arthur of my failure. I beg of you.

"We will limit Gwyneira and her bodyguards to your own men, Kay, Bedevere, Illtud, and myself. One of us will be with her at all times. I have promised to be her guardian here, and we will sell our lives cheap to vouchsafe hers!"

The earnestness of my appeal seemed to touch Aircol, as the lines in his face became less rigid, less severe. "You are right, Malgwyn. I do desire this union." He turned away for a second and spoke to me without looking. "You have a daughter yourself, I understand."

"Yes, my lord. A child named Mariam."

He spun around. "Then you know how it feels to be a father. Gwyneira would tell you that I am overprotective, aye, overreacting to this, this, thing," and he pointed at the parchment.

"That I would," Gwyneira said, speaking for the first time. "Father, if I am to sit beside Arthur, it is my duty, my responsibility, to win the people over. Why should they not consider me a meretrix, a common woman? I am unknown to them."

Aircol threw me a quick look. Both of us realized that she was ignoring the most important aspect—the access the doer of this deed had. And we both knew that nothing we said would convince her of the significance of that fact.

"I will take this to Arthur immediately," I promised.

"Then I will give you that chance. But I will speak to him myself when the opportunity permits."

"Please understand, I do not seek to hide this thing. I simply seek to correct it without endangering all that you have worked for."

"Very well." Aircol paused, the ruddy cast retreating from his face. "I am sorry that I reacted so badly, Malgwyn."

Poor Aircol, the thing that would eventually spell his doom, I feared, was that he was a good man.

"You owe me nor any man an apology for that, my lord. She is your daughter, and I would think less of you had you had any less anger than you did."

The redness had faded from his cheeks completely then, and he sat next to Gwyneira. "She and little Vortipor are all I have, Malgwyn. Some fathers do not value their daughters as they do their sons, but I am not one of these. She is every bit as clever as her brother. Aye, and she has a talent for diplomacy that I am afraid will forever elude Vortipor."

At that, Gwyneira blushed. "Forgive my father, Malgwyn. He has the blindness common in a parent. These little things," she said, pointing at the parchment scrap, "have no meaning. They do not frighten me."

I stood, took the bit of parchment, and let a frown paint its way across my face. Something in the writing was familiar, but I could not remember from where. "You should be frightened, my lady. Whoever did this has the ultimate weapon."

Then, both Gwyneira and Aircol looked at me with astonishment. "How so?"

"They are unknown, and it is always the unknown that harbors the most danger."

CHAPTER THIRTEEN

I will have guards stationed around the hall every second of every minute of every hour!"

I had never seen Arthur so enraged. He was stomping around the main room in Kay's house like an angry ox.

"No, my lord, you will not." I will admit that I took some pleasure in overruling the Rigotamos. It was not something I could do often, but it did please me. And at my insolence, he advanced on me with red, angry eyes, but Bedevere calmed him with a light touch on his shoulder. "Listen to me, Rigotamos. If you surround your hall with soldiers, you will simply be doing what this scum wants. He wants you frightened. He wants you showing your fear!"

Arthur's chest heaved beneath his tunic. "What would you have me do then, Malgwyn? You think you have all the answers! What would you have me do?"

I too breathed deeply. "I have few answers, my lord. But you have trusted Kay and Bedevere all of your life. Trust them now. Trust me now. From this moment until the wedding, let us move Gwyneira to mine and Merlin's house. When she is needed at your hall for ceremonial functions, we can spirit her in through the kitchen." The idea had come to me as I made the inevitable trip to see Arthur.

"Your house is safer than my hall? Explain that to me, Malgwyn!" Arthur was furious; the veins in his neck threatened to explode through the skin. At that moment, I feared that I had gone too far at last.

But Kay and Bedevere immediately saw my plan, and Kay rescued me from my own stupidity. "Arthur, we will place one of the serving girls in Gwyneira's place at the hall. No one will know that we have moved her. And it will be easier to guard her at Malgwyn's house. It is not a public place. But your closest advisors, aye even you yourself, are always visiting there. Aircol was seen there just this morning. We can keep a much closer watch on her, and perhaps catch this rogue if he tries something else at your hall, without putting Gwyneira at further risk."

At that, Arthur stroked his beard, twisting the ends of his mustache as he did when in deep thought. "Agreed." He turned on me then. "Malgwyn, I give you great freedom in dealing with me. And I have devolved great responsibility on you, trusting in the decisions you make, and I have great respect for your ability to untangle the skeins of these affairs. But you are not the Rigotamos. I am. And I will be the one the people judge for your actions. Never forget that."

And with that, he swept from the room.

Chastised, I hung my head.

Bedevere slapped me on the shoulder. "Take heart, Malgwyn. He could have ordered you beheaded."

"Perhaps he should have," I said. "I have been singularly unable to find who killed those girls at the White Mount and in Aircol's town. And I sought to lighten my mood by irritating

Arthur. I was wrong to do that. Arthur deserves better from me."

"Nonsense," Kay answered. "You simply forgot your place for a moment. Arthur allows all of us too much freedom, but it is a freedom that must be unspoken and as invisible as possible. And, most important, it is a trust and a freedom that must never be betrayed." He paused. "Malgwyn, I know you curse the man who killed these girls in such a brutal and vicious way. We all curse them. But, in the greater world, their deaths are simply a pity and of little consequence. Do not torture yourself so over it, and do not accord them more importance than they deserve. Larger issues are at stake."

I was so angry with myself that I stood rooted to the spot. And I was angry with Kay for dismissing those dead girls so easily. They had been beloved by people, and that alone made them important. It took the grip of Bedevere's hand on my good arm to shake me from my reverie. "Come, Malgwyn. Arthur considers you as a brother. His anger will fade. We have work to do."

❖

Merlin hired two women from the town to clean our house. We were neither of us very good at that sort of thing, and we periodically commissioned someone to clean.

I went to Ygerne's house to see if her anger had abated, but she was not there, and none of the children could tell me where she had gone. Owain had taken Mariam and some of the other children to the market square in front of Arthur's hall to see the goods for sale and to watch the arrival of the lords of the consilium.

The wedding was to be held the next day at Arthur's hall.

His famous cruciform church, still nothing more than foundation trenches, had failed even yet to get the blessing from Coroticus that Arthur desired. David, Mordred, Gawain and some of the others had arrived the night before. Gaheris and young lord Celyn were expected that afternoon as were the envoys from Rome and Gaul. Lauhiir, who was still technically a member of the consilium, was, of course, enjoying Coroticus's hospitality and sanctuary. He would not be joining us just as Melwas, ensconced on the great tor with his new friend Guinevere, would stay away.

Arthur had not demanded my presence to welcome the new arrivals. Aircol would be present, but Gwyneira, now tucked away in our house, was not attending, watched instead by Kay, Bedevere, and Illtud. Merlin had moved in with Kay as would I. But I would take my turn guarding Gwyneira as well.

That night would be the first of two great wedding feasts. Arthur had had his hunters scouring the forest for game. We would dine on rabbit, pig, deer, and drink wine from Italy, Gaul, Syria, and Judea. Of course, there would be fish from the great seas, hurried in fresh by riders, and great salmon from local streams. And river mussels and oysters. We would have leeks and onions and rape. And Arthur had decided that all food left over from each feast be distributed among the people. No one would go away hungry.

Even as I thought these things, I wandered the back lanes to the northeast of Arthur's hall and saw servi and others hauling food, amphorae, and storage jars to the kitchen. The scene reminded me of an anthill I once watched for a time. The little fellows streamed in a line, each carrying some burden, food for their colony or some object to add to their home. They were remarkably focused, rarely deviating from their path and only then to find an alternative route around some obstacle. I admired their focus and determination, unwavering. And so the servi and other servants seemed in their haste to prepare for the first great banquet.

"Fight!" The shout echoed through the lanes, followed quickly by another that chilled my blood.

"Malgwyn, quickly, Mariam!"

The echoes had not faded as my feet sped me to their origin.

It was yet early, and no new lords had arrived, so the market square was filled with villagers appraising the vendors' wares. Only at that moment, it had been cleared and three combatants, it seemed, were squared off.

Owain stood with fists raised, feet set, facing his opponent. My heart fell when I saw why. His adversary had a hand firmly clamped on Mariam's upper arm. And though I should have known, or at least expected, facing Owain was Aircol's son, Vortipor.

I had no idea what the dispute was over, though Mariam would certainly seem to be involved, but I started to wade into the coming battle.

Until a hand on my shoulder pulled me back.

Aircol.

"Let them resolve it," he said.

"With all due respect, Lord Aircol, that is my daughter," I whispered through clenched teeth.

"And by our ancient laws and traditions, any who strike a noble can be executed," he countered. "But my son needs to learn humility, and your daughter's friend seems ready to provide a valuable lesson. Rest easy, Malgwyn. I will not allow any harm to come to your daughter. Trust me, as I trust you."

And at that, I surrendered. At least a part of me, if the truth be known, was anxious to see Vortipor knocked on his backside.

Aircol's appearance quieted the crowd some, and it was easier to hear the combatants.

A quizzical look marked young Vortipor's face. "I do not see," he said to Owain, "why you would risk death over this. I simply said that I would like to buy her and asked the price."

Aircol stifled a chuckle, but I was enraged. How dare the little princeling! If Owain did not feed him dirt, I would!

Mariam shook her arm loose. "We do not buy and sell free people at Castellum Arturius," she advised him.

This seemed to confuse Vortipor, who cocked his head to the side and said, "Then what use are they?"

And then my daughter showed just how much backbone she had.

Taking a step forward, she launched her foot into Vortipor's privates, sending him flying backward into the dirt, his hands clutching himself and moaning loudly.

"Now that, Malgwyn," Aircol said, "was a lesson well deserved. And your daughter is a child to be reckoned with. Try and forgive him, Malgwyn. His mother was much like him, and no matter how hard I tried, I have not been able to smother his haughty nature."

"Give my daughter another chance and she will beat it out of him." I was much pleased with Mariam.

As we two old fathers laughed, a roar like that of a wounded bull sounded, and we looked back to the market square as our tongues froze in fright.

Mariam had turned and taken a few steps away from Vortipor.

The little prince had regained his feet and, moving awkwardly, had pulled a dagger from his belt and was advancing on Mariam.

Both Aircol and I leapt toward him, in a vain hope to intercede before his dagger found Mariam.

But we needn't have bothered.

Young Owain very expertly swept the dagger away with his left hand and with a tremendous swing of his right sent Vortipor sprawling backward once more, this time unconscious.

Rather than cheers for a well-placed fist, the crowd audibly gasped.

Owain had struck a prince.

True to his word, though, Aircol strode forward and thrust forward his hand for Owain to take.

Blinking and uncertain, my little friend searched the crowd until he found me. I nodded quickly, and he took Aircol's hand.

"Well struck, young man! You will become a mighty warrior."

With Owain's safety secured, the crowd then released its applause.

I reached Mariam and wrapped my arm around her. "Where did you learn to kick like that?" I asked her, once assured that she was unharmed.

She smiled at me. "In the lanes, Father. He is not the first to lay hands upon me."

I tousled her head and hugged her again.

"Were you two old fools going to let these children kill each other?"

Ygerne.

Her fury was so great that you could almost feel the heat.

Both Aircol and I were struck dumb.

"I suppose I should be grateful that you took time away from your noble friends and matchmaking to notice your daughter," she fumed, taking Mariam in one hand and Owain in the other. Then she turned to Aircol. "And you, teach your spawn some manners or keep him at home!"

With that, she stomped off down the lane, her two charges in tow.

I started after her, intent on learning why she was so angry, but Aircol's hand on my shoulder stopped me.

"You will gain nothing but more of her fury if you go to her now. Let her calm. Your woman?"

"Aye."

"A fiery one." He smiled then. "Let us go and see to Gwyneira."

I motioned toward the still unconscious body of Vortipor, lying in the dirt.

"Leave him. Perhaps it will add to the lesson so ably administered by your daughter's friend."

While it seemed but a child's fight at the time, years later, that single fist, so well struck, would come back to haunt me, Owain, and Mariam.

❖

"Did you and my father rescue my brother from himself, Malgwyn?"

The voice startled me, startled Aircol. All the more because it was a voice not intended to be heard in the lanes, at least not then. Gwyneira. I spun and saw her standing there in a peasant dress. Glancing about to see if anyone was watching us, I hustled to her side and slipped my good arm about her waist.

"My lady, why are you out of the house? More important, *how* did you get out of the house?" My tone was more of a guarded hiss than actual words.

She smiled at me and wrapped her own arm around my waist. "Why, Malgwyn! I didn't know you found me attractive," she whispered.

"Girl," Aircol began, "you will stop this nonsense!"

Her life in danger and yet she could tease me. She was either incredibly foolish or a truly remarkable girl. "Woman," I threatened through clenched teeth, "noble or no, I will personally haul you over my knee and spank some sense into you. Keep smiling and pretending to be happy and we will get you back to safety."

"But I am happy out here, Malgwyn. I am not happy caged up like some criminal."

"Gwyneira, someone in this town means you harm. I have pledged to you and your father to protect you from that. But I cannot fulfill that promise if you do not cooperate."

"Very well, but I needed to see what my new home really looked like, without people knowing who I was, changing their behavior to fit my status. Do you understand me?"

"Of course I do, my lady. But too many people saw you arrive with your father. It was not exactly secret."

She laughed and those beautiful doe-like eyes laughed at me as well. Had she been ten years older or I ten years younger, I would have challenged Arthur to mortal combat for her hand. But she was not nor was I, and no matter how beautiful Gwyneira might be, Ygerne held my heart in her hands. Still.

I firmly turned us toward my house, where a stricken Kay

was in the lane looking back and forth. "Do not worry, Kay. I found our wayward maiden." Kay's shoulders slumped in relief.

"May the Christ bless your life, Malgwyn! I thought my own was forfeit. I turned away but a moment and she had scampered out."

"This one is headstrong, Kay. We may have to tie her to a chair."

"And then I shall walk out through the lanes carrying the chair with me." Gwyneira was not going to remain quiet long.

"And then I shall tie you to a post. You will not walk down the lanes with that."

By then we had reached the house, and I firmly, if gently, shoved her in.

"Malgwyn!" she cried.

"My lady, your safety is part of my charge. I will not allow you to compromise it."

"Nor should he," said Aircol.

Aircol's face held a grim set, but it was aimed at Gwyneira, not at me. "You are even more headstrong than your mother. But I am your father, and you will both obey and honor me, even if that means that Malgwyn does indeed have to tie you to a post."

She dropped her head at Aircol's words and mumbled a soft "Yes, Father." But I could not tell if she was truly chastised or simply telling him what he wanted to hear. I suspected the latter. She disappeared to change behind a partition we had set up to give her some privacy.

"My lord, what will you do with your son?"

Aircol rolled his eyes. "I am tempted to put him on a horse and send him back home, alone."

I knew he did not mean it, but I had to smile.

"He will mature."

"If he lives that long," his father grumbled. "Gwyneira needs to be properly dressed, which she is not. I was coming in search of you when my son chose to entertain us. A new guest has arrived, an unexpected but welcome one. Ambrosius."

I jerked my head back in surprise. "Ambrosius Aurelianus?"

Aircol nodded. "Aye, the old Rigotamos. And he wishes to meet the bride and give his blessing. I cannot deny him that."

Old Ambrosius! He had stepped down as Rigotamos nearly two years before, when Arthur was elected by the consilium to succeed him. It had been a time ripe with conspiracies and death. I was surprised that he had roused himself from his fortress at Dinas Emrys, far to the north. He had another home closer by, near unto the great stone circle, but it was also near unto Saxon settlements and he had ceased to feel safe there. I did not blame him. Any proximity with Saxons was too much for me. They could not be trusted. And, besides, they smelled.

"Come," Aircol invited. "I am sure he will be happy to see you. He visits me on occasion and he speaks well of you. Aye, it was Ambrosius who first told me of you. He holds you in high regard."

I cocked my head to the side in confusion. I never knew that Ambrosius thought much of me one way or the other. I had fought under his and Arthur's banners, to be sure, but we had not shared a special bond of any kind. Such was life, though. A man never really knew what others thought of him, sometimes until it was too late.

As if by intention, Gwyneira appeared from behind the partition, now properly attired for meeting a lord, and the three of us, with Kay trailing behind, made our way across the lane, stepping gingerly to avoid the puddles born of a brief rain shower, and into the rear of Arthur's hall.

❖

Ambrosius had grown even fatter in his retirement. He was arrayed in a crimson tunic and leather braccae, wrapped by a wide belt decorated with more iron studs than I had seen on any other belt in my life, including Arthur's. His hair had turned white and desperately needed a comb brushed through it. Ygerne would be outraged that the former Rigotamos would appear in public without being properly groomed.

"Malgwyn! My dear friend," Ambrosius shouted, slurring a few words and already deep into a wine amphora. By rights, he should have acknowledged Gwyneira first, but in his present state, I was not sure if he was aware she was there.

"My lord, it is always good to see you," I said, kneeling, but he motioned for me to rise, nearly slipping from his place in the process. Yes, he was deep into the wine.

At that he turned his attention to Gwyneira. "Let us see this bride of Arthur's, Aircol. Let us see if she is fit for a queen."

Gwyneira stepped out from behind her father and dropped her head in respect.

Ambrosius straightened and looked her up and down with a wavering head. "By the gods, Aircol! She is indeed suitable for a queen. Were I not already in retirement, I would petition you for her hand myself."

"I am pleased that you approve, my lord," Aircol answered with a smile.

"Now, put her back into hiding before I forget how old I am."

Gwyneira dropped her head again and stepped back without turning. She had comported herself well, and I was as proud of her as Aircol was. I moved to join Kay in returning her to my house, but Ambrosius waved at me.

"Malgwyn, stay. I would speak with you."

I exchanged looks with Kay, but he just shrugged and left with Gwyneira.

"Sit, Malgwyn."

I pulled a chair close and lowered myself into it, curious now. Ambrosius and I were not strangers by any means, and though friendly, we had never been particular friends.

"How may I help you, my lord?"

Ambrosius took a sip from a beaker of wine. "We were approached by a man on the road from Dinas Emrys. He gave his name as Rhodri and he lives in an old villa along the road."

I nodded. "Aye, we met him on our own journey back from Aircol's fort. He seemed a good, if simple, man."

"He recognized my banner and stopped us on the road. He asked if we were headed to Castellum Arturius and if we expected to see you."

"Me?"

Ambrosius nodded. "I thought it was an odd question as well. You are quite well known, but I could not fathom why such a simple man, so far from these lands, would both know you and wish to send you a message."

"A message? What sort of message?"

"He said that there had been a killing reported the morning after your party left."

"A killing?" The hairs on the back of my neck were tingling, and I felt the pit of my stomach grow heavy.

CHAPTER FOURTEEN

Some girl had been raped and abused by some horrible thing or creature. He said there was much blood and rent flesh and that the people were saying she had been assaulted by a dragon, though I have never heard of a dragon raping a woman." Ambrosius finished in a near mumble, raising his beaker and draining the rest of the wine. Then his head dropped and his eyes closed, a not unfamiliar pose for the old king.

I leapt to my feet, shocking Ambrosius's guards so much that they drew their swords. "Was it Vala? Rhodri's daughter?"

"What?" Ambrosius roused himself enough to open one eye. "Vala? I know no Vala."

"Was the murdered girl Rhodri's daughter?"

"Oh." A spark of understanding flared in Ambrosius's eye. "No, the daughter of some family that lived a short distance to the west of the road. Really, Malgwyn. I do not understand why you would want to know about these things."

"Thank you, my lord," I said, without meaning a word of it. At that moment, I wished he had lost the whole story in the bottom of his beaker. "With your permission, my lord, I have matters to see to."

"Of course, Malgwyn, of course. But allow some time to spend with your old commander, to relive our glorious deeds on the fields of battle."

"I would be honored, my lord."

At that, the wine got the better of him, and Ambrosius drifted back asleep.

⁂

Though I had felt low before, this news took me even lower. As I left the feasting hall, I snatched a skin of wine and headed for my old hut just beyond the main gate. I told no one where I was going, though I faintly remember hearing Bedevere hail me from a distance. But he must have assumed I did not hear him, as he went on his way.

I grunted at the guards at the massive timber gate and stumbled down the snake-like entrance, constructed to prevent the use of a battering ram. Ignoring the greetings from around me, I fell into the door of my old hut, pulled the plug from my wineskin and drank deeply.

Three girls, torn from life by the hand of some monster. Dragons, Ambrosius said. Druids, more likely, I thought. And one Druid in particular, Wynn. What other answer was there? He was present at the White Mount; he was present at Caer Goch; he may have been present on our return. He certainly had appeared in Castellum Arturius within hours of our own arrival, indicating that he may have followed us from Caer Goch. Yet, by all the old and new laws, as the guest of Mordred, his person was inviolable. Once again, Mordred was vexing me.

People had loved those girls. And someone had ripped them from that love for no reason that was apparent to me, but to discredit Arthur, to make real a curse laid on him by that blasted Druid. And I felt in my heart that I knew the killer and yet I could not touch him. I took another pull on the skin, letting the sour warmth fill my stomach. Once I had found comfort in that, but now I was punishing myself. As if to punctuate the thought, I drained the last of the wine. I fumbled at the door, waved at a passing boy and sent him for more.

I do not remember much about the next few hours, except turning up the skin and the wine pouring down until my stomach revolted. Sometime after dark, I remember hearing the sounds of horses and soldiers passing my hut, heading into the fortress for the feasting. Not long after that I passed out amid the sour and fetid smell of my own vomit.

✣

"I seem to recall another situation like this." The voice stirred me from my drink-induced slumber. My eyes, matted with tears and dirt from my hovel's floor, pried themselves open and searched blurrily for the voice's owner. Of course it was Arthur, looking almost exactly as he had that night some two years before when he had found me in very nearly the same position.

"Go away and let me die," I croaked, the words barely audible.

"I cannot do that, Malgwyn," he said in his most reasonable tone. My ears perked up. Usually, when he spoke like that, someone was about to lose their head. "Either you arise, clean yourself, and get back to work or I will drag you out into the market square and gut you like a hog at the slaughter."

I pushed myself up on my one good arm. "Three children are dead, and you care nothing about it. All you care about is solidifying your position as Rigotamos and chasing Guinevere into Melwas's arms."

And then my head exploded and I was flung against one of the walls so violently that it shook.

"Enough, Malgwyn! You wallow in self-pity as if it is a warm bath! Do you want me to care about these girls? Then show me who killed them! I will personally take his head and display it from the walls! But until then, *enough* of this!"

I straightened myself and felt the back of my head where it had collided with the wall. My fingers came away damp and crimson.

Arthur knelt beside me, kneading his wool-wrapped hand, the knuckles already bruising from striking me. "Malgwyn. I know that your heart is true. I know that you wish for the same things that I wish for—truth and justice, a good life for all of our people. But men, women, children are going to die. You cannot save them all, nor can you find each and every killer. If I had a thousand Malgwyns, maybe we could make this true. But there is only one of you, and you pledged to serve me. Now, serve me."

I pulled myself up until I was sitting against the wall more than lying in front of it. My hand inched up and felt the puffiness of my swelling lip. The wine still twisted my stomach in its grip but its fogginess was leaving my brain. I looked up at him, standing above me, no anger now in his face, only sadness.

"I hoped you had put this behind you."

"So had I." I looked away, unwilling to face him. Arthur was right. I had solved nothing by wallowing in my own filth. "I take it the feasting has ended."

Arthur dragged an old chair over and lowered himself into it. He had split his mail shirt at the hips so that it would spread and not bunch up. "The formal part has finished. The lords and their chief lieutenants are still drinking in the hall."

"Mordred?"

He nodded.

"The Druid?"

Arthur laughed. "No. I told Mordred that his hospitality only guaranteed the Druid's entry and safety in my city. It did not mean that I had to break bread with him."

"Good for you. Arthur—"

"No," he interrupted, holding his hand up. "I know that these killings have touched a memory that you would rather remain buried. I know that each time you see one of these girls, you are seeing Gwyneth again, ravaged by the Saxons. That memory will haunt you for the rest of your life, but do not allow it to ruin all of your days."

He rose. "Rest here this night. I need you at your best over the next few days. Tomorrow is the wedding. There is time yet for someone to try to destroy this alliance. You have always had an eye for spotting trouble where none appeared to exist. I need that eye now. Once we have the wedding behind us, we will have more time to deal with other things. Perhaps, just perhaps, we will finally be able to relax a bit. We will speak no more of this, but I expect you to live up to your pledge. Your friend David arrived in time for the feast," he added, almost as an afterthought.

"What of Guinevere? Is there any news? I cannot believe that she is willingly with Melwas."

Arthur shrugged. "Ask Ygerne. She spent the better part of the day with Guinevere at the tor, just returned right before the feasting."

"What did she tell you? She is not speaking to me right now."

At that he laughed. "Then we have something in common as she refuses to talk to me as well." And then he was gone.

Sleep came, but not easily. I needed to seek out Gareth's men and see if they had learned anything. But every time I threatened to arise, my stomach threatened to revolt yet again. Almost without knowing it, exhaustion turned to an uneasy sleep. And I woke to the dim light of dawn streaming through my door. Clouds tried valiantly to hold the sun at bay, but they were losing badly. I knew how they felt.

✣

A few hours later I was clean and garbed as a king's councilor should be, though my head still pounded from the wine the night before and my face wore a frown to match the pain. Even a heavy draught of Merlin's willow bark extract had only dulled the throb.

I went to Ygerne's house, and she slammed the door in my face. But as I was leaving, I heard Mariam call for me. As I turned, she leapt into my arm.

"Where have you been, Father?"

"I had business for the Rigotamos," I answered, kneeling and adjusting her onto my knee.

"Mother says that you fell into a wineskin."

"Your mother is out of sorts with me."

"Why?"

"I only understand part of it, Mariam. Like you, she is angry with the Rigotamos for marrying Gwyneira rather than Guinevere. But more than that, I do not know."

Mariam's little face, framed by her golden hair, wore a thoughtful frown. "She has not felt well lately. But she is truly upset over the Rigotamos's wedding. She went to Ynys-witrin yesterday, after that horrible Vortipor attacked us, to see Aunt Guinevere and stayed all day."

"Did she say anything when she returned?"

"No." Mariam shook her head. "She has been very quiet. Lord Arthur came to see her last night after she came home. She slammed the door in his face as well. Father?" She cocked her head to the side. "Isn't a wedding supposed to be a happy time? I mean, I am sad for Aunt Guinevere, but it seems like no one is happy. And somebody should be."

"You are right, Mariam." And she was. "Go, run and play. I will come and see you later."

"Father?"

"Yes."

"Don't go swimming in a wineskin again. It makes Mother mad and you smell."

She scampered back to the house and I turned toward Arthur's hall, duly chastised by my own daughter. Rounding a corner to a lane that would take me past Kay's house, I literally collided with someone. We both went flying, he into the mud from the previous night's rain and me into the side of a house, rattling the wall.

I say "he" because it was the Druid, Wynn.

Pushing myself to my feet, I had the pleasure of seeing the Druid's white robes splattered with mud. I glanced about and saw no sign of Mordred or his men.

"Looking for any witnesses so you may kill me?" The Druid wasted no time with pleasantries.

"The thought did indeed occur to me. But, you see, were you to be found dead, I would be the first suspected. And since you are here under Mordred's grant of hospitality, and Arthur is bound to honor it, my life would stand forfeit. I do not propose to give my life for such as you. If you are guilty of those acts as I believe you are, then ultimately I will be able to prove it and you will be punished."

Wynn did not speak immediately, choosing to brush, forlornly, at the mud on his robe, succeeding only in smearing it. "I did not kill those girls. Lord Arthur brought that upon himself by defying the gods and desecrating Bran's head. He is responsible for this string of evil, a string that even now winds its way around his throat and will choke the life from him. That is why I am here."

"You killed the girl at the White Mount, and the girl at Caer Goch, and the girl near the old Roman villa on our journey back. And you did it all to prove the effectiveness of your own curse."

The Druid stopped swiping at his robe and looked at me curiously. "I killed no one. Arthur's and your arrogance caused those deaths. Your arrogance and ill treatment of the people and their beliefs murdered those girls. If you are seeking to blame someone, blame yourself!"

In one motion, faster than even I thought possible, I pinned him by his scrawny neck against the wall of the house with my one forearm. He choked and white, foamy spittle burst from his lips and clung to the hairs on my arm. "I think you are here so that I may choke the life from you."

His eyes began to bulge and my senses returned at the same time. I released him. "I will prove that you killed those girls and then your life will be mine, or I will catch you in the act of killing another and your fate will be the same."

At that moment, Mordred and two of his men appeared in the lane. But by then, a foot or more separated me and Wynn.

Mordred was no fool, though. He could tell by the way that the Druid rubbed his throat and from the blood in my eyes what had happened. He stopped in his tracks, placed his wool-wrapped hands on his hips and began to laugh.

"Early in the day for the wine, isn't it, my lord?"

Mordred just shook his head, his long hair flapping in the breeze. "We are getting old, Malgwyn, you and I. Just a few years ago, the Druid would be dead. You have learned restraint."

"And you, my lord? What have you learned?"

He stopped laughing and gave me a penetrating stare. "Why, the same thing. A few years ago, I would not have stopped to laugh. I would have avenged the insult to my guest by running you through."

I smoothed my tunic. "Then we both have something to be grateful for."

Mordred clapped Wynn on the back, an action that caused the Druid to cringe. "Come, bard, let us find some of that wine Malgwyn mentioned."

The quartet moved off, but Wynn kept his eyes on me as they disappeared down the lane. No one had ever focused such hatred at me. I could not conceive of anyone bearing such hatred yet being innocent of the accusations laid against him. Only the knowledge of his own guilt and his own exposure could brew such hatred. At that moment, I knew that I was right. But at that moment too, I became convinced that Mordred was involved.

I spent the remainder of that day at Gwyneira's side. Kay, as Cup-Bearer, was in charge of the ceremonies. Dubricius, the episcopus for all of Britannia, had agreed to perform the marriage, something that enraged Coroticus. But he was a mere abbot; Dubricius was an episcopus. And that was that.

I managed a clandestine meeting with Gareth's men, but they had little to report. The Druid had been on his best behavior. Morgan had kept to his small hovel near Arthur's hall, venturing only to the kitchen and the hall itself. "But that will change," said one of my spies.

"How so?"

"Lord David is expected at any moment."

And, again, that was that.

Bedevere stayed with me. Any threat to Gwyneira would end the moment she and Arthur were married. Once the deed was done, attacking her served no purpose. The alliance would be concluded; Aircol would join the consilium. And his popularity already assured him of a place second only to Arthur. Indeed, according to Bedevere, Mordred and David were already suggesting that perhaps Aircol should become Rigotamos, supplanting Arthur.

But Aircol was not stupid, nor was he as greedy as his newfound supporters. "Do not believe the tales that Mordred and David are spreading," he told me a few hours before the wedding. We were in my house. Gwyneira and two of her ladies were behind the partition preparing her for her marriage. "My allegiance is to Arthur ap Uther."

"I never believed otherwise, my lord."

"I missed you at the feasting last night."

"My apologies. I had just received some bad news."

He nodded. "I heard. Another of these young girls savagely abused and murdered. You are a warrior, Malgwyn. I know how valiantly you fought in the recent rebellion. I know your deeds earned you an invitation to the consilium, an invitation you rejected. You have seen more death and destruction than most men, even in this bloody day and age. Why have these three deaths among so many affected you this way?"

To his credit, his tone was more that of a *philologus* than a lord. It was as if he truly wanted to understand what spurred me on.

"I had not realized it before, but Arthur said last night that when I see these girls, I see my wife once again, lying in the burning ruins of our house, just as foully ravaged. Perhaps that is the answer. Perhaps it is that I see no reason for it."

Aircol laid his hand on my shoulder. "No man can argue that you have not seen your share of tragedy, Malgwyn. But sometimes God puts us to a test, to see how we bear such tragedies, to see if we emerge stronger from the challenge. Faith in Him and his son, the Christ, will sustain you in the darkest times."

A dark cloud blurred my vision, a cloud with a lining of red. "My lord," I answered bitterly, "just as I reject the gods of the Druids, who demand human sacrifice for their appeasement, if what you say about your god is true, I would have to reject him as well. I can conceive of no divine being that would savagely kill innocent young girls to test another."

"Then," a new voice entered the conversation, "we will have to redouble our efforts to bring you to the Christ."

Episcopus Dubricius.

Retreat seemed a valid strategy. "Please forgive me, my lord. Nerves are strained; it has been a difficult time."

The episcopus, a portly man who obviously kept a well-stocked larder, smiled broadly as he greeted Aircol. Dubricius wore what I took to be his best brown robe. Each of his fingers held a well-wrought ring, and three ornate necklaces draped his neck, one holding the emblem of his office.

I had not met Dubricius before, not really. I had observed him from a distance on a few occasions, in earlier times, when he had been slimmer and he wore a wild, unruly beard. But now his beard was neatly trimmed and the plump cheeks beneath were reddened from an excess of wine; his nose had an unhealthy purplish hue. He had been residing at Mark's seat at Castellum Dore, but his home was actually in the old Roman town of Ariconium. It looked as if he had thoroughly enjoyed Mark's hospitality.

"Prayer will relieve your burdens." He stopped and looked to my missing arm. "You are Malgwyn ap Cuneglas. I have heard of you."

Intent on being on my best behavior, I bowed and said as humbly as I could, "I am honored, my lord episcopus."

"Yes," Dubricius continued, "I have heard of your excesses and arrogance. But Coroticus still holds out hope of your salvation. I shall pray for the same." With that he turned away and I no longer existed for him.

Quite obviously, Dubricius and I were not fated to be friends. Summarily dismissed, in a way, I wandered out into the lane to find Illtud running toward me.

"Is he here?" panted a breathless Illtud.

"Is who here?"

"The episcopus. Dubricius?"

"He is inside. Is there a problem?"

He stopped long enough to catch his breath. "I . . . to . . . talk about . . . my decision." Illtud looked quickly around to see if anyone had heard him.

"Illtud, you cannot become a brother of the Christ in secret," I chided him.

"I know. I just do not want it known yet."

"As you wish. But I would wait a bit to talk to him. He is inside with Aircol, Bedevere, and Gwyneira."

At that, some of the urgency fled from his features. "What is the new plan?"

"Bedevere and I are to remain at Gwyneira's side until just before the ceremony. Then we will escort both her and Aircol to the hall. The market square will be lined with soldiers, both ours and Aircol's. Aircol will escort Gwyneira to Arthur's side and Dubricius will marry them. The great feast will follow. On the morrow we can rid ourselves of David, Mordred, and the rest. Perhaps then things can go back to normal."

Illtud nodded. "And perhaps then I can pursue my heart's desires."

"I will be most sad to see you go. We have weathered many storms, fought many battles together. Your service has been an honor to Arthur and to your family, and your friendship has been an honor to me."

A touch of dampness glinted at the corner of his eye. "Do you know why Arthur trusts you so much, Malgwyn?"

I shook my head.

"Because of all of his men, myself included, you remind him the most of what he wishes to be."

My look must have told Illtud that I believed him crazy. "Arthur wishes to be an old, one-armed man who cannot find his way clear of a wineskin? I think you have been sampling too many of Merlin's potions."

"You are a good man, Malgwyn, with the freedom to

pursue justice without worrying about the demands of being a king."

"I am just another weapon in his arsenal."

"If that is true, then you are a weapon with a mind of your own." Illtud laughed.

At that moment, Bedevere emerged from my house, stepping his caligae carefully over a mud puddle. "Malgwyn, Arthur wishes us to deliver a message to the camps of the visiting lords."

"What sort of message? And who will watch over Gwyneira?"

"I was going for Illtud, but I see that he is already here."

"Whatever the Rigotamos orders I will do," he said. With an informal salute, Illtud ducked into the door.

Bedevere looked about quickly and grasped my good arm, turning me from my house and into the lane. "No word of this must slip out. Arthur is worried. It appears that Melwas has spoken to the villagers of Ynys-witrin and hinted that Arthur's wedding is wrong and that Lady Guinevere is the rightful queen."

I waved a hand. "Arthur worries for no reason. To claim the throne by right of your mistress is no claim at all. Besides, in a few hours it will not matter. Gwyneira and Arthur will be wed; the deed will be done. The people will not rise up against Arthur because of this. If he starved them and tortured them, maybe. But not because of who he chooses for a wife. I doubt that Guinevere even knew what Melwas was saying. If she had known, she would certainly have told him not to." I stopped as a sudden realization hit me. To Bedevere's amazement, a laugh erupted from me.

"What?"

"Melwas is just frustrated in his quest."

"His quest?"

"Melwas wishes to bed Guinevere. That he's trying to raise public sentiment against Arthur tells me that Guinevere has not succumbed to his charms, at least not yet."

Bedevere grinned as he grasped my message. "Poor Melwas." And we continued on our journey to the camps of the consilium circling the base of Castellum Arturius.

✤

Although Mordred maintained a house in the castle, he had chosen to encamp with his troop of horse at the base of the hill along with David, Gawain, Gaheris, and Tristan, no longer a de facto prisoner, who now commanded a troop of his father's men sent for the festivities.

We found David, Mordred, and Tristan at Mordred's camp, along with little Morgan ap Tud, sitting at a campfire placed before an old leather tent. Such tents had been a common fixture in Roman camps. When the Romans had finally abandoned us, we reverted to our old tribal ways, warring among ourselves almost as often as with the Picts and Scotti and then the Saxons. But under first Ambrosius and now Arthur, much of what had been Roman about us had been revived, perhaps not everything, but much. Except, that is, for the legions.

Our success against the Saxons had been won by our cavalry, moving quickly and striking hard. Our foot soldiers served honorably and fought bravely, but it was the horse that won our battles. Ambrosius and Arthur had seen its potential, and they developed new strategies to exploit its strengths. Now, a strong cavalry force was necessary for a lord of the consilium, and taking a troop of his finest men to ceremonial occasions was expected.

But Bedevere's concern, as mine, was that we not find ourselves surrounded by men loyal to other lords at the wedding.
I did not truly believe that, after pushing so hard for this
wedding, any of them would do anything to prevent it. Aircol's
seat at the consilium's table was too important; the inclusion of
the lands of the Demetae was too valuable strategically. But
after the discovery of the threatening note in Gwyneira's quarters, we could afford to take no chances. And, of course, there
was the Druid.

"Welcome, Bedevere, Malgwyn!" David shouted as we drew
nearer to the fire. "Join us. We were sampling the wine and telling lies about our glorious battles."

"A delightful offer, my lord," Bedevere began, "but we come
on the order of the Rigotamos."

All three lords sat up a little straighter at this pronouncement. I said nothing, rather studied their faces as Bedevere
spoke.

"Only members of the consilium will be allowed to enter
the castle and attend the wedding. Your soldiers and personal
escorts will not be admitted."

Mordred bounced to his feet. "That is unacceptable! We
would be at Arthur's mercy!"

Bedevere turned his square jaw toward Mordred. "You have
pledged your obeisance to the Rigotamos. You are already at
his mercy. Threats have been made against the lady Gwyneira. Our precautions are only prudent."

I watched carefully, but saw nothing but surprise and alarm
on the quartet's faces. Tristan, chastised after nearly two years
as a prisoner, wisely stayed quiet.

"Is she well?" Morgan asked solicitously. "Does she need
my assistance?"

"No, Morgan," I said, suspicious yet of this creature of David's.

"You must admit, Bedevere, it would give Arthur a prime opportunity to eliminate us," David said slowly. "Perhaps he should rethink his position."

"Please, Lord David," I said softly. "What would it profit Arthur to kill all the lords of the consilium save his favorites? You all have vast lands and people loyal to you. Such an action would spark another civil war. And many of the lords, like Gaheris and Gawain, are good, honorable men who would themselves challenge Arthur if he were to act so brutally. No, David, this is only about ensuring the safety of Gwyneira. And are you ready to stake her life and yours that none of your soldiers have sold their loyalty to her enemies?"

Mordred and David exchanged quick glances. In truth, their objections were pro forma. They were so used to objecting to anything Arthur did that now they did it almost without thinking. And they truly did desire the alliance with Aircol.

"As you wish," Mordred begrudgingly agreed. "But we do this under protest."

"Wine, Master Malgwyn?" A familiar voice sounded at my elbow.

I turned to see Talorc, the servi boy. "Talorc! I am surprised to see you here and not at the hall making preparations."

The Pictish boy dropped his head sheepishly. "Cerdic lent me to Lord Mordred."

To keep him out from under foot, I supposed. "Be honored, Mordred. You have a true hero waiting upon you."

"That will keep his head attached to his neck as long as he keeps my beaker full of wine," grumbled Mordred. As if to emphasize the point, he halfheartedly threw a slap at Talorc, who dodged the blow, but fell to the ground.

With the trio laughing at Talorc and mumbling about suspicious lords, we left and headed to Gawain's camp farther along the base of the hill.

❖

Gawain and Gaheris were brothers to Mordred, sons of one of Arthur's uncles. But they were as different from Mordred as Druids were to Christians. Gawain was as brave a man as any I had known. Gaheris was a born diplomat, better able to resolve disputes than an army of ambassadors. Visiting them was a delight. They expressed no concerns and pledged to follow Arthur's instructions.

❖

Bedevere and I continued on our circuit of camps, though I dreaded the next with all my heart—Lord Celyn, son of Caw, brother of Huaill and, my favorite *monachus*, Gildas. Celyn had particular reason to hate Arthur.

In years past, when Ambrosius was Rigotamos, Celyn's father Caw refused to both acknowledge the consilium and pay obeisance to Ambrosius. Even worse, Caw's son, Huaill, had organized a band of pirates who were terrorizing shipping between our western shores and the lands of the Scotti. I had been with Arthur when we raided their camp. Huaill, as arrogant a man as ever lived, spat at Arthur. And though he was strong, he was not up to single combat with Arthur. It took but moments and a single splash of blood and Arthur held Huaill's head in his hand.

Though Caw vowed revenge and refused to join the con-

silium, he ordered his youngest son, Celyn, to pledge obeisance. We all knew that Celyn was more spy than ally, but at
least he kept communication open between the consilium and
Caw, who ruled a wide territory in the far north. Another son,
Gildas, became a brother of the Christ and lived at the abbey
at Ynys-witrin.

When Arthur was elected Rigotamos, Celyn had tried to
snatch the sword, the symbol of the office, from the Caesar Stone
before Arthur could. I stopped him with a well-placed backhand
and Lord David demanded my arrest. But Ambrosius overruled
him. Celyn had retained his seat in the consilium, but his blue
eyes always seethed with anger when he saw me.

Just as he did when Bedevere and I arrived at his camp.

I was in front of Bedevere, and Celyn, seeing only me at
first, leapt to his feet and his hand shot to his sword. But the
man standing next to him laid a hand upon Celyn's shoulder
and gently held him back. Gereint ap Erbin, the last of the
consilium to be in attendance.

"Be easy, Celyn," Gereint cautioned the young lord. The
pair was as distant in appearance as their lands were on our
island. Celyn was a lord in the far north, near the lands of the
Picts, and his blond hair and blue eyes seemed suited to that distant kingdom. Gereint was tall and dark in both eyes and hair.
Of all of our lords only he was clean shaven, in the manner of the
Romans. His lands lay to the southwest, among the Dumnonii.

The scent of leeks was in the air, and I noted a steaming
pot, suspended by a strap from a tripod, hanging over the fire.
Celyn was not taking advantage of Arthur's kitchen as the
other lords were.

"Lord Celyn, Lord Gereint, it is good to find you both
here," Bedevere said in greeting.

"Lord Gereint," I nodded, watching from the corner of my eye as Celyn glowered.

"How be it, Bedevere? Is our Rigotamos ready for marriage at last?" Gereint attempted to soften the mood.

"Nearly. We have come to tell you that entry to the wedding will be limited to yourselves; your troops will not be allowed."

Even as alarm spread on Celyn's face, Gereint nodded in approval. "Taking no chances then."

"This is unacceptable!" cried Celyn.

"Why is it, Lord Celyn," I asked, "that your response to almost everything is to argue against it?"

"Lord Bedevere, if Arthur persists in this, I will absent myself from the ceremony in protest." Celyn believed that not responding to me was an insult. But, then again, I had thought the same thing. Suddenly my face went red, not from anger, but from embarrassment.

Celyn was much like his brother, Gildas. Though, in Gildas's defense, the monachus was less prone to verbal outbursts.

Gereint patted Celyn on his back. "Come, Celyn! You would miss all that fine food and drink? The horn will be full for our pleasure!"

"But Gereint—"

"Arthur has no need or desire to place you in jeopardy, but there have been unusual incidents over the past fortnight. And Arthur is not one to court God's anger," Bedevere explained as gently as he could.

Swallowing hard, I smiled at the young lord. "Lord Celyn, the occasion would be the less for your absence."

Even Bedevere had to stifle a laugh at my awkward diplomacy.

But my olive branch had the desired effect. Celyn looked

at me for the first time with a smile. "How kind of you, scribe. I mean no disrespect to the Rigotamos, and of course I will attend under his conditions."

As we walked away, Bedevere patted me on the back. "See, Malgwyn? You have learned some restraint in your old age."

That both Bedevere and Mordred had accused me of the same thing bothered me. Perhaps I was losing my edge.

CHAPTER FIFTEEN

The time had come. Kay had done his work well and the market square had been encircled by banners, the white with a red cross for Arthur and Aircol's green with a white cross, alternating. Garlands of fresh late-summer flowers hung from the posts that supported the banners.

After the twelfth hour, only citizens of the town, the lords and distinguished guests, and Arthur's soldiers were allowed into our citadel. Despite their objections, David and the others did not seem ill at ease without their bodyguards. I had stationed myself at the main gate to observe their entry, but try as I might, I discerned no concern, nothing that would indicate they were planning some mischief.

I had tried to see Ygerne again, but Mariam stopped me at the door and said that she was sick and would not go to the wedding.

"And you?"

She cocked her head to one side and smiled sadly. "I will stay here with Mother. She needs to be cared for."

I leaned down and kissed her cheek. "I will tell you all about it later."

With that, she had disappeared inside the house, and I had trudged off to my house to check on Gwyneira after first stopping at Kay's house to retrieve my new clothes. Vivianne, a local seamstress, had made me a fine pair of braccae and new crimson tunic. For this occasion, I wore a linen camisia beneath my tunic and felt horribly decadent. Only the very rich or very noble (and I suppose they were the same) could afford such luxuries. But after my all too recent return to the wineskin, I decided that I needed it to remind myself of my station. In truth, I could instantly see the attraction. Woolen tunics, especially the sort that I was used to wearing, scratched the skin, sometimes so badly that it left it red and itching.

Once properly arrayed, I attended to my charge—Gwyneira. She was alone in my and Merlin's house, already dressed in a beautiful white gown with a wreath of flowers about her head. To my delight, she had refrained from using chalk to whiten her cheeks or berries to redden her lips. She was as fresh and natural as the smell of spring breeze.

"My lady, you are just the sort of queen who will capture our people's hearts."

"If I ever get the chance to meet the people," she answered with a frown.

"Do not fault us for protecting you. Once the marriage is made, all threat to your person will vanish."

"Why do you insist on that? If someone wishes me dead, will they not still wish me dead after I am married to Arthur?"

"The only reason anyone in our lands would wish you dead is to sabotage the alliance with your father. When the marriage is complete, the alliance will be fact. Your houses will be bound. Killing you then serves no purpose. And, my lady, I have to believe that it was more an attempt to frighten you than a true death threat. Killing either the intended bride of a Rigo-tamos and more especially the actual woman of our high king is not something to be done for the thinnest of reasons."

She looked at me with her eyebrow cocked. "Perhaps. But purpose might be found by those whose aims are not political."

"What other enemies could you have, my lady?"

At that she fell silent.

"Have you spent much time with Arthur?" I changed the subject.

Her lips curled into a smile at that. "Some. He is quite handsome and very kind. But I worry."

"About what?"

"Whether I shall be able to please him as a good wife should. It is no small consideration."

I felt my face redden and I swallowed hard. "Have you spoken to your mother about this?"

"My mother died long ago, Malgwyn, when Vortipor was born. But why do you ask?"

It was impossible for me to look at her. The heat in my face and beneath my tunic was nearly unbearable. But I had sworn to help her. "The question of how to please your husband is not something that I feel comfortable answering. But I will try. This night, after you retire . . ."

And then she laughed so loud, I fairly leapt from my seat.

"Oh, Malgwyn, you are a tonic to my mind! I need no advice on coupling. I meant as a queen, at his side."

The wave of relief that washed over me near drowned me. And I must have shown it as Gwyneira burst into another fit of laughter.

"M-m-m-my lady, I apologize for misunderstanding!"

She waved a hand at me dismissively. "Malgwyn, I may be young but women talk about these things. And we have just as many dogs running in our lanes as you do here."

I straightened my tunic. "Then, my lady, if your question is whether you will make Arthur a good queen, then I can assure you that you will. I am not accustomed to paying compliments, but you are an exceptional woman, wise beyond your years, and we are fortunate to have you among us."

At that, Gwyneira stepped quickly to my side and kissed my cheek, and I reddened even more.

"It is time." The pronouncement came from the doorway. Aircol and Bedevere were standing there, ready to escort Gwyneira to her wedding.

She smiled at me once more, took a deep breath and hooked her arm in her father's. Arthur's bride was ready.

Nightfall was no more than an hour away. Already the lanes danced with the light of a thousand torches. With Bedevere and me flanking them, they were led across the lane into a side door of the hall. No one was loitering along the cobbles; most folks were crowded into the market square. I looked this way and that, searching thatched rooftops, dark corners, anywhere an enemy might hide. The marriage would be made inside Arthur's hall. After Dubricius had wed them, they would emerge through the double doors onto the square and greet the people. And then the celebration would begin, and I could rest a little easier. Perhaps even Ygerne would come to her senses and forgive me.

Inside the hall were Dubricius, garbed in his finest robes and jewelry, Arthur, likewise arrayed, the lords of the consilium, the brothers Riocatus and Faustus, the emperor's envoy, and all the rest.

Such weddings were not common in our world. Ancient law recognized many forms of marriage, but since faith in the Christ had begun, such distinctions were usually ignored. Most often, a man and woman would simply begin keeping house together; any words they spoke were private. The agreement would have been struck between their parents, a business arrangement. In recent years though, more and more marriages were blessed by an episcopus or sacerdote, rather giving God's blessing on the union. For two committed believers in the Christ as Aircol and Arthur most assuredly were, a marriage granted by episcopus Dubricius was the only proper course.

Once Bedevere and I had delivered Aircol and Gwyneira to the hall, we stepped back and moved quietly to the main entrance. I had begun to think that our precautions were silly, that the message had been, as even I had said to Gwyneira, merely to frighten. A quick survey of the gathering drew no suspicious looks or expressions. Rather, they all seemed delighted. Perhaps I was seeing conspiracies where none existed.

From that distance, we could not hear the words that Dubricius spoke, though I recognized that he was speaking in Latin. Slowly, but steadily, we were using less and less Latin in our language, reverting back to our old tribal tongues. Latin was still the written language, but other than formal ceremonies such as this, it was rarely used in conversation.

And, even as I mused about languages, it was over. We knew from the cheer that erupted at the front of the hall. The crowd parted and we could see Arthur and Gwyneira, arm in arm, advancing toward us with Aircol and Dubricius bringing up the rear.

On cue, we swung open the double doors and the roar from the crowd outside smothered the cries from inside. Though the sun had now set, the square was brightly lit by torches. I was delighted to see Mariam perched atop Owain's shoulders. She looked so happy, waving her arms and cheering the couple. The scene reminded me of a more somber one, when another large crowd had overwhelmed the market square as Arthur was poised to behead Merlin. Instinctively, my eyes began sweeping the rooftops, but no Saxons with bows marred their outlines, only cheering, happy townsfolk.

Arthur led Gwyneira to the center of the market square and held her hand high between them. "This is my queen, and you will serve and obey her as you do me!" he proclaimed in a voice that swallowed even the loudest cries in its deep, bass timbre.

Then the festival began in earnest.

❈

"Come, Malgwyn! Our work has been done this day! We can at last catch our breath and relax! Arthur is married. The alliance made!" I had never seen Bedevere so happy. He didn't even kick the dogs that were crowding the door to Arthur's hall, baying for scraps from the tables.

With a grin on my own face, I slapped him on the back. Indeed, we had done our work well. And while safeguarding Arthur and Gwyneira would always be our responsibility, a critical time had passed without the horror that we had feared.

Cerdic had done his job well. While Arthur and Gwyneira had been greeting the people, he had been hurrying the servi as they arranged the hall for the feast. Hardly an inch of the giant room was unoccupied either by people or food.

The lords of the consilium were blissfully celebrating, all animosity and intrigue set aside on this night. Even his chief rivals, David and Mordred, seemed genuinely happy. And that was cause to celebrate. Gwyneira fairly glowed. Aircol and Arthur laughed and joked with Gawain and Gaheris. Even Celyn seemed in a good mood, though he still glowered whenever his glance chanced upon me.

With David's company in attendance, Morgan had more old friends, and he had relaxed a bit, drinking his share of mead. I saw him at one point waving a roasted chicken leg in the air and trying to sing. He needed to remain a medicus.

Despite my still rumbling belly, I gladly accepted a flagon of wine, intent, however, on moderation.

Most of the night passed in a blur of songs and wine and food. Talorc and the other servi were kept busy simply refilling beakers and restocking the platters with food. Once I wandered out into the market square to catch some fresh air and saw the Druid Wynn, a smile on his face, taking a flagon from Talorc. I remember thinking that perhaps I had misjudged Wynn.

Three bards, one from nearby, one from Aircol's lands, and one sent by Lord Mark, regaled us with tales of our ancestors, of Brutus who first settled our lands and old King Leir, son of Bladud. Their words were prettier than their voices, however, and I wandered away from the entertainment to find Kay.

Strangely, I found him on the rampart, looking off at the

watch fire at Ynys-witrin, out of sight and nearly sound of the festival. "No interest in the celebration, Kay?"

He looked down at me from his great height, and I detected a wan smile. "I have worked so much arranging this day that I find I have no energy to enjoy it."

"I understand," and indeed I did. Many of us, close to Arthur, had been surprised when he named Kay as his Cup-Bearer. His temperament was ill-suited to such mundane tasks, and his anger flashed frequently when confronted with recalcitrant servi unused to a firm hand. But he had borne his responsibilities with honor and had managed the marriage with efficiency, if not skill. That his mood should be dark seemed natural.

"Well," I continued, "it is behind us now, and we can return to matters more fitted to our talents.

At that he looked down at me and grinned. "That will be a pleasant change." The grin disappeared then. "Did you know that Arthur plans to free some of the servi tomorrow?"

"In truth?"

"Aye." He nodded. "Talorc and one or two of the others. Aircol has requested it."

"I understand Talorc, but what of the others?"

Kay shrugged. "They have been attentive to Gwyneira's needs or some such nonsense."

"You do not agree with freeing them?"

"I think that some will see it as a sign of a weak character. Freeing old servi who have spent a life serving you is one thing, but to free the young who have yet to prove themselves is dangerous."

"Everyone knows of Arthur's distaste for slavery, and his

enemies already think him weak or they would not be his enemy. So I see no harm in it."

"It is of little consequence," Kay said. "The girl will make a fine queen."

Something in his tone told me that he had left something unsaid. "What, Kay? Are you troubled?"

"Aircol and Gwyneira are good people, good followers of the Christ. But two of her servants do not understand their own station. With my leave, Cerdic asked them to help with serving the feast. I assumed he would approach Gwyneira first to secure her permission. But you know Cerdic, used to having his own way, he went to them directly. They did not take it well, complained to Gwyneira, who is now petitioning Arthur to replace Cerdic as chief cook."

I laughed, not at Kay but at the situation. "We must be prepared for more than a few changes. Guinevere's likes and dislikes were so well known that we automatically took them into account. So, your trials are just beginning anew?"

"I'll weather this new storm." He paused for a second and then put on a smile I was not sure he truly felt. "And you, Malgwyn? Now that your present task is finished, how will you occupy yourself?

"I'm certain that Arthur will find work for me, and I have some unfinished business of my own."

"The dead girls?"

"Aye. I did not have the time nor freedom to truly concern myself with those. I intend to take that time now."

"Now that so many days have passed, how can you come to the truth of it?"

"I had no chance to question anyone about who or what they saw. That is how I will proceed, and I'll look at the places they breathed their last as well. Ambrosius brought me word of yet another, killed near where our party passed on the road back."

He nodded. "I heard of this. Think you that this Druid did it?"

"I can see no other logical answer, Kay. 'Tis not as easy to sort out as Eleonore's death. We understood quickly that taking the hearts was to direct guilt to Merlin. But the brutality of these acts makes no sense to me." I paused. "Kay, I have not had the chance to tell you how saddened I was by the death of Nimue. I know you had taken a fancy to her and perhaps envisioned making her your woman."

"True." Kay nodded. "I have come to the conclusion that such a life is not for me. It seems I have the worst fortune in that regard." Kay straightened then to his full height, looming far above me. "Come, Malgwyn! Let us store these matters away for tomorrow. Tonight, let's help our friend celebrate his marriage!"

❖

The fire in the center of the room roared, but not as loud as the gathering of lords. Ambrosius was declaiming on battles fought and won, although I noticed that some of his victories seemed as defeats at the time. David, Mordred, and Gawain were in deep discussion. Celyn was whispering in the ear of a common woman, a true meretrix, one of several around the room. Vortimer's brothers, Faustus and Riocatus, were speaking to Dubricius. The envoy from Rome had retired for the evening. He was an old man who had not wanted to come, but in those days, a prudent man did not refuse a request from the emperor, whoever it happened to be that day.

Arthur and Aircol entered from the private quarters.

Gwyneira was not with them, nor was I surprised. I suspected that once the feast had ended we would see little of her on this night. Both men were cheered as they walked to the center of the room. In one motion, David jumped to his feet and snatched up a beaker of wine.

"Let us drink to the health of Arthur and his new bride!" he shouted over the general clamor.

We all stood and took up our beakers and other drinking pots. As one, we saluted Arthur and drank his health. The Rigotamos blushed, just a bit, but enough to show he was uncomfortable in this new role.

Not to be outdone, Bedevere offered the next salute. Soon everyone but Merlin, who had fallen asleep in the corner, had paid homage. And we were feeling a bit more than tipsy.

My legs gave way underneath me, and I fell into a sitting position on the hard-packed dirt floor, struggling to stay upright.

As the room began spinning around me, I heard, rather than saw, Mordred bounce to his feet and proclaim, "My lord Arthur! Before you enter upon the life of a devoted husband, a decidedly boring and unexciting life," and laughter shook the posts, "I think you owe the consilium one last duty as a bachelor!"

Gawain sprang to his feet as well. "A ride!"

"A ride!" Bedevere took up the call.

Soon, every lord in the room was shouting, "A ride! A last ride!" Even me.

Arthur and Aircol had been no strangers to the drink on this night, and a broad grin walked its way across Arthur's face. I was pleased for him. For the first time in nearly two years as Rigotamos, the consilium seemed as one. Even as he tried to stifle the cries, Aircol took them up, and Arthur was forced to concede defeat. It was an age-old tradition, usually tided to Beltane or Samhane, the ancient celebrations, and it was one that Arthur could not ignore.

Arthur snagged a passing servus. "To the stables! Prepare our horses! We ride!"

CHAPTER SIXTEEN

The night was warm and quiet, the pleasing scent of wood smoke in the air, until we began our ride. The villagers must have thought a crazed pack of Saxon raiders had descended, so loud were our cries. In truth, if they were brave enough to glance out of their cottages, they would have seen a dancing parade of torches, lighting a band of drunken lords, swaying in their saddles and howling at the moon. Only Morgan and Merlin had failed to join us; both were besotted with mead and sound asleep.

Drunk as I was, I kept a close eye on Arthur. It would not be difficult to create an accident—a jostling of his horse, a stinging whip to the animal's hindquarters, sending the rider tumbling. Accidents happened, sometimes fatal ones. More than one lord had broken his neck in a fall from a horse. And Mordred and David would not mourn for long if such misfortune befell Arthur. But all seemed as it should be, all of us enjoying our ride.

We rode out the Via Arturius, across the river Cam and out toward Ynys-witrin, passing small hamlets and villages.

The summer had been dry, and much land that was usually underwater now lay revealed, damp and rotting. Sweeping to the west, we tore into the old Roman town at Lindinis.

Pulling up to rest our mounts at an old, abandoned Roman villa, we eyed the broken-down house. "I believe," Mordred shouted, "I'll see if anyone is at home."

Snatching the reins quickly to the left, he aimed his horse for the entrance, intending, I supposed, to ride into the atrium.

Almost immediately, even above the sounds of our raucous, drunken band, we heard an odd sound like that of an over-ripened squash exploding against a rock. Then, much to our surprise, Mordred flew backward from his horse, falling to the ground and rolling into a groaning bundle.

We sat, stunned, until Mordred raised his head and we saw the blood running down his face. In his impatience, he had missed seeing the lintel and it caught him directly in the nose. Thrown to the ground, he cursed us, his horse, the long departed Romans, and his battered nose, now painted a shiny red in the torchlight.

As Mordred struggled back to his feet and climbed back on his saddle, Kay whistled for our attention.

"A race! To Castellum Arturius and once around the hill! First man to enter the gate wins!"

"But what prize?" Aircol asked.

"An amphora of my best wine," replied Arthur, getting into the spirit of the affair.

With a renewed shout of joy, we all kicked our horses and lunged toward home. At that precise moment, with the night air cooling the sweat on my face, and despite Guinevere's sorrow and Ygerne's anger, I had never felt happier.

I was mired well back of the leaders when the uppermost ramparts became visible, the wine clouding my eyes, judgment, and strength. From my position, it appeared that Bedevere and Celyn were battling for victory. A whiff of wood smoke from the campfires circling the hill flavored the air. I glanced up at the moon and guessed that we had been three hours on our ride.

By that time, I was so far in the rear that I slowed my mount to a walk. Horse racing was for younger warriors than me. After a few moments, I heard the jiggle of bridles and the creaking of leather coming up behind me. Twisting about, I saw that Arthur and Aircol were joining me on either side.

"Well, Malgwyn, it is finally done," Arthur said.

"Aye, my lord. It is that. What are your plans now, Lord Aircol?"

"Home. To Caer Goch. Now that we are allied with the consilium, there are some changes I must make in my defense arrangements. And we have agreed to send an envoy to the northern tribes and seek better relations."

"Ready for another journey, Malgwyn?" Arthur asked.

My head whipped around. "My lord, you cannot be serious! I have just returned from nearly a month away!" But then I saw the smile hiding behind his beard. Aircol burst into laughter.

"A plague upon both of you!"

Their laughter continued to ring across the flatlands. "Be at peace, Malgwyn," Arthur counseled. "Your services will not be required this time. An emissary from Aircol will be better received than one from me."

He spoke the truth. Arthur's relations with our cousins to the north had always been precarious. It had been the Picts from beyond the great Roman wall in the north that had caused Vortigern to first send for the Saxons. They had raided across the wall and killed many of our people, stolen animals and food. Our mutual hatred of the grasping Saxons had brought an uneasy peace. Aircol's relatively good relations with those tribes had been a major reason for striking an alliance with him.

I breathed a heavy sigh of relief. I had other plans for the days ahead, and traveling to the land of the Picts was not among them. The most important puzzle facing me now was why Ygerne had turned so angry with me. I had never been very good at understanding women, and with Ygerne I seemed to be even worse. But I did love her, not in the same way that I had loved Gwyneth, but just as strongly. At that moment, however, I was exhausted and would settle for my own bed.

We rode up to the main gate, where a mass of cheering men surrounded another whom we could not see.

With the help of a guard, I climbed down from my mount and pushed my way closer to the gaggle of men. One, obviously the victor, was now being held up by the others. A blond head bobbed up above the rest. Celyn. I had to laugh. The boy lord had proved himself good at something.

A handful of stable boys had arrived and were leading the horses away. Bedevere appeared at my side. "More drink, Malgwyn?"

I waved him off. "The only thing I wish right now is my bed. And you?"

He yawned and stretched. "I will make certain the guard is set and then retire to Kay's house." Slapping me on the

back, Bedevere smiled. "You are not the only man whose patience and fortitude has been stretched to the limits, old
friend."

"I know. Perhaps now we can get back to normal life."

With that, I wandered off through the lanes to my house,
intent only in curling up beneath a fur blanket. Merlin was
already abed when I entered, and I fell into a deep sleep almost
immediately.

"Malgwyn!" A bear was roaring in my ear, and I wondered
how it got into my hut. I turned away and buried my head deeper
in the furs.

"Malgwyn!" If I ignored it, I thought it would just go
away.

But then I felt a hand on my shoulder, jerking me upright.

I blinked and tried to focus. 'Twas Bedevere. And the expression on his face was one I never wanted to see again. Fear. And
not just ordinary fear. The veins in his neck pumped angrily;
the skin of his face was white.

"What, Bedevere? What has happened?"

"Come! Now!"

I reached for my caligae, but Bedevere snatched at my tunic. "There is not time!"

With that he dragged me through the door and onto the
cobbled pavement barefoot. I hopped and limped behind him
as the not always smooth cobbles tore at my feet.

"In the name of all the gods, Bedevere, what has happened? You can let go." I glanced up at the sky. I had not been
abed more than an hour if that.

But Bedevere did not speak, just pointed to the side door of
Arthur's hall, and then shoved me in.

A handful of lords were lolling about, speaking in hushed whispers to each other while keeping an eye on the door to Arthur's chambers.

And then I stopped, my eyes growing wide as the realization hit.

I brushed off Bedevere's hand and walked cautiously to the open door.

With a deep, deep breath, I stepped in, and then shuddered in horror.

Little Vala had been right. Someone in that wagon had been marked.

Gwyneira was dead.

❊

By then I had become accustomed to the scene—the bloodless face, the splayed legs, the crimson stain painting her thighs. But for the room, I could be looking at the girl at the White Mount or the one at Caer Goch. Gwyneira's eyes were closed. In the maelstrom that was my thoughts at that moment, I wondered if she had been found that way or if someone had closed them later. Having faced any number of the dead, I had noticed that they rarely closed their own eyes, especially those who died by violence.

Arthur was there, pacing angrily with short, quick steps, his eyes reddened. Aircol, his long white hair hanging down over his face, sat in a chair, head bent, obviously stunned, seeming far more fragile than I had ever seen him.

I wanted to close my eyes and believe it all a dream. The servants must have just cleared the feasting hall; I could still detect the hint of roasted chicken and vegetables in the air.

Walking to the bed, I reached down and touched her face. Not cold, but no longer warm either.

Then something odd happened to me. My vision cleared and rather than the self-pitying mess I had been the night before, I grew angry, but it was a cold anger, a chilling fury as I'd never felt. I walked to Arthur and put my hand on his shoulder.

He spun about quickly, his hand shooting to the hilt of his sword, his eyes wide.

"I will find this killer, my lord. And we will punish him no matter who he is."

Arthur smiled wryly. "Do we not already know, Malgwyn? And did I not chastise you for worrying? Perhaps if I had given you leave . . ." His voice drifted off.

At that, Aircol rose from his seat, stood over Gwyneira's body, touched lightly her leg and turned to us. "Arthur, I am a man of my word, but this I promise you: Someone must pay for this or I will withdraw from the consilium."

"Someone will pay, my lord," I interjected. "I swear it."

He looked at me with his eyes narrowed in doubt. "You swore to protect her, and yet this has happened. Perhaps if you had been more faithful to that oath, this one wouldn't be necessary."

"My lord—" I began, but Arthur cut me off.

"Lord Aircol, Malgwyn was not the only man charged with keeping Gwyneira safe. If you fault him, you must fault them as well. In the short time I knew your daughter, her potential to be a great queen became obvious. I mourn with you. In even that short time, I had already come to . . ." The dampness at his eyes told what his voice didn't. "I cannot return life to her, though I wish with all my heart that I could. If you want justice, then Malgwyn is the man to bring that to you. He is skilled in these things."

The older lord, his face lined more deeply than at any time I had seen him, turned his gaze upon me. "You will have your chance, Malgwyn. But the guilty one will be subject to my punishment, not Lord Arthur's. That is only fair, only just."

I glanced quickly at Arthur, who nodded almost imperceptibly. "I understand."

Then Aircol turned around slowly. "Though I do not think your task is difficult. Obviously it was the Druid that did this thing and killed those other girls."

"That is the only conclusion I am able to draw at present, my lord. But," and I hesitated, "at least one other possibility exists." Morgan was not with us on the ride. Yet again, I could not discount him.

"Who?" Both Aircol and Arthur asked almost in unison.

"I would rather not say until I have made further inquiries." The looks on both their faces told me how little they liked my response. "I promise you both that if my suspicions are confirmed in the least, you will be the first to know. The Druid is absolutely the most likely."

"Then why not simply hunt him down? Bring him to me now!"

"My lord, I do not think that a good idea." Merlin. I had not even noticed his entry. "The Druids are still much respected by many of the people, particularly those in the north near your borders. If word circulated, and it would, that you had summarily executed a Druid priest, it could bring more trouble than you would wish. Malgwyn has a way with these things. And when he has finished, no one will be able to doubt the identity of the doer of these deeds."

"He is right, Aircol," Arthur added. "And if you wish to blame someone for this, blame me. Malgwyn wanted desperately to pursue the killer of these girls. I resisted, forcing him to focus on other things. I never dreamed that the same killer would strike within my own house. So I hold more blame than anyone."

Gwyneira's father did not speak immediately. For a long second, he stared at his daughter's lifeless body, gray and growing cold. When he spoke, it was in a voice devoid of all but the darkest of emotions. "I blame all of you." He turned to me. "Can you promise me that you will find justice for my child?"

"I will pursue this as if my own life depended on success."

Aircol met my eyes. "It does."

I matched him, stare for stare. "I would accept nothing less." With that, I looked to Kay and Bedevere. "One of you find and fetch the Druid Wynn. You will probably find him at Mordred's camp. The other bring the servi from the kitchen. They would have been cleaning up and may have seen something." The orders came naturally. I glanced around the room. Too many people. And I needed to more closely examine the body. "Rigotamos," I began, "I need some quiet to better study what has happened here."

Arthur immediately took my meaning. With a pair of quick hand gestures, he began emptying the room. Merlin was at the back, and I motioned for him to stay. In a matter of seconds, he and I were alone with Gwyneira's body.

"Well, Malgwyn," Merlin began. "This was unexpected."

I grinned despite the grimness of my task. "Out in the villages and the countryside, it is easy to commit such act and then disappear. But here, in the Rigotamos's own chamber, that takes a confident man."

"Or a very stupid one."

"Aye." I moved closer to Gwyneira and pulled the gown back from her womanhood. I winced at the sight of her thighs, the white skin torn and raw. "Merlin? A torch."

The stiffness that accompanied death had not yet touched her body. I pushed open one of her eyelids to find the little dots of red on her sightless eyes—the sign of suffocation. Her head wobbled loosely and I felt of her neck with my one hand. It took only a second, and I detected the break. Though she had been smothered, her neck had been broken as well. There was no way to tell which had proved fatal.

Merlin moved the globe of yellowed light closer, and then I could see the bits of brown bark and yellow splinters dotting her legs. The injuries here were far more severe than in the first two girls. Gouges, easily a half an inch deep, marred both of her thighs. Her maidenhead was ripped beyond recognition. But I noticed too that the gashes were deeper and more plentiful on her left thigh. Whoever did this wanted her to hurt.

It was puzzling. I had assumed that the attacker had knelt in front of the body and performed his desecration, his target already being dead. But there was more blood here than at the others, spread over a wider area, which meant that her heart was still beating when she had been ravaged.

A thought struck me. I lifted her chin and motioned for Merlin to bring the torch closer. Under the brighter light, I immediately saw what I suspected. Her throat was horribly bruised, but more so on the front and left side. And as my eyes grew accustomed to the light, I saw finger-like bruises on her left cheek. Turning her head, I observed a single bruise on her right cheek. I placed my hand across her mouth and saw that my fingers nearly fit on the bruises, but not quite. Whoever covered her mouth had a hand smaller than mine. That was odd, as I had a small hand for a man.

Arising, I cast about the chamber for the offending object but I found nothing that would have created such horrible wounds. Merlin, too, scavenged about but he found nothing either.

"He must have carried it away with him," I mused. "I do not understand why he does this. Raping a woman I can understand. That speaks to anger and control. But this, this butchery. I see no manner in which a man could gain satisfaction from this."

Merlin cocked his head to the side. "I think, Malgwyn, that if you could understand the why you would know the who."

The chamber door opened and Bedevere stepped through. "Kay found the Druid in Mordred's camp as you expected. We have placed him under guard at the barracks."

"Did Mordred object?"

"No. He seemed glad to be rid of him. I suspect, if the truth were known, that Mordred couldn't care less about the Christ or the Druids or any gods or goddesses."

I nodded. "The servants?"

"We have gathered them at the kitchen."

"I will join you in a moment."

Bedevere ducked out and I turned to Merlin. "I know that you are right, but I cannot fathom why it should be so. People kill because it profits them to do so, or it proves their superiority, but even in that they gain something."

"I agree. And the only profit I see in this is to crush the alliance with Aircol. But I cannot name a single lord that would wish for that, except for perhaps Melwas. But even he profits from this alliance. It leaves Guinevere available for his suit."

"Do not forget Morgan. We know that he is David's creature. David is used to manipulating others to do his bidding. And he did not join us on the ride."

"Neither did I," Merlin reminded me.

"True, but you could not have killed the girl at the White Mount or the one at Aircol's town. You were with others."

He nodded. "Shall we have Morgan taken into custody?"

I thought for a moment. "No, if he did this thing, Gareth's men will have some knowledge. And a medicus does not mutilate like this unless someone else has directed it. A man of Morgan's nervous disposition will seek shelter with David. We should wait and watch him, for now."

"But not forever. Still, I agree that the Druid is the most likely."

"Please, Merlin, stay here and keep the others out. I will not have her stared at." With that, I turned, took a deep breath, and walked into the feasting hall and amidst the growing mob of lords and their servants.

"What has happened, Malgwyn?"

"Malgwyn, speak!"

"Is she dead?"

"Who did it?"

"Why are you not wearing your caligae?"

I was pelted by questions, but I ignored them and slid out the side door and back onto the cobbled lane.

Old Cerdic hung his head so low that I could see the bald spot growing beneath his curly gray hair. He was more subdued than I had ever seen him. The servi were lined up, five girls and three boys, including young Talorc. The Romans, I have been told, did not trust testimony from servi unless they had been tortured. Thank the gods that was not a practice resurrected by Arthur. In my experience, even people who knew nothing would tell you something in hope of making you stop the torture.

"I need to know," I began, "what each of you observed from the time that the lords left to ride with Arthur until we returned and Lady Gwyneira was found dead. Search your memories carefully, for even the smallest detail might prove valuable."

They all avoided my gaze.

"We have no reason to believe that any of you did this thing," I assured them. "But you were the only people in and around the hall after the rest of us left."

"My lord," Cerdic stuttered. "We have no idea how someone could have done this. They must have found a different entrance. We saw no strangers."

Each of them nodded vigorously. "He is right, my lord," Talorc said hurriedly. "We saw and heard nothing out of the ordinary."

"Nothing?"

Cerdic licked his lips nervously. "The Lady Gwyneira had already retired when the lords left, Malgwyn. We did not see her afterwards."

"She asked for nothing? No one checked on her?"

The old servus shrugged. "No. And why should we look in upon her? If she needed us, she would call us."

I felt sorry for him. An overly solicitous servus could easily be punished for intruding. Yet here I was chastising him for not being so.

"Besides, my lord," one of the girls added, "she was with the visitors most of the time."

My head jerked straight. "What visitors? Wynn, the Druid?"

Cerdic looked at me as if I were mad. "The Druid did not come. But the Lady Guinevere and your woman, Ygerne."

"Who permitted them entry?" I could barely control the tremor in my voice.

Again, Cerdic's face was painted with confusion. "They said they had your permission, Malgwyn."

CHAPTER SEVENTEEN

D id they not?" Cerdic asked, so innocently that had I not known the truth I would think that he was playing the fool.

To compound my troubles, Arthur and Aircol walked into the kitchen at that precise moment. The Rigotamos looked from me to Cerdic and back again. Arthur needed no alarum or signal. My shock was too new to be hidden and I wore it like a badge.

"What? Speak, Malgwyn!"

I did not answer immediately because my mind had just resolved a question that had been nagging at me for the last few days. And that answer was one that chilled me to the bone.

"My lord," I began, hesitating. "My lord, Cerdic has just told us that Lady Gwyneira had two visitors this night."

"Then one of them must have done this!" Aircol said quickly. "Let us take them and learn the truth!"

"We should not accept the first answer that comes to us, my lord," I cautioned, lowering my face into my one hand.

But Arthur knew me too well. "Malgwyn . . ." he began in a low, rumbling voice.

" 'Twas Guinevere and Ygerne." I said it so softly that I almost mumbled.

But neither lord had trouble hearing. Arthur grabbed my shoulder, squeezing it so tightly that I winced. "Is this some joke, some jest?"

I looked up at him. "No. It is not. But Arthur, you know them. They could not have done this terrible thing!"

He saw it in my eyes though. He knew me so well, too well.

"There is something you are not saying, Malgwyn."

Perhaps if I had had more time to plan, I could have avoided the answer then on my lips. "Arthur, I told Ygerne of the murdered girls. She knows how they were ravaged."

"And she spent the day with Guinevere not two days ago," the Rigotamos finished for me. He walked slowly to a chair in the corner and lowered himself. When he looked up, it was with a face deeply lined, the face of a man much older. He looked to me. "Malgwyn, what have they done?"

"They have killed my daughter and your queen," shouted an enraged Aircol, red-faced and the veins pumping rhythmically in his neck. "And you will see justice done or I will do it for you!"

"No, my lord, I will see them dead myself," Arthur said coldly. I knew the pain coursing through him. His entire world had been shaken in just moments. He had lost both the woman he loved and the woman he was coming to love.

"Lord Aircol, let us not move hastily," I began, with none of the urgency that should have marked my words. No man or woman should know the pain I felt at that moment. My stomach ground in an ache so severe that it felt as if twenty swords had been thrust into me and twisted.

Arthur saw it, and knew it did not bode well. His anger was so great that he snatched me up by my tunic.

"What have you not told us?"

I shook him off.

I searched for a reason not to reveal what I now knew, what had come to me just moments before. I loved both Guinevere and Ygerne. I wasn't certain that I could survive the loss of one, let alone both. I wasn't certain that I wanted to.

"If you know something more, you need to tell them." Bedevere spoke softly, his lips near my ear. "It is not like you to hide things."

I swiveled about and grimaced at him. "My lords, the note left earlier in Gwyneira's chamber, calling her a meretrix?"

"Yes," Arthur prompted.

"It was written by Guinevere."

"I suspected as much," Aircol said with both a hint of satisfaction and that of finality.

"How can you be certain?" Arthur pressed. I could look into the lines etched on his face and knew that he ached as I did.

"I have a sample of her hand in my house. I thought when I first saw the note that there was something familiar about it, but I did not make the connection until Cerdic spoke of Guinevere."

"Could it not be just as easily in Ygerne's hand?" Arthur wanted any answer but the one that I was about to give him. "One person would make their letters the same as any other."

I shook my head. "Ygerne cannot write."

"Are you certain?" The panic on his face told the truth more readily than anything else could. He knew what it meant.

"It matters not," said Aircol. "They were both there and each had a hand in this. They share equal guilt!"

One of the girls—I no longer remember which—spoke up then, making my life worse than I ever thought it could be. "But my lord, they did not come together. First Lady Guinevere came. But she left. Then Ygerne came."

Arthur and I looked at each other, aghast. Had there been any food in my belly, I would have spewed it across the room. Had he not been Rigotamos, I believe he would have wept.

Could either Ygerne or Guinevere have done this thing? There was no question that they were innocent of the killings at the White Mount and Caer Goch. But I had told Ygerne of them. And she had spent the day with Guinevere. Might they have concocted this scheme in some kind of spavined attempt at revenge?

Half of me said they were not capable of such. The other part said that both had exhibited bizarre behavior—Ygerne's unfathomable anger and Guinevere's flight to Melwas's arms. But they couldn't be! I would not give up Ygerne, no matter what she had done!

Arthur must have seen the determination growing on my face. In a soft voice, he spoke to a confused Bedevere. "Lord Bedevere, find both Ygerne and Guinevere and bring them to the barracks."

I had never seen Bedevere look so distraught. It was as if he felt our pain. Kay, seeing his dilemma, moved beside him. "I will fetch Ygerne. You go for Guinevere."

As they left, I turned to Aircol, who wore a grim smile seeded firmly on his face. "My lord, I tell you now, I do not believe that either of these women did this thing. They stood to gain nothing from it, especially not Ygerne."

"Who knows why women act as they do? I am far older than you or Arthur and I have never understood them." At that, he placed his face within inches of mine. "But do not think for a second that I will sit by while you or Arthur protect the killer of my daughter, whether it is your woman or your cousin." He stopped and looked from Arthur to me and back to Arthur again. "You wooed me like a woman with your belief in the Christ and your commitment to truth and justice. Now, we will learn how just you truly are."

Anger climbed up and across Arthur's face. "You sought this alliance as fiercely as we did! I mourn for Gwyneira too, more than you know, but she will not be avenged by you throwing accusations around. Did Malgwyn hide any knowledge? No. He freely told us what he had learned, even though it sent the finger of suspicion pointing at both his cousin and his woman."

For a fraction of a moment, I thought that they would come to blows. I had forgotten the servi, but they had not forgotten us. Cerdic had seen many things in his life. Wars and traitors and treachery. Some said that as a boy, Cerdic was present when Vortigern cast out his Briton wife. Whatever his true history, the blustery, gray old cook stepped very high in my regard as he positioned himself between the two lords, Arthur and Aircol.

"You accomplish nothing by this," he declared with narrow eyes and in a firm voice. "Act like the lords you are and not like petulant children. You are both far too old for that."

In any ordinary place and time, I would be watching Cerdic's bloodied head rolling on the floor. But an odd thing happened. The lords stepped back, hanging their heads to the ground, well chastised by the old servus.

Kay and Bedevere left on their missions. I turned to the other servants. "Speak not a word of any of this. Disobey me and you will not live to regret it." With wide eyes, they nodded in unison. "Now, return to clearing the hall."

Of course, I knew that each of them would be bribed by the other lords. It was for that reason that I waited until they were out of the room before I continued.

"I can tell you more, my lords. Whoever did this thing came from behind her. With the right hand clamped over her mouth to keep her quiet, the left hand held the stick or branch that ravaged her."

Aircol cocked his head to one side, his face holding a skeptical look. "How can you possibly know these things? You were not there."

And then support came from an unlikely source, indeed a source that should never have been present. "Lord Aircol, I can personally vouch for the truth of Malgwyn's method."

I turned quickly. Tristan, who had managed to find us.

Aircol looked from me to Tristan and back. He knew of the trouble between Tristan and Arthur, part but not all. "You swear it?"

The young lord nodded slowly, but firmly. "Malgwyn does not countenance such fancies as alchemy or magic. No one knows his abilities better than I."

Though it came at an awkward moment, Arthur actually chuckled at the statement. "The first time that Malgwyn explained these sorts of events, I too doubted them. But Tristan speaks the truth."

"My lord, the wounds on her left thigh were deeper. And the killer's fingers left bruises on her face, on the left side of her face. The only way to accomplish that is to be behind her, wrapping your right hand across her mouth and assaulting her with the weapon held in your left hand. But, that could also indicate that the bruises were left on her face when he subdued her, and she was either freshly dead or unconscious when he attacked her." I did not tell them about the hand being smaller than my own, convincing myself that it was not relevant.

"Unless," Merlin's voice came from the door, "there were two people involved in this."

"Which does not seem to be the case," I answered without looking at him. Normally that would be an insult, but we had grown used to each other over time.

Aircol appeared not to have heard our last exchange. The frown on his face and the narrowing of his eyebrows told me that he was trying to understand what I had said about the wounds. Finally, he nodded, as much to himself it seemed as to us, and said, "What do we do now?"

"You will take your rest. On the morrow, we will mourn your daughter's passing and prepare for her burial."

"And then?"

"And then we will seek justice for our queen."

❖

My next visit was one that I dreaded with all my heart. The barracks. Ygerne. As I left the kitchen and started along the cobbled lane, I saw that Arthur was beside me. "This is not a trip for you to take, Arthur." No one else was with us, and I could dispense with my customary formality.

"You do not truly think that either woman did this?"

I stopped and turned to him. "I do not know. I can tell you that it makes no sense for Ygerne to be involved if Guinevere is not. But it makes a great deal of sense for Guinevere to be involved."

Arthur bristled at my statement. "Why? I see no difference! After all, it was Ygerne who you told about the killings, not Guinevere."

"Please, Arthur! What possible reward could Ygerne gain from killing the girl?"

He frowned and looked away. "Preferment when I married Guinevere," he almost mumbled.

"But if you were going to marry Guinevere, you would have done so already. If you wish to blame someone, blame yourself. You tossed Guinevere aside. 'Twas Guinevere who left the note and Guinevere who probably killed the girl. Guinevere is of my blood, Arthur. Do you think that I wish to see her dead? Do you think that any of this is easy for me? I do not like it any more than you do, but everything points that way."

"You wish for it, so it is." He paused and stared at me intently. "Understand this, Malgwyn. I was growing to love Gwyneira, perhaps as much as I loved Guinevere. I will see her avenged. But no one will pay for this deed unless you can prove without question that they did it, or unless they confess it freely."

"And how often does that happen," I scoffed.

"Make it happen." The look on his face, the tightness at the corners of his mouth, told me everything about his intentions. He would protect Guinevere; I would protect the truth.

"I will follow the path of truth. You may follow what you will."

"You will make certain that suspicion does not fall on Ygerne," he accused. "Do not pretend that you are not capable of hiding the truth to protect your own interests. We both know that is not the case."

The heat rose in my neck and spread across my face. "I will make certain that suspicion falls only on the one who deserves it." I had hidden facts before, but I was not aware that he knew of it. Perhaps he was just guessing. Perhaps not. But I knew at that moment that the truce between us was fragile indeed. I was certain of one thing; he did not realize that the pain he felt at Guinevere's possible guilt was doubled for me. And that pain was so severe that it nearly sucked the air from my lungs. Without another word, he spun about and left me to my task.

The guard at the barracks gate looked embarrassed. I recognized him immediately as one of the men who had ridden with me during the recent rebellion. "Malgwyn, we have treated her well."

"Did she offer much resistance?"

The gruff soldier shook his head. "It was almost as if she expected us. She came along meekly."

"That does not sound like Ygerne."

He laughed. "No, it does not."

I passed through and made for the door. Taking a deep breath, I opened it and stepped inside.

"So, he did send you." Her voice was just as harsh as it had been the day before.

"You would do well to temper your tone. This affair does not bode well for you at all."

She brushed that flaming red hair from her face and squinted at me. "Why? If Arthur or Aircol demand it, you'll see me put to the sword."

"Think you so? Think you that little of me?"

"Why should I not? You watched as Arthur betrayed Guinevere and married the little meretrix. Why should you not look the other way now?"

I winced at her words. They would not serve her well. "Gwyneira was no whore. She was just a young girl promised in a marriage in which she had no say."

Ygerne looked at me then, with a piercing gaze and a growing horror. "You were in love with her."

I threw my hand up. "Because I do not believe she was a whore? Ygerne, you make no sense whatsoever! What has happened to you?"

She pursed her lips. "You!"

Getting any worthwhile information was seeming less and less a possibility. Perhaps I had misjudged Ygerne. This was not the woman I had come to love. "Will you tell me what happened when you went to see Gwyneira?"

"Why? You will not believe anything I say."

"Ygerne, you may remain quiet or you may help me find the truth. Someone is going to die over this. Right now, you and Guinevere are the most likely. I do not believe that either of you did this, but you are giving me no weapons with which to fight your cause."

She crossed the room and settled into a chair. "You must promise not to tell others what I am about to say."

"Why?"

"Promise." Not a request, a demand.

Obviously, she was not going to tell me unless I acceded. "Very well."

Ygerne sighed deeply. "The girl was dead when Guinevere went to see her. She came to my house, upset, frightened. I went to see for myself. It was just as she said."

"When you went to see her the other day, did you tell her of the killings I had described to you?"

"Of course. I was trying to take her mind off of Arthur."

"So you told her of killings that a Druid priest claims are the gods' vengeance against Arthur? And that is supposed to steer her thoughts away from him?" I shook my head, but she was not in a mood to agree. I decided to move forward.

"And then what happened?"

She looked up at me quizzically. "Nothing happened. I returned to Castellum Arturius. I did not see her again until this eve. Malgwyn, she did not do this thing. The sort of cruelty that I saw in Arthur's chamber is not within her."

"Why did you not raise the alarum when you found her so?"

A look of incredulity spread across her face. "Of course, Malgwyn! That was my first thought. And my second was that I would immediately be thought guilty! I knew that you men would be back soon enough and she would be found. And there was no power on earth that could help Gwyneira."

I could not quibble with her analysis, though I did not think that anyone we left behind would have immediately blamed her. "What happened when you returned home?"

Ygerne shrugged. "Guinevere was gone, back to Ynys-witrin, I assumed."

"And you did nothing? Told no one?"

"Understand me, Malgwyn. I did not know this girl. I do not like killing but her death does not touch me in any special way. Arthur used Guinevere for his pleasure and then tossed her aside when a younger woman was handed to him. This serves all of you right for playing with people's lives, bartering them as if they were goods to be sold."

"That is the way of it everywhere."

"The Saxons do not treat their women thus. They accord them property and status. And the Picts do likewise."

"Ygerne, how would you know what the Saxons and Picts do?"

She looked at me as if I were a dolt. And perhaps I was. "People talk, Malgwyn. And we have traders passing through who treat with both."

I had given little thought to such things, merely accepting affairs as they always had been among us. Apparently, though, our women had. I did not have time then to ponder the meaning of that, but it was something to consider later.

"Well, now it is time for you to talk to Arthur and Aircol and tell them what you have told me."

She leapt to her feet with fire in her eyes and that red hair flying about her shoulders. "I will not! I told you, Malgwyn. What I have said is for your ears alone!"

"And what does that accomplish but keep the eye of suspicion turned to you?"

"Exactly! As long as there is some doubt, you can convince them to wait."

"Wait for what, Ygerne? You did not see Aircol, or Arthur! They will have revenge!"

But Ygerne did not respond in kind, rather she smiled softly at me. "You will convince them, because it will give you time to find who truly did this thing." She paused and walked across the room, leaning against a wall. "I do not think you would betray your noble sense of justice to save me. But you know that I did not kill Gwyneira, and you know that Guinevere did not either. Or at least you hope that is true. So, you will not rest until you find the true killer. That is what I depend upon, Malgwyn."

My heart fell. Part of me wanted to feel pride that she respected me so much. But another, larger part was saddened that she did not believe I would protect, defend her. Then was not the time to worry about such things, though.

"Unfortunately for your plans, Ygerne, the servi remembered that Guinevere came first and you second. And I finally realized who left the note for Gwyneira calling her a meretrix."

Ygerne lowered her eyes.

"You knew?"

She did not answer, turning away from me.

The truth hit me like a Saxon spear. "You put it there."

"We thought it a harmless jest."

"Calling a poor child a *meretrix* was a jest? You and my cousin have a strange sense of humor."

Then she turned and looked at me with something approaching a smile. "It was meant more for Arthur than the girl."

"Your choice of targets seems a bit askew."

Her attempt to soften did not work. She realized it and changed her tactics. "It was ill-advised. I do not dispute that. But Guinevere did not kill that girl any more than I did."

I hung my head and crossed to her side. "And I do not doubt you, but I fear that Arthur and Aircol will. Why should they not? The servi have already told us that you and Guinevere were the girl's only visitors. I told Arthur that I recognized the hand on the note as Guinevere's, though I did not know that you played a part in that. And they know that I told you of those blasted deaths on the road. What more do they need? If I did not know the two of you, I would think you guilty, and your silly actions have done nothing to make anyone think otherwise."

Twisting her head, she brushed a strand of hair from her face. "Right now, you are upset at the girl's death and with me and your cousin. But when you calm, you will realize that there are other answers as well."

"It does not matter that there are other answers. What am I to tell them now?"

"That I will not speak. That I said nothing."

"You are playing a dangerous game, Ygerne. You know that I love you, but there is nothing stopping Arthur from serving up your head to satisfy Aircol."

"Yes, there is," she answered.

Before I could ask her what she meant, the door burst open and Illtud bounded into the room.

"What?"

The soldier who would be a priest hung his head, his long hair hanging in sweat-laden locks against his mail shirt, and caught his breath. Finally, he met my eye.

"We have a problem."

CHAPTER EIGHTEEN

I jerked my head toward the door, avoiding the glare in Ygerne's eyes, and followed my friend out into the night air.

"Bedevere just returned." Illtud wasted no time. "An envoy from Melwas met him on the Via Arturius. Melwas has announced that he has Guinevere under his protection and that he will not surrender her to Arthur and Aircol." He paused and breathed deeply. "He has closed off the road at Pomparles and to the north and east as well. Ynys-witrin is closed to all."

"Is he mad! That is a virtual admission that she is guilty. Arthur will have no choice but to assault Melwas's fortress and take Guinevere by force!"

"Could this be another rebellion?"

I paused and considered events. "My heart tells me no, but my head tells me maybe. David cannot be trusted any more than Mordred can. Both lust after Arthur's seat. I suspect, though, that they are waiting for some hesitancy on Arthur's part, some indication that he will not challenge Melwas. That would leave an opening for David, probably, to ally with Aircol against Arthur." I turned and saw Bedevere approaching from the great hall. "Quickly! Fetch Arthur and bring him to Kay's house!"

Bedevere, within hearing now, shook his shaggy head. "No, Malgwyn. Arthur gathered the soldiers here and those in the encampment below and started off for Ynys-witrin."

"Then you must stop him!" The vision of Arthur, probably still cloudy from drink, and his soldiers, certainly still reeling from mead, clashing with clear-eyed soldiers at Melwas's fortress was one of horror. "Bring both him and Aircol back here to Kay's house. But whatever you do, they must be stopped! They will be slaughtered!"

It took my friend but a second to realize that I was right. He spun and raced back up the lane. I breathed easily for the first time in the last minute. Bedevere was an excellent rider and had one of the fastest horses among us. He could easily catch Arthur. And though he would resist, Arthur respected Bedevere enough to listen to him.

"To Kay's," I told Illtud.

✳

We did not have long to wait. A hastily gathered band still moves slowly, and Bedevere caught them just a few miles from Castellum Arturius. I wish I had been there; those who were told me it was a dramatic scene. Arthur threatened to behead Bedevere, but he stood his ground and brought Arthur around. But they were both smart enough to do this outside Aircol's presence, in a glen off the road.

When I next saw Arthur, the circles around his eyes had grown deeper and darker. His tunic was streaked with sweat, and like Illtud, his long, chestnut hair hung about his shoulders in wet, tangled strands.

Old terra cotta lamps filled with oil were scattered about, their flames dancing on the walls so that it seemed a hundred people were in the room rather than just our small band— Arthur, Bedevere, Kay, Illtud, Merlin, and me. We had convinced Aircol to seek some rest. On the morrow, he would face a task no father should see.

"What did Ygerne say?" Arthur wasted no time.

I shook my head sadly. "Nothing. She refuses to bear witness against Guinevere or even to defend herself."

"Then they were in this together. Both shall have to suffer. And the Druid?"

"Illtud came to me with this news before I had the chance to question him. But I have heard no one say that he was seen about the lanes at all."

Everyone nodded in agreement.

"Perhaps if we behead Ygerne now," Arthur continued, "that will pacify Aircol enough to allow us time to gather forces to besiege Melwas." As I write these words, they seem to evoke a tone of calmness, of casual brutality. But that was far from the case. The air was laden with the scent of sweat and fear and pain, laden so heavily that each breath seemed a torture, unbearable.

"My lord, that would certainly seem the simplest path," I said, choosing my words carefully. "But let us consider the matter. I have spent only a few moments with Ygerne, too little time to be confident of anything. I have not questioned Guinevere at all. And let us not forget Wynn, the Druid, and his proximity to each of these deaths."

Merlin squinted at me. "No one saw Wynn near the hall. You just said so yourself."

"No one that we have spoken to yet." If Merlin was to oppose me, I was in serious trouble, and so were Ygerne and

Guinevere. I turned to Arthur. "Remember Eleonore's death? Kay and I questioned nearly everyone that lives along the lanes and those without the castle as well. These matters cannot be understood without a little time.

"I have my, um, other agents to speak with as well."

Arthur understood, and he reached up and tugged at the ends of his mustache. I knew what he was thinking, and that was my advantage. He did not want to believe that Guinevere was responsible for this any more than I did. But the precarious edge I was walking was that Arthur would gladly sacrifice Ygerne to save Guinevere. He was no monster as some lords seemed. He wanted the guilty party to pay. But he had to punish someone. And the longer it took, the more trouble he would have from Aircol, and the more his enemies would try to exploit the situation.

Kay, though renowned for his temper, emerged as the voice of caution. "Rigotamos, we have a more immediate problem. Melwas is defying your order. And by isolating Ynys-witrin he has, essentially, taken up arms against the consilium."

That must have given Merlin an idea. His thick eyebrows arched, and I watched a smile stretch his thin lips. "Kay is right, Arthur. You should call a meeting of the consilium immediately to deal with this."

The old devil! He knew exactly what that would do. It took Guinevere's guilt or innocence out of the game. Everyone would know that Guinevere was at the heart of it, but by classing Melwas's defiance as defiance of the consilium as a whole, it made it very awkward for his enemies to do aught but support him.

Arthur looked at me with a tired smile. I would have at least a little more time to resolve this affair. Glancing to the window, I saw that the sun would soon be poking its head into the sky. "Bedevere!" Arthur barked. "You and Kay alert the consilium that we will meet at my hall when the sun is at its height. Merlin, will you alert Dubricius and Coroticus that we must bury Gwyneira this morning." He turned then to me. "You know what you must do."

I nodded. Sleep would elude me yet another night.

✤

By the time that the sun had truly climbed from its bed, I was somewhat organized and quite nearly sober. Though I feared that my stomach would rebel, I stuffed it full of bread. I was unsure of when I would have a chance to eat.

And I sought out Gareth's men. Or rather they sought me out. "Master, the little medicus simply disappeared," one said, munching on some of the bread I had brought.

"Disappeared?"

"We lost him for a moment when the lords left for the ride," related the one called Dylan, who had helped us at Caer Goch. "He did not go back to his hovel, and he did not leave the fort."

So Morgan could not be counted out quite yet. Very well. "What of the Druid?"

"You will not like it, Master Malgwyn," Dylan cautioned.

"Tell me."

"He left the fort when the lords left and went straight to Lord Mordred's camp. He did not venture out again."

"He did not venture out that you saw," I corrected him. I was not yet ready to absolve Wynn of any guilt. Gareth's men were good, but not infallible.

"What now, Master?"

"Keep an eye on the medicus."

With my belly rumbling, I went to meet the little band allotted to me for this task—Merlin, Illtud, and my young friend Ider, who had served me so well during the dark days of the past rebellion. We were well balanced. Merlin brought maturity and a pragmatic approach, something I was just learning. Illtud added the warrior's mind. Ider offered the voice of innocence that was often indispensable to such quests. I was bedeviled with a need to do the right thing, the just thing.

On my way to Arthur's hall, I met Coroticus, scurrying to the stables for a horse. "I see you have heard," I greeted him.

His gold cross, emblem of his office, swung wildly about his neck as he rushed along the lane, but he stopped at seeing me. "Malgwyn! I knew Melwas was headstrong, but I never dreamed he would do this."

"Has his lust for power swallowed his good sense?"

Coroticus smiled wanly. "He is in love, and that is worse."

Although I had my doubts about the abbot's sincerity, he certainly seemed to be genuinely distressed. Then again, if Melwas had truly sealed off Ynys-witrin, that would reduce the number of rich benefactors coming to see the abbey and filling its coffers.

"You must help me, Malgwyn."

"And what can I do?"

"I propose to let the Church resolve this."

I laughed. I did not mean to, but I did. Arthur might agree to such an arrangement, but if he did it would be seen as a horrible weakness on his part. Arthur was a devoted believer in the Christ. Most of the lords considered themselves such as well, but only a handful like Kay and Bedevere truly believed. A few, like Mordred, leaned more toward the old gods.

"I am serious, Malgwyn."

"Forgive me, Coroticus. I just cannot see the consilium allowing the Church to make decisions for it."

He scowled at me. "In time, you will learn to fear the Church."

"I thought the teachings of the Christ were those of love?"

The grimace on his face grew. "See that you do not get caught in the middle. One day, Malgwyn, you will have to choose who you truly serve."

"Then I have no choice," I told him. "Thank you for allowing Ider to stay behind to help me."

The abbot's features changed then, softened. "Use him well. He is one of the brightest among us. I see a great future for him, if you do not corrupt him." With that, he resumed his journey and I mine.

At the great hall, I found Dubricius donning his robes as several of the lords milled about. He would be presiding over Gwyneira's burial. He saw me and finished adjusting his attire. "Master Malgwyn, a moment?"

I nodded, my eyes narrowing in suspicion. I had great respect for the teachings of the Christ, but some of His sacerdotes and presbyters troubled me, including Dubricius.

"Episcopus?"

He motioned for me to join him to the side, away from the others.

"I have heard of your experiences at resolving these things. I know too that you are completely loyal to Arthur."

"I am completely loyal to the truth, episcopus. More often than not, I have found Arthur's loyalties are the same."

Tugging at his fur-lined collar, he studied me with a cocked eye. "It is in everyone's interests that this dispute be resolved amicably. Even if that means making choices that are contrary to one's desires. No other consideration is as important."

I reached out with my one hand and stopped his continuing fidgeting. "Are you telling me I should allow Ygerne to be killed if that will allow this situation to be settled without bloodshed."

And then I learned why he was an episcopus. Gently but firmly, he removed my hand from his person and looked me straight in the eye. "That is exactly what I am saying. I am pleased that I am not misunderstood."

"No," I said, shaking my head. "You are not misunderstood." Stepping in closer, I bumped against him intentionally and he moved back. "I do not need your advice or approval. If you think I do, then you are mistaken."

"Do not challenge me, Malgwyn!" he rasped, a bit of fear lighting his eyes. "You will find that I am not without influence."

"Then do not tell me how my inquiries should turn out before I have even conducted them. You bury the dead, episcopus. I will find the ones who did it."

Even now, fifty winters later, I can still see the surprise in Dubricius's eyes. He was so accustomed to being deferred to that he had no ready answer for an open act of defiance. Yet he found one.

"Should it come to a stand-off between you and me, Malgwyn, you'll have no trouble recognizing me. I will be the sober one."

At that Aircol entered the feasting hall and Dubricius swept away to join him. The arrow had been well aimed and hurt. I did not crave the mead or cervesas as I once had, but, after the events of two days before, I could not expect anyone to believe that. It had been a costly lapse of judgment.

Young Ider bounded over to me then, with that limitless enthusiasm I had come to associate with him. His newly shaven tonsure made his head seem to poke like a new sprout over his rough brown robes. I had chided him the night before that his tonsure was in sore need of attention. Obviously, he had taken me at my word.

In a few moments, we had been joined by Merlin and Illtud. Merlin and I often saw things differently, and that was one reason that I prized his opinion so. But I could not recall when so much depended on our actions. Ygerne. Guinevere. Our alliance with Aircol, aye, the future of the consilium itself. Certainly the rebellion had been terrible, but something about this lacked the openness of a rebellion. Something rancid flavored the air in this matter, something foul and hidden.

But before I could begin assigning tasks, a grunt and raised eyebrow from Merlin turned me around. Lord David stood behind me with a smile on his face. A handsome man whose face bore few of the wounds of excessive living, David had secretly sided with Lauhiir in the recent war. But when it became obvious that their plans had unraveled, he deftly switched sides and I had been unable to convince Arthur of his complicity.

"Malgwyn? A word?"

David would not want the others to hear what he had to say. We had no secrets from each other; he had told me frankly where he stood during the rebellion because he believed I would be dead before I could tell another. That did not happen.

I stepped away from the others and joined David.

"I do not have to tell you that I will make use of this situation to my own profit."

I nodded. He paused, as if deciding whether or not to continue. "But know this. Aircol's seat on the consilium is worth allowing Arthur to remain as Rigotamos for a spell longer. Others do not see it that clearly."

"Are you saying that you know something of this affair?"

His eyes flitted nervously from me to Merlin to Illtud and back. "I am saying that I have my suspicions, but, in truth, that is all I have."

"Very well. Thank you for your candor."

"Even rivals find moments of cooperation valuable."

"If I have learned anything in Arthur's service it is that few things are clearly defined."

"Then there is hope for you yet," David said with a smile.

"But none for you," I countered, turning away before he could reply.

What did that mean? Was David preparing to betray Morgan, in much the same way he switched sides and betrayed Lauhiir?

"Time is wasting, Malgwyn," Merlin reminded me. I could tell by the urgency in his crackling voice that he was more than worried.

"Illtud, you and Ider talk to everyone that lives along the lane on the eastern side of the hall. If this person did not come through the feasting hall, then they would have to have come in that way."

"You are proceeding as if Ygerne and Guinevere are innocent," Ider said.

"I am proceeding as if we have already spoken to the servants, who were in the best position to see who entered from the feasting hall. We know that Ygerne and Guinevere had been there; now let us see who else might have been there."

"And what will you and Merlin do?" Illtud asked.

I paused for a moment, glancing at David, across the room

now. He caught my eye and smiled. "Merlin and I will question the guards on each of the gates and see if we had visitors from outside last night. Then we will attend the meeting of the consilium. There is something more here, but I do not know yet whether it is important or not." Breaking from my reverie, I jerked my chin up. "Go and see what you can learn."

They disappeared from the hall just as I felt a dagger point in my back, rather low down on my back, and a familiar voice rasped in a low whisper, "I will kill you where you stand."

CHAPTER NINETEEN

❦

"WHy, Master Vortipor," I said, turning slowly around. "You have me at the disadvantage." My tone was jovial, but the dagger point was most serious, as was the pressure with which he pushed it against my back.

"Fine," the little lord said with a gleam in his eye. "I shall gut you like a pig," he continued, switching the blade to my belly. "You were charged with protecting my sister and you failed. For that failure only one punishment will do. And your daughter dishonored me."

And then his dagger went flying through the air, clattering against one of the beams in the ceiling before falling to the earthen floor. "And only one punishment will do for you!" Aircol shouted, swatting the little boy's behind. "Now, go and mourn your sister's death and terrorize your betters no more."

Vortipor puffed his lower lip out and slinked off, brooding.

"Forgive him, Malgwyn. I have done a poor job with him. He has learned not how to use power and station wisely, but how to use them to torment people."

"He is young, my lord. All youngsters are cruel at such an age."

"As you say, Malgwyn." He paused and took a tentative step toward me. "I wanted to apologize to you for my words last night."

With the wave of my one hand, I silenced him. "They were the words of a father distraught over his daughter's death. I would have done no differently if it had been Mariam lying there."

Behind his flowing white beard, I saw his expression grow grim. "Lords have long been criticized for their brutality, Malgwyn. Patrick, the old episcopus to the Scotti, enraged Ceredig with that letter of his, but he was right. You cannot remember the Roman days, nor really can I. But I remember my father telling me that law and justice were the first casualties. Those with wealth and power used them viciously. I do not want to strike out blindly. I want only the guilty to pay. The Christ teaches mercy. So I shall be merciful. What I must know is whether or not I can trust you to find who is truly guilty."

"You can trust me," I answered, "to do my best. That is all I can promise."

"What drives you, Malgwyn?" he asked, shaking his head. "What makes you search for the truth of these things so passionately?"

"Should we not always wish for the truth, my lord?"

"Wishing and achieving are often two different things. You have a knack, I am told, for achievement." At that, he turned away as four of the servi carried Gwyneira's body into the feasting hall. Wrapped in a white shroud, she was to be buried in the same ground that held my Gwyneth and my brother, Cuneglas. I had thought that he would wish to take her back to Caer Goch, but he said no. "For however short a time, this was her home; these were her people. She should rest among them."

Later, perhaps, when time had passed and the present situation was resolved, Arthur would likely build a more impressive tomb for her and her remains would be translated there. But for that day to arrive, much had to be done.

Arthur had sent three troop of horse to cover the three approaches to Ynys-witrin: the southern road to the old Roman bridge at Pomparles, the northern lane leading from the Roman town of Fontanetum, and the eastern passage, a massive bank and ditch entrance commissioned by Melwas and just recently completed. I knew that dispatching the troops would heighten tensions, but I knew also that Arthur had little choice. Whatever his motivations, Melwas had challenged Arthur, and the Rigotamos could not be seen to shrink.

Merlin and I stepped out into the market square, into a beehive was more to the point. In all my years, I had never seen such activity, such scurrying about. The cobbled lanes reverberated with the clatter of hooves, matched only by the jingle of mail shirts, swords, and the creaking of leather.

"Merlin, would you wait for me here. I have a visit to make."

His old eyes crinkled into a smile. "Of course."

Threading through the throngs of people, I made my way to Ygerne's house. My Mariam was playing in the lane with the other children as Owain stood a silent but careful watch, leaning against a wall with the air of a much older boy. She turned and saw me approach and dashed toward me, her blond hair flying behind. "Father!"

I knelt and wrapped my arm about her. "I am sorry to have been away for so long."

Her cheeks were red from play. "I am sorry about the new queen, Father."

"I know. I am too."

She pulled back a bit and put on her most stern face. "Mother did not do this. You must release her."

"Soon, little one. Soon. Until then, Owain will keep you safe. Isn't that right, boy?"

He bounced off the wall he had leaned against. "Yes, Master Malgwyn. Though they complain about my cooking."

I laughed and it felt good. "I will have Cerdic send over a girl to cook until this affair is resolved. Take care of these babes, Owain, or you will answer to me."

Rubbing Mariam's blond hair gently, I reluctantly turned away and headed back toward the hall.

※

"Malgwyn!" The voice had almost a warmth in it, which was more than unusual as it belonged to Mordred. Merlin sneered, but I was curious.

"Mordred. And how are you today?"

He moved close and took my arm in his hand impatiently. "No matter what you might hear, Malgwyn," he whispered, "I had nothing to do with this matter."

"You say that as if you know who did."

He did not speak, but his eyes told me much.

"Mordred, you and I are not friends, and I suspect we never will be. But perhaps you will answer one question for me."

Brushing one of his braids from his face, he raised his eyebrows. "Perhaps."

"Why is it that so many people seem to understand this far better than I, yet no one wishes to tell me anything?"

He smiled then, with those perfect white teeth of his. I often wondered how he kept them until once I saw him cleaning them with the end of a broken stick, the wood fibers frayed. "By joining the consilium, Aircol immediately became one of its most powerful members. No one is demented enough to want to admit knowledge of his daughter's death, especially not to you. But that does not mean that they do not have such knowledge."

"And why should they be threatened by me? I am no lord of the consilium."

At that, Mordred threw his head back and laughed. "No," he agreed. "You are not. But you could have been. And you rejected it. No one knows quite what to make of you. You seem to desire no power, but look at yourself now. You have great power, and it has flowed to you not because of the lands you hold or your wealth. Nor do you profess to be a believer in the Christ, even if just for the advantages that such a declaration can bring you. Those advantages are the things that lords understand. You, they do not understand. And they do not trust what they cannot understand."

I was amused by his recital. "And you, Mordred? Do you understand me?"

He smiled in a way that chilled me. "Oh, yes, Malgwyn. I understand you, just as you understand me. That is why a day will come when you and I will have to bring an end to our enmity. And when I have dispatched you, I will celebrate your feats and curse the decaying mind that brought you to such a tragic end."

Then it was my time to laugh. "You are better than one of Merlin's tonics, Mordred."

He nodded and wandered off. Our laughter confused poor

Merlin, who could only see two sworn enemies smiling and amiably chatting with one another.

"Come, Merlin. Let us go study Arthur's chamber once more. Perhaps with her body removed something more will reveal itself."

We searched the walls and the two entry doors. We searched the bedding. No signs of anyone forcing the doors. No signs of a hidden entrance, not that I expected to find one. Our structures were simple ones, of timber and wattle. Even the great stone roundhouses in which many of the old folk still lived had few surprises.

"Malgwyn," Merlin said finally. "There is no answer here. Whoever did this thing left nothing more for us to find."

I felt the heat rise in my neck, and I slammed my fist into the wall. "Then where are the answers, Merlin! Where?"

My old friend threw his arms in the air. "I do not know, Malgwyn. We may have no other possibilities than Guinevere and Ygerne."

I raised my one hand. "No, Ygerne said they did not do it and I believe them."

"People lie. You know this. Do you believe them because your head or your heart tells you so?"

Looking back at him, I felt a tired smile stretch my face. "Both, I suppose."

"People also make mistakes, Malgwyn. You and I know that better than most."

Something in his tone of voice was out of order, out of character. "Merlin, the world knows about my mistakes. But what mistakes have you made?"

He waved the question off with a tired hand. "Perhaps later, when we have weaved our way clear of this affair."

When Merlin did not want to speak of something, he did not speak. I did the only thing I could and gestured to the door. Time to seek Ider and Illtud.

❖

We found the pair in the lanes northeast of Arthur's hall, staring down at something near a house. Ider had just taken a step in our direction when he looked up and saw us approaching.

"Malgwyn, hurry!"

I hastened forward, but Merlin, as was his way, never broke stride nor quickened his pace. As I neared, Illtud reached down and plucked something from the ground, thrusting it at me. In the morning light, the black encrustation did not sparkle, looked dull despite its sharp edges. They had found our murderer's torture tool, lying not five feet from the lane leading out the northeast gate.

Ider cocked his head to the side. "Why would it be discarded here? Were the culprit Ygerne, it would have made more sense to drop it between the hall and her house."

"And were it Guinevere, this would be right along her path out of the fort and to Ynys-witrin," Illtud pointed out.

But I shook my head as I studied what was, really, just an ordinary stick of firewood, the sort cut for Arthur's hall and a hundred other houses. "Whoever killed Gwyneira would have had blood splattered all about them. Had Ygerne seen Guinevere in such a state, she would not be so certain of her innocence."

"She was certain enough that you would stake their lives on it?" Merlin had caught up with us.

"I believe so. And according to her story, Guinevere came straight to her house after leaving the hall. Surely if she had had this thing with her, she couldn't have hidden it from Ygerne."

Illtud frowned. "Could she not have started toward Ynys-witrin and then panicked, dropping it here and turning back to Ygerne's?"

He made sense, though I hated to admit it. Merlin looked at me with a sad smile while Ider stood there expectantly, waiting I am sure for a clever reply by me that would absolve Guinevere of all guilt.

"Yes, old friend, she could have. This does not proclaim either woman's innocence, nor does it prove their guilt." Even as I said it, Ider's shoulders drooped. "Have you found anyone that saw anything?"

Illtud shook his head. "No, the people here in the back lanes saw nothing. Those who live closer to Arthur's hall saw only the servants, soldiers, and lords. It was a hectic night for all, Malgwyn. What will we do now?"

"Go and speak with the guards on the gates from last night. I will go to the barracks and speak to the Druid."

"Think you still that the Druid had a hand in this?"

"I refuse to speculate. Gwyneira's death came as such a shock to me. After all the deaths on the road." I stopped and shook my head. "The lords will be back soon from the bury-ing, and I need to have questioned the Druid by then. You two go about your chores and we shall ours. We will meet back at the feasting hall in time for the consilium's gathering."

"As you say," Illtud said and then jerked his head, motion-ing young Ider to follow him.

Illtud and Ider stalked off for the northeast gate as Merlin and I turned our feet toward the barracks.

I studied the piece of wood once more, without the others watching over me. I saw nothing new save the blood-encrusted end. It had been freshly cut, the axe bites at the opposite end exposing the white meat of the wood, untarnished by the elements. I wondered if the axe that cut the wood could be identified from the marks it left. Perhaps. But then I would only know from which wood pile it came, not who wielded it against Gwyneira. And to track it down would take more time than I had.

"Something, Malgwyn?" Merlin asked.

I shook my head. "Just a thought. Let us go and see the Druid."

⁂

Wynn threw us a foul look as we entered. Merlin chuckled. The guards had tied the Druid's hands, raised above his head, to the same post that had held Merlin when he stood accused of killing young Eleonore. Druids had shown their faces then as well, but they emerged innocent in that affair, at least the true ones did. I thought Wynn many things, but innocent was not one.

"Is this your idea of hospitality?" Wynn's voice cracked. I guessed that he had been left without water. Merlin looked to me and I nodded. He shuffled over to the post and untied Wynn's hands. I took a water gourd from a table and tossed it to the Druid, who caught it awkwardly as he tried to rub the pain from his wrists.

"Do not think for even an instant that I have any sympathy for you," I told him coldly. "You wish for nothing more than Arthur's downfall and that because his beliefs do not match yours. The killing at the White Mount, the one at Caer Goch, and that on the journey back were all within your ability, and I believe you committed them simply to prove that your 'curse' on Arthur was real."

Wynn seemed less intimidating in that barracks room, his robes torn and dirtied, a bloody cut at the corner of his eye. Mordred may have given him up willingly, but it seemed that Wynn had not gone willingly. "You may believe what you wish," he said finally, after downing a healthy swallow of water. "That does not make it true. I tell you once again that I did not kill those girls."

"But you do not deny killing Gwyneira?"

He narrowed his eyes. "And how could I do that, Master Malgwyn, when you forbade me entry?"

"Yet you found your way in after the marriage itself. As we speak, every guard, every soldier, every man or woman who was here is being questioned. If you were anywhere near Gwyneira, I will know by nightfall. And you will be dead by morning."

Wynn looked at me with a smile both on his lips and in his eyes. "By morning, Malgwyn, you will have discovered that I was not in the town and the consilium will be poised to assault Melwas at Ynys-witrin. When that happens, I doubt that you will be concerned with a simple Druid priest. Besides, your reputation has spread far and wide. You wish only the guilty to be punished, and without proof, you will not punish the innocent. You are known for your sense of justice and truth."

"I am known too for my fondness of mead, but here I stand before you, sober and serious. Do not believe all that you hear, Wynn. It would not be wise. Where were you last night, after we departed for the ride?"

"I was in Mordred's camp."

"Even until we returned?"

Wynn nodded, pausing only long enough to take another swig from the water gourd. "Even then. I had no place else to be. Indeed I was even then preparing for my next trip."

"To where?"

The Druid smiled, and I got the feeling that he was enjoying this. "Away from here. Malgwyn, I did not kill those girls nor the Lady Gwyneira either. You may try all you wish, but you will never be able to prove that I did these things because I did not."

He said this with such confidence that another thought struck me.

"But you know who did." I said it flatly, without the hint of a question.

At that, the Druid smoothed his robes and smiled once again. "Even if I do, I am under no obligation to tell you."

To Merlin's horror, I nodded as if in agreement. "That is true, Wynn. And I am under no obligation to release you. And I have no intention of doing that."

"You cannot hold me hostage!" Wynn's eyes grew wide and I enjoyed that.

"I can and I will. Even during the Roman days, Druid, authority came with much power. It is even more so now, though Arthur wishes for only fairness and equity. I am his official iudex pedaneous, his investigator, and Aircol's as well. As long as I think you may hold answers, I will hold you. Besides, as long as you're tied to a post in here, you can do little mischief out there."

With Merlin on my heels, I pivoted quickly and left, the whining of the Druid as music in my ears.

"We have no choice but to lay siege to Ynys-witrin and take the woman Guinevere and Lord Melwas!" Celyn was a bloodthirsty little lord. From the look on Arthur's face, I could tell that he was not impressed with Celyn's reference to Guinevere as "the woman." Nor was I. In that one simple sentence, Celyn had laid bare our charade.

The lords were seated around the great round table in the center of Arthur's feasting hall. Only a handful of members were absent, and those the ones that had not attended the marriage. Where they chose to sit said much about their allegiances. Near unto Arthur, on either side, were Kay, Bedevere, Ambrosius, Gawain, and, surprisingly, Tristan. Opposite were David, Mordred, Gaheris, and Celyn son of Caw. The chairs on either side of Aircol were empty. Merlin and I sat apart from the table so that we might see everyone.

"How might we best proceed?" Aircol asked, ignoring Celyn's pronouncement. He was maintaining his temper and this was good.

"Both Lord Arthur and Lord Aircol have the right to seek retribution for this deed," Bedevere began. "But do we truly know that Guinevere played a part? Should not that question be answered before we begin a war?"

It was a fair question, and one that neither Arthur nor I were particularly happy to answer. Bedevere thought he was helping, but in reality, I would much rather have talked about Melwas's misdeeds than Guinevere's. But too many people knew some if not all of what had transpired. Merely the rumors were enough to force me to give an accurate accounting, something I felt compelled to do anyway but wished to delay as long as I could. One thing that I knew: Once the decision had been made to attack Melwas, Guinevere's guilt would be assumed and with that probably Ygerne's as well.

And with Ygerne in our custody, Arthur would push for her immediate execution and then use that to press for negotiations with Melwas, praying for time to let tempers calm.

"Malgwyn?" Ambrosius prodded.

I ransacked my brain for some way to avoid discussion of the murder. But I saw none. "This is far too soon for me to report any results." My retort was weak. "Let us make this first about Melwas's disobedience. When we have resolved that, we can turn to the issue of Gwyneira's death."

"You are much too clever a man for such a poor sally," said Mordred, reveling in my discomfiture. "Were it not for Gwyneira's death, there would be no reason for any of this. Now, delay no more!"

I had lied before. Everyone lies. But I had tried to confine my lies to the unimportant and the necessary. And Gwyneira's death could hardly be classed as unimportant. "Very well. My investigation has uncovered few things for certain," I began, but the quick grumble that erupted around the table told me to stop all pretense. "After the lords and their men went off on the ride, only two people were seen entering Gwyneira's chamber—Ygerne and Guinevere. We are holding Ygerne at the barracks, but she refuses to say anything." She had actually told me much, but I had promised not to reveal any of it. I knew Ygerne well enough to know that breaking her confidence could cost me much pain. "Guinevere is, of course, with Melwas and thus I have had no chance to question her."

"And the Druid?" David entered the fray, but I sensed something odd in his tone, a gesture of, of, kindness, support? I was uncertain, but it was unexpected.

"We are holding him at the barracks as well, but he has given little useful information."

"Was he seen inside the fortress?" This from Arthur, looking now for any hook on which to hang his hopes.

"None of the guards at the gates, none of the servants, no one we have questioned as yet saw him." And then Lord David truly puzzled me, for he seemed saddened by this news.

"Then, it is decided!" declaimed Celyn, who was quickly becoming more than an aggravation. "We demand that Melwas hand her over or we assault his fortress!"

"A moment, Lord Celyn. Are we a land that believes in justice, or are we to forget that which sets us apart from the Saxons?" I had never seen Arthur speak more forcefully or certainly. It saddened me though to know why he was so passionate in his defense of justice. And it saddened me that I approved wholeheartedly of his tactics.

"I have not yet finished my inquiries either, Rigotamos. These things are not immediately resolved." The plaintiveness of my request was not lost on either Aircol or Ambrosius. And it was Ambrosius who finally spoke up.

"This is a matter that should not be decided either too hastily or with too much delay. And, if we are to attack Melwas and remove him from the tor, we need more soldiers than we have. It is a formidable place to assault with even twice the men we have."

"And Melwas has now built a fortification on the high ground to the east," Mordred pointed out. In the wettest weather, there were only three approaches to Ynys-witrin and hence the tor.

From the south across the bridge near the old Roman shrine or from the east via a narrow neck of land.

Ambrosius frowned. "If I speed a rider at once, I can have another hundred men here by morning." He stopped and remembered his place, turning to Arthur. "Rigotamos, I suggest that we give Malgwyn two further days to complete his investigations. In the meantime, we can well use the time to strengthen our forces, and, perhaps, negotiate a better solution to this."

I could fair see the flames burst forth from Celyn's nose as he pawed the ground like an angry stallion, but a hand on his shoulder from Mordred held him in check.

Deadlines.

I hated deadlines.

And then Illtud spoke and made it worse.

"I am a peaceful man, my lord Rigotamos," he began, at which Celyn snickered until Gawain cuffed him on the back of the head. "But I have seen enough of life to know that cruel times often require cruel actions. Charity is an aspect of the Christ, but one abused in a king. One thing that I have learned from my friend Malgwyn is that justice and mercy are often in opposition," Illtud said. "If you wish to spark Melwas to action, you must raise the stakes. He knows that a siege of the tor will take many weeks. The one person that Melwas will listen to is Guinevere. We must appeal to her as much as Melwas, play on her emotions."

I could not see exactly where Illtud was going, but my stomach began a rumbling.

Arthur began tugging his mustache and spinning the end between his fingers, never a good sign.

"What is it you are suggesting, Illtud?" Ambrosius asked.

"If we couple the deadline given to Malgwyn with an act designed to make Guinevere come forward on her own."

"And what would that be?" I was beginning to see his direction and I liked it not.

"Malgwyn, you have questioned Ygerne and you have questioned all of the servants. They say that only she and Guinevere entered the girl's chamber. Ygerne admits such and will not publicly deny her involvement. Indeed she chastised the Rigotamos for entering into a marriage with Gwyneira. I know that she is your woman, Malgwyn, but even you cannot deny that these facts weigh heavily against her."

I did not need Illtud to point that out to me. I could strangle Ygerne for her stubbornness. And I could strangle Illtud for turning my own methods against me. "Your point?"

"We all know that Ygerne and Guinevere are close; Guinevere, after all, is your cousin. Perhaps if we send word to Melwas that we intend to attack in two days and to underscore our resolve that we will behead Ygerne as Guinevere's conspirator, perhaps that will spur action by Guinevere."

"And should it not spur action?"

Ambrosius laid a hand on my shoulder. "Malgwyn, no one knows more than I of your sacrifices. And certainly no one is more grateful for your service. But you know as well as I that no impartial iudex would be able to ignore such evidence. Especially when Ygerne refuses to defend herself."

"Does that not speak of guilt to you?" Aircol asked. We were straining his good will. That I could tell.

"I think it speaks of stubbornness more, my lord. But I take your meaning. So, if it does not spur the action desired?" I asked Arthur.

"Then, Malgwyn, we shall have to behead Ygerne and assault Melwas." In his defense, he said it softly and without any pleasure.

"And?" I could not let it rest.

Arthur waited a long second before answering, his eyes never leaving mine. When he spoke, it was firm and decisive. "And Guinevere must lose her head to the sword as well."

❖

No one could mistake the import of this, least of all Aircol. The old man looked at Arthur with a gleam of respect, but said nothing, merely nodded. Even David and Mordred seemed surprised. They exchanged sudden, quick glances.

"Who among you has troops close enough to be summoned?" The Rigotamos had become the general once more.

Three of the lords spoke up, swiftly dispatching riders as they did so. Arthur turned to Kay. "Speed a rider to our eastern garrison. Fetch two troop of horse. With any luck, they will be here tomorrow morning. Mordred!"

"Yes, my lord." For once Arthur's cantankerous cousin offered no snide comments.

"Take command of the troops we have already here. Establish a camp at the old Roman shrine to the south of Ynyswitrin and await my arrival."

"At your command, my lord," and Mordred scampered off, shouting orders left and right.

Arthur stopped and looked at those of us left. "My Lord Aircol, I assume you will wish to commit your troops to this matter?"

With a nod and a grim smile that only highlighted his wrinkles, Aircol agreed.

"Then take them and join Mordred."

"And you?"

Arthur glanced about quickly. "I will follow shortly, as soon as I have made further dispositions and made arrangements for our supplies."

Gwyneira's father found his mount and departed. Arthur gathered Bedevere, me, Illtud and Merlin away from the now frenzy-filled room. "Bedevere, I trust you and Illtud only with this. Go to the defenses Melwas has constructed to the east. Take two of my troops. Do not allow yourself to be seen. I do not want Melwas to know you are there."

Merlin nodded, his long gray locks dipping with each bounce of his head. "You do not wish him to feel trapped, yet."

The Rigotamos smiled. "I wish there to appear that there is an escape route. But I want it closely watched. One of the others might be bribed to let Melwas flee, but you two will not."

He turned to Merlin. "I want you with me to give me counsel, and you have established a stronger rapport with Aircol than I."

Though I had not noticed him until then, Morgan popped up before Arthur. The Rigotamos tapped him on the shoulder. "Organize all the servi save those attached to my kitchen. Prepare the wagons with supplies to treat the wounded if we attack. Then bring them on to the old Roman shrine."

Morgan's eyes held a question.

"Any of the servi can show you where it is. Now, be off!"

And the medicus scampered out. For a moment, I considered again whether he could have done these things. Appearances said no. But appearances sometimes lied.

"And what about me, Arthur?" I was afraid that I already knew the answer.

He cut his eyes around at me in that manner of his, that

THE BELOVED DEAD / 301

manner that said I had better listen and take heed. "You know what your task is."

"I am to find who truly killed these girls, and you have given me two days. How generous, my lord!" The bitterness on my tongue was unmistakable. "And if I cannot?"

"You are to find who truly killed Gwyneira. If that is the same person as he who killed those girls, all the better. My bride has been foully murdered, Malgwyn. Her death is the only one of concern right now. You saw the consilium, Malgwyn. They wish this alliance with Aircol as we all do, but they also smell a chance here to undercut me, and they will exploit it to the fullest. Unless you can find a different answer, or unless Ygerne and Guinevere surrender and defend themselves. Otherwise, I will be forced to execute them both."

"But if anyone has to be executed, you would prefer that it be Ygerne."

He narrowed his eyes. "Just as you would prefer it be Guinevere."

"Do not pretend you know what I want, Rigotamos. I will find the truth, no matter how painful it is."

Arthur's eyes softened then. "Malgwyn, you and I are already suspect in this. If we do anything that can be seen to favor the killer of Gwyneira, everything we have worked for will be lost." He stopped then, his eyes softening. "This affair can end several different ways, Malgwyn, most of them badly. For it to end well, that, old friend, will be up to you. This time, if you fail, it will not be your own head, or even Merlin's on the block, but Ygerne's and Guinevere's. And I fear the consilium will fall apart and drag our people into chaos once more. You have until the sun reaches its height two days hence."

And with his chestnut hair, tangled and damp with sweat,

drooping behind him, he spun and strode from the hall, leaving me alone, staring at the walls and wondering where to
begin.

In all of my life, both before and after, I had never felt such
a weight on me. Guinevere, my cousin and childhood
playmate—Ygerne, who had emerged from the carnage of revolt as the love and stanchion of my life. I hungered for the
truth of these killings, but I cringed inside at the thought that
it might be named Guinevere or Ygerne. I prayed to the old
gods; I prayed to Arthur's God. And then I set about my task.

PART FOUR

ꟿNYS-WITRIN

CHAPTER TWENTY

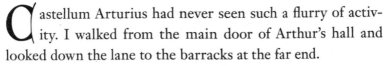

Castellum Arturius had never seen such a flurry of activity. I walked from the main door of Arthur's hall and looked down the lane to the barracks at the far end.

Chaos would have seemed organized.

Soldiers raced about, like ants fleeing from a destroyed hill.

Cerdic's raspy voice rose above the cacophony of chirping, shouting oaths, orders and curses at Talorc and the other servi as they loaded the wagons.

And mothers herded their children into their houses, away from the clambering hooves of horses and soldiers.

Children!

I had completely forgotten about Mariam, Owain, and the others. Spinning around, I near fell to the ground. Striding with careful, measured steps toward Arthur's hall was Owain, dragging a sword behind him.

"Owain! No!"

With eyes narrowed, he pulled the sword in front of him and clumsily raised it. "You will not stop me, Malgwyn! The Rigotamos intends to kill Mother Ygerne. I will not let him!"

Word had indeed spread quickly. I ran to him, snatched

the sword away with my one hand, and pushed him to the side with my stump. "This is not the way, Owain!"

Out of the flow of people, I knelt beside him and tried to hug him, but he pulled back, as firm a set to his jaw as I had seen on any grown man. "No! They murdered my mother! I will not lose Mother Ygerne too!"

I reached out and took him by the neck. "And you think I wish to lose Ygerne? Come to your senses, boy. The other soldiers will stop you before you get close, and they will not even allow you the honor of dying for your cause."

He dropped his head at that and took on the look of the little boy he really was. I did not wish to disgrace him or make little of his intent. He was honorable, but reality was necessary, though bitter its draught.

"Believe me, Owain," I said, as earnestly as I could. "I will do everything in my power to keep Ygerne safe. But you have to understand that she brings much of this on herself."

Owain shook his head. "No."

"Yes. She refuses to speak of what happened that night. She refuses to deny that she had something to do with the Lady Gwyneira's death." And publicly that was true. In privacy she had told some things, but I promised to hold her words close and not share them with anyone.

"But why?"

"She thinks that remaining silent will also protect Guinevere."

"And will it?"

"I do not believe so. Owain, Arthur has given me two days to find an answer to all of this. I need you now more than ever. You have proven your bravery by protecting Mariam from Vortipor. You must watch over Mariam and the other children now while I sort through this affair. If Ygerne and Guinevere are to be spared the sword, I cannot worry about the children's welfare. That is your responsibility."

The tears disappeared from his eyes as if by magic. "What must I do?" The gods bless the boy! No hesitation. No question.

"Keep them safe and fed. Do not let them into the lanes when it is like this. Guard them with your very life. I am depending on you, boy!"

He said nothing, but the firm set to his jaw and the severity of his look affirmed his understanding as clearly as any words scratched on parchment.

"Good. Now, take your sword." I stopped. "Where did you get it?"

Owain screwed one side of his face up in guilt. "It is Kay's extra."

When this was over, I had to talk to Merlin about the lessons he was teaching this boy.

"Well, go back home and see to the children."

As I watched, he turned and headed back to Ygerne's with purpose and confidence in his step. I wished that I could feel the same.

Watching Owain's retreating back, I suddenly realized that Arthur had left me with no one to help. But then, out of the corner of my eye, I saw a solitary figure loitering about the door to the feasting hall, looking lost.

"Ider!"

The lone figure turned quickly at my call.

I was not certain how to read the expression on his face.

Though he had seen much during the rebellion, Ider was still very naïve. But, the young monachus looked, well, excited, an emotion alien to most brothers of the Christ that I knew. And he was just what I needed.

As soon as he saw me, he dashed across the market square, his monachus garb flapping about him. "Malgwyn!" In his haste, he stumbled on a stone and nearly fell on top of me.

"What . . . is . . . happening?" The words came out in a staccato rhythm as Ider rushed to catch his wind.

I explained the situation to Ider as best I could. "Melwas refuses to hand over Guinevere, thus defying the consilium. Arthur has ordered all available troops to be gathered at the old Roman shrine near the River Brue. He is giving Melwas two days to hand over Guinevere or face an assault."

"And the consilium supports this?"

I nodded. "Ygerne is already being held. She refuses to speak about Gwyneira's death. She even refuses to deny that she had a part in it. As a way to force either Guinevere to surrender or Ygerne to speak, Arthur has ordered that Ygerne be killed on the bridge should our demands not be met two days hence."

"And your orders?"

"Why, to sort out the entire matter in two days," I answered, the sarcasm unhidden.

Then my young monachus friend pursed his lips and stared at the sky. "You will need my help, of course," he said with a certainty that made me laugh. But as I stared at his reddened face and carefully tonsured head, I realized that I did indeed need his help, that his help might be crucial.

I grabbed his arm with my hand and steered him toward

my house. "Come, Ider. I need to change clothes and you need to help me."

✦

"Malgwyn, this is dangerous!" Ider was horrified as my plan took shape. "And a blasphemy!" he added, even as he straightened my robes.

I ran my hand over my now expertly shaven tonsure and clean-shaven face. "Ider, do you believe in a God of mercy?"

He nodded.

"I do as well. And this is a mission of mercy."

Ider frowned. "I am not stupid, Malgwyn. You are dressing as a monachus to slip past Melwas's defenses and gather information for Lord Arthur."

"Young friend, you think me too much Arthur's errand boy. Although, if Arthur had thought of that, he would have ordered it. I do this not for Arthur, but to discover the truth." I stopped. My answer surprised even myself, even as I realized that I was correct. A voice in my head told me that if I discovered the truth of Gwyneira's death that I would learn who killed those other girls, the one's unworthy of Arthur's notice, but who were beloved by their families and were now dead. "But you are right. I do wish to get inside the abbey.

"You are a bright and curious man, Ider. Do you remember during the rebellion last year?"

"Of course."

"Do you remember that despite all of our patrols, Lauhiir got inside the abbey and so declared sanctuary?"

Ider's head dropped. I had guessed correctly.

"Oh, my young friend. You've been keeping secrets from me."

His face popped up, red. "No, Malgwyn! I only learned of the tunnels later!"

Properly attired as one of the monachi, I patted him on the shoulder. "I know. I figured that one as young and curious as you would know all such secrets of the abbey. But what I need now is for you to guide me to one of the entrances. Where are they?"

The young monachus hesitated, turning away. "Malgwyn, I promised the abbot that I would never reveal that."

"Ider, I will not tell Coroticus of your help. And if he should find out, I will not allow him to harm you in any way."

At that, Ider looked completely incredulous. "How can you stop him? He is the abbot!"

I simply smiled. "I know, but he and I have an understanding. Now, stop this nonsense and tell me!"

Ider drew back, and I was immediately ashamed. He had done nothing to earn my reproach.

"Please, Ider. It is important or I would not ask it of you."

That soothed him somewhat, and his shoulders slumped a bit. "There is one, in the village, below the abbey."

"Is that the one that comes out near the old well? At the corner of the vetustam ecclesia?"

"Yes. That's how I found it. It is cleverly concealed inside the vetustam, in that corner that lies nearest the old well."

"But I've been in the vetustam many times, and I have never seen any such entrance!"

And now it was Ider's turn to smile at me. "Have you not seen the large chest in the southeast corner?"

"The big one? The one that they say holds the relics of Joseph the Arimathean?"

"Aye. That chest is never moved. But soon after the rebellion,

I was in the vetustam and noticed that the dirt had been disturbed. I moved it and beneath was the entrance to the tunnel."

"And you told Coroticus?"

"Yes, and he ordered me to forget about it, and he threatened me with expulsion from the community if I ever betrayed its existence."

"But you did not forget about it." I already knew the answer so there was no use to make it a question.

He smiled sheepishly. "I needed to know where it went. I followed it until it emerged near both the old Roman wharf and the small community of believers." I knew where he meant. Out on the lower western slope of Wirral Hill, a newer group of sisters had gathered and built a chapel. They were more like the hermits of old than the new breed of monachi spreading across the land.

But the location made sense for an entrance to a secret route. It lay far down the slope from the village, and it would be sheltered from most eyes.

I clapped my young friend on the shoulder. "You once told me that you desire to be like me in sorting out these matters. I think you are well on your way."

With the sun at meridian height, Ider and I, now arrayed as monachi with hoods about our heads, mounted horses and threaded between the now constant stream of soldiers and wagons. Though rain had not been a recent visitor, the ground was moist, and the hooves of a hundred horses had turned the Via Arturius into one long, muddy track.

So intent were the soldiers on their tasks that none gave us a second look. The bulky robes of the monachi allowed me to hide the fact of my missing arm quite well. Aye, Mordred passed within ten feet of me yet never raised an eyebrow. But then Mordred probably had never envisioned me as a monachus. He knew me all too well and I him.

"What will you do once you are inside Melwas's defenses?" Ider asked as we neared the old Roman bridge at the southern end of Wirral Hill across the River Brue.

"We will do what has to be done. You will make certain that Coroticus does not know that I have slipped into his lair, and I shall find Guinevere and talk some sense into her."

"If your mission is peaceful, why would Coroticus not welcome it?" I prayed that Ider would one day cease being so innocent.

"If I am successful, then this affair might be resolved without violence. Coroticus and Dubricius would rather the Church accomplish that than me."

"But surely they would not hinder you?"

At that his naïveté simply became too much for me. I stopped and took his shoulder in my one hand. "Ider, you are a good and decent man, but your superiors cannot lay claim to the same title! They do whatever it takes to better their own positions, not because it is the right thing to do! Right has little to do with it!"

"They are men of the Christ!" Ider's face had grown red in anger.

"They are men! And men will seek that which profits them most!"

He hung his head. "You must think me a child."

"No, Ider. I think you an earnest young man who has been sheltered from the world a bit too much. Do not worry. Stay with me a while longer and you will make up for that."

At that, Ider smiled, the hurt fleeing from his face. "Of that, I have no doubt."

"Good," I answered. "Now let us thread our way through this mass of humanity."

⊹

As we approached the old Roman bridge at the River Brue, we paused to take stock of the situation. On the far side of the bridge, I could see Melwas's soldiers gathering. They had constructed no blockade as yet, but I could just make out a pile of hastily cut logs lying to the side of the road. And two of them were casually inspecting those seeking to cross the bridge.

"Look, Malgwyn!" Ider pointed at the soldiers. "They search only the people, not the monachi."

He was right. Even from a distance, I could see the guards waving robed and hooded monachi through without so much as a cursory glance.

"Melwas dares not offend Coroticus or Dubricius." I paused and shook my head. "I still do not understand why Melwas courts disaster over Guinevere. He must know that Arthur will have no choice but to attack if he continues to defy the consilium!"

"Perhaps," Ider ventured, "he loves her."

The look I gave him left nothing to be sorted out.

But the young monachus squared his shoulders. "If that were Gwyneth threatened with a beheading, would you not face a thousand men alone to protect her? Are you not now taking a grave risk to clear both Ygerne's and Guinevere's names? Would you not defy Arthur?"

The boy was becoming irritating, but he was not wrong. Still he did not understand all of it, about the girls at the White Mount and Caer Goch, of the girl along the road back, of

Gwyneira and my promise to her. But I chose to ignore him. This was not the time to explain.

"You are well known to Melwas's men?"

Ider shrugged. "They have seen me."

"Then we shall walk straight through with our hoods up. As we pass them, nod and show your face, but do not speak. They will assume we are both brothers of the abbey."

"And then?"

"And then you will show me where to enter the tunnel and you will continue on to the abbey alone."

Uncertainty flashed in his eyes once again. "Why?"

"I have told you. Coroticus must be distracted."

"Malgwyn, I am a brother of the Christ! I should return to my duties."

"Ider, look around you. The soldiers of the consilium are gathering to lay siege to the great tor. Your own superiors are frantically searching for a solution that does not involve violence. Moments ago, you were ready to ride into Hell with me. What has changed?"

Ider turned away. "This is different than the rebellion. That was easy to understand. Lauhiir had rebelled against Arthur. But this, this is different. Melwas has not yet taken arms against the consilium. All he seems to be doing is protecting Guinevere from these accusations."

" 'Seems to be,' " I repeated. "We have no idea exactly why Melwas has chosen this path. But you are correct. Men will do many things for the love of a woman.

"Trust me on this, Ider. We can avert a great disaster here. But only if we act now. I need you, my friend. Never before have I needed your help so much. Do not think otherwise!"

Still, I saw hesitation in his eyes. I drew him over to the side of the road, to a fallen log. "Sit."

"Ider, do you really believe that either Guinevere or Ygerne did this thing?"

He shook his head quickly. "No. Not the women I know. But Arthur rejected Guinevere. Could not that have spurred her to some act of revenge?"

I ignored his query. "And Ygerne? What could she seek revenge for? Have I rejected her? No."

"But she is Guinevere's friend," he persisted.

"Ider, you and I are friends. Would that friendship permit you to help me kill a girl in such a brutal fashion? Or to help me hide such a deed?"

He shook his head as a gust of wind blew the mud-laden smell of river reeds around us. The wrinkles in his youthful forehead told me that he was still disturbed.

"What is truly bothering you?"

"You are not of the Christ. You admit such yourself. But I have never seen you truly speak or act against the Church, until now. In the rebellion time, aye, even in the death of Eleonore, you were not at cross-purposes with the Church. It's even said that Patrick favored you above many."

"Patrick," I said softly, "was a good, kind man, who labored in the Christ's cause with all the strength in him. I am the better man for having known him."

"Yet now, you ask me, who is of the Christ, to betray those placed in authority over me?"

"No, Ider. I ask you to help me find the truth. Were I to ask you to ignore evidence that points to the guilt of a man, then, yes, I would cast you in the role of betrayer. But we all seek the same ends, Ider. Coroticus, Dubricius, and I want only a peaceful resolution. That we seek it down separate paths does not change our intentions, rather it ensures our ultimate success."

Ider looked at me with something like relief on his face, and I was embarrassed. I had turned him to my task with glibness and a modicum of truth.

"Then I will show you."

As I had predicted, the guards gave us barely a second glance as we passed across the old Roman bridge and through the breastworks being thrown up by Melwas.

The consilium had made the old Roman shrine their headquarters, establishing temporary defensive works on the southern approach to the bridge. The lands to either side were swampy, under water in some places, far too muddy to sustain a horse assault.

The wider approach on the eastern side of the tor was better defended by a bank and ditch, begun by Lauhiir and then completed and strengthened by Melwas.

All of these things I noted as we made our way along the base of Wirral Hill toward the small village at Ynys-witrin. My ruse would only work to get past the guards at the bridge. Brothers going in and out of the abbey precinct through the vallum were unlikely to be fooled. If I could penetrate the abbey grounds, with Ider's help, I could learn where Guinevere was. By speaking to her, I hoped to do one of two things: learn truly who had killed Gwyneira or convince her to surrender to Arthur and purchase yet more time for my inquiries.

"We are nearly there, Malgwyn," Ider told me as the abbey entrance drew in sight before us.

"Then it is time for you to continue toward the abbey. I will walk as if I'm headed to the other community to the west."

"As I explained, you will find it at the back of an old hovel, covered by what seems to be a wooden pallet over a storage pit. I really wish you would let me go with you."

"No, I need you to make certain that no one is about in the vetustam ecclesia when I emerge. You are needed there more than at my side."

He nodded. I clapped him on the shoulder and watched him walk for a few steps toward the abbey. Satisfied that all was aright, I started toward the hovel in the back lane of Ynys-witrin.

I made it almost to the entrance of the tunnel.

My plan had started out well. But most plans were that way. Then, something would happen to alter its path.

Like the whining voice of Melwas.

"Master Malgwyn! I wondered when you would visit me."

CHAPTER TWENTY-ONE

L ord Melwas! How goes it with you?"
    I was brazen if nothing else. My cheery greeting took
the grubby little lord by surprise. "Why, my lord, you knew
that I had taken the vows?"

This was new information, and Melwas did not deal well
with new information. But one of his aides leaned in and whispered something in his ear. A smile broke across Melwas's face.
"Malgwyn, you are ever the jester! Come be my guest!"

At that I found my good arm held by one soldier and my
stump by another. I shook them off.

"Be careful, Melwas. From a distance it might appear that
you were arresting a monachus. That would not bode well for
negotiations over Guinevere."

Rather than look thoughtful or pensive, as if he were con-
sidering my words, Melwas grinned a rotting-toothed grin.
"You are assuming that I intend to negotiate."

The smile on his face gave me great pause. In some hidden
corner of my mind, I had always assumed that Melwas would
ultimately wish to negotiate new lands, that he would give in
at the last moment and surrender her, but only in return for

new titles or property. Oh, he would claim it was all in defense of Guinevere, but he would seek some profit. It would have been too late to save Ygerne, but Guinevere might live another day. I saw now how naïve that had been on my part. At that moment, I saw how completely besotted with my cousin Melwas had become. He was mad, not drooling mad, but insane nonetheless.

He would, indeed, go to war over Guinevere.

Unless he saw how futile his cause was; he was not suicidal.

His soldiers laid hands upon me again and this time I did not shake them off.

Nor was I surprised when, as we drew closer to the village, I saw Ider standing next to Coroticus and Dubricius, his head hanging in shame.

He had betrayed me.

Coroticus wore a smug expression. Dubricius seemed pleased. "You see, Lord Melwas," the abbot began, "it was as our brother Ider said. Arthur and the consilium sent Malgwyn, dressed as a monachus, to spy out your defenses. This is the sort of duplicity that you can expect from them. And this is why you must allow the Church to work as a neutral party for a peaceful solution."

I straightened quickly. Something was wrong in this. Ider knew what my mission was; he knew it had nothing to do with spying out Melwas's defenses.

And while everyone else listened carefully to Coroticus, Ider did something completely out of character for the earnest young monachus. He winked at me.

That could mean only one thing. He knew something that I did not, and it would have doomed our plan. Somehow, he believed that by betraying me, he was helping me. But unless I knew what he apparently knew, I could not judge his success.

I tried to focus on what Coroticus, Dubricius, and Melwas were saying. But after Coroticus's diatribe, none of which I heard, they had moved off a step or two and lowered their voices. All I could discern was Coroticus making some sort of plea about two being better than one.

After a moment, Melwas waved to the soldiers and they began marching me off toward his fortress at the base of the tor, exactly where I did not wish to be. My stomach nearly revolted as I realized that Ygerne would be beheaded in less than two days, and I had little chance now of preventing it.

❖

"You look silly in those robes, Malgwyn."

Only one person would say that to me.

Guinevere.

"And the tonsure makes you look as some sea monster."

I had just been tossed into a small wooden hut within Melwas's compound and the door bolted shut. Blinking my eyes to adjust to the dim light, I could make out my cousin, sitting on the dirt floor. A platter of cheese and bread lay near her, and I saw that a flagon of water hung from a wooden peg.

"You are a prisoner?" I had just assumed that she would have the freedom to roam where she wished within Melwas's defenses. Indeed, I thought she was the little toad's consort.

"You think I would willingly become Melwas's woman? You are no kin of mine, Malgwyn. My relations think better of me," she chided.

"Then what happened?"

She brushed her blond hair from her face. "I was not as

devastated as you might think at Arthur's news. I have my own spies, and I knew that David and the others were urging him to marry Aircol's daughter." Her words were firm, but I heard a sadness despite her bravado.

Still, I chuckled grimly. It seemed that we were forever underestimating Guinevere.

"The day after Arthur told me, Melwas appeared at my cottage. He started out politely, offering his patronage, but when my face betrayed my horror, well, he turned nasty."

"How so?" I asked. If he had raped her, there would be no corner of our patria in which he could hide.

"He progressed to demands very quickly, and when I scoffed at his demands, four of his soldiers threatened to abduct me, and I saw quickly it would be folly to resist. I pretended to go along with it."

I nodded. "He put word about that you were now his consort."

Guinevere scowled. "If I were in need of a new patron, it would be Kay or Bedevere or perhaps even Gaheris. At least they are pretty to look at." She paused. "Is it true?"

"What?"

"That Arthur and Aircol are condemning me for Gwyneira's death. That if Melwas fails to hand me over that they will lay siege and take me by force so that I may pay for her death."

Melwas was indeed a madman, but not so insane that he had told Guinevere of Ygerne's fate.

"You made certain that no other conclusion could be drawn. You were one of the last two people to see Gwyneira alive. You were proven to be the author of the note. What were they supposed to think? I take it that that's how you ended up in here?"

She nodded. "For the first bit, I had the freedom of the area. But after I had slipped away twice to Castellum Arturius, Melwas put me in here and said it was for my own protection."

"Why didn't you just stay at Arthur's castle?"

"The first time, when I delivered the note to Ygerne, it was jealousy that sent me back. The second time, last night, after I found poor Gwyneira so foully murdered, I thought I had nowhere else I could go."

"There is more to tell you." It was time that she knew about Ygerne. I explained how events had transpired after Gwyneira was discovered, how Ygerne refused to say anything publicly in some effort to cast the torch of suspicion away from Guinevere. How Arthur had given Melwas two days to hand her over and how Arthur planned to execute Ygerne in a final effort to make Guinevere surrender.

"And Arthur has given you two days to find out who truly did this?" It was more a statement than a question.

I nodded.

"Why is Ygerne being so stubborn?" Guinevere exclaimed. "She knew nothing about Gwyneira until I told her."

"She thinks her silence keeps you safe."

"Marry her, Malgwyn, if we all survive this. She is one to keep. She has complete faith in you, you know. She does this only because she believes that you will work your magic and resolve this affair."

"Hmmph! I find that unlikely. She will not let me in her door."

Guinevere hid a smile behind her hand. "That is another matter."

"Tell me what you remember of that night."

"Why, Malgwyn? We can do nothing from here."

"True. But we have yet a little time, and the only thing that I can do is to talk to the one person I have not yet made inquiries of. Unless and until I can give them the murderer, where we are is of little consequence."

So Guinevere began, telling essentially the same tale that Ygerne had told me. "I went there not to do her harm, but to see if we could reach a sort of understanding."

"An understanding?"

"I have many friends among Arthur's men and the town folk. I did not wish to lose them all. But in order to keep them, I also needed to make my peace with the child. I needed to walk the lanes without fearing an encounter with her."

"How did you know she would be alone?"

"How could Arthur and his nobles ignore a chance to ride once more?"

"And so you used me for permission to see Gwyneira."

"I knew that no one would question your word."

"Then what happened?"

"Then nothing. I went in and found her dead, the blood still very, very fresh."

"And no one else around?"

"No one. Merely the servants clearing the feasting hall."

"In the lanes you saw no one, not the Druid or . . . Mordred or David or . . ."

She held up her hand. "I saw no one I knew and scarcely anyone else. The stalls selling wine and mead had closed. Only the drunken lords of the consilium were about."

"What of Morgan ap Tud? The medicus?"

Guinevere shook her head. "No, not him either. You do not think little Morgan could have done these things?"

I shrugged. "He is David's man. And I believe David capable

of anything. At the White Mount and then again at Caer Goch, Morgan's whereabouts cannot be determined. The night of Gwyneira's death, he managed to elude two of my, uh, watchmen."

"You mean two of your spies."

I stood and paced about. "This makes no sense. Someone had to kill her. She did not do this to herself."

"Who knew of the method by which the other girls were killed?"

'Twas a fair question. But she did not like my answer. "You, Ygerne, Bedevere, Arthur, and Merlin. Oh, and Wynn, of course."

The scowl she threw my way was as withering as a summer sun at midday. "You are not being helpful. Did not the parents of these girls know how they died? Could not one of them have believed that it was one of Arthur's men who did this? Could not one of them have killed Gwyneira in the same manner out of revenge?"

My cousin was much like me in the way her mind worked. But I had already considered this possibility and dismissed it. "No, I met their families, well, except for the last one on the journey back from Caer Goch. And no one we have spoken to saw anyone unfamiliar."

"Malgwyn!" The door had opened and a smiling Melwas stood in it.

"My lord," I acknowledged him with a bowed head.

"I would speak to you, alone." I knew Guinevere did not like that, but I had little choice.

"It would seem that I am at your service, whether I want to be or not."

"If you will excuse us, Lady," he said, bowing in deference to Guinevere.

Her sharp eyes shot daggers at him. "My cousin I will excuse. You are but a little toad."

Melwas threw his head back in laughter. "Ahh, those little pet names you have for me! How delightful!"

I stood and we left the hut with Guinevere glowering behind us. For a moment, I thought about strangling him and taking our chances with his men, but two of them appeared from either side of our little prison.

From our vantage point, we could see as far as Wirral Hill and beyond the faint glow of campfires near Pomparles. Melwas stared into the distance for a long moment before turning back to me. "We do not know each other well, Malgwyn."

"No, my lord, we do not."

"Although I expect that I will have to kill you soon, I thought we should become better acquainted."

"That seems unnecessary, my lord."

Melwas nodded sadly. "But you are Guinevere's cousin, and should circumstances allow, I might let you live."

He seemed totally detached from the situation.

"Melwas, are you not aware that the consilium is raising an army to assault your position? That you have no escape route?"

The little lord laughed, a belly-deep chortle. "But Malgwyn, what better way to convince the lady that I truly love her than to defy the consilium in her defense." His eyes twinkled at me and I shuddered.

We were in deep trouble. He was serious. Melwas honestly thought that Guinevere would see his insane actions as proof of his abiding love for her. What a fool!

326 / TONY HAYS

"Melwas, my lord, that is not going to happen! Every lord in the consilium demanded this marriage to ally Aircol to our cause. But then Gwyneira was murdered. The alliance is yet threatened. The only way to satisfy Aircol and bind him to us is to find the guilty party, and at this moment, that seems to be Guinevere. Arthur will assault the tor with all the strength he can muster in just more than a day from now. If you stand between the consilium and the Lady Guinevere, you will be crushed!"

He shook his head. "I do not think that will happen, Malgwyn. When Guinevere stands with me, arm in arm, Arthur will see his error. He will understand. Besides, if he attacks, the abbey will be destroyed. Neither Arthur nor Aircol would do that to their precious church."

"You have not heard anything that I have said. You are mad!"

"I am a man in love who will not be denied. Be grateful, Malgwyn, that I have spared your life. Were it not for Coroticus and Ider, your head would have already leapt from your shoulders. You are a meddling busybody and we would all be well shed of you. I have no need of you. When I receive my new—" He stopped suddenly. And I saw his plan immediately. The little lord intended to negotiate his way to new lands by suddenly appearing to listen to reason at the last moment. I did not doubt that he wanted to take Guinevere to his bed; she was a beautiful woman. But, like most lords of his ilk, he sought personal advantage as well.

"Besides, they cannot muster enough men in so short a time to successfully assault the tor."

I thought I saw a flaw in his plan; well, in truth I saw a herd of them. "But though you 'turn' reasonable, that will have nothing to do with saving Guinevere. You will have to surrender her."

"Malgwyn, Malgwyn. She has been promised sanctuary by Dubricius in the abbey. Lauhiir yet enjoys safety within its precinct."

"Lauhiir was a different matter. My lord, I will warn you once more. Lord Aircol demands justice for his daughter. He will have it and sanctuary will not stop him. If you do not hand her over to them, they will assault."

Again the fat little lord grinned. "Now, Malgwyn. Who is better suited to judge the actions of nobles? Their equal or a one-armed scribe?"

"Argh!" I threw my one hand into the air and returned to the hut without his leave. He had lost all command of his senses. The small of my back tensed, in case the little worm struck me, but he didn't, and I pulled the wooden door to behind me.

And, after I told her of Melwas's lunacy, Guinevere and I spent our time in the narrow hut thus—she voicing new possibilities and I countering them with the facts.

By the time that I noticed that it was nearly as dark outside as inside, we had talked until our tongues were sore and our food was gone. And we were no closer to solving the puzzle.

"Are we to be fed no more? Or does Melwas think you need to be thinner?" I asked, more for lack of anything new to say.

Guinevere slapped at me, but without malice. "I always liked it, when we were children, when you would tease me. No matter how ill my mood, you could always make me feel better with your teasing. Melwas will send food soon. He profits nothing by starving us."

I was not really listening, and Guinevere noticed. "What troubles you?"

"My friend, the monachus Ider, he betrayed me to Melwas. I want to believe that it was because he had learned something important, something that would have made my original plan unworkable. When I was placed here, with you, I thought this was it, that he discovered that you were truly imprisoned. But we have not heard from him."

"Perhaps Melwas has not allowed him access."

"Perhaps."

"You think too much, Malgwyn."

At that, the door swung open on its leather hinges, the glow of an old Roman lamp revealing a tired Coroticus. Alone. He stepped in and pulled the door shut behind him.

It may have been the shadows cast by the lamp, but Coroticus looked more worn than I had ever seen him. He sat down on the floor with a heavy sigh.

"Malgwyn, we have had our differences, but I have always had respect for your abilities." He paused. "We need more than that this time."

"Why?" Guinevere asked, alarmed.

"Melwas is truly insane. He believes that he is protecting you from certain death, and he believes that his actions will persuade you to love him."

I shook my head sadly. "Does he not realize that Arthur and Aircol will kill him without a hint of regret?"

"It is not without its romantic attraction," Guinevere conceded.

"Please, cousin."

"It may not be that easy, Malgwyn," Coroticus said. "He has effectively sealed off all of the approaches to Ynys-witrin, and the sky was covered in clouds late this afternoon. A hard rain tonight will turn the abbey and the tor into an island once more. A siege will take a long time, and the people of the village will suffer."

I struggled to my feet. "Coroticus, every conceivable piece of evidence points to Guinevere and Ygerne, either acting separately or together. Aircol will force Arthur to produce Ygerne at Pomparles in a last ditch effort to get Guinevere to surrender. When that does not work, Ygerne will be executed according to the laws, and the consilium's forces will launch an immediate assault. They will not lay siege."

"They will if the rain makes the levels impassable."

"Perhaps."

"Are you certain of their intent?"

"That was the decision taken at the last conference before I left. I have no reason to believe that their plans have changed. In truth, the only reason that I think Aircol agreed to wait two days was to give the lords time to assemble a goodly force."

"Can they?"

"Without doubt. Every lord present pledged his support and most have large forces within two days' ride."

"A full scale assault will doom the village. Nothing will be left. The abbey will be destroyed!"

"It would seem, Coroticus, that you will get your wish. Go, and negotiate our way out of this disaster."

My heart fell into my stomach.

Coroticus looked ill.

"What?"

"Though we have not been confined here, Dubricius and I are as much prisoners as the two of you. Melwas will not let us beyond his defenses in order to treat with the consilium."

"Does he expect the consilium to simply concede?" I exploded.

"He is quite mad, Malgwyn."

I thought of Bedevere and Illtud, blocking the other approaches, but telling Coroticus of them was as good as telling Melwas. The abbot would use anything to his advantage.

Guinevere stood then. "Is there not anything you can do, Coroticus, to convince him of the folly of his path?"

"Perhaps if I already had Arthur and Melwas in the same chamber, I could, but that will not happen. And some among the brothers are being just as insane. Why, Ider is now counseling Melwas to move the two of you to the vetustam ecclesia; in case the worst happens, he can claim sanctuary for himself and the two of you. But all that that will accomplish is to ensure the destruction of the abbey!"

"You are correct. If the assault begins, sanctuary will have no meaning. They will be like dogs with the taste of blood in their mouths. They will clamor for more." I stopped, losing myself in the yellow-orange flame of the lamp for a moment. A smile broke across my face as Ider's purpose became clear. What a clever monachus!

"Coroticus, go to Melwas and support Ider on this point! Assure him that neither Arthur nor Aircol would dare desecrate the abbey, and that it is a good and logical plan should all else go awry."

Guinevere and Coroticus looked at me now as if I were mad.

"Malgwyn!"

"Go, my lord abbot! Do as I say!"

"In the name of the Christ, Malgwyn, I pray that you know what you are doing," Coroticus murmured. But he did not object any further and left us alone again.

"Tell me what you are planning, Malgwyn," Guinevere asked.

"Not yet. First, while we wait for our food, help me understand how a man or anyone could profit from abusing these poor girls in the way that they were."

She narrowed her beautiful eyes at me, but without a spoken objection we began to talk.

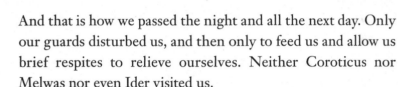

And that is how we passed the night and all the next day. Only our guards disturbed us, and then only to feed us and allow us brief respites to relieve ourselves. Neither Coroticus nor Melwas nor even Ider visited us.

"So, you have five young girls dead from brutal and horrible assaults, assaults that seem to be unprovoked—"

"—five girls?" I almost missed it. "You mean four."

Guinevere looked at me quizzically. "No. I mean five. Young Nimue was killed thus as well."

The walls of the little hut seemed to close in around me, and I found it hard to breathe. "No one said aught of this to me. They said only that she was dead. How do you know that she was killed in the same manner?"

Guinevere blinked in near confusion. "Malgwyn! Ygerne helped to prepare her for burial. Who told you of this?"

"Arthur and Kay."

She grunted. "Well, of course they would not have told you. They never looked upon her. A vigile found her in one of the abandoned houses in the old Roman village. He assumed that she had gotten drunk with the wrong sort. Ygerne said that there was little blood on her gown."

"But they said that she had been found the day after our departure for the land of the Demetae."

"That was true. But Ygerne said she was already stiff and beginning to bloat as the dead do in hot weather."

"Why didn't she tell me this? I will have to think through everything again!"

"By the time you returned, Ygerne was so out of sorts with you that she could scarcely speak. But what difference does this make?"

"Don't you see, cousin? The Druid Wynn did not enter our town that night. He came here instead, to Ynys-witrin. We saw him with Melwas in the village. He could not have killed Nimue."

Nimue. Such a pretty child. On the eve of her freedom to have her life ripped from her. Damn this bastard to Hell! If I survived Melwas and this insanity, I would not rest until I choked him to death with my one hand!

I remembered how happy she seemed when Arthur released her, how embarrassed she seemed by all the attention. As I thought these things, I heard the door open and someone enter.

I smelled food.

Onions.

Maybe it was the memory of Nimue. Maybe it was the smell of onions. Maybe it was Arthur's God in His Providence, guiding my brain.

But suddenly, the answer appeared.

I knew who had killed them all!

I knew as surely as I knew that the sun would rise on the morrow. Looking up, I saw that it was Coroticus who had brought our platters. I leaped to my feet and grabbed his arm, scattering the food about the cell.

"You must have us moved to the vetustam ecclesia, Coroticus!"

The abbot winced at the fierceness of my grip. "I have tried, but he seems not to be interested."

"Then redouble your efforts. Triple them! If you wish to have an abbey this time tomorrow, then Guinevere and I must be moved immediately!"

Coroticus studied my face, probably trying to decide if I had gone mad myself. He turned to Guinevere and God bless my cousin, she nodded.

"I do not pretend to understand him, Coroticus. But we both know that he is seldom wrong in these things. Do as he asks."

The abbot, his face lined thrice over by the weight of this crisis, nodded and left without a word.

"Who was it, Malgwyn?"

"Not yet, cousin. I need to think carefully, need to plan carefully. I will get but one chance to resolve this and it must work."

"But what if Coroticus does not succeed?"

I brushed my hair from my pounding forehead. "He will."

"How do you know?"

"Because he must."

CHAPTER TWENTY-TWO

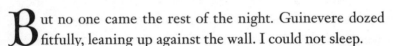

B ut no one came the rest of the night. Guinevere dozed
fitfully, leaning up against the wall. I could not sleep.

Merlin had been wrong, but not completely. He had suggested that when I knew why these deeds were done, I would
know the who. But, now that I knew who had killed those
girls, I understood the why. Or perhaps the "why" and the "who"
revealed themselves to me at the same time. It saddened me for
more than one reason. I understood why the girls had been
killed. It was not a good reason, but it was an understandable
one. We were all to blame in a way.

As soon as I understood these things, my tired mind concocted a way to accomplish what Arthur said I must. I had run
my plan through my mind a thousand times but it was all for
naught if we were not moved to the old church, the vetustam
ecclesia. And it rained; it rained as if it might never rain again.

The hastily built hut was rife with leaks, forcing Guinevere and me into one reasonably dry corner. I suspected that
the levels were soaked, if not actually flooded. It would make
the consilium's assault both more difficult and more bloody.

"Why do you not just call in Melwas and Dubricius and

tell them who is guilty of these things?" Guinevere asked as the sun began to poke its head above the eastern horizon.

"Because Arthur was right. In order to prevent both your death and Ygerne's, I must be able to either prove it absolutely or make the killer confess. I cannot prove it absolutely, and Melwas wants this coming battle. He has lost all sense of reality. He will resist any resolution that takes control away from him. Therefore I must maneuver events to force the murderer to confess."

She nodded. "Why will you not tell me?"

"The person who did these things is unlikely. I believe if I approach this in the correct way, he will reveal himself. I believe he will be unable not to. If you or anyone else knows, your eyes may give it away before I am ready, and my plan will fall apart."

"Then it was the Druid Wynn? Or Morgan?"

"Be patient, cousin."

The door to our little prison opened and Coroticus presented himself. "Melwas has agreed to have you moved to the vetustam ecclesia."

From the looks of him, the abbot had spent all night haranguing the lord. His robes were wet and smelled of mud and rain. His tonsure needed trimming. But it was his eyes that disturbed me the most. They were very nearly dead, just a bare spark of life, and then only deep in their sockets.

"I would ask how you managed this miracle, but I fear the answer."

He slumped to the ground. "It was not my doing. Melwas went up on the tor and what he saw frightened him."

"What could he have seen to cause him such a change of heart?"

Coroticus smiled. "The consilium has mustered nearly two thousand men and Arthur has them building boats."

"Boats?" I asked.

"Boats," he confirmed.

And that explained it all. Melwas did not have enough men to guard the entire circumference of Ynys-witrin and the great tor. With flat-bottomed boats or boats of shallow draft, Arthur's soldiers could float across the flooded levels and invade the isle at any point. The idea had come from Merlin, I was certain. He had mentioned it to me on more than one occasion after Lauhiir's abortive rebellion.

"So he's not completely mad."

The abbot shook his head. "And he is finally allowing Dubricius and me to cross over and parlay with the consilium."

"Then go, but leave Ider behind with us."

Coroticus narrowed his eyes. "Why?"

"I will need him."

"You will be in the *vetusta ecclesiam*."

I smiled.

"Very well, but I must speak to Ider when this is all over."

"No, you will not. Or Dubricius and I will have a long talk about you."

The abbot scowled. "You are every bit as evil as you have accused me of being."

Guinevere looked from one to the other of us in confusion. "What are you talking about?"

"It is unimportant," Coroticus answered and left. Moments later, two of Melwas's soldiers appeared and walked with us from the fort, around the women's community and into the abbey grounds. Word of Arthur's tactics had obviously spread. Soldiers rushed to and fro. The sisters were hurriedly storing away food. As we moved through down the slope and through the apple orchard between the women's community and the abbey, a fascinating sight appeared. The brothers, instead of preparing for a siege as were the women, seemed to be standing about dithering, wringing their hands. All, that is, except one, Gildas.

The youngest brother of Celyn was a statue of peace in a landscape of chaos. He stood near the old church, his fingers laced over his belly, waiting as Coroticus and Dubricius left the abbot's hall and headed in his direction. So Coroticus had turned to the child monachus as his aide in this affair. Just as well; it would keep him out of my way.

The vetustam ecclesia was known throughout our lands as the most ancient of churches. Old stories told of the tin merchant, Joseph the Arimathean, having built it after the Christ was crucified. Aye, some said that the Christ had come to these lands as a child with Joseph.

Once a simple wattle structure, it had been encased with lead to help preserve it. Only one door provided access, in its western wall. Inside was an altar at the eastern end. And in the southeastern corner was the intricately carved box that held the abbey's relics, the bones of the Arimathean, not the two mysterious cruets he was said to have brought with him. No one knew where those were secreted nor, exactly, what they contained.

The soldiers shoved us, very unceremoniously, into the chapel, tossing a goatskin of water in behind us.

"Your lover is not a good host," I said, feeling more relief than I had in more than a day. But the wallop I felt at my back stopped my good cheer.

"Do you think me so common that I would truly take up with that madman?"

I turned to confront a Guinevere with the reddened face of the truly angry. "Cousin, no! It was a mere jest."

The lines in her face smoothed, a bit. "Malgwyn, do you not realize how Arthur's decision crushed me?"

"Surely you knew that at some point he would be pressured to wed?"

"In truth, cousin, I believed that enough time would have passed to allow us to be married."

"Such wishful thinking, Guinevere. Such a romantic. I always believed you to be a woman who lived firmly in reality."

"Do not be fooled, Malgwyn. I can be every bit as cunning and cold as those you pledge your fidelity to."

"Of that, I have no doubt. And that may serve you well in the hours and days ahead."

She cocked her head and looked a bit like Mariam at that moment. "Of hours, I understand. Of days, I do not take your meaning."

As was so common with me, I had said too much. And now I had no choice but to answer. "As soon as this is resolved, the consilium will be casting about for another advantageous marriage for Arthur. I doubt that you will be on that list."

Her head drooped. I did not think that I had ever seen her so dejected. But her face bobbed back almost immediately. "Do not count me out yet," she said, her voice strong with defiance. "That would be unwise." Something in her words made me glad that I would not be one of those thwarting her plans.

Before I could embarrass myself further, Ider arrived, and before I could open my mouth to give voice to my complaints, the young monachus raised a hand for silence.

"I did exactly what you do, Malgwyn. I did what was necessary. As soon as I learned that Guinevere was more hostage than consort, and hidden away within Melwas's fort, I knew that you would be arrested straightaway. It seemed logical to me that one of us should remain in favor with the church and Melwas."

Shaking my freshly tonsured head, I smiled. "It seems that the apprentice is teaching the master now."

"Do not compliment me yet. The distance from the tunnel's exit and Pomparles may not seem far, but you may have to swim for it, something you are not well suited for," he pointed out.

"True. Melwas will not look kindly on losing his hostages and he will prevent us if he can. The troops of the consilium will not be able to tell at a distance who we are and may attack."

Guinevere nodded. "I take your meaning. How shall we deal with this?"

"We have no way to alert Arthur's men. If Ider will be so kind as to provide a diversion on this side, I believe we can at least cut our risks in half. Do you know how the men are armed? Will it simply be a race?"

Ider grimaced. "No, Melwas has bowmen along the southern approach, more to keep Arthur's men from encroaching too closely. But he will turn them on you if he sees you. What sort of diversion must I provide?"

"I am afraid, Ider, that that will be up to you. Come, help me move this chest. We can waste no more time."

❖

The tunnel was narrow, more of a rabbit hole than a true passageway, or so it seemed that way to me. My monachus's robes made it all the more difficult. Paved with flagstones, the tunnel had been constructed with some care. Stout beams spaced at regular intervals supported the roof.

In later years, I would see similar structures in the far west of our lands. But those were designed for storage and for hiding from marauders.

"Does anyone know who built these?" I asked, essentially in the dark as only our small torches provided any relief from the pitch black of the tunnel.

"I asked Coroticus, but he said no one really knows," Ider answered, his voice seeming hollow and distant.

"What is at the end?"

"Just a wooden door."

"Go then. We will find our way. When you judge we have had time to reach the other end, begin your diversion. We will need them looking away from us for as long as we can."

"Is it near the midday yet?" Guinevere asked.

Ider shook his head. "You have more than an hour."

With that, he disappeared, leaving Guinevere and me to brave the dank, dark tunnel alone. Somewhere down its length, I heard water dripping against the stones.

"Come. We have little time." I stepped forward, comforted to feel Guinevere's hand clutching at my tunic.

We inched along the mostly straight trackway, slipping occasionally on the slick flagstones for some time. The small torches gave us little warning of what faced us. Once I heard what sounded like a rat scurrying along, and a sound like something slithering, but I had no desire to find its source.

"We should move faster, Malgwyn," Guinevere hissed behind me.

I turned to answer and then realized that her voice sounded different, or rather the sound of it in this tunnel had changed. "What?"

Without answering, I took three quick steps forward, stretching my one arm out so that the torch might reach farther into the blackness.

At the edges of the yellow globe of light, I saw what I feared, what I had not even thought of until that moment. A landslide had partially blocked the tunnel. One of the wooden supports had rotted and collapsed on itself, spilling dirt and rock into the opening until only one tiny hole could be discerned in the upper corner of the slide.

I rushed over and held the torch close to the cavity. It was large enough so that I could see through to the other side. The landslide had been a recent one, I saw, as my hand sank into the soft earth. The blockage was not too thick, but it would take time to clear it.

Behind me, Guinevere gasped as she realized our predicament.

After a moment of silence, broken only by our labored breathing, Guinevere's voice sounded. "Come, cousin. You will see what your one arm can do."

So did we both.

✦

We shifted rock and dirt behind us like furious demons, for what seemed like hours. But though my head ached and my heart felt ready to burst through my chest, I knew it could not have been that long.

In the dim, dim light of our fading torches, I looked to

Guinevere and knew I was glad I did not have a looking glass. Her face was near covered in dirt and her gown looked more like a rag. Somehow the front had been ripped down almost revealing her breasts. My head turned in embarrassment, but her voice stopped me.

"Now is not the time for that, cousin. Besides, they are not the first you have ever seen."

I grunted and returned to our task with that passion born only of desperation.

Ygerne's life was hanging by less than a tortured thread from Guinevere's gown.

Sharp pains ripped through my fingers with each handful of earth. I knew that at least some of my fingernails had been torn, and I guessed that Guinevere suffered the same.

Though we did not speak, only one vision drove us then—Ygerne kneeling, head bowed, awaiting the sword blow that would end her life. Two people were truly responsible for this horror. And both would pay!

Even as I thought this, my arm slipped through into a void. I snatched up my nearly extinguished torch and saw that we had cleared enough space to wedge ourselves through.

"Here, cousin," I urged her. "Help me through."

"That would be better done from the other side, Malgwyn."

I shook my head, though she could not really see it. "We do not know what is over there. Better that I go first."

"No, better that I do, and then I can pull you through by your arm."

She was right. Bending down, I let her use my back to hoist herself into the opening. I could hear her grunt, and the sound of dirt and rock sliding down beneath her.

"Guinevere?"

Nothing.

"Guinevere!"

The sound of spluttering and spitting burst through the hole. "Yes! I am all right. I just got a mouth full of dirt. Here, reach through!"

I did. And with yet more grunting and the ripping sound of my robe tearing from me, I tried with all my might. But my strength was gone.

My fingers, slick with sweat and mud, slipped from Guinevere's grasp. That Ygerne might die because I could not pass through a hole in the earth was a sin, greater than any other sin.

"You are not helping, Malgwyn," Guinevere said, almost in the same voice she had used when we were children at play. "When this is over, I shall tell Ygerne that you did not care for her enough." And somehow that fleeting bit of youthful teasing put vigor back into my legs and I willed myself forward.

This time, our grip was strong, and together we pulled me through the hole, my robe catching and ripping as we went.

Then I was through, and the world became a blur in shades of darkness.

Groaning, I righted myself. I could sense rather than see Guinevere. "I would tell you, cousin, how bad you look, but I would be lying."

Though the pains in my arm, legs, and hand were great, I forced myself to my feet. "We have little time to waste, if any."

We slipped and slid along the wet stones, headed almost frantically for the end of the tunnel, not certain how far it was or what we might encounter on the way.

The end of the tunnel took us both by surprise. After feeling our way down the pitch black for what seemed a Roman *schoenus* but was probably only a few hundred feet, my fingers struck wood.

I put my shoulder into it, but it gave just a little.

"What is wrong?"

"Something is on top or against it."

"Then put your back into it," instructed Guinevere.

And I did.

And it gave, tumbling me out onto the ground behind the hovel. We were very nearly due north of the bridge, and the rains had truly swollen the river and the levels.

With Guinevere pushing at me from behind, I climbed out, flipped around, and helped her out as well.

My eyes flew to the sky. The sun was at meridian height!

"Come! We have no time!" And I set off along the edge of the water, the fatigue paining my legs forgotten.

"What shall we do?"

"Ider will have given up on us by now. Indeed, we may be too late. We will cross the water east of the bridge. Some of that stretch is still probably low enough that we can wade. What we cannot wade, we will swim."

We crossed the ground with more speed than we thought possible.

Suddenly, we rounded the new, palisaded sisters' community and came within sight of the bridge.

"*NO!!*" My roar resounded like that of a wounded bear.

In the distance, kneeling on the bridge, was Ider, head bowed, awaiting the blow from Aircol's sword hovering above his neck.

I looked behind me at Guinevere, catching but a glimpse of the beautiful noble lady she was. Her hair hung in clumps; scratches marked her face. Her gown was shredded from waist up, and her bosom lay naked before me. I could only guess what I looked like.

"NO!!" I shouted again, as loud as I possibly could. And it worked well enough to steal Aircol's attention. And everyone else's.

Heads on both sides of the bridge turned toward us, and then arrows split the air. Melwas's archers.

I grabbed Guinevere's hand in mine and splashed into the flooded levels.

Though there was much shouting, I could not tell who was saying what. Aye, I could not tell much at all. Above the din, I heard someone shout "Hold!" but I did not know if it was Melwas, Arthur, or someone else.

I only knew that Ygerne might well be dead, and for reasons I could not fathom, Ider was next.

I was blessing the inaccuracy of Melwas's archers when I felt the nip of an arrow at my ear.

And Guinevere yelped.

The water was at my chest now and I did the only thing I knew to do. "Grab my waist," I ordered Guinevere.

But then a figure, something like the water nymphs my old dad had told me about, splashed past me.

Blood dripped from the arrow wound to Guinevere's cheek.

"No, cousin. You grab mine."

She was truly an extraordinary woman.

Neither of us could look up long enough to judge our position. My one arm was so exhausted that I despaired of holding on much longer.

More arrows split the water about us.

And I swallowed a mouthful of brown river water, choking me, burning my lungs.

Then Guinevere screamed.

CHAPTER TWENTY-THREE

For a moment I believed that she had been struck again by an arrow.

Then something hard and wooden banged against my head.

And as had happened before in my life, a hand grabbed me and pulled me from the water.

"We have saved a drowning rat from the waters," Merlin's voice cracked.

"But what fate have we saved him for," Bedevere answered.

As my eyes cleared, I realized that I was aboard one of Arthur's flat-bottomed boats.

I jerked forward. "Ygerne? Ider?"

"Both yet live," Bedevere assured us.

"For the moment," Merlin added.

"Forever," I said.

Neither man answered, just gave me an odd look.

"Malgwyn, Ider has confessed to committing all the killings. When Ygerne was brought out on the bridge as Arthur had promised, he broke into tears, rushed across the bridge and threw himself on Aircol's mercy."

And Guinevere, who now had a wool blanket draped across her bare breasts, said nothing but gave me a curious look.

"It works quite well, Malgwyn. Guinevere and Ygerne are innocent. But why do you look so disapproving?" Merlin finally asked.

"Guinevere did not do this thing. Nor did Ygerne. I know now who did."

"Ider, of course."

"Do not bother, Bedevere," Guinevere said in a shaky voice. "'Twas not Ider, and Malgwyn will not tell you."

Moments later, three of Arthur's soldiers waded out and helped pull our boat ashore.

I looked about. Coroticus had spoken the truth. The consilium had gathered at least two thousand. They were lined up back down the road to the south, staying to the dry and avoiding the swamp. The bulk of the boats were farther south, along the ridge. Only a handful were here, on either side of the bridge. If this was a sample of what the consilium could do when united, the Saxons were indeed in trouble.

With Bedevere's help, I sloshed through the water and regained land.

Ider was a true friend. I had underestimated his bravery. But he had provided just the distraction we needed. It was now time for my own.

I swooned.

"Malgwyn!" Merlin rushed to my side. My old friend did not miss a step when I winked at him. He rose and gestured for two of the soldiers. "Can't you see this man is injured? Bring him to me at the bridge." They hesitated. "Now!" stormed Merlin in his deepest and strongest voice.

Moments later, with Bedevere carrying Guinevere behind us, we mounted the bridge itself. Arrayed before us were Arthur, Aircol, a still kneeling Ider, my dear Ygerne, Dubricius, and Coroticus. On the far side of the span were Melwas, two of his chief lieutenants, and young Gildas.

"You!" Arthur shouted at a soldier. "Fetch Morgan ap Tud!"

"My lord Rigotamos," I croaked. "A word."

Arthur approached with something like a smile on his face. He knelt beside me. "You accomplished that which I thought impossible. You have provided a confession."

With a weak finger, I beckoned him closer. "A false confession, one that can be dismissed with a single stroke. Guinevere and Ygerne have not yet escaped Aircol's sword."

To his credit, Arthur maintained his smile, though it was a bit more strained, stretched at the corners. "Why would he confess to something he did not do?"

"To help me. To help you. Bear with me, Arthur. I have the answer, but it is not what you would expect. You will yet have your confession, I think.

The short, slender physician Morgan ap Tud arrived with his bag of herbs. "Some wine, Morgan," I said more loudly. "I beg of you."

Arthur rose and looked about. "You!" He pointed at one of the soldiers. "Go back to the shrine and have Cerdic send some wine!"

Morgan ap Tud leaned close, listened at my chest and grinned at me. "You will be fine."

"But not all of us will be, Morgan. Not all of us."

He blinked and stepped back, a look of consternation and confusion marking his face.

Aircol directed a soldier to watch Ider, and he approached me. "I thought you had run away, Malgwyn. What means this bizarre appearance?"

"I brought you Guinevere, my lord."

"Yes, you did. But you see we have already found my daughter's killer, this rogue sacerdote."

"I do see that, Lord Aircol. But are you certain?"

"He has confessed it. Are you telling me that a sacerdote would lie?"

"You are telling me that a sacerdote would kill."

A hint of a smile creased the lines at the corners of his eyes. "Malgwyn, I want revenge for my daughter, and I am just tired enough of all this delay that I will take it where I can find it. If not the monachus, then Guinevere and your woman will do."

Suddenly I caught a glimpse of where little Vortipor learned some of his manners. "I wish revenge for your daughter as well. But I will take it from the ones who did it."

They had rested me against a log. Up the road toward the shrine I saw Cerdic and Talorc running with bloated goatskins. In their wake came David, Mordred, and Celyn, hurrying to see what had happened.

As they administered the wine, Dubricius and Coroticus approached.

"I should have known that you would reappear, Malgwyn," the episcopus said. "I should have let Melwas kill you when he wanted to."

"My lord, I am like a weed in a garden. Just when you think I have been eliminated, I spring back up."

Coroticus held his tongue, but I caught a bit of a smile on his lips.

Struggling to my feet, my chest still bare, I faced Arthur

and Aircol. "My lords, you charged me to find out who killed Gwyneira and the other children." That was something of a misstatement, but I did not intend for them to forget the others, the lesser dead some would call them.

"I think we already have done that, Malgwyn," Dubricius said.

Looking then at Ider for the first time, I saw how much his "diversion" had cost him. "This man killed no one. Ider is a good and loyal friend, and more brave than any of us would have believed. But he is no killer."

Gildas and Melwas inched across the bridge, anxious to see what was happening.

Ider's shoulders sagged in relief.

"Yet he confesses it," said Dubricius.

"Episcopus, he was not at the White Mount when the first girl was killed thus. He was not at Castellum Arturius when the girl Nimue was killed thus."

"What!" exploded Arthur. "She did not die in such a manner."

"Indeed she did!" retorted Ygerne, speaking for the first time. "You knew only that she was dead. Merlin, her guardian, had already left for Caer Goch. You and Kay were worried only about pleasing this man and his daughter. I cleaned her for the grave."

If a king can be truly embarrassed, Ygerne had accomplished it with Arthur. Had the Rigotamos been anyone else, her life would have been forfeit if only for her tone. But it was Arthur, and he was not any other man.

"Then," asked Dubricius, "why would this monachus confess to something he did not do?"

"Because he is my friend, and because he wishes only the

guilty punished. He delayed events, at great risk to himself, so that Guinevere and I might escape from Melwas."

"If he did not do these things, and Guinevere and this other woman did not, who did?"

If I had been Dubricius, I would have grabbed a shield. Ygerne's face was red with fury. She was not fond of being called "this other woman."

"Someone that none of us would have ever dreamed capable." I paused. My plan hinged on this one moment. For the killer to reveal himself, the next few moments had to work just right.

Looking about, I saw that I had everyone's attention—Arthur, Aircol, Bedevere, Dubricius, Coroticus, Ygerne, Guinevere, the other lords, Ider, even Morgan. Melwas and Gildas had crossed the bridge now, too curious to ignore the drama then playing out.

"*WHO*, Malgwyn?" Arthur thundered.

But I tarried yet a second longer and then began. "The Druid Wynn was nearby when all the killings took place. He had excellent reason and plentiful opportunity." That was not exactly true, but close enough. "Morgan ap Tud!"

And the little man jumped.

"You too were nearby when these killings occurred. Aye, you suddenly appeared at the White Mount just after I had been attacked by the killer!

"And on the return from Caer Goch, you disappeared during the attack by the Saxons. You emerged from the forest only after it was over."

Morgan took a step back, fear widening his eyes.

"And the night that Gwyneira died, you did not go riding with us and you disappeared from view."

"No, Malgwyn!"

I advanced on him. "No one would ever suspect a medicus of this sort of mutilation."

"But why, Malgwyn? Why would I do this?" It looked for a moment as if Morgan might have a heart seizure as Kay and Bedevere moved toward him.

Shrugging, I took a few more steps about the growing circle. "Who knows? Perhaps some lord intent on Arthur's downfall." I could not resist the thrust at David, and I was finally in place.

"But you were not the only one with the opportunity." I stopped and stabbed my finger in the chest of yet another. "What say you, Cerdic?"

The old cook took three steps back, and I feared his shaky old knees would give way. "Malgwyn, I . . ."

"You were there when each and every girl was killed. You are a servant, and no one pays much attention to servants." I advanced slowly on him.

His knees did give out then, and he fell to them. I will never forget the trembling around his eyes, nor their tears. "Malgwyn—you cannot think that I—"

"What else am I to think, Cerdic?" I glanced quickly about. Had I accused Aircol himself, I would have not have commanded the others' attention so absolutely. But this was not the end. I drew close and leaned over him, my eyes close enough to see the spittle on his lips and in his beard. "Were you not with us when all these things happened?"

"Yesss . . ." he spluttered, "but—"

Abruptly, I pulled back from him, two and then three steps, turning half from him with a self-satisfied smirk on my face. "And where were you, Cerdic, when the Scotti attacked us? When, I have learned, another unfortunate child was killed?"

354 / TONY HAYS

It was as if he had forgotten that, and he did just what I hoped he would do—his eyes flew to another.

And the guilt in that second set of eyes told the tale.

"Take him, Bedevere! Now!"

Three soldiers slammed the wriggling, writhing figure to the ground. I walked to him and looked down.

Talorc.

Talorc, the Pictish slave boy.

His face held fear, but something more. Something proud and arrogant yet.

"I could not fathom why the sticks of wood smelled of onions. But then, you work in the kitchen.

"When I studied Gwyneira's corpse, I noted that the marks left by the hands that had broken her neck were small, not man-sized. At first, that just seemed to point at Ygerne or Guinevere. But it fits you as well."

One of the soldiers snatched up Talorc's right hand and thrust it in the air. A small hand, not yet fully matured.

And, just as I was about to say more, I was roughly shoved aside.

Aircol, angry yet confused, stood over Talorc. "Why, boy? Why? You saved her life from the Scotti. Arthur had agreed, at my request, to free you in honor of your bravery. I—"

Before Aircol could continue, Talorc turned white as a spirit and roared like a wounded bear.

"NO! No!"

I strode forward then and, kneeling, took his young throat in my one hand. "Gwyneira, I think I understand. But what of the others? Why them? They were just children, the daughters of . . ." Of village leaders, of decurions, just as Gwyneira had been the daughter of a king. I needed nothing else, at least not then.

Releasing his neck, I motioned to the soldiers who jerked him to his knees.

"You did these things to punish the fathers, did you not? To seek revenge for your enslavement?"

He smiled then, in a most foul way.

"You hated them, though you didn't even know them. They represented everyone who had mistreated you."

His eyes narrowed, just slightly. "They deserved it. They all did."

"Even Nimue? She was but a slave like yourself." I desperately wanted to understand why she had to die.

"She did not deserve freedom. She had done nothing to warrant it."

"So you killed her because of her good fortune?"

"She died because she had not earned her freedom. Because she refused me my right." I no longer recognized his face, so twisted in hatred and anger was it.

Enough of this. "And you have earned this." With a quick nod, one of the soldiers snatched up a hank of hair on his head and stretched out his neck.

I snatched a dagger from Aircol's belt, a pretty new one, took but a single swipe.

Talorc died as the blood flooded from his throat, but the anger, the hatred, only left his eyes when they too had died, open, yet vacant.

CHAPTER TWENTY-FOUR

Talorc's death brought silence to the gathering. Life was brutal in our lands, but seldom had anyone seen such a sudden and bloody taking of life. I had allowed no defense, indeed no opportunity for anyone to stop me. Yet I had fulfilled my promise to Gwyneira and to the beloved dead.

As his body lay slumped over in a pool of blood, I motioned for Illtud, who had joined us on the bridge. It took but a moment to explain to him what I needed.

"Are you certain?"

I nodded.

And he departed, without Arthur's leave.

Coroticus looked more than a little relieved. "What of Melwas now, Rigotamos?" he asked.

Young Gildas, fingers still clasped over his stomach, smiled. "If my lord abbot and the episcopus will allow me . . ." They nodded. "I believe I have a solution to this situation."

We all turned then, to see what the monachus was about. Lord Celyn, in particular, seemed anxious to see what his brother had to say.

"Since it is obvious that Guinevere was not guilty of these

crimes as you believed, and thus Melwas was preventing a horrible wrong, I suggest that he be forgiven his defiance."

Melwas, little toad that he was, nodded quickly. He was not so mad after all.

"With the following condition: As penance for his deeds, he should grant certain of his lands to the abbey." Gildas would go far in the church. That much I saw immediately.

"And what should he owe the consilium for his act of defiance, no matter its cause?" asked Mordred, anxious to be a factor.

For a wonder, Dubricius and Coroticus remained quiet and allowed Gildas to take the lead.

But Celyn's brother proved his youth. He blinked a few times and looked amazed. "If he has satisfied the Christ and His servants, then it is unseemly for the consilium to demand anything more."

To a man, the lords of the consilium looked at the rotund monachus in equal amazement.

"This affair is separate from that of my daughter's death, Rigotamos, and I am newly come to the consilium," Aircol said.

"You have an idea, Lord Aircol?"

Aircol stroked his beard. "I think it meet that Lord Melwas surrender his portion of the lead mining to the other members of the consilium for one year."

I could not hold the chuckle in. That would put a stop to much of his imported wine and other goods. Since it fattened all the lords' purses, there was no need to take a vote.

With Guinevere released and Talorc dead, the great crisis had passed, and the lords began organizing their troops to return home.

Yet we were left with Cerdic.

The bridge had cleared but for our small band, circled now around the old cook. Two of Arthur's men held his arms. The Rigotamos circled Cerdic, tugging at the ends of his mustache.

"I do not know what to do with you. You have been with me nearly as long as I have taken breath in this world. At war or at home, you have done your job with only a minimum of complaining."

"My lord," Cerdic began, more controlled now. "I knew only of the one girl on the journey back from Caer Goch. I saw Talorc slip away into the forest, and I feared he was trying to run away. I followed him and spied him working his butchery on that poor girl."

"Cerdic," Arthur said sadly. "When you saw how Gwyneira died, you must have realized that the boy did it. You are many things, old friend, but stupid is not one."

Rather than argue with the Rigotamos, Cerdic merely bowed his head.

We had no prisons, no dungeons, no place to hold prisoners for long, not really. As much as I liked Cerdic, his offense could not go unpunished. To do so would weaken Arthur in the eyes of Aircol, and others. And, as though Arthur were reading my mind, he nodded, more to himself than to anyone else.

"Lord Kay."

"Yes, my lord."

"Take Cerdic to the barracks and confine him there. At such a time as is convenient, take one of his eyes. He will remember then not to withhold information."

Aircol nodded approvingly. "I did not think his offense merited his death."

"There has been too much death already," Arthur said.

In truth, Arthur's decision was very wise. Of Talorc's execution, much would be said of its speed. No one would doubt his guilt. But in those days there was still a belief that the old Roman system of justice was to be admired, with its courts and judges. My old dad often said though that under the Romans justice was bought and sold more freely than the lead they mined. As time passed, it would be Arthur who was blamed for the killing. Time twists tales. Aye, in the last few years I have heard it said that 'twas Bedevere who was missing part of his arm. I have been swallowed up by time. And that suits me well.

For Cerdic's punishment, Arthur would be praised for his restraint. Other lords, Mordred, for example, would have condemned him. No one knew, as I did, that Arthur would tell Kay to make certain that the old man was well and truly drunk before his eye was taken.

But as the soldiers removed Cerdic from the bridge, the cook looked at me with undisguised hatred. By using him to force Talorc to reveal himself, I had cost him his pride as well as his eye.

"You have made an enemy," Ygerne said. Now that the guilty one had been punished, those under suspicion were ignored. I looked down at my love. Her red hair needed brushing, and beyond the circles beneath her eyes, she looked well. "Did you have to betray him?"

"Do not feel sympathy for Cerdic. He brought this on himself. Had he told us what he saw in the forest, we might have saved Gwyneira's life. But to answer your query, yes. Talorc was very cunning. I had to put him off his guard. Ambrosius had told me that another girl had been murdered on the journey back. I remembered then that Cerdic had appeared from those same woods after the Scotti attacked, and he had been very reluctant to give any excuse. When I realized who had done these things, so many elements suddenly made sense. I guessed, and rightly so, that Cerdic had caught Talorc about his mischief. So I twisted matters to make first Morgan and then Cerdic look guilty. Cerdic's instinct when accused of killing the girl was to look to the true culprit. Had I not done that, he would never have betrayed Talorc."

"You were guessing? That seems a great chance to take."

"I was confident that I had read affairs correctly."

Ygerne nodded. "Why then did Talorc scream so wildly when Aircol told him he had asked for his freedom?"

"That is a story for another day."

I looked about. There stood my cousin, shivering a bit, her shoulders yet bare. "What now, Guinevere?"

"I shall go home," she answered with a tired smile.

"Not back to Melwas's fort?"

"I think the little toad understands how affairs stand."

"If you need anything, cousin, all you must do is ask."

She stepped close, leaned forward, and kissed me on the cheek. Her lips near my ear, she whispered, "Marry her, Malgwyn."

Pulling away, she nearly bumped into Aircol. "Forgive me, my lord."

The lord of the Demetae took Guinevere by her shoulders. "So, you are the maker of all this trouble?" he asked, but the twinkle in his eye played his tone and his words false.

"My lord, had I not been held captive by Melwas, I would have come straight to you and proven that I did not do this thing. I will not pretend that I was happy about her marriage to Arthur, but I did not wish her harm."

"Yet you left her a threatening note."

Guinevere hung her head. "The actions of a spoilt child."

"Yes," he agreed. "They were. But your honesty speaks well of you."

He took another long look at her, and then moved past.

"Malgwyn!" Ygerne's voice carried urgency. I looked up and saw young Ider confronted by Dubricius and Coroticus, with Gildas smirking as he looked on.

Poor Ider! I had forgotten him in the excitement. Without another word, I left Ygerne with Guinevere and approached the small conclave.

"Is there some problem, Coroticus?" I asked, the warning in my voice unmistakable. I knew something of Coroticus that no one else knew, and I would use it if I had to.

The abbot looked no better and somewhat worse than he had earlier. "Malgwyn, this is not the time."

Dubricius narrowed his eyes at me. "This is a Church matter, Malgwyn, hardly the business of drunks."

I did not move. "Coroticus, what is going on?"

Despite his superior's look of disdain, the abbot finally answered. "My lord episcopus has decided to cast Ider out from the community."

No wonder the boy looked ill. His life had been spent in the Christ's service. "And what has he done to deserve such a punishment?"

"Quite simply, he confessed to murder and lied before God."

"He confessed to murder in order to save Ygerne's life."

"It does not matter. And besides, he lied before almighty God."

"Episcopus, if you discharged monachi or sacerdotes or even episcopi for lying before God, He would have no servants."

"Oh, how clever you are, Malgwyn. But my decision is made. I do not seek nor need your approval."

Coroticus looked ill indeed, but he shrugged his shoulders as if to say, quite rightly, that there was nothing he could do.

"Then he shall come and serve me," a new voice said. Arthur had joined us. Now he stood, rubbing his wool-wrapped hands together, and considered Ider. "Any man who is willing to lay down his life for another in a just cause can sit at my table. I am always in need of new advisors, even, occasionally, on Church affairs."

Dubricius's heavy jowls sank in disbelief. "That is unacceptable!"

"Episcopus, let me explain it in terms even you can understand. You have no say in this matter. None."

"He is right, episcopus," Coroticus said, a little uncomfortably.

"The Church is ascendant in all things," Dubricius replied. "Do not think that you cannot be dismissed as well, Coroticus."

The warning was ominous, but the abbot suddenly straightened and strode toward Dubricius with a purpose. "Do not think you can rid yourself of me so easily. Ider acted foolishly. But my father in Aquae Sulis has stronger connections in Rome than even you. You would do well to remember that."

For the first time in my acquaintance with Dubricius he seemed truly frightened. He spun about, gestured to Gildas, and they hurried back toward Ynys-witrin, with Coroticus following in their wake.

"Well, Master Malgwyn, can you think of some service that this young pony can do for us?" Arthur enjoyed teasing.

"He is impetuous, my lord. But perhaps that can be made

to serve us." I reached toward Ider with my one hand and tousled his tonsure.

Arthur slapped him on the back. "Do not worry, boy. Your days of serving the Christ may not be over yet. But in the meantime, entering the service of the Rigotamos will give you fine experience against that day." He looked about, saw Bedevere and called him forth. "Lord Bedevere, see what use you can make of this new recruit."

Bedevere chuckled and Ider smiled at long last. Off they went together.

"Shall we escort the women, my lord?" I looked about but Ygerne and Guinevere had gone.

"Perhaps we should escort each other. Tell me, what errand did you send Illtud on?"

"Give me yet a little time to see if anything comes of it. If he is successful, it will rid us of one problem."

"Malgwyn, you are forever taking liberties." Arthur chuckled. "But you have done what I thought impossible, so I will humor you." He looked about, the wind catching his cloak. "Where has Aircol gone?"

I had not noticed him leave, and I climbed upon a half wall of logs, intended for a fortification. Swiveling back and forth, I finally saw him, a lone figure riding slowly along the lane, headed toward Gwyneira's burial place.

"What of Talorc, Arthur?" I asked, hopping down from the pile. Flies had gathered about the dead boy. I felt no dishonor at being the instrument of his death; he had certainly felt none when he killed the children. But I understood him now, and Wynn had not been completely wrong when he said that we were to blame.

364 / TONY HAYS

"Arthur?" I ceased musing and looked to the Rigotamos, who stared at the slave's body fixedly.

"Let him glut the ravens. The people need to know how we deal with such as he."

"Rigotamos, I pray to your god, the three gods, all of the gods, that we never encounter another such as he."

We walked south along the Via Arturius then, silent, while all about us, the clanking chains and creaking leather of an army disbanding filled the air.

"Arthur," I began, reluctantly, "my conduct in this matter has not been—"

He stopped me with a hand on my shoulder, squeezing it gently. "No, Malgwyn. You are a victim of your own conscience and no man can be condemned for that. You saw a series of children savagely murdered and you were not allowed to do anything about it. That burned within you, as though you yourself were guilty. When you learned of yet another death, that misplaced guilt surged up from your stomach like tainted meat."

"But even before that, I behaved toward you like an unruly child."

Arthur smiled and shook his head. "Malgwyn, you were angry with me, and rightly so. I had cast aside your cousin in favor of another. I kept you from searching for the killer of these girls. But even in all of that, you judged me well enough to know how far you could push. The Christ help me if you ever turn against me.

"You have the luxury of doing the right thing, the just thing. A king by election, not by birth, does not have that freedom, not always. You know that I wish to be just, and I need you at my side reminding me of that."

I nodded. It was moments like that which reminded me why I had followed his banner so many years before.

But one more frayed knot had yet to be repaired in this tapestry of frayed knots.

CHAPTER TWENTY-FIVE

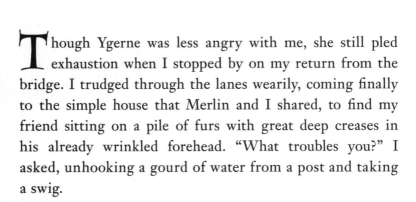

Though Ygerne was less angry with me, she still pled exhaustion when I stopped by on my return from the bridge. I trudged through the lanes wearily, coming finally to the simple house that Merlin and I shared, to find my friend sitting on a pile of furs with great deep creases in his already wrinkled forehead. "What troubles you?" I asked, unhooking a gourd of water from a post and taking a swig.

"A matter has been weighing heavily on me, Malgwyn. Can I trust in your silence?"

"Of course." For a second, my weariness disappeared. Merlin was more than my friend; he was my teacher, indeed something like my father.

For a long moment, he was silent. "You know that I have never married."

I nodded.

"But that does not mean that I have no children."

This took me completely by surprise. "What are you saying, Merlin?"

"Malgwyn, I know you. Have you not often remarked, at least to yourself, on how much Owain and I favor?"

So many pieces fell into place then. Nyfain, the boy's mother, had been a woman of uncertain fidelity even when her first husband was living. His death simply brought her lusts out into the open and then the marriage to poor Accolon did nothing to change her ways.

"Are you certain?"

He cast a jaundiced look my way. "Have you any doubts?"

I could not help but laugh. "No, even Paderic could see the resemblance."

"I should have acknowledged him years ago, but now I am afraid that to do so would cause more harm than good."

It did my heart good and lightened my mood considerably. "When we have sorted out this affair, Merlin, we will sort out that one. Does Arthur know?"

"No, but I suspect he has guessed."

"Do not look at this as a problem. See it as an opportunity." I glanced about the room and realized that, once again, we were without food in our storage pits. "Come, let us see if we can scavenge some food at Arthur's kitchen. At least Cerdic will not be there to complain."

"What of Wynn, Malgwyn? I had forgotten about him."

"He will keep. Come, my stomach howls for food."

✥

And keep Wynn did.

I spent the time waiting at a stone mason's shop near Lindinis, where I supervised the carving of four memorial stones commissioned by me and a fifth commissioned by Arthur. Such stones for women were uncommon in our world, but, as I have been told so many times, I am an uncommon man. I needed to honor those poor children who had been stripped from us. Arthur needed to honor his queen.

Though little Mariam fussed at me for my absence every time I saw her during those days, I needed the relative quiet of Lindinis. I needed it to consider all that had happened, and all that was yet to happen. Others were seeking solitude as well. Merlin mentioned that Kay had absented himself from the fort without saying what he was about. Arthur stayed secluded in his chambers, emerging only occasionally, and then without much comment. He sent a message off by his fastest horse, but he would not answer when anyone asked. Each evening, when daylight was stealing away, Arthur could be found atop the parapet, staring across the lands in some sort of reverie.

As the stonemasons cut the memorials, I took my seat on an old log and tried to understand how force should be used and how justice should be applied. We lived in a world where strength, though not everything, was truly one of only two things of consequence—the other being wealth. And though I saw no place for truth and justice in that, I could not resist the urge to pursue them. Someone needed to.

Then, one day as I sat and watched the workmen, my attention was drawn to a woodworker in a nearby shop. He was using an old Roman lathe to turn a piece of wood into some object. I watched for a moment, fixed on the thin curls of wood he shaved from the stick, leaving a smoother, almost shiny surface in its wake.

I reached into my pouch, forever and always hanging from my neck, and pulled the bit of worked wood out, the wood I had found in poor Hafren at the White Mount. And now I understood all that had happened on that dark night so long ago. And the smile that had once marked me as "Smiling" Malgwyn returned, for another enemy was soon to die, and I took great pleasure in it.

The waiting ended after a fortnight, when our old friend Illtud returned, looking weary, bedraggled, and accompanied by three men.

Word of their arrival reached me at Lindinis by a rider dispatched by Arthur. The stones were nearly finished, and once my next chore was completed, I would take them to be set up. I mounted my own horse and rode at a trot to Castellum Arturius.

Arthur met me at the main gate. He was not happy, but his anger was checked by his curiosity. "Your guests are disposed as you requested." He paused. "I must question your judgment in having them brought here."

I waved him off with my one hand and dismounted. "It needs to be done this way, Arthur. I promise you. My intent is not to subvert you, but it is better this way."

"Why have you been so secretive?"

"To protect you. Please, humor me a little longer."

With his hand brushing back his long hair, the Rigotamos stared at me with undisguised confusion. But after a moment, he followed as I mounted the lane toward his hall.

The great timber hall was quiet. The aisles and great feasting table were empty. I motioned for Arthur to sit, with Bedevere and Kay flanking him. Mordred, Gawain, Gaheris, and David had arrived earlier in the day, summoned by Arthur at my request. Merlin I kept at my side. I would not sit. Illtud stood just inside the main door. My "guests" were nowhere to be seen.

"We are here as you requested. What is this, Malgwyn?" Arthur demanded, his patience truly worn thin. Guinevere yet refused to see him. With Gwyneira gone, he did not understand, but I did. She was protecting herself.

I nodded to Illtud. "Bring the Druid."

Keeping the Druid Wynn prisoner had brought condemnation on me by David and Mordred. Arthur certainly could have granted Wynn's freedom, but he did not. He knew that I had a reason for begging his indulgence. And he was loathe to accommodate either David or Mordred in any way.

I took a deep breath, straightened my tunic with my one hand, and prepared to begin. Roman justice might yet have another day of life left in it.

"I wanted you all here because I think you all have a contribution to make to this. Too often we impose punishment quickly, fatally."

"As you did with Talorc?" Mordred said, but I ignored him.

"That cannot be done in this case."

"What is this nonsense, Arthur? This is why you dragged me here?" David's annoyance dripped from every word.

"Be silent!" Arthur commanded, banging a fist on the table. The room fell quiet.

"We know that the Druid did not kill any of these women. It is an affront to the gods to keep him imprisoned or to punish him," Mordred argued.

Arthur rose and placed both hands firmly on the table. "You will be silent or I shall order you both gagged."

Mordred and David looked about then and realized that

none of their aides were there. Arthur had conveniently gotten them out of our path.

Silence reigned.

And Illtud entered with the Druid Wynn, hands tied before him. Dark circles rimmed his eyes and his hair hung in greasy locks. I noticed some sores on his bare feet. All of it did my heart good.

I had no sympathy to spare that day.

"Bring him here," I ordered, pointing to the space between the table and Arthur's chambers. Illtud shoved him roughly to the hard-beaten earth, tossing his staff to the ground beside him.

"I protest!" shouted Mordred, leaping to his feet. "This priest came here as my guest!"

"And he was treated as such until he became suspect in the murder of Queen Gwyneira. You turned him over willingly. If you would wish us to use the ancient rules of hospitality?" and Arthur's voice trailed off.

Mordred sat down immediately. By the ancient rules of hospitality, Mordred could himself be found guilty of any crime committed by one of his guests.

Wynn struggled to his knees, his face smudged with dirt. He did not even attempt to disguise his hatred of us. "Is this where you condemn me on false charges?"

"No, Wynn. This is where we discuss your crimes against our people."

He spat on Arthur's floor. "I did not touch those girls. This is not my doing. It is your doing, all of you. You treated that boy like an animal and he repaid you for your 'kindnesses.'"

"You know much about him for not being involved."

Wynn pursed his lips. "I have long observed how the believers of the Christ talk of love, redemption, forgiveness, but
then you treat your people as swine for the butcher."

"Druids sacrifice innocents to appease their gods," I said,
shrugging. "Better a live pig than a dead child. Yet, for a man,
Druid or no, who claims to know nothing of this, you seem very
well acquainted with his reasoning."

He did not like my statement. Shrugging, he rose to his
feet. "The soldiers talk."

"The soldiers care little about why the boy would kill. Are
you certain that you know nothing of these deeds?"

"That is what I said," Wynn insisted.

"And you certainly did not know that Talorc was involved?"

"I had no contact with the boy."

There!

A flicker of surprise. Two flickers.

But not from Wynn.

From Mordred and David.

"You have something to add, Lord Mordred?"

He fair jumped from his chair.

"Wynn was your guest and lived in your camp. Did you ever
see him with Talorc?"

Mordred did not want to answer. Those hawkish eyes,
flashing back and forth, and the nervous tongue licking his
lips, told that tale all too well. But he was too smart to defend
the Druid, not when he did not know what I was about.

"Mordred?" Arthur prodded him as he would a stubborn
horse.

Arthur's cousin brushed his braided lock from his face.
"Yes, I saw him talking to Talorc. Cerdic had loaned me the
boy to help serve in my camp."

"They spoke? Often?"

Mordred nodded begrudgingly.

"About what?"

"I do not eavesdrop on priests and slaves."

"And you, Lord David? Did you see these conferences?"

A proud, handsome man, David was also more clever than his ally Mordred. He could hide his lies better.

"I did, but like Lord Mordred, I have no idea what they were talking about." And that was the lie. But David was not my quarry on this day.

"Are you certain?" I narrowed my eyes. "You came to me just after Gwyneira was killed and—"

"I might have heard a little," David admitted, rushing to cut me off. "The Druid frequently told the boy that Aircol would never live up to his promise to see Talorc freed."

"Frequently?"

David hated me yet, and well he should. He had no greater enemy than me. But on this one issue, he had no choice but to cooperate. "He seemed to badger the boy unmercifully about it."

Turning back to Wynn, I suppressed the pleasure I felt at forcing Mordred and David to serve my purposes. "You see, Druid, even my enemies put the lie to your words."

"They are servants of Arthur's," he said, turning away. "They will say that which pleases the Rigotamos."

I chuckled despite myself. "You obviously do not know Mordred and David that well," and that drew nervous laughter from everyone.

"So I counseled with the boy. That proves nothing. It was easy for Aircol to say he would press for Talorc's freedom, but it did not happen, did it?"

"Events hardly allowed for it. You insured that."

Arthur cocked his head and nodded slowly, slightly. He understood then what I was about, but the frown that next appeared on his face said that he did not see success along this path.

David was becoming impatient. As was Mordred and even Gawain. But they were not truly my audience, and I had now done what I needed to do. I had caught Wynn in a lie. I had shown that he had poisoned Talorc's mind against Aircol. Now it was time to reveal the last lie.

"Wynn, you have said that you never touched any of these poor children."

He nodded, eyeing me carefully.

"But then why were you in the forest near where Fercos's daughter was killed right afterward?"

A hint of alarm flashed in his eyes. "That is impossible. I was nowhere near there."

I walked over to his staff and picked it up. Cradling it under my half-arm, I moved to the table and placed it there. "Then, perhaps, you could explain how a bit of your staff appeared where poor Fercos's daughter was killed?"

I pulled the large splinter with the smooth face from my pouch and laid it next to Wynn's staff. "I found that in Hafren's wounds when I cleaned her."

"A lie! A complete lie!" Wynn proclaimed.

But the lords all stood and looked at the items. They were not a perfect match, but when David realized how neatly the bloodied splinter matched the little gap at the bottom of the staff, the shock in his eyes turned to revulsion.

"She was but a child, Druid!"

In unison, they all turned to look at Wynn, who finally understood.

"Tell me, Wynn. Was it you or Talorc who knocked me down in the copse at the White Mount?"

Wynn's eyes began that flickering back and forth that animals begin when they are hunting an escape.

"What I do not know is whether you left that splinter behind when you showed Talorc how to ravage her or whether you took your own pleasure when the boy had left?"

He began inching toward Arthur's chambers, but Illtud moved to stop his escape.

Kay's face held yet a question. "Why this performance, Malgwyn? You could have simply shown us your evidence."

My eyes found Arthur's face, a sad smile growing upon it. He understood then.

"The performance was not for us, Kay," Arthur said. "It was for them."

And he gestured behind Wynn, who fell to his knees then, his jaw slack, his eyes tortured, howling like a wounded beast.

For emerging from Arthur's chambers were three identically dressed men with long beards, white robes, and intricately carved and polished staffs.

Druids!

CHAPTER TWENTY-SIX

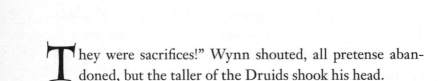

T hey were sacrifices!" Wynn shouted, all pretense abandoned, but the taller of the Druids shook his head.

"This is not our way. Beltaine has passed and Samhain has
not yet arrived. Besides, we cannot pass the duty of perform-
ing ritual sacrifices to one who is not an initiate."

Wynn's jaw took on a firm set. "They needed punishment!
They have turned from our gods!"

"Our gods do not need our help, but our devotion. And we
only kill for proper sacrifice and then only at the proper times.
These are things you know well." The Druid turned then to
Arthur. "We are grateful to you for sending for us. Stories
abound of Lord Arthur and the Christ. I am happy to see that
you are understanding of other beliefs."

The Rigotamos forced a smile onto his face. "It seems my
councilor Malgwyn is equally understanding." If Illtud's mission had been for naught, I would not have wanted Arthur to
know. But I had suspected that there were good men among
the Druids, and I was right. But I also suspected that I would
receive another lecture about knowing my place.

The expressions on Mordred and David's faces were priceless. Both had begun to see this as a way to further undercut Arthur, not in a rebellion, but in a whispering campaign. *"Arthur killed a Druid priest. Arthur betrayed the old gods."* That would not happen now.

The old Druid looked to Wynn yet again. "You have dishonored our gods and our ways. You turned the emblem of your office into a weapon and have it up against a human being. These acts demand punishment."

He turned back to Arthur. "You will no longer be troubled with this one," he said. "We will deal with him in our own way." He gestured with his staff, and his two companions took Wynn by each arm.

The flame in Wynn's eye became wilder, and he writhed and twisted in a vain effort to free himself, the cords of his muscles near to snapping. When he realized he could not escape, such a howl rose from him that it seemed more animal than human. "Malgwyn! I beg you! You know what this means!"

"You seek mercy from the wrong man, Wynn."

The small group of lords parted and allowed the four Druids to depart, Wynn still twisting and contorting at each step.

Mordred and David approached me. "You realize," David began, "that we could not know that Talorc had done these things, or that the Druid knew that either?"

I nodded. "But you had your suspicions."

"Only after Gwyneira was dead, and by then it was too late," Mordred pointed out. "The Druid was of a mean disposition. We thought he just enjoyed taunting the boy."

"He will taunt no one ever again," I said, not without a good deal of satisfaction.

"Aye, you maneuvered well in this, Malgwyn," David conceded. "When it becomes known that Arthur surrendered

Wynn to his fellow Druids, the people will be pleased. Obviously, you bear closer watching."

"Be careful, Malgwyn. Such successes will make you the target of assassins," Mordred added. And then the two were gone.

Before I could react, Kay had slipped up beside me. "I need your help," he whispered.

"With what?"

"Just follow me."

Kay climbed atop the great table. "If it please my lords, I wish for the Rigotamos, my friends Bedevere and Malgwyn, Merlin and Gawain to come with me." He paused. "Oh, and someone fetch Morgan ap Tud."

"To where, Kay?" Arthur grumbled. "There is work to do."

"Please, my lord, suffer me this one favor."

And despite all that had happened, he did.

❖

"Kay, what is this about?" I hissed two hours later as we rode along the little finger of dry land, back near the bridge at Pomparles.

"Just a bit farther," he answered with a smile. At that he turned us away from the main road and off toward the old Roman shrine, where we were greeted by a rather odd assortment of people.

In the shade of the great yew trees stood Coroticus, Guinevere, Ygerne, even little Mariam and Owain. I glanced at Arthur and saw that all annoyance with Kay had fled. Guinevere was here, and the happiness in Arthur's eyes showed clearly that his heart had lightened in one bound.

But where the shrine had been was now only a mass of

tumbled stone and broken beams. A pile of wood, readied for a building, stood nearby, along with a handful of workers, men from a nearby village.

"We are here now, Kay," Merlin said. "What have you wrought here? What is this?"

Morgan ap Tud was with us, but he looked upon me with distrust and anger. I had not taken time to speak to him since that day at Pomparles.

Kay, standing so tall and straight, crossed the clearing and mounted a stump. "Rigotamos, am I not in charge of your household? Am I not your Seneschal?"

Arthur nodded, but Guinevere's presence was distracting him. I knew he burned to go to her, but she was giving him no sign that he would be welcome.

"Then it is time for me to get about my task. Except for Coroticus, you are all members of Arthur's household, so attend to my instructions. Owain!"

My little friend glanced around nervously. "I did nothing wrong, my lord. I swear it!"

Kay chuckled. "You think yourself an orphan."

It was Owain's turn to straighten, to square his shoulders. "I do not complain about my place in life. The Christ and His Father have been good to me." His speech was a pretty one, and I suspected that he had had help with it.

"That is good, because you are not an orphan."

I knew then what Kay's game was.

Owain was confused. "My lord?"

"Meet your father!" He swept an arm toward Merlin. "Merlin, acknowledge your son!"

Obviously I was not the only one Merlin had sought counsel from.

Owain could not have been more confused. He looked at Merlin and then at me. "Malgwyn?"

"It is true, boy. Merlin is indeed your father. Your true father, not a substitute."

He started over to a waiting Merlin, but stopped halfway across the clearing. "He should have told me before this."

But Mariam marched over and shoved him toward Merlin. "He lives with Father, Owain, and you know how slow he is."

And the laughter truly rang as Merlin knelt and took his son in his arms. "I hope you do not mind having a tired old man as your father," Merlin said.

"You are already as a father to me." The boy was certainly his father's son.

With the sort of flourish that only Merlin could accomplish, he produced a pair of old but beautiful scissors, rendered in silver, and a shining golden comb. In his most severe voice, he said, "As has been the custom of all of our peoples for more years than one can count, I formally accept you, Owain, into my family." And, as prescribed by ancient law, Merlin combed and trimmed Owain's hair. The men cheered, and the women cried.

"Well, this has been worth the ride, Kay," Arthur began, impatient, turning to leave, but his Seneschal held up a hand. Reaching into his pouch, he pulled out a vellum document.

"Attend to this letter from Aircol."

At that, Arthur's eyes narrowed. I sensed a sudden storm brewing. He knew nothing of this communication and did not like it. I have learned over the years that no king likes to be surprised in front of others.

"'My Lord Kay, Your letter was unexpected but welcome. As to your request. Though my daughter was a noble, subject to being thrown into any marriage at my whim, she believed in love, wished for it, hoped for it. Before I met the Lady Guinevere, I would not have given you the answer you desire. But I took her measure and believe that my daughter, your queen, would approve. The long ago acts of an impetuous child should not ruin her life forever, and the Christ believed in forgiveness. So, should the Rigotamos desire to marry Guinevere, and should she welcome his suit, I will not object and I will denounce anyone who does. May the Christ and His Father keep you.'"

Kay was clever. By courting Aircol's approval in secret, he had effectively cut off any dissent from the consilium. And there would be dissent—David, Mordred, even Illtud, who adored Guinevere, would balk at this union. The marriage with Gwyneira had been sought simply to insure Aircol's membership in the consilium, to ally his vast resources and lands to our cause. By gaining Aircol's approval of Guinevere first, and holding him in the consilium, Kay had proved himself a diplomat of the first order. No lord could object too loudly or risk making himself an enemy of two of the consilium's three most important lords.

But Kay's cleverness aside, that did not guarantee Arthur's acceptance. In truth, it had been Arthur's decision to set Guinevere aside in favor of Gwyneira. We were in dangerous territory here, as we were toying with Arthur's concept of being a good king.

As narrow as Arthur's eyes had grown, they were now opened wide.

"Kay, you forget your place!"

"No," said Guinevere, "he does not. He reminds you of yours. You are a man, a stubborn, frustrating man, but I love you, and I fear you."

"You fear me?"

Guinevere grinned, with a hint of a tremble. "And why should I not? You quite willingly abandoned me for a child unknown to you." The trembling stopped as her ire grew. She turned to Kay. "You are a good and decent man, Kay. And I thank you for your thoughtfulness. But I fear that I will have to think upon this a bit longer."

The look in Arthur's eyes then was priceless. He was stunned, more so, I think, that she had the temerity to refuse him before he had even asked than that she had chastised him.

He grumbled, started to speak, stopped, started again, and finally lapsed into a brooding silence.

"Perhaps this will help," Coroticus said, moving beside Kay. "I will marry you and the Church will recognize the marriage."

For many years I had been happily unaware of the world and its many machinations. Now I was very much a part of it, and I enjoyed being privy to secrets. But here I was, councilor to the Rigotamos, and there were intrigues and conspiracies sprouting about me like the spring crops.

"Perhaps, Arthur," I said, "you should name Kay as your 'Chief of Spies.'"

I was suspicious though, of this abrupt turnabout. "And what brings about this change of heart, Coroticus? Just a fortnight ago, Guinevere was a disgraced woman of the community and unworthy to marry a king."

Guinevere sent me an arrow-tipped look, but she was curious, too.

Coroticus cleared his throat. "I believe that Dubricius was wrong, and so I have reversed his decision."

"Ah, so you did not like his manner and this is a way to oppose him and still remain popular."

"Malgwyn!" Ygerne chided. "Must you always reduce things to motives?"

"I–"

"Be silent, Malgwyn," Arthur snapped. "If these things are true," he asked Kay, "why are we here? You could just have easily told us this at Castellum Arturius."

"That is true, but I have more to tell you," Kay said, turning from Arthur and facing his audience. "At my request, Arthur granted me these lands. I have pulled down the pagan Roman shrine and intend to build a chapel here. It shall be called Lantokay, Kay's chapel in our tongue. Your marriage chapel, Rigotamos, if you choose to marry again. It is my gift to you and our new queen, whoever that may be." He nodded as a sign of respect to my cousin.

At that, Guinevere allowed the tears to flow freely. Arthur, too, was moved, but he simply looked away, unwilling to reveal the moisture forming in the corner of his eye.

Coroticus came and stood beside me. "You are a brave man, Coroticus, challenging Dubricius on this," I granted. The episcopus had let his displeasure with a marriage between Arthur and Guinevere be known.

"Not really. Dubricius is afraid of me."

"Not enough to save Ider."

The abbot shook his head. "Ider overstepped. Some time away from the abbey will only make him more valuable. See that you treat him well."

Across the clearing, preparing to mount his horse, was Morgan ap Tud. I trotted over to him.

"Morgan?"

He stopped and turned. "I appreciated being invited to this gathering, but I fail to see how I have contributed to it. After your accusations on the bridge, I have been expecting Arthur to order my return home at any time."

"I am sorry, Morgan. I felt certain that you were not the guilty party, but I needed to lull both Cerdic and Talorc, to allay their fears. Shock often brings the truth. You are an honest man, and I have told Arthur this."

The hard look on his face softened. "Thank you, Malgwyn. That means much."

"I have but one question for you."

"Please, ask!"

"Where did you go the night Gwyneira was killed? I had you followed, yet you disappeared."

At that the little medicus grew crimson, "Malgwyn, men have certain needs . . ."

And we both laughed.

This had been a good day. A killer revealed. A father and son reunited. A king and the woman he loved put on a more honest, truer path. Only time would tell if they could navigate that path together.

"Will you be visiting me tonight?" Ygerne asked, as Coroticus moved to congratulate Merlin, grasping and then clinging on to my half-arm.

"Will I be welcome tonight?" I rejoined.

"Oh, Father," Mariam chastised me. "Do not be difficult."

Mariam had grown so much in the nearly two years that I had reentered her life. I laughed then, and it felt more than good. It felt right. But there was one more chore before this long day was finished.

❖

I had seen these sites before, as had Bedevere, these places of ritual. This one was not difficult to find. Fires had been set in the four corners of the clearing, deep in the forests northwest of Arthur's castle, on the summit of an old fort long since abandoned.

Neither Bedevere nor I spoke a word as we rode up. Nearly a hundred people had gathered, some just watching, some helping the three priests with their work.

Though they saw us, sitting atop our mounts at the edge of the clearing, they made no move to hurry us away. From the look of wonder in Bedevere's eyes, I could tell he was surprised at the sheer number of people.

We did not speak, did not break the silence. Of the people, some worked. Some chanted. We watched.

My nose twitched as I caught a hint of rain riding the western wind.

After a few hours, as the midnight approached, more people arrived. The chanting had risen. Suddenly, a piercing scream broke the night.

I leaned forward in my saddle. Through the flickering yellow light of the fires on the far side of the clearing, I saw Wynn hauled into the clearing, still struggling, now naked.

Many of those down in the clearing put their hands to their ears as Wynn's screams grew louder and he disappeared from view in the great object the Druids were building.

With a blend of back power and ropes, they raised the object to a standing position.

"The Wicker Man," Bedevere whispered.

"Aye, with Wynn in his belly."

We watched again in silence as fire was put to the great wicker figure by the oldest of the Druids. We listened as Wynn's screams turned from fear to pain, and that sickly sweet smell of burning human flesh washed the scent of rain from the air. And still he screamed.

Until.

Until he was silent forever.

We rode away then, content in knowing that the affair was finally ended. The Druids had punished their own, and we had punished our own. I had found justice for the dead, the beloved dead.

Bedevere and I dismounted at the barracks and headed back up the lane toward Arthur's hall.

"What of Owain now?" Bedevere asked. "Will he come live with you and Merlin?"

"No, no. He is safe and happy with Ygerne. And he sees Merlin every day as it is."

"Have Merlin teach his son some manners. Arthur heard about the little assassin seeking him with Kay's sword. He wasn't amused."

We both had a chuckle at that, and I bid Bedevere a good eve, and he trudged off toward Kay's house.

"So it is ended?"

The voice came from behind me. I turned to see Arthur, Guinevere, and Ygerne entering from one of the side lanes. Arthur and my cousin were arm in arm and I was pleased to see it.

"Ah! So you have reconciled."

Guinevere frowned at me. "We have agreed to explore the future. I am still uncertain of him."

Arthur turned red.

"Well, you are about late," I said.

"We were watching the great fire from the parapet," Guinevere answered. "The Druid?"

"Aye. Justice has been satisfied."

"Has it?" the Rigotamos asked.

"What mean you?"

"That the Druid should die for his acts, I agree. But was Talorc truly responsible? We enslaved him. We treated him thus."

"Arthur, I do not argue the injustice of slavery. But no one forced him to abuse those girls. No one forced him to steal their lives away."

"The Druid encouraged it."

"When I realized who the killer was, I knew then the why. Sometimes it is not easy to understand the motives of a man. And we do not even try to understand slaves. To think that they feel no hint of resentment at their captivity and their treatment is more than foolhardy. If that were so, why have there always been laws against slaves having weapons? The boy killed the daughters of men important in their villages and towns. He wanted to punish the fathers by raping and killing the daughters. He believed that he was taking some measure of revenge and that that was right and proper. Talorc was old enough to make his own choices. He chose to kill. He deserved his punishment.

"In truth, Arthur, I do not think that the Druid introduced him to this. I think that the Druid happened on him killing Fercos's daughter by accident. Once he knew Talorc's secret, Wynn knew how to manipulate the boy. At some point, I think Talorc came to enjoy the act, came to feel that it gave him power in some way."

"And the splinter from the Druid's staff in the girl?" Arthur asked.

"I think Wynn stayed about after Talorc had killed her, and he could not resist the temptation to extract his own revenge. He simply did not realize that we would involve ourselves."

"Some people are broken," Ygerne added. "Once, in my village, a powerful man, a decurion, was caught removing a dead maiden from her grave and trying to lie with her."

Arthur nodded. "I have heard such tales."

"Sometimes I fear for you, Malgwyn," Guinevere teased. "You are a hard man. You dispatched Talorc without hesitation, and you delivered the Druid up to the Wicker Man for his feast."

"With all due respect to the Rigotamos, the only justice we find in this life is that which we make for ourselves. Sometimes that justice needs be harsh and immediate. And I want only justice, only the truth."

Arthur chuckled softly. "Then I suspect your life will be filled with disappointment."

"Perhaps, but I can do nothing else." I hesitated for a moment, long enough for Arthur to notice.

"A question?"

"A favor. On the journey back from Caer Goch, we encountered a family living in an old villa, a man named Rhodri. They are a good people, but struggling to survive."

"You wish me to send for them and resettle them here near our home?"

"There is a small girl, Vala. She—"

Arthur stopped me. "Oh, the girl that Bedevere spoke of, who can predict death?"

"Who is to know if that is true? But you know that children of that nature are often treated harshly in hard times. The people blame them when crops fail, when the rain does not come. I would not have that happen to this family. They freely shared their food with us. And they sent word to me of that death."

"I will have Bedevere fetch them as soon as his duties allow."

We had almost reached Arthur's hall when Ygerne, mostly silent until then, coughed.

"Malgwyn, we must speak."

Arthur and Guinevere exchanged glances and started to leave us alone, but Ygerne stopped them with a hand. "No, better that you should hear this now."

My stomach rolled around. It seemed I was about to hear why Ygerne had been so angry with me for so long. I was not certain that I was ready.

As was Ygerne's nature, she did not hesitate. "Mariam is to have a new brother."

That was not what I had expected her to say. So stunned was I that I did not speak except to blurt out, "What?"

Her eyes sparking and that red hair fair glowing in the torchlight, she squared on me and slapped me in the stomach. "I am carrying your child, you dolt! The fortune tellers say it shall be a boy. Have you nothing else to say?"

Truly I did not know what to say. Though I knew enough to pull her against my chest and hold on tight. But for the rest of my life, I would count that single moment, drowned by the congratulations of my Rigotamos, Arthur ap Uther, and my cousin Guinevere, as the happiest of my life.

This was a good land, our Britannia, and we were about to bring a new life into it.

GLOSSARY AND GAZETTEER

Aquae Sulis—This was the Roman name for what is now Bath, England. Excavations have shown that many of its buildings were refurbished and continued in use throughout the fifth and sixth centuries.

braccae—Breeches worn by both Saxons and the Brythonic tribes. The only extant examples come from peat bogs in Europe. There was a certain disdain by Romans toward the Gallic tribes for wearing pants.

Breton—A native or inhabitant of Brittany, or the Celtic language of the Breton people.

Brittany—That area of Gaul known as Brittany. Settlements by some of the Brythonic tribes were located there during the fifth and sixth centuries.

Caer Goch—An Iron Age hill fort in south Wales.

camisia—A type of undershirt worn beneath a tunic.

Carmarthen—The legendary birthplace of Merlin.

castellum—Castle, but not in the High Middle Ages sense with thick stone walls, towers, and damsels in distress. Usually a defensive position with stacked rock and timber defensive rings.

Castellum Arturius—For the purposes of this novel, Cadbury Castle at South Cadbury, Somerset, is the location for Arthur's castle. Excavations during the 1960s identified it as having been significantly rebuilt and reinforced during the late fifth century by a warlord of Arthurian-like stature, although no explicit evidence linking the site to Arthur himself was discovered.

Castellum Mark—Castle Marcus near Fowey in southeast Cornwall is believed to have been the site of King Mark's headquarters. Nearby was found the famous Tristan stone, a gravestone believed to commemorate the historical Tristan, making it the one contemporary piece of evidence for the historicity of a character in the Arthurian canon.

cervesa—The Latin name for the beer made by the local tribes during the Roman occupation. According to tablets unearthed at Vindolanda near Hadrian's Wall, Roman soldiers were not shy about drinking cervesas.

consilium—A council. Gildas refers to a *consilium* ruling pre-Saxon Britannia that ended in Vortigern hiring Saxon mercenaries to help put down the raids of the Picts and Scots. It is safe to assume that any warlord that exerted influence over large areas in central and western England would have done so at the behest and the agreement of such a council of lesser kings.

Dumnonia (Dumnonii)—A tribe residing in the area of Cornwall and throughout the west lands. Mark is thought to have been a king of the Dumnonii during the general period of Arthur's life. Christopher Snyder suggests in *The Britons* that people in the post-Roman period referred to themselves by tribal designations.

Durotrigia (Durotrigii)—A tribe residing in the area surrounding Glastonbury down through the South Cadbury area to the southern coast.

fibula—A brooch used to pin cloaks and other clothing together. Sometimes they were jeweled and quite ornate. Others were made in the shape of crossbows.

iudex pedaneus—A Roman official assigned to investigate crimes and offenses. It is known that such titles were still used in post-Roman Britannia.

latrunculi—A term applied to groups of bandits that ran rampant during the fifth century, not to be confused with a Roman board game of the same era.

levels—The remarkably flat terrain from the Polden Ridge and South Cadbury in the east and south and stretching to the Mendip Hills in the north and northeast, really only broken once and then by the cluster of hills that is modern-day Glastonbury.

Lindinis—A Roman town near what is now Ilchester, just west of South Cadbury.

Londinium—As would be expected, this is the Roman name for what is now London.

meneds—The *meneds* is the ancient name for the Mendip Hills of northwest Somerset.

mortaria—A type of bowl with knots or beads in the bottom to make it easier to grind vegetables to a pulp.

peplos—A type of gown worn by women, having a Roman cut.

philologus—A teacher.

Pomparles Bridge—Located between present-day Street and the edge of Glastonbury. Legend has it that it was from this point that Bedevere set Arthur's funeral bier off for Avalon. Although the current bridge is not ancient by any means, fieldwork has shown that there may have been a Roman crossing in this vicinity.

presbyter—A Latin term applied to priests or other church officers. Remember that this was a time before parish priests.

sacerdote—A term used to describe priests, interchangeable with *presbyter* above. There may certainly have been differences between these two terms at the time, but such distinctions, without documentary evidence, are impossible for modern readers to discern.

schoenus—A Roman mile.

tigernos—The Celtic word for "lord," sometimes used to designate local lords, but believed by some scholars to have been combined with the word "vor" to produce the name "Vortigern," or "overlord."

vallum—A ditch, possibly holding a wooden palisade, used as both a defense and a boundary marker for monastical sites during the fifth century and onward.

Via Arturius—"Arthur's Way." A roadway or lane actually ran from Cadbury Castle to Glastonbury. It has become known as Arthur's Way. Two major Roman roads near Cadbury Castle were the Via Fosse and the Via Harrow.

Via Caedes—"The Killing Way." Obviously, this is a creation for the series, but skeletons were found along the main roadway entering Cadbury Castle. They were victims of an ancient massacre, probably at the hands of Romans and probably in reaction to the rebellions of Caractacus or Boudicca.

vigile—The Roman equivalent, in a sense, of both a policeman and a fireman. In Rome, they watched for fires as much as any crime.

Votadini (Votadinii)—A tribe residing in what is now northern England and into the lands of the Scots border as far as the Firth of Forth. One story of a chieftain named Cunneda (Kenneth) suggests that part of the Votadini migrated to northern Wales, but, according to Snyder, that possibility has been discounted.

White Mount—Said to be the location of the White Tower at the Tower of London.

Ynys-witrin—According to some sources, this was the early name for what is now Glastonbury. It is believed that a Christian community may have resided there during the Arthurian age.

The idea that serial killers are a modern invention has always struck me as short-sighted and arrogant. The same
basic factors that drive serial killers today have been around as
long as humans have. Mothers and fathers mistreat their children, sometimes to the extreme. Those with twisted minds
see killing as a way to gain power, to take control over something. The difference today is that communications have im-
proved in such a way as to make these killings all the more
visible. In the distant past, in post-Roman Britain, word of
mouth was the only channel for dissemination.

Once again I have chosen to weave certain Arthurian traditions into the tale. A mythic king of the Britons, Bran became involved in a war with the king of Ireland in which only
seven men from Bran's side survived. Mortally wounded, Bran
ordered that his head be severed after his death and buried on
the White Mount (Tower Hill) to ward off invasion. And Arthur is said to have gone to the White Mount and exhumed
the head because the people should not rely on such a talisman
for protection.

Lord Aircol Lawhir was a real person, a king of the Demetae in the region of Wales known as Dyfed. We actually know more about his son, Vortipor, than we do him. Gildas, in the *De Excidio*, complains about Vortipor, and his memorial stone has survived. Aircol is also known by his Latinate name, Agricola, but having already used that name in *The Divine Sacrifice*, I chose not to confuse my readers. His daughter, Gwyneira, is sadly fictional, however. I would like to have met her. Melwas's abduction of Guinevere is first mentioned in *The Vita Gildas*, approximately contemporary with Geoffrey of Monmouth's work. Melwas is mentioned as lord in the "Summer Country," usually thought to mean Somerset. He is mentioned again in an anonymous poem called "The Dialogue of Melwas and Gwenhyfer." Oddly, Arthur does not figure in the poem much, but Kay does. When Chrétien de Troyes added to the literature later, Melwas becomes Melagaunt, from which twentieth-century filmmakers extracted *First Knight*. Poor Guinevere, as Geoffrey Ashe says, seems to have been abduction prone, it happens to her so often. But the legend of Arthur removing Bran the Blessed's head from the White Mount stems from the Welsh Triads.

One of the stories surrounding the alleged exhumation of Arthur and Guinevere at Glastonbury in 1190 is that the famous lead cross that accompanied the burial referred to Guinevere as Arthur's "second wife." But if Arthur was married twice, who was his first wife? So there you have the central elements around which I concocted this tale, and it is a tale, a novel of murder, a piece of fiction.

The reader will note that a new character has appeared at Arthur's court, one Morgan ap Tud, a physician. He originates in the *Mabinogion* and is thought by some to have been the model for Arthur's sister, Morgan le Fay.

Anyone familiar with the Arthurian legends and Arthurian fact will see that I use scholar Geoffrey Ashe's theories frequently. I have also profited from Dr. Christopher Snyder's work on the history of post-Roman Britain and Christopher Gidlow's *The Reign of King Arthur.*

As usual, I've relied on a plethora of archaeological studies, particularly of Cadbury Castle in South Cadbury, England, and Glastonbury and the surrounding area. For those interested in Cadbury Castle, my website, www.tonyhays.com, has a number of new photographs of the hill fort as it now stands.

I find myself amused by these scholars who insist that Arthur was some sort of Celtic god made mortal over the millennia. They accuse those who believe in a historical Arthur of making an *a priori* assumption that he was real, when they themselves are making an *a priori* assumption that he was not. The various twists and turns they make to prove their theories remind me of Ockham's razor. When all is said and done, the simplest explanation is almost always the correct one.

Any mistakes I've made, and I'm sure there are some, are mine and mine alone. For those, you have my apologies.